PAYBACK

Something was wrong. Sergei Tal knew it deep in his bones, in that part of him that was still more animal than human. But he couldn't worry about details. He had to get out of Moscow, fast.

He opened the front door and let himself out onto the sidewalk. The usual bright lights of his nightclub were out now and the street was shrouded in darkness, broken only by two streetlights, each of them a half block away.

Turning left, he started down the deserted street toward his car, a black Zil limousine. The sound of a car coming fast down the street caught his attention and he looked up. It was a cab.

He stepped off the curb near his car as the taxi slowed, then glanced up and saw Kamenski leaning out the back window. Tal reached inside his jacket for his pistol, but he was too late.

A fusillade of bullets tore into his stomach, his chest, and carved a tattoo across his body up toward his left shoulder. He grabbed the fender of his limo, but his strength ebbed away with his blood and he slid down into the street.

PINNACLE BOOKS HAS SOMETHING FOR EVERYONE—

MAGICIANS, EXPLORERS, WITCHES AND CATS

WARREN MURPHY

HONOR AMONG THIEVES

PINNACLE BOOKS
WINDSOR PUBLISHING CORP.

For Bob and Bonnie Gallagher,
Ralph and Penny Rudolph.

PINNACLE BOOKS

are published by

Windsor Publishing Corp.
475 Park Avenue South
New York, NY 10016

Copyright © 1992 by Warren Murphy

First Printing: November, 1992

Printed in the United States of America

Chapter One

"If I get told to fire one more shot at one more rock, I'm going to swallow this pistol and pull the trigger."

"Go ahead. That's why they always have us use blanks. So that nobody gets hurt."

"And that's another thing. I didn't become a policeman so I could play with toy pistols and toy bullets. Suppose we get attacked. What am I going to do, throw my blank cartridges at them?"

"You'd have a better chance of hitting somebody that way than by shooting at them. You couldn't hit a lake if you were standing on the bottom."

"*Ebi korovu*, my good sergeant." Go screw a cow.

The second man laughed at the vulgar Russian slang expression but the laughter did not seem to come naturally to his face. His eyes were hard and his mouth not much more than a thin slit in his face. His skin was weathered and scarred and his ears cauliflower lumpy, a souvenir of the years he had spent as a boxer. His knuckles bore the signs, too, callused and twisted things, broken more times than Sergeant Mikhail Federenko could remember. He was forty-nine years old. He looked sixty-nine.

He clapped one of his big hands around the shoulders of the younger man and said good-naturedly, "Who knows, Georgi? Maybe soon, Cowboy will have something for us to do."

"You'll forgive me if I don't hold my breath."

"Breathe all you want. But keep your eyes open. We are not in Moscow."

They were sitting on the side of a small hill in the former Soviet republic of Uzbekistan, only a few miles from the country's unmarked and basically unguarded border with Afghanistan. Fifty feet farther down the hillside, four more men were absorbed in playing dominoes.

While all six were members of the militsia, the Soviet Union's national police arm, they were not wearing the normal dark blue uniform with shoulder boards, but instead were dressed in tough khaki work clothes that looked like military fatigues.

One of the players, a husky man with a bristling black mustache and curiously Oriental eyes, slammed his last domino down onto the blanket the four men used as a table.

"All of them," he announced. "That's another ruble each."

Two men carefully examined the long string of dominoes that trailed across the blanket. The third man threw his two remaining dominoes down onto the blanket and grumbled, "Pigsticker."

Mustache said, "If you can't afford to lose, you can't afford to play."

"I'm just tired of being out here in this damned wasteland." He looked up the hillside to where Sergeant Federenko and the younger policeman sat side by side. "When do we do something?"

"When Cowboy says we do something. Until then we just call it maneuvers," the winner said. He watched the other two men disgustedly give up trying to find an error in the play of the game. "I figure if we stay out here another two weeks, I will own all of you, your wives, and your children."

"I concede," one of the others said. "Let's stop playing and I give you my wife now."

"And your children?"

"No. I need them to support me when I retire in fifty years."

"You'll die of boredom first."

"No. Cowboy will not let us die of boredom."

"He better hurry," one of the losers said. "One more day and I turn up my toes."

"Wash them first. God will throw you out of heaven if you show up with dirty feet."

"There is no God. That was a precept of the Soviet state."

"There is no Soviet state," one of the other men grumbled. "That is a precept of God's."

"And man's," the fourth man said. He rose to his feet with a painful clicking sound in his knees. "I am going to the latrine," he announced.

Without looking up from the notebook in which he was writing down how much each man owed him, the winner said, "Take a gun."

The standing man grunted, looked around him at the barren land that seemed to stretch to the horizon in all directions, but picked up a Kalashnikov automatic rifle from a handful that were stacked in a pyramid nearby before stumbling off toward a slit the men had dug in the ground some fifty yards away.

His name was Vadim Barabonov, and he did not need

to be reminded that they were very close to the Afghanistan border and that thus their lives were in constant danger.

A cousin of Barabanov's who had served with the army in that unsuccessful war had come back, filled with horror stories about the savagery of the Afghans.

"We found one of our men," his cousin had said. "The rebels had captured him. They had staked him to the ground and then the women carefully cut open his stomach and pulled his intestines out. He was still alive. And then in the cavity, they built a wood fire and they cooked their meal over it. When we got there, the poor bastard was still alive and his guts were burning and these bastards were standing around eating, smiling, laughing. Our lieutenant ordered us to turn around and we did and we heard a shot, and when we turned back, our soldier was dead. The lieutenant did it himself but he didn't want any of us to see it. And then we took turns blowing the shit out of every one of those evil bastards."

"You should have stayed the hell out of Afghanistan," Barabanov had said.

His cousin had replied, "I am a soldier. I go where they send me," and Barabanov had snorted in contempt and now, here he was, himself in Uzbekistan, sweltering in the summer heat, only a mile from the Afghan border, wasting time, and constantly looking over his shoulder to make sure none of those sadistic evil bastards was sneaking up on him with a knife and a sack of charcoal.

He urinated into the slit trench and when he returned, he saw the two other men coming down from the hillside.

The two men who had been on the hill slowly trudged back to where the other men were gathered. The younger man was named Georgi Golovin, and at twenty-six, he was the youngest member of the militsia squad. He looked frail and his skin was pale and his hair so blonde

8

that in certain lights it looked as if he did not even have eyebrows. A few months before, he had come back from a week's vacation with a mustache he had grown in an effort to look older. It had not worked and he had succeeded only in looking like an oversized boy with a dirt smudge on his lower lip and the other policemen had derided him so unmercifully that he shaved it off that night.

Georgi said to Sergeant Federenko, "I don't want you to misunderstand. The only reason I mind being out here is that I don't know if my family's all right."

"Your family's all right," Federenko said. "If something was wrong, they'd let you know." The sergeant spoke with the sure authority of his rank.

"Hah! If something was wrong, they wouldn't even think of me," Golovin said. "What do they care about me?"

"True. But you're one of Cowboy's men. They wouldn't mess with Cowboy. They would let you know."

"You've been with him a long time, haven't you?"

"Here, with the squad, three years since it started. I was the first man he chose." He could not keep the pride out of his voice.

"You like him," the younger man said in a flat voice. It was neither question nor declaration, only conversation.

"Don't you?"

"He frightens me," Golovin said.

"He should. But he is the best cop in Russia. I would rather be here with him, peeing in a hole in the ground, than be the President's chauffeur and have a dacha in Zhukovka."

"But we're here almost a week. We play war games. We shoot blanks at make-believe targets. We hike like soldiers. Why?"

"Because Cowboy wants it that way," said the sergeant.

"Where is he, anyway?" Golovin said.

"He will get here when he gets here," Federenko said in a tone that signaled the conversation was over. He called out loud, "On your feet. Time to go for a walk and shoot some more rocks."

The other four men groaned and one of the losers in the domino game mumbled under his breath as he slowly rose to his feet, "To hell with Cowboy."

The man was improbably tall by any standard save that of a basketball league, but for a Russian he seemed like a giant. In truth he was six feet four, but with the tall ten-gallon hat on his head, and the high-heeled Western-style boots, he seemed to be near the seven foot mark.

He wore dark brown trousers and a lightweight tan jacket.

He had driven his military-style Jeep slowly down the main street of the little town of Termez, just a ten-minute drive from the Afghan border. It was afternoon and the dusty main street of the Uzbekistan town was clotted with small groups of men who lolled back from the road, under the shade of scrawny-looking trees, starting small wood fires under their woklike *khazans*, special iron pots where the men, following an ages-old tradition, cooked meals of horsemeat and noodles and then spent the afternoon in gossip and insult. No women were to be seen because no women were allowed at the afternoon ceremony.

The tall man parked his dusty dented vehicle outside the squat gray concrete building that housed the militsia office, jumped out, and walked inside. He could sense the stares of some of the men clustered along the road but ignored them. A visitor to town here was big news. He would give them something to talk about for days to come, he thought.

Inside the building, as she saw him approaching her desk, Svetlana Turchin ran her hand alongside her right ear, smoothing down the lock of hair that she knew had a tendency to spurt out from her head.

She had been working at the Militsia office in Termez for three months and had expected police work to be exciting. But instead she found herself surrounded by a lot of old men, bureaucrats who were not interested in crime, criminals, or police work, but only in not getting into any trouble, and the biggest excitement in her life was in constantly finding new ways to reject the advances of her boss, Major Markin, a fat and furry man with large pads of black hair on the backs of his knuckles, whom she regarded as the most repulsive man she had ever seen.

Boredom described her days and that was, she knew, why she felt her heart flutter as the tall man drew near. He *was* coming to her desk. His face was lean and tanned, with green eyes that had laugh wrinkles at the corners. His nose was sharp and straight and his mouth was wide, and could that have been a hint of cruelty in the set of his lips? His jaw was square, the kind of jaw she always associated in her mind with cosmonauts and war heroes.

She brushed a hand through her light blond hair again and then the man was standing in front of her, and he was waiting, and finally he cleared his throat, and she felt embarrassment sting her face red and she said, trying to be businesslike, "Can I help you, sir?"

"I am here to see Major Markin," the man said in a voice that was soft but not at all gentle.

She began to rise from her chair. She was glad she had worn her new bra this day, even if she had had to stand on line for it for three hours the last time she had vacationed in Moscow. And this very night, she was going to start her new diet. Absolutely, this time without fail.

"And your name?" she said as she turned from her desk.

"I am Lieutenant Lev Rostov," the man said.

She looked back at him over her shoulder. "Cowboy?" she said, and the tall man grinned.

"Some call me that," he said. He watched her walk toward Markin's door. He glanced at her desk and saw a pad of interoffice memo paper on the desk, and when she went inside the major's office, he peeled off the first few sheets, rolled them, and stuck them in an inside pocket of his light tan jacket.

Lev Rostov stood in front of the major's desk, holding his cowboy hat under his arm. Markin did not ask him to sit and he now seemed to spend an inordinate amount of time reading a one-paragraph memo before he pushed it aside and looked up at the lieutenant.

"So, Lieutenant Rostov, what brings you here?"

"Merely a training mission, Major," Rostov said politely.

"What kind of training mission?" Markin asked.

"I'm sorry, sir, but I'm not at liberty to say. Moscow has ordered secrecy."

"Oh, really?" Markin said. He waited for an answer, but Rostov did not offer one.

After a long pause that seemed to intimidate Markin more than Rostov, the major said, "Then how do you explain this?"

The major snapped a yellow communications form from the incoming pile of papers stacked neatly on the left side of his desk. As he cleared his throat to read, Rostov looked at the other pile of papers on the right side of his desk, ready for his signature, to see how they were addressed.

Markin read aloud, " 'Ascertain immediately status of Rostov special unit. Advise Rostov training period over; he should return to Moscow soonest.' It is signed by Colonel Alexei Svoboda."

The lieutenant said, "I'm very glad, Major, that you passed this on to me. I will prepare immediately to move my men out of here and return to headquarters."

"So what were your men doing here?" Markin asked again.

And even though the message to Markin gave him no authority to ask for such information, Rostov answered.

"For the last four weeks, Major, my men and I have been engaged in training situations at various spots in our country. We have also been engaged in training local militsia to be able to recognize illegal narcotics more quickly. This is, as you know, part of our squad's broad mission, dictated to us by the headquarters staff. We conducted such a training session in Tashkent and I thought, while we were in this republic, I would spend a few days with my men out in the countryside, toughening them up." He smiled. "Uzbekistan is a demanding place. I thought if my men could survive here, they can survive anything. As of course, sir, you well know."

Rostov's handsome face was bland and open as he spoke. Markin said, "You are not here on official police business?"

"No, sir. Only training."

"You do not need our help in any matter? I would be only too glad to assist in any way we can."

"No, sir. But thank you for your kind offer. And, of course, now that we have our orders to return, we will be out of your jurisdiction almost immediately."

Markin thought for a while, then said, "Very well. But let me tell you, Rostov, the next time you come, it would be best to consult with the commander at the start. This free-lancing may work in the United States where *everyone* is a cowboy, but not here, not yet. You understand?"

"Perfectly," Rostov said. "You have my apologies, sir. The next time, I will follow protocol much more precisely."

"See that you do," Markin snapped. He looked back down at the papers on his desk and dismissed Rostov with a cavalier wave of his hand.

13

So that's the famous Cowboy? he thought. He snorted to himself. *Sent him out of here with his tail between his legs. Just another big-reputation publicity hound.*

Svetlana had reapplied her makeup and even found her false eyelashes in the bottom of her suitcase-sized purse. She smiled at Rostov when he left Markin's office.

She had to talk to him and she built up the nerve to ask, "Everything all right, Lieutenant?"

"Yes," Rostov said. "What is your name?"

"Svetlana."

"Svetlana, I won't be here long and I did want to see your city. Would you be free tomorrow evening to show me around town?"

She cleared her throat, then nodded her head.

"Good. I will pick you up here after work," Rostov said. He smiled at her and said, "We'll have a wonderful time."

She nodded dumbly, even as he started to walk away. Then he stopped and came back to her desk, leaving over, close enough for her to smell his aftershave, whispering to her.

"I think it's best if you don't mention it to the major," he said. "In fact, don't even mention my name to him."

She nodded but raised an eyebrow.

"I don't think he cares for me," Rostov explained.

How could he? You are a hero policeman, and he is but an overfed paper-pusher. She thought but just nodded again.

Rostov stood up straight. "The major mentioned the name of your armorer, but it's slipped my mind. What is it?"

"Sergeant Ardenov," Svetlana said. "Do you know where he is?"

"In the basement?" Rostov said.

"Yes."

"I have to see him," Rostov said. "Perhaps you would call him and tell him I am on my way."

"Yes. Yes, I will."

"Thank you," Rostov said. He touched her hand lightly. "Until tomorrow. And again . . ." He pressed his right index finger across his lips, signifying silence, and nodded with his head toward Major Markin's office door.

"I understand," Svetlana said, and watched him go, before she picked up the phone to call Sergeant Ardenov.

It was very curious, Sergeant Ardenov thought, as he helped the big policemen load two cases of ammunition and a case of gas and concussion grenades into the back of his small drab police Jeep. No one outside the local militsia captains were ever allowed to withdraw ammunition, and especially not some big visiting cowboy from Moscow.

But he had a neat list of supplies he wanted written right on a memo from Major Markin's office. And hadn't Markin's secretary called him personally to tell him that Lieutenant Rostov was on his way down to the armory?

Who was he to argue?

He loaded the last box onto the back of the small vehicle and grinned at Rostov.

"Going bear hunting?" he said. He had heard of this Rostov. Around the department, he had the reputation of being the man who got the big cases, the one who made the really big arrests. Real police work. The kind Sergeant Ardenov used to do himself before the arthritis had finally crippled him up and made him useful only as a property clerk.

"Something like that," Rostov answered with a grin. "Except sometimes *these* bears can shoot back. But you'd know all about those kind of bears, wouldn't you?"

15

"Seen one or two in my time," Ardenov answered proudly. "Give them one for me," he said.

"I'll write your name on every bullet," Rostov replied, "so they know who they've been fooling around with." He hugged the grizzled old sergeant, and mumbled, "You will tell no one that I have been here."

"Yes, sir, Lieutenant."

"No one. Understand?"

"Yes, sir."

Rostov nodded, and threw the older man a precise military salute, then drove quickly away from the police building.

He drove south out of the town, the setting sun aggressively orange on his right.

He reached his men fifty minutes later. Darkness was settling on the land and the men had already built a large campfire, around which they were seated, when his Jeep pulled up in front of the big communal tent at the bottom of the scubby hill.

All the men got to their feet as he stepped into the flickering light of the campfire. Sergeant Federenko nodded.

"I hope everybody's well-rested," Rostov said.

"Bored is more like it," the sergeant said lightly.

"Not for much longer. We're moving out tonight." He hesitated a bit, then added, "On foot," and smiled as the men groaned.

"And when we're done with this drill and we fire a lot more blanks at a lot more rocks, then are we going home?" asked the man who had won at the domino game. His name was Yevgeny Astafyev, and after Sergeant Federenko, was the most veteran squad member.

Rostov saw the other men nod, and said softly, "This one's not a drill. This is the real thing." He squatted next

16

to the fire and poured a cup of black tea from a battered old metal pot.

"I know you men have been wondering what we've been up to for the past few weeks, so I'll tell you." He sipped at the tea and burned his lip on the cup. "Damn!" he snapped, and bit off and spat away a piece of blistered skin.

"This does not go past this campfire," he said. "You understand?"

He looked around at each of the men. They all nodded.

"Three times in the last six months, we've had a chance to break up a major drug operation. All three times, they were tipped off and the arrests fell through. This time, it's not going to happen that way."

He looked around and felt suddenly very close to his men. He had handpicked each of them and he knew that in a crisis, they would stand by him. There was the tough and shrewd Sergeant Federenko, and young Golovin, whom Federenko seemed to have taken under his wing. Astafyev, the man who had asked the mocking question, was the squad's lover, always chasing women, but a sound policeman despite that.

There was Vadim Barabanov, sluggish and slow with no imagination, but with the determination of a bulldog. And Ivan Gorlov, who had joined the militsia after flunking out of law school and had become their chief paper-pusher. And Leo Tarkovsky, who had been raised right nearby in the city of Tashkent and who outworked everybody on the squad because as an ethnic Uzbeki, an Asiatic group often despised by European Russians, he thought his performance could strike a blow against prejudice. Each had his strengths and each his faults, but not one had ever used drugs and Rostov doubted if anyone could have assembled a better squad to combat the narcotics dealers.

"I don't know where the leak has been coming from,

but I couldn't take any chances. So I didn't even tell headquarters what we were up to. I just got us authorization to do this training mission and we've been working our way down toward the Afghan border. That's where the drug sale is supposed to take place tomorrow. Meanwhile, Moscow doesn't know what we're doing. That's why I didn't even bring special ammunition or grenades, lest somebody start talking too much. So no one up there is going to tip anybody off this time. This one belongs to us.''

He stood up and tossed the contents of his cup into the fire. It sizzled, but the wood burst back into flames only a moment later.

''Any questions?'' he said.

''One,'' the sergeant answered.

''I know the question,'' Rostov said. ''Why didn't I tell you earlier? Because you didn't need to know. Sometimes it's best to be in the dark.''

The sergeant smiled, his false teeth—his own had been left in boxing rings a generation ago—glinting pearl white in the flames, and said, ''Besides, if Moscow comes down on somebody with both boots for this, we'll be off the hook. You'll be the only one hung out to dry.''

''Don't make me out to be noble,'' Rostov said. ''That hat doesn't fit. Now, Sergeant, issue these men some ammunition. And grenades. It's in the Jeep.''

''That's the way to go, Cowboy,'' Tarkovsky yelled, and all the men laughed.

''And then let's get moving,'' Rostov said. ''We've got a lot of ground to cover and we've got to be there before daybreak.''

Chapter Two

Macungie, Pennsylvania:

Eugene Palmer strolled into the Weird Fellows Hall and took the stool at the corner of the bar where he had sat regularly every Monday, Wednesday, and Friday for the last six months.

He was a smallish husky man with blond wavy hair and regular features that were made almost good-looking by the fact that he seemed always to be smiling.

Sandy, the bartender, acknowledged his arrival with a nod and, without being asked, poured a glass of Dry Sack sherry over the rocks and put it in front of Palmer.

It was a salesman's drink, Sandy thought. Enough alcohol to get a buzz on but not enough to wipe you out. Guys who drove a lot for a living and depended on their cars drank like that, especially since the damned state police had gone nuts banging everybody for DWI—driving while intoxicated. And Palmer would have just three drinks, no more, no less, and when he was done, he would go whether it took him an hour to drink them or all night.

He would leave a ten-dollar bill, which worked out to six dollars for the drinks and a four-dollar tip, and he would mind his business and speak only when spoken to, and the rest of the time he would watch the baseball game on television, and he would never raise his voice or get nasty, and when his time came he would leave and he was, all in all, the kind of customer bartenders lived to find.

"Evening, Gene."

"Sandy."

"How's it going? Make any money today?"

"If I wanted to make money, I would have become a bartender," Palmer said casually. "Who's playing tonight?"

"The Phillies on Channel Twenty-nine." The bartender looked at the clock over the bar. "On in twenty minutes."

Palmer nodded, and when he seemed to be concentrating on his drink, Sandy took the hint and left.

Mona Charbonneau pulled her battered silver Ford Escort into the Weird Fellows parking lot, turned off the motor, and pulled down the visor to check her makeup in the mirror she had attached there with two-faced tape.

Behind her, she saw a white Chevy pickup with three young men crammed into the front seat drive slowly down the narrow road in front of the hall, but this was Pennsylvania where everybody drove a truck and she paid no more than fleeting attention to the vehicle.

Her makeup, she decided, looked good. She was a pretty redheaded woman, a few years past forty, but she convinced herself she looked no more than thirty-five. She sat in the car, messing with her hair which already looked fine, and realized that she was just stalling.

20

She wondered how she would be treated inside the Weird Fellows Hall. The last time she had been there was six months ago with Howie, but then Howie had left her and she had been sitting home alone at nights—and a little of that went a long way—and now she had decided she needed some company.

Howie was not coming back; not that she minded much, because he was a nasty drunk with a slow wallet and a fast fist, and his idea of an evening's entertainment was to sit around the house, drinking beer and watching sitcoms until he was blotto, when he would drag Mona to bed and roughly try to take her. Usually, he was too drunk.

And that was another thing she needed.

She got out of the car, not bothering to lock the doors. She noticed the white pickup drive by again in the opposite direction. She tucked her well-filled soft pink sweater neatly into her skirt, smoothed the skirt, and walked toward the door of the bar. She heard someone whistle from a passing truck. That made her feel good.

Third inning and the bar was filling up nicely. In small private clubs like this one, the members ran a whole fleet of fund-raising activities ranging from bingos to cake sales, but the truth always was that bar revenues had to pay the freight for running the rest of the club.

Sandy had been surprised to see Mona Charbonneau come in. After Howie had left her, the bartender had figured that Mona was out partying every night in Allentown, the nearest big city, especially the way Howie had always complained that his wife had round heels and wanted to pop into bed at all hours of the day and night. Howie used to say she only married him because he was the only man she had ever met who could keep her satisfied in bed.

Somehow Sandy doubted it. Most nights Howie was

at the hall, he could barely walk when he left. That didn't sound like any demon lover to him.

But she had come in, looking nice and being friendly, and sat at a corner of the bar near Gene Palmer and, wonder of wonders, they had started to talk and now they were sitting side by side like old friends, gassing away. Maybe he had been wrong, Sandy thought. Maybe Palmer was just a lonely guy, looking for female company.

Nothing wrong with that, he thought. *And if Mona's still here around closing time, maybe I'll take a little run at her myself.* Unless she was with Gene Palmer. No sense in messing with a big tipper.

"So then he left me. Without a note, without any explanation. Just up and left. Like wham, bam, screw you, ma'am."

"Sounds like a jerk to me," Gene Palmer said. "Good riddance to bad rubbish."

Mona nodded, and moved her body over on her bar stool so that their thighs touched lightly.

"That's the way I figure it too," she said. "So what's your tale of woe?"

"Nothing much," Palmer said. "Widower for five years, salesman, working out in California, moved here when the company closed down."

"What do you sell?" she said.

"Army helicopters."

"There are no helicopter plants around here," Mona said. "Or army bases, for that matter."

Palmer snapped his fingers. "Maybe *that's* why it's so tough to make a buck."

Mona giggled and moved still closer to him. She let her hand fall casually onto his leg.

"Maybe us lonely people have to take care of each other," she said.

"If we don't, who will?" Palmer said. He smiled and Mona thought he had a nice gentle smile.

The white Chevy pickup had parked amidst a bunch of cars and trucks in the closed gas station next to the Weird Fellows Hall.

Three young men had gotten out of the cab and walked to the alley alongside the building where they pulled ski masks from their pockets and yanked them over their heads.

"Okay," one said. "We've got about fifteen minutes. Sassy will call the cops in . . ." He glanced at his watch. "In one more minute and she'll get them to go over to the other side of town. By the time they figure out it's a phony, we'll be done and gone here."

"Okay," the other two mumbled.

"And don't forget. Take their wallets, but keep your eyes open for pay envelopes too. This is payday and anyway a lot of them bring money so they can play poker after the bar closes, so a lot of them should be loaded. Get it all."

"How about jewelry, watches and stuff?"

"Grab that too. Grab everything."

"Let's go, I'm getting nervous," one said.

"We wait until we hear the police si-reen, then we know we're home free." He took a .38 Police Special from inside his belt and checked, for the hundredth time, to make sure it was loaded. Through the mouth slit of his ski mask, the other two could see him grinning.

From far away, they heard the sound of a siren.

Eugene Palmer saw the three of them come in the front door of the tavern and knew immediately what was going on.

He leaned close to Mona and said, "Don't panic. There's some trouble, but just do what they say."

23

She did not understand what he was talking about so she giggled and squeezed his thigh. They were both on their third drinks now—hers was Scotch on the rocks—and she was a little drunk.

Only one of them with a gun, Palmer thought. *That makes them kids. Trouble. Kids are nuts.*

Somebody yelled out, "What the hell is this, Halloween?" just as the masked man with the gun planted himself in the middle of the bar and shouted, "Don't anybody move. This is a stickup."

Palmer noticed that the gunman's voice quavered slightly. *Kids. Today's kids are pains in the ass.*

Sandy, the bartender, moved closer to the beer taps where Palmer knew he kept a small handgun.

But the man with the gun cocked the pistol and said, "Don't get cute, bartender, or somebody'll get hurt. Get your hands up. All of you."

There were sixteen people at the bar, all men except for Mona Charbonneau. Mona's lips were quivering. She was frightened and did not know what to do, and Palmer patted her reassuringly on the leg with one hand while he halfheartedly raised his other hand above his head in compliance with the holdup man's orders.

The two other bandits had gone to the far end of the bar and were working their way up, stripping wallets and wristwatches from the customers at the bar.

Some of the men grumbled but no one seemed willing to challenge the holdup men. Two of the men groaned when their pay envelopes were lifted from their shirt pockets.

They had worked their way almost down the whole bar when the man with the gun tapped one of them and said, "Empty the register."

The other man nodded and ran around behind the bar and started to scoop the change out into his jacket pockets. The third man came around the corner of the bar to Palmer and Mona.

"Okay, your wallets," he said.

24

Mona nodded toward her tan leather purse, next to her on the bar, and the robber rooted around inside and came out with her wallet, which he stuck into his jacket.

Palmer noticed the man in the middle of the floor, holding a gun, glance at the clock over the bar.

"Hurry up," he snapped.

The nearest robber turned to Palmer. "Your wallet."

"Back left pocket," Palmer said.

"Get it yourself. I ain't no fairy."

Palmer shrugged, pulled out his wallet with his left hand, and handed it to the man.

"And your watch."

Palmer shook his head.

"Your watch, I said."

"No. Can't have it."

"Why not?"

"It's a present from my wife."

"Tell her to buy you another one," the robber said.

"She's dead," Palmer said.

The robber nodded for a moment, as if that made sense, then bawled out, "This guy won't give me his watch."

The one emptying the cash register had come back around the bar, and now the gunman walked over toward Palmer. He kept the gun fixed on Palmer's face.

"What's the matter here?"

"He won't give me his watch."

"A present from my wife," Palmer said. "You can't have it."

The gunman said, "This your wife?" He waved the gun in his right hand toward Mona, then reached out his left hand and fastened it on Mona's breast. "She looks like a whore. What do you think of that?"

"I think you're a rude son of a bitch," Palmer said, and shot his right leg up from the knee, burying the toe of his shoe in the gunman's testicles.

As the gunman buckled over with an exhaled "whoof," Palmer whipped his hand around the top of

25

the gun, the webbing between his thumb and index finger jammed into the hammer so the gun could not fire, and he yanked it from the man's hand. Even as he did, his other hand shot out and punched the second holdup man on the jaw, sending him reeling backward.

Then Palmer was on his feet, herding the two men toward the center of the room. The third gunman fled out the door. No one thought to chase him, and then, when they all realized what had happened, the men in the bar cheered.

"Okay," Palmer said. "You two down on the floor. Face down. Put your hands behind your head."

The leader was slow to comply, and Palmer swiped his legs out from under him with his own leg and the man fell heavily onto the linoleum floor.

Palmer looked toward Sandy at the bar and said, "Better call the cops."

The television crew—a reporter and a cameraman— had been in Macungie to shoot a nighttime feature story on a local haunted house, but no ghosts had arrived and they were on their way back to the offices of Local Channel 68 when they heard the report of the attempted robbery over the police radio in their van.

"What the hell," said Dave Kinnock, the reporter. "Let's go over there. Maybe we'll come away with something tonight."

The cameraman who was driving looked at the green numbers on the digital clock over the dash. "If it's good, we could still remote it in for the eleven o'clock show," he said.

"We'll never be that lucky," said Kinnock.

The police had the two holdup men in custody—they turned out to be teenagers from the next town over—and had already issued an alarm for the one youth who had escaped.

Lieutenant Chet Dorney, who had been roused from his home to come to take over the case, was talking to Gene Palmer and the others at the bar when a patrolman came into the Weird Fellows and whispered something in his ear.

Dorney nodded and said, "I'll be back in a few minutes. I've got something to take care of."

He stepped outside to meet the TV crew from Channel 68.

Palmer told Mona, "Screw this, I'm leaving. I should have left right away."

"Can I go with you?" she said.

"Ahhh, maybe it's not a good night for it," he said. "Let's get together some night without guns."

She looked both disappointed and used to disappointment. "All right," she said. "I'm in the phone book if you change your mind."

"I'll remember," Palmer said. He got up, left twenty dollars on the bar to cover his and Mona's drinks, and walked outside. As soon as he got outdoors, however, bright camera lights shone in his face.

He heard Lieutenant Dorney say, "And this is the real hero of the evening. Mr. Gene Palmer."

His eyes squinted down, Palmer could see the young newsman coming toward him.

"No, no," Palmer said.

"Just a word, Mr. Palmer," the newsman said.

"I've got nothing to say." Palmer tried to brush by, but the police lieutenant grabbed his arm.

"Mr. Palmer here disarmed the robber and then overcame both of them."

"Weren't you afraid?" the newsman asked Palmer, who was riveted in place by the big policeman's hand on his arm.

Palmer tried to pull away again, failed, and sighed.

"No. You could tell they were kids and didn't know one end of a gun from the other. I have to go now."

"Just a few more questions," the newsman said. "You sound like an expert. Have you had any experience with guns?"

"No," Palmer said.

"How did you know the holdup men were kids, as you put it?"

Palmer shrugged. "They didn't know how to split up or to control the bar. They kept getting themselves all jammed up together in one spot. Nobody knew what they were doing."

The TV man chuckled. "You certainly sound like an expert."

"I read cop books," Palmer said.

"We understand you're a newcomer to Macungie, Mr. Palmer. What do you do for a living?"

"I sell paper carnations. You know, like magicians use in their act. Say, you're not going to use any of this film, are you?"

"We already are, Mr. Palmer. You're live, right now, on Channel Sixty-eight, On-Line News."

Palmer groaned. He tried to pull his arm free from the lieutenant's grasp but still couldn't shake loose. Finally, he turned to the cameraman and smiled at the TV camera's red light and said, "And I'd just like to say hello to my mother if she's watching." He held up an index finger declaring himself Number One. "Hi, Ma. I did it for you." Then he stuck his thumbs in his ears and waggled his fingers at the camera.

The lieutenant dropped his arm and Palmer walked across the parking lot to his car.

He saw Mona Charbonneau standing by her own car, fumbling with the door handle. She saw him and smiled, and Palmer said under his breath, "What the hell, why not? Everything else is ruined," and walked over to the woman.

* * *

Fifteen miles away, in his small brick house in Allentown, Daniel Taylor, special agent in charge of the Lehigh Valley office of the Federal Bureau of Investigation, was sitting in front of the TV set, drinking Coors beer from the can, his shoeless feet propped up on a coffee table.

His two young children had had trouble getting to sleep tonight and his wife was in their bedroom calming them down.

When Eugene Palmer's face came on the TV screen, Taylor sat bolt upright on the sofa. His knee knocked over the can of beer and it spilled on the table, but he did not even notice.

"You son of a bitch!" he screamed at the top of his voice.

As he watched the interview, his wife came into the room.

"Daniel, the children."

"Screw the children," he shouted. "Shut up."

She looked at the screen and saw a pleasant-looking fortyish man explaining how he knew some holdup men were just kids. So what was the big deal?

She looked at Taylor again. He was staring at the TV screen and mumbling under his breath.

She leaned forward to hear his words. He was saying, over and over again, "Die, you bastard, die. Die, you bastard, die."

And when Palmer said on the screen, "I'd just like to say hello to my mom," and then insanely stuck his thumbs in his ears and waggled his fingers, Taylor groaned again and buried his face in his hands.

Mrs. Taylor left the room, shaking her head. Sometimes he got this way. Working for the FBI put a lot of pressure on a man.

29

Chapter Three

Russia:

The trip was almost over, and Vladimir took both hands off the wheel and rubbed his aching eyes. Even without being steered, the ton-and-a-half truck plodded straight ahead, its wheels sunk into the deep ruts that years of traffic had carved into the unpaved dirt road.

He glanced in the sideview mirror and saw an identical truck following him, fifty yards back. The sun had just come up and the long morning rays painted the gray side of the truck a garish yellow, the color of egg yolks.

There were two men in the second truck, and for a moment, Vladimir let himself wonder if they had families who would miss them. Then he put the thought out of his mind. No sense in complicating things. They were complicated enough. No one would miss this pair of drifters.

He pressed on the accelerator as the truck started to

lug going up a long grade. And then he was at the crest of the hill, and he could see a small utility vehicle waiting for him in the valley below.

Almost done, he thought. *And it can't be too soon for me. But first to deal with these Afghans and get away without being killed.* He warmed himself with the thought that this night he would sleep in a soft, warm bed. And, he hoped, not alone.

"Damn. He must be made of iron," the passenger in the second truck said as Vladimir's vehicle disappeared over the crest of the hill. "Doesn't he ever get tired?" The passenger's name was Boris.

Pimen, the driver, grunted and sipped from a thermos of now-cold tea perched precariously on the dashboard of the truck. He made a face of disgust as he swallowed. "It's easier for him," he said. "Maybe he's made the trip before. He knows the road."

"Well, I hope he knows it well enough that we don't wind up in Afghanistan. Those Afghans are crazy bastards. They'd yank the eyeballs from our head for these two loads of guns. I don't want to run into any of them."

"What are you, an idiot?" Pimen spat. "Of course we're going to see some Afghans. You think we drove all this way south to get a suntan?"

"But . . ."

"But nothing. We've got two loads of guns. Obviously that sleepless bastard in the other truck is going to sell them or trade them. Who else but Afghans?"

"I don't like it," Boris said sourly.

"We don't have to like it. We just have to like the two hundred rubles each that we're getting for driving."

The truck topped the hill and down below they saw Vladimir's truck slowing to a stop next to a smaller vehicle.

"And here we are," Pimen said. "Two hundred rubles. I'm going to buy the biggest steak in town."

"We're not back in Moscow yet," Boris said.

The two Afghans were the same ones who had met him on his previous trip, when Vladimir had first negotiated the deal. They wore long loose headdresses above loose, knee-length white tunics. Their khaki pants were bloused into their boots. Across their backs were slung assault rifles, and on their hips they carried the eighteen-inch-long curved knives that during the war had become known to the Russian people as almost a symbol of the fierce Afghan guerrillas.

The two men were leaning on the hood of their small truck and they nodded at Vladimir as he hopped down to the ground and approached them.

"A pleasant journey?" one said in accurate, but almost stilted, Russian.

"Uneventful," Vladimir said. "You have my goods?"

The man nodded. "And you, ours?"

"Yes," Vladimir answered. "Let's look things over."

Glancing nervously about him, he walked to the back of the small truck which was only slightly larger than a Jeep, and pulled aside a canvas, uncovering four metal cases, each just a little bigger than one cubic foot.

He opened one in the back, shoved his hand down into the crate, and brought out a tightly woven cotton bag, tied around the top with string.

He heard the second truck stop with a tortured squeal of its tired old brakes.

He slid the string from around the neck of the bag and dipped his right index finger into the white powder inside, then licked it from his fingertip.

He thought about it a moment, then smiled at the two Afghans who had come alongside him.

"Fine," he said. "And of course it's all like this?"

"It all came from factory at the same time," the Russian-speaking man answered. "All identical."

"Good. You'll want to inspect the weapons?"

The Afghan looked at him blankly, not responding, making it clear that the idea of *not* inspecting the weapons was one no sane man would even consider. "Of course," the Afghan answered.

Vladimir retied the top of the cotton bag and inserted it back into its carton. There were twenty-four identical bags, each containing two kilograms of pure cocaine.

Forty-eight kilos. It would be worth a fortune back in Moscow, Vladimir thought.

He led the two Afghans back toward his own truck. Boris and Pimen were sitting on the front bumper of their truck, parked ten yards behind Vladimir's, smoking cigarettes. They looked nervous as the three men approached, but the Afghans ignored them and one of them clambered up over the tailgate of the truck and vanished inside the canvas curtain.

The sounds of wooden crates being jimmied open echoed in the still, warm air.

Then the Afghan jumped lightly down to the ground and nodded to his companion.

"Fine," the second Afghan said to Vladimir in Russian. "Then we are done."

Vladimir smiled and clapped the man on the shoulder in a friendly gesture.

And then a voice, amplified by a bullhorn, roared out over the small valley.

"Hands up. Don't anybody move. You're all under arrest."

Cowboy Rostov and his six men had reached the spot where the transfer was to be made an hour before daylight. Cowboy had sent four men to the other side of the small valley, and stayed on the near side with the rest of his squad.

At his orders, they had uprooted all the scrub brush they could find in the barren area and covered themselves with it in a crude form of camouflage. Rostov did not know if either of the "traders" would have a helicopter at their disposal, but the camouflage might fool somebody who was not paying enough attention. However, he did not expect a helicopter. The fact that this valley had been chosen for the arms-for-drugs switch proved that the suspects were getting careless. It was a place made for ambushes. "Bushwhacking," they called it in the Hollywood western movies that he loved to watch. He would have liked to put a couple of his men at the entrance to the small valley, but there was no protective cover there. The hillsides would have to do.

And then his men had hunkered down to wait. It was a hot and boring four hours before the trucks had arrived and Rostov climbed out of the protective covering of sparse greenery and bellowed his orders at the five suspects below.

At the first sound of Rostov's voice, the Afghan who spoke Russian snarled a curse, yanked his gun from his shoulder, and fired a burst up the hillside, even as he rolled under the ammunition truck. The other Afghan followed.

Boris and Pimen, at first, seemed confused. Then both men got to their feet and looked up at the ridge, where they caught glimpses of armed men in khaki, and they stood and raised their arms over their heads in a sullen dumb fashion.

"Not so goddam fast," Vladimir snarled. He pulled a pistol from the holster on his belt, and squeezed off a shot too. Then he grabbed Boris around the neck from behind and, using him as a partial shield, shoved him toward the small utility vehicle that held the cocaine.

"Stop it, I don't want to get shot," Boris yelled. His voice sounded almost tearful.

Vladimir put the pistol to the younger man's temple. "Then keep moving," he snarled.

The two Afghans under the truck were now spraying both hillsides with automatic fire, and the policemen were unable to move up onto the ridge in firing position.

Vladimir pushed Boris into the passenger seat of the drug vehicle, then clambered over him to get behind the wheel. The key was in the ignition and the small truck started right up. With a skidding of gravel and sand, Vladimir pulled past both weapons trucks and started back down the road, the way they had come. Bullets from the police pinged around him; one shattered the windshield, and Vladimir punched the rest of it out with the butt of his pistol.

Now he heard the sound of grenades exploding, and behind him he could see the white cloud of tear gas settling down into the small declivity in the earth.

Close. But I'm going to make it, he thought. *And I've got the drugs.* The truck started up the grade of the road leading out of the valley, and Vladimir pushed the pedal down, then turned, put a bullet into Boris's temple, and shoved him from the cab. In the rearview mirror, he saw the body hit and roll.

And then he saw something else. Racing on foot down the hillside, through the clouds of gas, braving the fire, was a tall man wearing a white cowboy's hat. Vladimir could see bullets kicking up around his feet, but the man must have been charmed, because somehow the shots missed him, and he climbed into the driver's seat of the second arms truck and began to turn it around.

A moment later, he was lugging up the hill after Vladimir.

* * *

Following Rostov's orders, two men split off from his group and worked their ways in opposite directions to each end of the small valley.

They came down along the road from both directions into the valley, and when they had worked near enough, both started spraying automatic fire underneath the remaining arms truck where the two Afghans were holding out.

One stray bullet hit Pimen in the leg and he fell heavily, then rolled to the side of the roadway to try to escape.

With his body out of the way, both Russian policemen dropped to the ground and poured full clips of fire under the arms truck. At the same time, the other militsia ran down the hill toward the truck.

As they ran, they screamed, "Geronimo!"

None knew what it meant; it was just a word that Cowboy had taught them.

There was no return fire, and Sergeant Federenko barked an order to stop shooting. The little canyon was quiet. Rostov's men were crouched off to the sides, weapons still pointing at the weapons truck. Carefully, Federenko stood at the side of the road, ready to dodge if someone should fire at him. When there were no shots, he walked over toward the truck. Holding his gun ready, he bent down and looked under the truck at the bullet-riddled body of the two Afghans. Even though his eyes were tearing with the residue of the tear-gas grenades they had thrown, he could see the men's eyes open in death.

He stood up and waved his men forward, and as he did, Pimen, with the eyes of a wounded puppy, looked at the men approaching down the side, then raised his arms up into the air and cried, "Mercy, mercy. I surrender."

Sergeant Federenko saw him and smiled. "Cowboy

36

will be happy,'' he told Vadim Barabanov. "At least we've got one. Take good care of him.''

Barabanov, heavy-footed and clumsy, slogged across the road to tend to Pimen's wounds.

Georgi Golovin ran up to the sergeant.

"Cowboy's gone. Should we go after him?'' he asked excitedly.

"In time,'' Federenko said with no apparent concern. "Some things he likes to do on his own. Go over there and help Vadim bandage that one's leg.''

When he reached the top of the hill, Lev Rostov saw the smaller truck down below him, and he knew that the big lumbering vehicle he had, loaded down with the weight of arms and ammunition, would not be able to catch it.

He had just one chance.

Cowboy jammed the accelerator to the floor even as the truck started down the hill. He saw that the hill leveled out briefly before starting up the incline on the other side.

If he could only build up enough speed. . . .

The truck rumbled and roared down the hill. Its growing momentum added to the speed Rostov was able to get from the clattering engine and it bounced down the slope after the drug wagon. Rostov could see he was narrowing the gap.

Now, if he could keep the truck's speed at its maximum, momentum might enable him to gain even more ground going up the hill on the far side . . . and that might give him a chance.

He must be crazy, Vladimir thought as he saw the truck lumbering closer to him. He tried to get more speed from his own truck but it was pulling the hill now and did not respond to his pressure on the accelerator. He was slowing, but he realized it did not matter. He would still beat the other truck to the crest and after that the road was straight for many miles. He would just simply run away from him then.

Too bad. In a life of crime, he had found out that a lot of cops were just simply crazy—and they were always the easiest ones to kill. He wished that he had a chance to teach that lesson to the driving maniac behind him.

Still gaining, he noticed. *Nothing to worry about*.

Now or never, thought Cowboy. He had narrowed the gap between the trucks to only about thirty yards but the drug vehicle was almost at the top of the hill. In an instant, it would be over the crest, out of sight and out of reach.

Still holding down the accelerator, Rostov fought the pressure of the wind to push open the driver's door of his own truck and then, without hesitating, he jumped from the vehicle. He jumped in a peculiar fashion, facing the front of the vehicle but pushing his body backward, jumping toward the truck's rear. As he did, he yanked the steering wheel clockwise so the truck headed off to the right, out of his line of fire.

He hit the ground running, sucked in a large breath of air, and dropped to a crouch, then leveled his small Kalashnikov automatic at the rear of Vladimir's vehicle, which was nearing the hilltop.

Rostov pulled his elbows into his waist to try to steady the notoriously inaccurate weapon, then squeezed the trigger slowly. A solid rip of sound accompanied the heavy spray of fire and he panned the weapon slightly from side to side, aiming low, aiming at the spot where the drug truck's tires met the ground. It would give him the most margin for error, because even a shot that was too low had a chance of rebounding upward to find its target.

In just a split second, the weapon's clip was exhausted, but Rostov saw the other vehicle jolt, almost as if its engine had coughed before it crested the hill.

He had done what he wanted to do: blow out one or both of the rear tires.

He started running up the hill, even as he heard the dull thud of his own truck mashing headfirst into one of the few trees that were scattered about the alien landscape. The engine whirred for a moment, then stopped, and the only sound Rostov heard were his own footsteps as he ran.

At the top of the hill, he had to stifle a cry of triumph. He had gotten not only the wheels but the gas tank, and a small spit of flame was visible at the truck where the leaking gas had dripped onto the hot exhaust pipe.

The driver must have seen it too, because as the truck reached the bottom of the hill, Rostov saw the brake lights flash and then the driver jumping from the truck, hitting heavily, then scrambling to his feet and running off to the left, toward a rugged-looking tree-lined ravine.

The drug truck rolled to a stop, before igniting with a whooshing burst of flame.

The driver turned and saw Rostov, then kept running. Cowboy loped after him.

The ravine was like a scar dug into the face of the earth by God's fingernail. It was almost a mile long and heavily wooded on both sides. A small stream meandered along down at the bottom of it.

Escape should be easy, Vladimir thought. *At least, if there are no dogs.*

He turned down to the stream, hardly deeper than a creek, and ran along the rocky bed for several hundred yards, before picking his way back up the hillside. He stopped to catch his breath and picked a pair of cigars from the breast pocket of his shirt. He crumbled the dry tobacco between his hands and sprinkled it over the ground. That should take care of dogs *if* the damned militsia even had dogs.

Now he needed only someplace to hide. A cave, a fallen tree, maybe even a heavily greened tree that he could climb. If he could just elude them until dark, then he would just walk away and by morning be far from this place.

One of the drivers he had hired was still alive, and he congratulated himself for having the sense never to tell his drivers anything about him. All they knew was that his name was Vladimir, and there was no shortage of Vladimirs in Moscow.

Still, he felt badly about losing the shipment of drugs. That would not go down well with his superiors, especially since he was not bringing back the guns either.

But they would understand. Vladimir had handled a half-dozen drug transactions before, with never a problem, never a gram of drugs missing, and that kind of record had to be worth something. And besides, he had other resources. He knew who the bosses were, and before he let anybody punish him for bad luck that he could not control, he would go to the authorities. The bosses would know that too.

No, they will understand and they will protect me. And if I am apprehended, they will even provide me with an attorney. Despite his circumstances, the last thought brought a smile to his face.

He found a fallen tree, apparently broken off by lightning five feet above the ground. The long trunk of the tree formed a lean-to with the ground and it was still heavily greened with parasite weeds and brush. He clambered inside the natural tent and settled down to wait until dark, when he could make his escape. Then he heard a faint buzzing sound.

* * *

Cowboy looked down along the stream meandering through the ravine.

In case we've got dogs, he'll run along the streambed to kill his scent, he thought. *Then he'll just go to ground and try to wait it out until nightfall. He knows we probably can't get reinforcements here in time to stop him. He'll be someplace up near the other end. Let's see what kind of trail he's left. I want this bastard alive.*

The only sound Vladimir could hear was the buzzing of mosquitoes around his head. He had never known they were so bad here; they enveloped his head in a dark swarm. He could feel their needles piercing his flesh, sucking his blood. When he was young, he had read about mosquito swarms so vicious that they could drive large farm animals crazy, that they could kill grown men with their millions of stings, but he had always thought they were folk tales.

Until now.

They were killing him. They were biting his exposed skin and piercing his clothing and it was all he could do to stifle a scream and finally he could take no more and he scrambled up to his knees and then bolted from under the cover of the fallen tree out into a small clearing.

And there was the big policeman, wearing the cowboy hat, walking toward him from no more than fifteen feet away and Vladimir roared in tortured anger and raised his gun at the militsia man, but before he could squeeze the trigger, the cop's hand flashed to his side and slapped a long pistol from a holster he wore and put one bullet right between Vladimir's eyes.

"You son of a bitch, you made me kill you," Lev Rostov growled, and slowly replaced the gun in his holster.

* * *

The man had carried no wallet and Rostov could not find even one piece of paper in any of his pockets.

Slowly, methodically, he set about stripping the corpse of all his clothing to search the body. The shoes, he noticed, were of very expensive soft leather. They zipped up the side. He pulled them off, and stuck in the toe of one of the shoes, he found a driver's license. The heavy cardboard license was covered in plastic, apparently by some homemade laminating kit. It had been issued to one Vladimir Slepak, forty-two, and gave a Moscow address that Rostov immediately knew was fake.

He shoved the license into his pocket and stood up. For the first time, he took notice of the mosquitoes that were swarming heavily around him. He swatted one and realized that he would have to get out of there quickly before the swarm reached killer size. There was no way he could carry out Vladimir's body without falling prey to the mosquitoes.

From inside the belt of his trousers he removed a long hunting knife and, using its thick point as both a blade and a chisel, cut off the five fingers of the man's right hand, just where they joined the palm. Even as he stuck them into a plastic sandwich bag he carried in his pocket, he turned and ran down to the stream to follow it out of these accursed, bug-infested woods.

Chapter Four

Washington, D.C.:

"I hope it's important," the sleep-thickened voice said.

"I think it is," said Daniel Taylor from the phone at his desk in the FBI's darkened Lehigh Valley office. "I waited till now to call you."

"What is it, five-thirty A.M.? Thanks for nothing. What is it?"

The man in bed in Washington sat up and turned on the light on his bedroom end table. His wife began to grumble in her sleep and the man pulled the comforter up over her head. At least it would block out some of the noise. At most and with some luck, it might suffocate her.

"It's Peter Kamen." Daniel Taylor's excited voice crackled over the phone.

"What about him?"

"He's done it again," Taylor said. "Tonight, he was in a tavern and it got held up. He disarmed the robbers and held them for police."

"Not too bad," the man in Washington said.

"Except he hung around and then got interviewed on television. He's going under the name of Eugene Palmer."

"I know what name he's going under," the other man snapped. "I picked it for him myself. Anything else?"

"No," Taylor said slowly. "I just thought you'd want to know as soon as possible."

"Fine." The man in Washington paused. "How did you find out about this?"

"I was watching the late news on television and I saw his silly face in front of me."

"That's what I thought," the other man said. "You might ask yourself a question."

"What's that?" Daniel Taylor said.

"Were you the only one watching television last night? Or maybe somebody else saw him."

There was a stunned heavy silence on the other end of the telephone and then Daniel Taylor said, "Oh, shit."

"Exactly. I think you'd better get a move on. And then, come and see me."

Macungie, Pennsylvania:

The unmarked gray car pulled onto the quiet tree-lined street in one of the placid little towns that surrounded the big industrial centers of Allentown and Bethlehem.

The driver turned off the lights and the motor and let the car glide to a stop.

"Your FBI on the job," he grunted softly to his passenger, who grimly sipped from a container of black coffee.

The two men waited silently until they saw another quietly-gray car turn the corner from the other direction

44

and repeat the lights-out, motor-off, roll-to-a-stop maneuver.

Two men got out of the second car and came down the street. The driver rolled down his window as the men approached.

One of them asked, "What the hell are we doing here?"

"Taylor's got a wild hair up his butt. That house there . . ." He paused to point toward a small frame house with a wooden porch. An improbably-wide late-model Mercury sat in the driveway alongside. "The guy who lives there is in the witness-protection program. Taylor thinks somebody might try to take him out."

"Oh, for Christ's sake. For this they get me out of a nice warm wife? Who is this guy? What's the big deal?"

No one had a chance to answer.

It was not exactly an explosion, it was more like a sudden whoosh of air into a vacuum, but suddenly the sky was lighter. The two FBI men who had been standing alongside the car instinctively dropped to the pavement in confusion, and when they peered up a moment later, through the windows of the house, they could see flames racing around inside the building.

"Oh, shit, they got him," the driver groaned. He pushed open the car door to get out.

His passenger growled, "We're in deep now, guys," and he too got out and three of the men ran toward the burning house, from which flames were now licking out the windows.

The other FBI man jumped into the car and turned his radio to the frequency of the local police and reported the fire before running after his partners.

All four men charged into the burning house, without any apparent regard for their own safety, but once inside they knew they had lost.

The stairway to the second floor had been destroyed in

the explosion. A few loose steps jutted at awkward angles from a plasterboard wall, but there was no way to climb them and at the head of what had been the stairway they could hear the fire roaring.

The intense heat now sucked the breath from their lungs, and the smoke billowed heavily around them when the driver and senior agent of the group coughed through the smoke, "Screw it. We'd better get out of here. This guy's already a pizza. Let's leave him for the fire department."

The four men stood glumly across the street, watching the fire burn. Far away, they heard the whoop of the town's lone engine on its way toward them. Down the block, at least a hundred feet away, they saw a light come on in one of the houses, and heard the excited voices of people who had come out on their front porch and—

"What the hell is that?" one of the agents snapped.

He pointed across the street where the rear door of the Mercury parked in the driveway of the burning building opened and a man staggered out.

As he stared in what seemed to be dazed confusion at the burning building, the man idly tucked his shirttails into his trousers with one hand. In the other hand, he held a pint bottle of Seagram's Seven.

As the four men ran over to surround him, he dropped into a crouch and held the bottle by its neck in front of him.

"Eugene Palmer?" the team leader said.

The man looked at him suspiciously.

"Yeah?" he said.

"FBI. You have to come with us."

"Yeah? Let me see some identification."

The agent pulled his wallet from his pocket. He tried to flash it quickly at Palmer, but the man grabbed it from his hand and carefully examined the card behind the clear plastic shield. Then he handed it back with a big boyish grin.

"You had me fooled there for a minute," he said. "I thought you were the bad guys," Palmer said. He relaxed and lowered the bottle. "Let's go," he said cheerily.

The agents split into pairs and Palmer followed two of them to their car and got into the back seat. They pulled away just as the fire engine turned the corner into the street.

"What were you doing in that car?" the driver asked.

"Sleeping," Palmer said.

"Why were you sleeping in the car?"

"Well, I didn't start out sleeping in the car," Palmer said with an edge to his voice. "I picked up this woman and then we were in the car, drinking and fooling around and then I guess she left and I dozed off."

"Do you always do your fooling around in a car?"

"Not usually," Palmer said. "But tonight it seemed like a good idea 'cause I thought somebody might try to nail me at the house. I just didn't count on falling asleep."

The other agent twisted in his seat and looked back at Palmer. The man was sprawled across the back seat, his shirt still open to the waist, holding the bottle of whiskey straight up, trying to get out a last elusive drop.

"Mr. Palmer," the agent asked, "why would somebody want to blow up your house?"

There was a short pause before the answer came.

"Because I'm the most dangerous man in America." He finally gave up with the empty whiskey bottle and dropped it on the seat. He burped. A moment later, he was snoring.

Chapter Five

Moscow:

Olga Lutska, second assistant deputy prosecutor for the Moscow district, had never before tried a case involving Lieutenant Lev Rostov.

But, despite "Cowboy's" well-known reputation as sort of a militsia wild man, she expected no trouble with the case this day.

Her meeting with Lieutenant Rostov was scheduled for one P.M., an hour before the arraignment of Pimen Spatsky—forty-one, unemployed, charged with theft of people's property, drug dealing, and unauthorized sale of arms—was to begin.

She had skipped her lunch hour to read the reports and familiarize herself with the case, and when Rostov arrived, neatly dressed in civilian clothes and not wearing his ten-gallon hat, she ushered him into her office and said quickly, "I think we've got a very simple case."

Rostov slumped down in his chair and for a moment

Olga thought it was an unmannerly attitude to adopt and it annoyed her, but she pushed the feeling from her mind.

Rostov still had not said anything more than hello. That made her nervous for some reason and she said quickly, "I think Judge Alekhine can dispose of this one in a few minutes. He'll hold him without bail, and at trial, this Spatsky is looking at at least ten years."

Rostov sat up and shook his head. "I don't want him to be held. Not yet, anyway. I want him set free."

"What do you mean?"

"My squad and I are still investigating this whole case. Where the guns came from. Who organized the operation. Where the drugs were going to be shipped."

He paused and Olga said, "Yes, I gathered all that from your report. But I also gathered that Spatsky knows nothing. He was just hired as a driver. He didn't even know the last name of this . . ." She looked down at the papers on her desk. ". . . this Vladimir who was apparently in charge."

"That's right," Rostov said. "And Vladimir is still at large. Now if Spatsky gets sent to jail, that's the end of it and the mob will realize that he didn't talk—maybe that he had nothing to say—and that will be the end of it. But if we hold Spatsky for further investigation . . . if we hint to the court that he's a cooperative witness . . . the mob might get nervous and try to do something. That could be an opening."

"The mob?" Olga Lutska said with a faint hint of condescension in her voice.

Rostov nodded. "Yes, the mob. The Mafia if you wish. It is obviously behind this drug deal, just as it has been behind a half-dozen other cases of ours that sudden disintegrated at the last moment."

"I don't know anything about any Mafia," Olga said crisply. "And I don't know anything about any maybe they'll do this and maybe they'll do that. We have a man involved with stolen army guns and buying drugs, and I think if we deal with him harshly, we send a message to everyone else who might be thinking of doing the same thing.''

Rostov leaned forward and smiled, and Olga thought that he had a very nice smile.

"Look, Madam Prosecutor," he said. "You agree we have an open-and-shut case.''

"Yes. And Miss Lutska will be fine.''

"All right. In two weeks, we'll have the same open-and-shut case and we can send Spatsky away for as long as you want. But trust me. Give me and my men the two weeks to see what we can produce. I'm not asking you to change your opinion or your court case. I'm just asking you to delay it for a few days.''

The way he said it all seemed very logical. Olga had to admit that. She was silent for a long time as she read from the file on her desk. Then she looked up and nodded.

"All right. We'll see if the judge will go along,'' she said.

"We have Judge Alekhine?" Rostov asked.

"Yes. He's just been promoted to chief judge of the criminal courts.''

"Is he sane?''

"I beg your pardon.''

"I've not dealt with Judge Alekhine before. Is he sane?''

"I'm sure he's as sane as you are,'' Olga said.

Rostov grinned. "I can tell you don't believe that's much of a recommendation.''

"Judge Alekhine will be fine,'' Olga said. "I'll ask him to postpone formal arraignment for two weeks while the investigation continues.''

"And hint that Spatsky is cooperating with us.''

"All right. And bail?''

"A small amount," Rostov said. "As if it's his reward for being cooperative.''

"I'm not sure I like any of this," Olga said.

"Trust me."

She nodded again, then pushed all the papers of the file back into a leather briefcase and walked out from behind her desk. Rostov got up slowly and watched her walk away. *How does such a beautiful woman become a prosecutor?* he wondered.

She interrupted his thought. "I will see you in the courtroom promptly at two P.M.," she said.

"Of course . . . Olga," he said.

The courthouse was located on Petrovka Street, less than a mile from the Kremlin and only a few blocks from the big yellow building that housed the militsia headquarters.

Sergeant Mikhail Federenko waited on the steps of the courthouse, feeling out of place in a business suit that he felt made him look just like a lawyer.

That most lawyers did not have cauliflower ears or gnarled, often-broken knuckles did not occur to him. It was the suit that stamped the man. Federenko worked almost exclusively in plainclothes now as the second-in-command of Rostov's special narcotics squad, but the truth was he had always felt more comfortable wearing the official blue uniform with the big shoulder boards and the knife-creased trousers of the militsia.

This was in itself surprising because most Russians regarded the militsia as a second-rate organization and their usual nickname for policemen was "turnips"—which was not meant in any pleasant sense since the police had a reputation for being failed soldiers or country bumpkins who could not get any other kind of job in the big city.

But Sergeant Federenko did not give a damn what the average citizen thought. For all their criticism, he knew that they were still very glad to see that big blue militsia

51

uniform when something bad happened to them, and the truth was, he missed that feeling of being the public's protector. Working in plainclothes, no matter how important the case he was working on, was just not the same thing.

Without realizing it, but so that nobody would mistake him for a lawyer, he stood militarily erect on the wide stone steps of the courthouse, declining to smoke even though he wanted a cigarette, waiting for Rostov.

The lieutenant came up behind him quietly and said, "You look like one of those statues at the Kremlin."

The sergeant grinned. "Some of us are proud to be policemen," he said.

"I'll keep that in mind," Rostov said. "This is what's happening."

"You've met with Madam Beauty Queen?" the sergeant asked.

"Yes. She's passable."

"Hah," the sergeant said lightly. "This from a man who spent the night with some police secretary in Uzbekistan, when the woman really should have been at the gymnasium exercising off the pounds."

"You mistake the uses of gratitude," Rostov said. "Now be quiet and listen. We are going to be able to play this fish Spatsky for another two weeks. So you know what to do."

"When he comes out, follow him. Work the squad around the clock. Never let him out of our sight. And then what?"

"And then see what happens," Rostov said. "If somebody moves against him, let's get them and see where they can lead us."

"I understand," the sergeant said.

"You have the cars nearby?"

"Yes."

"Report back tonight."

"Yes, Cowboy."

* * *

Ten minutes till two. Rostov decided he had just enough time for a cup of tea at the small refreshment booth in the basement of the courthouse. He sat alone on a stool in the far corner of the room, sipping the thick Russian brew.

In addition to omitting it from the official report, he had not told the sergeant or any of his other men that he had killed Vladimir back in that mosquito-ridden ravine. He felt bad about doing this, about letting even his men think that Vladimir had escaped, but there had just been too many leaks, too many slipups on operations that Rostov had planned for him, to trust anyone now.

And besides, if his men thought that Vladimir was still alive, they might do a better job of trailing Pimen Spatsky, hoping that he would lead them to Vladimir.

He glanced at the wall clock, drained the cup quickly, and walked up to the second-floor courtroom.

The agreement carefully worked out between Rostov and Olga Lutska did not last for five minutes.

When they entered the courtroom, Rostov saw Judge Nikita Alekhine gesture toward the back of the room. A trim elegant man in his early sixties rose and came forward. He had been sitting with a dark-haired woman who Rostov decided instantly was the most beautiful woman he had ever seen.

The handful of spectators in court, mostly pensioners who had few other ways to spend the day, seemed collectively to sip in air. Of course, Rostov recognized the elegant man as Leonid Nabokov. He was nothing less than Russia's most famous criminal lawyer.

Nabokov nodded toward Olga and Rostov could see the woman stiffen slightly, even as she returned the polite nod.

Judge Alekhine held up a sheaf of reports. "We are fortunate today that Counselor Nabokov is visiting our courtroom on another matter. He has agreed to serve as counsel for the prisoner."

Alekhine nodded to a uniformed court officer who went into a side room and brought out Pimen Spatsky, wearing a light blue prison uniform, his hands cuffed behind him.

"This is your lawyer, Mr. Nabokov," the judge said.

"I didn't do anyth—" Spatsky began.

Alekhine cut him off by raising his hand.

"You will be silent," he intoned, "while I read this file."

Spatsky looked upset, but Nabokov patted him on the shoulder and gestured him to a chair behind a long table. As the prisoner sat down, Nabokov glanced over and his eyes met Rostov's. Nabokov smiled slightly and Rostov looked away.

"Counselor, please come up here," Alekhine said.

Nabokov went to the raised bench, leaned forward, and talked earnestly with the judge for a few moments.

Alekhine nodded and looked toward Olga. "Madam Prosecutor, what is the status now of this case?"

"Judge, the witness is cooperating with police. We ask that he be freed on small bail and this arraignment be postponed for two weeks."

"Your request is denied. In fact, all charges are to be dismissed."

Rostov was about to shout in anger, but Olga had already taken two steps toward the judge's bench.

"Your Honor, we are dealing here with a serious crime. The facts in the case are clear and undisputed."

Judge Alekhine was a burly red-faced legal veteran whose demeanor and bulbous nose showed that he had fought many legal fights and perhaps just as many battles against vodka. He leaned over the bench to respond. His voice was angry but Rostov could see that the judge's hands were trembling nervously.

"Young lady. Let me remind you . . . and the police who were involved in this fiasco . . . that this is no longer the land of the czars. Cases must stand on their own merits or honest judges will have no choice but to dismiss them out of hand. This case is riddled with error . . . errors of identification, of procedure, of intent. Just the simple fact alone that it was more than twenty-four hours before Mr. Spatsky was formally charged would be reason to dismiss this case, as Counselor Nabokov has been quick to remind me."

"Your honor," Olga said. "The prisoner was apprehended near the Afghanistan border. It took twenty-four hours just to return him to this jurisdiction."

"The letter of the law must be obeyed," Alekhine said, "even when it is difficult on policemen. The time of a busy court should not be wasted on frivolities such as this. Case dismissed, and I simply hope for everyone's sake that Mr. Spatsky does not choose to bring suit against anyone for false arrest."

He looked challengingly at Olga, who stared at him, then turned with a look of despair toward Nabokov as if expecting to find on the defense attorney's face some small bit of hope, of explanation. But Nabokov had his back to her and was leaning over talking to Spatsky.

Rostov looked toward the rear of the courtroom, toward the beautiful brunette who had been sitting with Nabokov. She was smiling. Her eyes met Rostov's and she winked.

Olga looked back at Alekhine, who met her gaze challengingly and snapped, "Next case."

Olga Lutska walked back into her office and angrily tossed her attaché case across the room toward her desk. It landed on the floor and she swore, then stopped when she saw Lieutenant Rostov standing by the window, smiling slightly.

"Do you still think that the system works to produce justice?" he asked.

She was angry, angry with Rostov, angry with the judge, and she snapped back, "Yes, dammit, except when you get a judge who ought to be committed to an asylum because he's lost his mind."

"Or maybe one who has been bought," Rostov said.

"By the Mafia, I suppose," she said sarcastically. "I'm sorry. I just can't believe that."

"Learn to believe," Rostov said. "Anyway, I just wanted to thank you for your efforts this morning."

She shrugged. "You seem to be taking this rather calmly."

"Well, I wanted Spatsky back out on the street and we seem to have accomplished that. Perhaps I owe you a vote of thanks for that."

"A very small vote of thanks," Olga said sourly.

"Perhaps I could pay that off with a very small dinner," Rostov suggested.

She was inclined to snap a rejection at him, but for some reason, Olga said instead, "That would be nice."

"Tonight," he said. "I will pick you up at eight."

"Fine."

Rostov started for the door and she said, "What kind of a policeman is it who is going to pick me up and doesn't ask me my address?"

"The kind of policeman who already knows where you live," Rostov said. And there was that smile again.

Pimen Spatsky, dumbfounded at being released, had walked down the broad steps of the courthouse, whistling, wondering where he would go now and deciding immediately that the first thing he wanted was a drink.

He had no job to go to, supporting himself by the occasional odd bits of work he could pick up loading or unloading trucks, and he lived in a shabby furnished room in the southeastern corner of the city, near the Moscow River, a room identical to the other thirty-nine rooms in the decrepit tenement building.

He did not notice Sergeant Federenko in his ill-fitting gray suit fall into step behind him. Nor did he notice the two other men, also members of Rostov's squad, who sat in a car parked illegally at the corner watching him approach.

Why had the judge dropped the charges? Spatsky was uneducated but no fool and he knew he had been caught dead to rights. Yet, somehow, he had been freed. He had tried to ask that fancy lawyer that the judge had assigned to him, but the lawyer had just turned away in disgust, as if Spatsky were a piece of garbage which smelled bad.

To hell with it. He decided that he would not question the wisdom of the gods; he would just accept it. *Take what comes. That is the way to get along in the world.*

He turned at the corner and crossed the next corner, still looking halfheartedly for a tavern. He regretted now not having made that Vladimir pay up in advance. Maybe if he went back to the bar where he had first met him, he would find him again. Certainly, Spatsky thought, he deserved something for the work he had done. It was not his fault that the deal had been upended by the militsia.

He had forgotten his new life's rule of taking what comes and was working himself up into a state of indignation when the rear door of a black Zil sedan opened, just as he approached it. A man called out, "Pimen."

He looked into the car's dark interior and the man beckoned to him, and when Spatsky took a step closer, the man lunged forward, grabbed his wrist, and yanked him into the car. It lurched forward from the curb, its forward motion slamming shut the door behind Pimen Spatsky.

Down the block, Rostov's two men saw Spatsky go into the car. They started after it, but just as they reached the corner, another car pulled out from the side street across their path. Ivan Gorlov jammed on the brakes. The other car stopped and the driver rolled down his window and shouted at them.

"Militsia. Get out of the way, you son of a bitch," yelled dark-faced Leo Tarkovsky, who sat in the passenger's seat of the police car.

The other driver shrugged, rolled up his window, and slowly pulled from the intersection.

When they got to the next corner, the Zil sedan carrying Spatsky was gone.

When they went back to try to find the driver who had blocked their way, that car was gone too. Sergeant Federenko was on the corner, his punched-face features twisted in anger.

"I saw him. I saw the bastard and I went after him, but he got away."

"Any license plate?" Tarkovsky asked.

"He had it covered with mud. We're screwed," Federenko said. "And wait until Cowboy finds out."

"*You* tell him," Ivan Gorlov said, rubbing his hands together nervously.

When he had been joking with Rostov on the courthouse steps, the sergeant had been wrong. Rostov had not slept with the secretary to the militsia commander at Termez because he had a liking for plump women but because he was slowly beginning to trust no one in Moscow and because the woman's brother was the head technician at the local police laboratory.

So when he had kept his promise and gone back to see Svetlana Turchin after his encounter with Vladimir at the drug drop, he had brought with him, packed in ice, the five fingers from dead Vladimir's right hand.

And then he had made love to the young woman and gotten an introduction to her brother and met him at the

58

police laboratory long after midnight, when the police building had been closed.

Svetlana had been left behind, and Rostov had been all business as he took the ice-packed plastic bag from his pocket and handed it to the technician, whose name was Viktor.

"Viktor, I need a set of prints from these fingers," he had said.

"Oh my God," the man responded when he saw the contents of the plastic bag. "Where did you get those?"

"That is not necessary for you to know," Rostov said. "Let me just say that it concerns an ongoing investigation."

His brusque manner had bullied the technician, as he expected, and the man took the severed digits to an examining table. He put on clear latex gloves, then carefully washed and dried the fingers.

Then he sprayed them with a clear liquid from an aerosol can. "This is a kind of stiffener," he explained. "We use it when taking prints from a corpse. It counteracts the decay of the flesh, at least temporarily."

Rostov nodded, and watched as the man sprayed each of the fingers, and then after a few minutes, Viktor handed Rostov a neatly printed set of black fingerprints on firm white cardboard. Rostov replaced the severed fingers in the plastic bag and stuck them into his jacket pocket.

"Viktor," he said. "You know who I am."

"Yes, of course. Lieutenant Rostov."

"These fingers are the only clues in a crime involving militsia corruption in this district."

"Oh," Victor said. His face clearly showed that he was trying to figure out what he had gotten himself involved in.

"Neither you nor your sister will be in any trouble as long as you remain silent," Rostov said. "And that means totally silent. You may not tell your family, your friends, not your sister, not your supervisor . . . not even Major Markin.'' He paused. "Especially not Major Markin,'' he added significantly. "Do you understand?''

"Yes, of course.''

"If a word of this is leaked, I will know where it came from. You understand that?''

"Yes.''

"Very good, Viktor. You have done a major service for the cause of honest law enforcement. The day will come when your contribution will be acknowledged.''

"I wish only to serve," Viktor had said.

He was so happy to see Rostov leave that he would never say a word, the Cowboy knew.

He drove back alone toward Tashkent where he planned to catch a plane back to Moscow. Twenty miles outside Termez, he stopped his small Jeep, walked out into a field, and dug a small hole with his hunting knife. Inside, he buried Vladimir's five fingers.

The first thing he had done when he returned to Moscow was to take the fingerprint card personally to the central records bureau and ask them to provide him with a name to go with the prints.

He was always amused at the crime movies that he watched in which police were able to take just one partial fingerprint and come up with the identification of a criminal in just a few minutes.

Maybe the FBI could do that. Maybe some kind of computer bigger than anything his agency had could do it. But the national militsia could not do it. It would take at least a day, probably longer, to identify the owner of the prints—that is, if he even had a police or military record—and Rostov had to call in a favor from the head of the records bureau to have the case given priority, without saying what it involved.

Now, two days later, back at his desk in the small ground-floor office near militsia headquarters, after the fiasco in court, he looked at the dark brown envelope on his desk, bearing his name, marked PERSONAL, and thought he recognized where it came from.

A single sheet of paper slipped out of the envelope. At the top was a photograph of the dead Vladimir.

The rest of it was his official police record.

GUBANOV, VLADIMIR: Age 39, arrested 12/1/86, possession of stolen car, charge dismissed; arrested 7/4/88, possession of narcotics, charge dismissed; arrested 9/12/89, possession of narcotics with intent to sell, placed on three years' probation; Department of Probation reports employment as janitor at Pink Elephant Club, Moscow.

Rostov skimmed the report and quickly found what he wanted. *Last known address.*

He jammed the paper into his pocket and strode from his office. As the door closed behind him, he heard the telephone ringing but decided to ignore it.

Chapter Six

Washington, D.C.:

On the fourth floor of the architectural monstrosity that was the Federal Bureau of Investigation headquarters, Archibald Semple looked across his desk at Daniel Taylor, who had just flown in from Pennsylvania.

"Didn't take them long to find him," Semple said.

Taylor shook his head. "He was on television on the eleven o'clock news. His house got smacked at five-thirty A.M. Makes you wonder sometimes."

"Wonder about what?" Semple asked.

"Does the Mafia have a stockpile of bombs just sitting around waiting to be used, waiting until some other Peter Kamen shows up to get his ass blown off? Maybe they have a whole weapons depot someplace. They just call up on the phone and say, we've found some guy who's been in the witness-protection program, so we want to send him a present. Maybe something nice in a fifty-pounder. Send up something like that. No . . . no card.

He'll know who it's from." He lit a cigarette even though the bureau did not like its agents smoking. "Scares the hell out of you, doesn't it?"

"Where do you have him now?"

"A hotel out near Harrisburg. I have two men with him, so he's safe. For now. But what do I do with him?"

Semple answered slowly, "I don't know. This is the fourth time in three years that he's come up for air."

"Are you serious?"

Semple nodded. He looked at a file on his desk. "First time, we had him in Omaha and he wound up saving some kid from drowning. Got his picture in the paper and the mob came and took a shot at him. Then he was selling insurance—and don't you know, he starts going door to door and he winds up trying to sell a policy to some Mafia goon. We got him out just in time then too. Then we bury him in Chicago and the dumb bastard wins the state lottery and winds up with his picture in the papers standing next to the governor. We're lucky we didn't get the governor of Illinois with his ass shot off too. So now he's got two million dollars coming to him and he doesn't have to work anymore and we've still got to bury him again somewhere else."

"I didn't know all that," Taylor said. Which was not exactly the truth. He had heard rumors of some of it, but he did not want Semple to ask him where those rumors had come from.

"So, we weren't doing you any favor, Dan, when we sent him out to you. And now he's done it again."

"He claims it's not his fault. He was just trying to stop an armed robbery. That's hard to argue with."

"It's never his fault. That's the problem. Peter Kamen is just a guy with a cloud over his head. Like that guy in the old Li'l Abner comic strip, Joe Blurfslurp or something. I almost think we ought to turn him over to the goddam mob and be done with it. Why don't you have one of your guys shoot him? Then they can claim the bounty. I hear he's worth two hundred and fifty thousand dead.''

"I guess that'd be bad for our image, if we couldn't protect the guy who sank the mob.''

"Yeah," Semple said sourly. "I guess so. So here's what you do. Go back, stash him someplace safe, and give me a couple of days to try to come up with something. And please . . . keep an eye on him so he doesn't get all of you killed.''

Harrisburg, Pennsylvania:

"Gin,'' said Peter Kamen as he laid down his hand.

"Dammit,'' FBI Special Agent Fred Keeler said as he tossed his remaining cards face-up on the table. "You are a cheating bastard.''

"Shhh. I'm counting. Let's see. Twenty for gin and you've got forty-four in your hand. That's sixty-four. And ninety-one. That's one-fifty-five. Four boxes. That's another hundred. Two-fifty-five. And doubled on the schneid, that's five-ten. At two cents a point, that's ten dollars and twenty cents. Add to what you already lost and let's see, let's see . . .'' He looked up with a grin. "You owe me forty-one dollars and forty cents. Call it forty-two even.''

"Call it forty-one even, you fucking thief,'' Keeler said.

"All right," Kamen said. "Forty-one. Your deal.''

"I've got to go to the bathroom. Don't mark the cards while I'm gone.''

"I did that the last time you went to the bathroom,'' Kamen said.

Over Virginia:

Why did the airlines always get copies of the current news magazines before his office did, Daniel Taylor wondered as he asked the stewardess for the new *TIME* magazine.

He thumbed idly through the pages, ignoring all the stories on foreign affairs since he had decided that his four-year-old son knew more about foreign policy than the editors of *TIME*. He turned the page and saw Peter Kamen—whom he had known as Eugene Palmer—staring at him. The picture showed Kamen with dark hair, the way he used to look before the FBI had stashed him in its witness-protection program and made him a blonde.

Taylor's stomach sank as he read the headline on the *TIME* article.

MAN ON THE RUN
Can Peter Kamen Escape a Mafia Hit?

He skimmed the story quickly and sighed in relief when he saw that *TIME* had not found out that Kamen was the same Eugene Palmer who had foiled a holdup and then had his house blown up.

Instead, the writers had used Kamen largely to headline a story on the entire witness-relocation program run by the government to protect people who had testified against the mob.

But Kamen was the star of the story, and *TIME* breathlessly reported that there was an open contract on his life, worth five hundred thousand dollars to the Mafioso who killed him.

The story went on to tell exactly why Kamen had incurred such expensive wrath. A lot of it Taylor had not heard before.

Kamen's original name had been Pyotr Kamenski. His grandparents had moved to Brighton Beach, New York, in the early part of the century. They had come from Odessa in Russia where the elder Kamenski had been a low-level but well-known criminal. No one had ever been able to figure out how he and his wife had been able to get out of Russia and into the country.

Kamenski's two sons had gotten involved in the illegal end of labor organizing in New York and during the Korean war had wound up with their throats cut in a garment-center warehouse.

Young Peter was now an orphan, his mother having died in childbirth, and he had been raised by his grandparents. But the apple had not fallen far from the tree and Kamen—his father had taken that name years before to "try to fit in"—had been in trouble right from the start. He quit school early and hung around with a gang of street toughs and was picked up at seventeen for auto theft.

The experience seemed to have straightened Kamen out for a while. He went back to school, graduated, then went to City College in New York to become an accountant.

But eventually he drifted in with the Brooklyn Mafia family. He was no strong-arm man, but he was quickwitted and worked for the Cosa Nostra as sort of an office manager. He had gotten married, but his wife had died young and he was childless.

He grew close to the mob and later testified that he had been "made a wiseguy" in the mid-1970s. Some might have regarded him as a rising star, but in the rigidly ethnic underworld where people whose families came from the "wrong town" in Italy were mistrusted, the grandson of Russian immigrants had no chance at all.

Peter Kamen did not seem to mind; no one had ever accused him of being overly ambitious, *TIME* reported.

And then in 1985, a federal investigation that had been going on for ten years revealed the existence of an international scheme to smuggle drugs into the United States. The couriers and the pushers and the muscle men were all Sicilian immigrants who had vanished into New York's landscape with modest jobs working in Mafia-owned pizzerias.

But the Mafia got wind of the federal investigation just before the government moved, and some heavy-duty "cooking of the books" managed to make it seem as if Peter Kamen, the outside Russian, had been the one who had created the plan, then administered it, and had collected all the millions in riches that came from the drug sales.

Federal agents arrested Kamen; the sixty-three counts of smuggling and drug selling were enough to guarantee him jail terms totaling more than three thousand years.

And so—"handed up by the people I thought were my friends"—Kamen became a witness for the state and, oddly enough, a willing one. The mob had guessed wrong in trying to pin the drug scheme on Kamen, because the quiet little mobster turned out to be an antidrug zealot; nothing else the mob did had ever offended him, but he detested their efforts "to poison all the kids."

Throughout the mid-1980s he testified at fourteen separate trials, and his testimony sent to prison sixty-one top Mafia figures. And then Peter Kamen vanished into the midst of the federal witness-relocation program.

Since then, *TIME* reported, there had been occasional reports that he had been sighted and occasional reports that attempts had been made on his life. The Justice Department routinely refused to comment on any aspect of its witness program, even to the point of refusing to say whether or not Peter Kamen is still alive.

The story concluded:

"But a report surfaced this week that the mob—and especially Gesualdo Ciccolini, the Brooklyn boss who alone escaped the Kamen-inspired purge—has raised the bounty on Kamen to a half-million dollars, half of it provided by the Sicilian Mafia which has never forgiven Kamen's exposure of their operation. If those bounty reports are true, it would indicate that the man who almost sank the American mob is still alive.

"But for how long?"

The story spilled over onto the next page of the magazine and then Taylor saw another strip of illustrations and cursed softly under his breath.

Those irresponsible press bastards had taken the last known picture of Kamen and published it, and alongside it they had reprinted it three more times—showing how Kamen would look if he had dyed his hair, had grown a mustache and a beard, had gained weight and had some small cosmetic surgery on his nose and hairline. The last picture showed what he would look like if he had dyed his hair blond . . . and there was the face of Eugene Palmer staring from the magazine page into Taylor's eyes.

Harrisburg, Pennsylvania:

"So how's King Rat?" Taylor said as the FBI agent let him into the motel room.

Peter Kamen looked up from the small card table.

"That's a curious thing for an FBI man to call me," he said mildly. "I thought we were on the same side."

"Oh, no," Taylor said. "I'm on the side of truth, justice, and the American way. You're on the side of confusion and chaos." He tossed the *TIME* magazine onto the table, spraying Kamen's playing cards onto the floor.

"Here. Read your latest press clippings."

Moving with studied slowness, Kamen opened the magazine, found the article about himself, and carefully read it.

"The press never gets anything right," he said.

"Oh? What's inaccurate?"

"My grandfather. They said he was a low-level hoodlum in Odessa. He was head of the Odessa mob and when

68

he came to America he was Meyer Lansky's buddy. They make him out to be a bum, but Grampa was no bum.''

"All you're worried about is your grandfather's reputation as a criminal? What about those goddam photos of you?''

Kamen shrugged. "Who cares? Next time I'll shave my head bald and they can start all over again. Or maybe red hair. I've never been a readhead. Anyway, I guess you've been to Washington, so where's my next stop?''

"Who knows? Maybe we should just turn you over to the Mafia," Taylor said.

Kamen smiled slightly. "Don't try," he said. "Or that'll be your last act on earth.''

The soft threat seemed to unnerve Taylor for a moment. He hesitated, then said, "We're going to stash you for a while until Washington figures out what to do.''

"Just where are you going to stash me?''

"One of the federal prisons near here. It's got private security rooms. You'll be safe there.''

"Okay," Kamen said. "For one week.''

"And then what?''

"And then I escape. I didn't sign on with you guys to do prison time.''

"You think you can?" Taylor said.

"I know I can," Kamen said. "And if you think I've made your life miserable up till now, just get me ticked off and see what happens. Wait until I get on the *Geraldo* show and talk about your witness-relocation program. You people don't know what grief is yet.''

Taylor shook his head and nodded to the two FBI agents in the room.

"Get him out of here, will you?''

Chapter Seven

Moscow:

Lev Rostov walked quietly up the steps of the dismal apartment building in the grimy western edge of Moscow.

The building reminded him of slum tenements he had seen ten years before when he had undergone special training by the KGB. After dinner each night, the trainees had to sit through two American movies, usually grim and gritty Hollywood indictments of American life, all of which seemed to share the philosophy that if someone is raised in a slum, it is society's fault if he turns to a life of crime.

Alone among the trainees, Rostov thought that this was hilarious. Russians had always been brought up in slums. Those that turned to crime were shot. No one ever thought to make a movie apologizing for *their* lives.

Rostov had not voiced his opinion. It was one thing to want to get out of the KGB spy school; it was quite another to make yourself a candidate to be shot as a potential traitor. No one had ever accused Lev Rostov of being stupid. In fact, it was his obvious brains that had caused him to be yanked from the army ranks and sent to the espionage school in the first place.

Two things had quickly become clear to him. The first was that the men were going to be trained to go undercover in the United States. That was obvious because of the nature of the training—a steady diet of American films and music and magazines. Special instruction in American slang and regional accents.

Rostov had gone along in lockstep with all the other recruits. But he found he had a deeper fascination with the United States than the other young soldiers did, and somewhere along the way, in the sixth month of training, the second thing became clear to him. If he was sent to the United States to infiltrate as a spy under deep cover, he would just vanish and become an American. And when Moscow rang his bell, he would not answer.

Rostov was too Russian to allow himself to get into that situation. Since he could not tell the KGB his true feelings, he let himself be flunked out of the spy school on the pretext that he was unable ever to learn to speak English in the American fashion. Many recruits failed that test.

It seemed to satisfy everyone in Rostov's case and he came back to Moscow and joined the militsia. There were no black marks on his record and the only reminder of the spy school was his nickname *kobcon*—Cowboy— which he got for his fascination with American film westerns and for the big-brimmed ten-gallon hat he convinced an old Russian haberdasher to make for him.

He had long since tired of the hat, but he understood enough about public relations to know that he was stuck with it; the hat was part of the legend of Cowboy Rostov, Moscow's drug-fighting cop.

The hallway of Vladimir Gubanov's apartment building was unpainted and unlit and now, in the growing darkness of early evening, dangerous to walk through. The steps were bare splintered wood and the whole building reeked with the smell of poverty, of potatoes that had grown too old, and of cabbage, that grand staple of Russian misery, that had been cooked and cooked and cooked in this building, so many times that its smell had soaked into the walls and leaked out, one poor scent at a time.

No one came out of any of the apartments to see him. He was quiet, but even if someone had heard him going up the steps, they would not have come out into the hall. It was the national policy of the Russian people to mind their own business. *Glasnost*, openness, might be the nation's official policy this week . . . maybe even next week . . . but it would take decades before it seeped down into the consciousness of the Russian people.

At the top of the steps he paused in front of Vladimir Gubanov's apartment. His hand went to the butt of the small automatic he carried in his shoulder holster, under his jacket. He knocked, twice, loud, because a loud brief knock was less liable to draw the attention of the other apartment residents than was a long continuous soft rapping on the door.

He waited a full minute. There was no answer from inside. No one peered out onto the landing.

He reached down and pulled his hunting knife from its sheath inside his tooled leather boots and inserted the heavy tip into the molding of the door, next to the lock. The wood was old, dry, ready to surrender at any excuse, and one twist pulled the molding loose. Rostov then pushed the tip of the knife into the locking mechanism, bit into the softer metal with the sprung steel of his blade, and then twisted hard. The lock slid back and the door pushed open.

With the heels of his hands, Rostov pushed the molding back into place, then replaced his knife and stepped inside the apartment, his hand again on the butt of his gun.

He closed the door behind him and looked around.

Vladimir Gubanov may not have had a fancy address in Moscow, but it was obvious that in income he was a cut above all his neighbors. A console color television set was at one side of the room and a stereo phonograph sat on shelves that appeared to be made of oiled teak.

His furniture was new, leather and expensive. His kitchen stove was clean and modern and there was even a microwave oven attached to the wall near the sink.

Rostov walked into the adjoining bedroom, looking for a file cabinet, but the bedroom was spare, barely decorated with an oversized bed, a dresser that held only clothing, and a closet in which hung a half-dozen good suits that Rostov knew he could not himself have afforded.

He satisfied himself that the bedroom was not hiding anything, even sprawling on the floor to look under the bed, and then went back out into the living room to search it.

Yelena Slepak was seventy-one years old and had worked most of her adult life as a *dezhurnaya* in an apartment building, occupied primarily by midlevel bureaucrats in the Agriculture Department. She had been— as were most of the people who held similar concierge jobs in other government-occupied apartment houses—a KGB snitch, reporting every day on the comings and goings in the building, especially on any foreign-looking visitors who might come to visit someone in the building.

But two years ago, she had been retired on pension. She knew she could not live on the meager sixty rubles a month she received, so she was forced to move into this dump.

Fortunately, during her years in the fancy apartment building, she had managed to save some money, and with her meager pension and this cheap and ugly apartment and eating hardly anything but cabbage and potatoes, when potatoes were available, she managed to survive, but every month her little stash of rubles grew smaller.

And then just two days ago, two very husky young men had come to visit her. They told her they had a job for her. It would pay fifty rubles a month.

"What kind of work is it?" Yelena Slepak asked.

"What you do best," one of them said. "Being nosy."

He explained that he wanted her to keep an eye on the apartment building for him and especially the apartment directly above hers. It was, she learned later, the apartment of Vladimir Gubanov.

"And what exactly is it you want me to do?" she asked.

"Let us know if anyone ever comes to that apartment," he said. "And tell no one what you are doing."

"Agreed," the old woman had snapped. "Pay in advance." The man had counted ten five-ruble notes from a very large roll of bills in his pocket and the two husky men had left.

Time now to earn my keep, Yelena thought. She had heard the footsteps going up the stairs outside her apartment and she knew they were not the steps of Vladimir Gubanov, because he walked heavily. He was a stomper. These were the footsteps of someone who walked softly.

She heard the sounds of footsteps again directly over her head and she wrapped her scarf around her thinning gray hair and walked quickly downstairs to the superintendent's apartment. No one answered her knock on the door, but she knew the key was kept over the doorframe and she let herself in.

The superintendent was the only person in the building that she knew had a telephone. She used it now to call the number the two husky men had given her. In the traditional way of the Moscow phone system, the telephone operator tried to grill her to find out who she was calling, but Yelena was old enough to know some of the tricks.

"This is police business. Complete the call immediately," she snapped, and a moment later she heard the clicking buzz of the telephone ringing.

"Yes?" a man's voice answered.

"You know who I am," she said. "Someone is walking around in Vladimir's apartment."

"We will take care of it."

The phone disconnected, and Yelena hung up and went back to her apartment to wait.

Vladimir Gubanov had been careful, but not as careful as he thought he was.

Rostov had not been able to find one single scrap of paper anywhere in the house. Not a telephone book, not a notepad, no stationery, no mail, nothing. If what the police were trained to believe was true—that everybody left a "paper trail"—then Vladimir Gubanov had never lived.

Except for one thing.

In a kitchen cabinet, Rostov found a large bin of potatoes and asked himself, *Now, does a man who owns all these fancy suits and shoes really spend a lot of time cooking potatoes in his apartment? Or does he eat in restaurants? He eats in restaurants.*

Rostov took the bin from the cabinet and spilled the potatoes onto the floor. In the bottom of the bin he found a small laptop computer in a carrying case. It was a Japanese Nishimoto model with a built-in screen.

Rostov took the computer out, placed it on the kitchen table, and plugged it into the wall socket. He turned it on and the small screen lit up . . . blank, as if awaiting directions.

So where is the disk that the machine uses? Rostov wondered. There was no point in having a computer unless you used it for something, and this one was not brand new. Some of the paint on the keyboard's letters was worn away from use.

Of course, it was possible that Vladimir had bought it used, already worn, but still why? And if he had bought it, would he not have bought the disk that the machine needed to be of any use?

Rostov sprawled out on the floor and began to look at the underside of everything in the room—table, chairs, the stereo cabinet. It was the favorite hiding place of the careless.

He found a disk taped under one of the two hard metal kitchen chairs. He placed it into the machine and called up the menu, to see what had been stored on the disk.

She heard footsteps again. There were two of them this time, both men, and the steps squeaked slightly under their feet even though they were obviously trying to be silent. Her two large young men.

Yelena Slepak felt an emotion very close to gratification. It was good to know that her eyes and ears were still valued and good to know that despite all the nonsense going on in politics . . . all that silliness about Westernizing . . . there were still people out and around who were men of action. They would appreciate what she had done. Maybe there would even be a reward.

The two men had stopped moving now. They must be outside Vladimir's apartment.

If he had been hoping for a list of people involved in the drug trade, Rostov was disappointed.

The small green-and-black monitor built into the computer showed only a long list of numbers and dates, and tantalizing hints contained in partial words and names and initials.

He hunkered down in front of the set, trying to decode the information he saw.

The first line read, "Mil. 25K."

Twenty-five thousand. Twenty-five thousand what? What was "Mil?"

The next line read, "Cou. 20K."

Again what?

And a third line read "ProsO. 15K."

And then came a list of dates and initials and amounts. He scrolled forward on the computer, but it was all the same. The dates went back two years. The most recent date, at the bottom of the long computer list, was only a week earlier.

Rostov leaned back in the kitchen chair.

Vladimir Gubanov had been involved in the drug trade in Moscow. Were these records of sales? Or of purchases from suppliers?

"Mil." "Cou." "ProsO."

"ProsO."

"ProsO."

What was it?

An abbreviation.

Prosecutor's office!

Cowboy Rostov sipped air through his pursed lips.

Payoffs. Could it be payoffs that were made to someone in the Prosecutor's office to protect the drug traffickers?

And "Cou." Was that the courts?

He scrolled again down to the bottom of the long listing. There was a record of "5K," made last week. And the initials "N.A.'

It was the ony time those initials appeared in the computer listing.

Were they the initials of Nikita Alekhine, the judge who had just set free Pimen Spatsky? The same judge who had only become the presiding judge in the criminal courts two weeks before?

Of course. This was a record of payoffs, of graft. Made to people in the court system . . . in the prosecutor's office . . . and, Rostov realized with a sinking feeling in his stomach, to the "Mil." To his own precious militsia. The drug dealers had someone inside the police forces. No wonder they knew about Rostov's raids before Rostov could pull them off.

He closed his eyes for a long second. The truth was that he had suspected it. Vladimir Gubanov was more than a truck driver who went to pick up a load of drugs. Those five-hundred-ruble shoes proved it. And so did all those expensive suits in Gubanov's closet. They were the kind of suits one wore to meetings. Meetings when you paid off some official that you had purchased.

He started to lean forward again, then froze when he heard a sound outside the door. Even as he reached for his gun and turned, he was moving toward the sofa, and when the door cracked open and a sudden spray of gunfire crackled into the room, Rostov had already dived behind the sofa. He buried himself deep into a corner as automatic fire ripped into the couch, sending small tufts of dirty gray foam puffing into the air.

And then the shooting stopped. But there was something else . . . a crackle and then a smell. Cautiously he peered up from behind the sofa and saw that the room was afire. Two Molotov cocktails, bottles filled with gasoline, had exploded onto the floor and the spreading liquid had already engulfed most of the room.

Rostov turned toward the computer, the disk, but there was nothing he could do. It had obviously been one of the targets of the firebombs and it was burning with a sticky yellow plastic flame. It was gone and so was the tape that was in it.

He ran for the doorway, but just as he got into the hall, another blast of furnace-hot air singed his face. The stairway below him was burning. He saw a woman lunge forward out of the apartment directly below Vladimir's. Her billowing black dress was afire. She staggered to the railing and then pitched over, falling into the central shaft of the stairs, down three flights. She hit the floor and did not move, and then, even far below on the first floor, her body was quickly swallowed up by flame.

The bastards have torched the whole building, he thought. *Is there anyone in this building?*

He began to shout, "Fire! Fire!" but there was no answering sound . . . only the snapping of the flames as they ate their way up the dry wood of the steps toward him.

He looked behind him into Vladimir's apartment. It was a furnace. He could not even get across the floor to the barred window. He ran into the hallway to the next apartment and, with the heel of his boot, kicked the door off its hinges.

"Fire!" he shouted again, but the apartment was still.

Cowboy ran through the small railroad set of rooms. The fire sizzled behind him. The building was so old, its wood so dry, that it was all going up like tinder.

There was an unbarred window at the end of the apartment he had just run into, and he clambered up onto the windowsill and saw, fifteen feet below, the roof of the smaller adjoining building, separated from him by a dozen feet of alley.

Rostov kicked the glass out. He felt the flames behind him.

He jumped across the wide opening and landed on the roof of the next building, rolling as he hit, stopping finally on his back. Far away, he heard the klaxon siren of a fire truck. The flames had already broken through the walls of the building he had fled, and through the few windows, he could see the fire coursing throughout the old frame structure.

He lay there for just a split second, catching his breath, then pulled open the door on the roof and ran down the stairs.

The fire engine pulled up just as he reached the street, and Rostov ran over to the captain commanding the truck. He identified himself and said, "Be careful inside. It's

79

a gasoline fire.'' The firemen began swarming into the building, looking for survivors, and Rostov looked around, to see if anybody watching the fire looked as if they might be paying too much attention to him, but there was nothing to see.

He shook his head and loped off down the street toward his own automobile.

A large moon shone overhead.

Rostov wondered if it was too late to have dinner.

Olga Lutska was feeling very good when she came home from the office, so good that she did not even mind her pet cat leaping toward her and then rubbing her head against Olga's legs.

The cat, named Trotsky by Olga in a wild burst of unlawyerly creativity, had been acting strangely for the past three days, squawking at night, hardly eating, and constantly rubbing her head against Olga's legs. At first, the lawyer had been concerned that the pet perhaps was suffering from some sort of virus attack, but the cat seemed healthy enough and now her behavior was beginning to annoy Olga.

The trouble is that the damned cat is spoiled, she thought. *Everyone is spoiled but me*.

''Shoo, shoo. Get away,'' she snapped, and pushed the cat away with her foot as she went in to take a bath.

She was ready an hour early, at seven P.M., and dressed in her best, she felt very fine indeed.

But as eight P.M. came and went, she began to feel not so fine.

At eight-thirty P.M., when she took off the high-heeled Italian pumps that her mother had stood in line five hours to buy, Olga Lutska was annoyed.

At nine P.M., when she took off her cocktail-length blue silk dress that had been handmade by a seamstress around the corner, Olga was angry.

And at nine-thirty, sitting in a robe, drinking from a snifter of brandy, Olga had become furious.

The nerve of that damned . . . damned . . . cowboy to stand her up. Did he think she was some *utka*, some whore from Arbat Street that he impressed with his damned badge and his silly cowboy hat? It was insulting.

To hell with him. He had probably run into some little *zopnik*, some little pansy that he had gone out with instead. She giggled as the brandy settled in her belly. Maybe the Cowboy liked boys better than girls. She did not really believe that, but it gave her a little pleasure to think about it, and perhaps even salvaged her pride a little. Sure, that was it. The famous Cowboy Rostov had run into some tight little fairy that evening and naturally had forgotten all about her.

The thought helped for a few minutes and then she was angry again. She poured an unaccustomed second brandy, then went into the bedroom of her small apartment and brought out her briefcase. Perching reading glasses on the end of her nose, she started to look over several police reports on trials she would be handling in the next week.

The knock on the door came at ten-ten P.M.

That was strange. It couldn't be Rostov because the *dezhurnaya* would have called her from downstairs if he had arrived. It must be one of her neighbors, come to borrow something—although it was a little late at night for that kind of activity.

"Who is it?" she said from behind the locked door.

"Lev Rostov."

She opened the door, but kept the security chain in place. It really *was* Rostov. He smiled at her.

Well, too bad. You can stay out in the hall forever for all I care. That was what she thought.

"What shall it be?" he said. "Dinner? Or dancing first? Personally, I'm in the mood for dancing."

81

"Try an oubliette for one," she snapped. "How did you get up here, anyway?"

"I told the old lady not to announce me. I thought you wouldn't let me in."

"I won't let you in now," she said.

Just then her cat sneaked out through the crack in the door and began rubbing against Rostov's boots. He bent over and stroked the cat's back and she raised her hindquarters and crouched down over her front feet, stepping from one hind foot to the other.

"In heat, I see," Rostov said.

"I beg your pardon," Olga said.

"Your cat. Your cat's in heat."

"I think she has a virus infection," Olga said. "What do you know about cats?"

"Nothing. But I know a lot about animals in heat," Rostov said as he stood up. "My uncle had a farm, you know." He paused. "So, may I come in? I come bearing gifts."

Olga arched an eyebrow and Rostov brought his hand from behind his back. In it was a withered old rose that looked as if it had come from someone's garbage pail. He also held a half-empty bottle of brandy.

The offering was so bizarre and unexpected that Olga smiled, softened, and said, "Well, how could I refuse such a gesture? Especially since you swam all the way to Holland to buy me that fine Dutch rose."

As she unlocked the door, Rostov said, "Actually I got it from the bar in a hotel I passed. They were just closing down. The brandy too."

As he came in, she pulled her robe closer around her and tightened the belt.

"You smell awful. Like a chimney sweep."

"Sorry. I was in a fire. That's why I was late."

"Oh, my," she said. "Where was the fire? Was anybody hurt?" She immediately felt guilty for having thought so badly of him earlier.

"In a tenement. An old woman died, I'm afraid. Somebody set it to try to kill me."

At her shocked look, he said, "And that's enough small talk, Olga, until I get a drink. And then I'll tell you the whole story."

The music of Borodin, her favorite romantic Russian composer, played softly on the big boxy stereo system. Olga and Rostov sat side by side on the nubby wool sofa, the remains of a trayful of sandwiches in front of them. Both sipped brandy. Trotsky, the cat, still rubbed against Rostov's boots.

In answer to persistent questioning, Rostov told her what had happened that night.

"But who would try to kill you?" she said.

"You laughed when I tried telling you today, but I'll try again," Rostov said. "The Mafia."

"That Mafia is an old wives' tale," she said sternly.

Rostov shook his head. "We've had one for years. And now that we're a democracy and our prosecutors believe in obeying the law and our policemen are afraid to bust open somebody's head to get answers, it's spreading."

"How do you know that? Is that knowledge or just a guess on your part?" she asked.

"Call it an educated guess," he said. "Do you know what my job is?"

"I should," Olga said. "You're in the press often enough. You run an antinarcotics squad. Isn't that so?" He had extended his legs next to hers on the coffee table. They both had long straight legs. She had always regarded that as very important in a man.

"Near enough to score a point," Rostov said. "And everything my men and I see on the street tells us that some single force is taking over the entire narcotics trade. And police in the other republics are telling me the same thing. Somehow, crime is consolidating. And if it happens, we will be in real trouble. A worse crime problem than anything the United States ever had to deal with.''

"I thought that's where the Mafia really came from. From the United States.''

Rostov shook his head, then leaned forward and poured a touch more brandy into both their glasses.

"No,'' he said. "The Mafia really started in Sicily. Of course, it wasn't much more than a collection of bandit gangs there. It turned into a real crime organization when it went to the United States. But even there, it's never been under the control of one family or one boss. There were always a group of crime families and they cut up territories and talked to each other, just so there wouldn't be any needless killing. But basically each family was on its own. Later, in the U.S., they stopped calling it the Mafia and named it La Cosa Nostra . . . 'our thing' . . . but it was the same. We're looking at something worse, darker, more serious here, than anything the United States ever had to deal with.''

"Why worse here? Russians aren't criminals by nature.''

"In a lot of ways, Madam Prosecutor, we're like a Third World country. The Mafia in America could infiltrate, but America was just so big, so vast, so powerful, that there was just no way the Mafia could rule the country. Here, we're basically just starting out. If the Mafia can get a foothold here and there . . . in the police . . . in the courts, in business . . . in construction, we could all wake up one morning and find that the mob is running everything, from the army to the police, to even the prosecutor's office.''

He looked at her sharply to see if that statement drew any reaction, but Olga just continued looking across the small living room.

"How does narcotics enter into it?'' she asked.

"I think it's a test case. Somebody or some group is

trying to control all the narcotics here. If they can do that, they'll have vast resources. They'll be able to buy out the criminals in every other part of our lives.''

She shook her head. ''It's hard to believe. A real Mafia in Russia. Do other militsia officers feel like you?''

He shrugged. ''Most of them are too busy keeping thugs off the streets, hooligans, purse-snatchers, car thieves. They don't have a chance to see a big picture.'' He sighed. ''Who knows?'' he said. ''Maybe I'm talking nonsense.''

''I don't think you're much given to talking nonsense, Lev,'' she said. ''Do you know who these top drug people are? Who might be running this newborn Mafia?''

''No. We had our best lead with Vladimir Gubanov. And then I had to kill the bastard. And whatever records he had went up in that fire. And Pimen Spatsky is, my men tell me, still among the missing.''

He sipped his brandy, found it suddenly too strong, and softened his drink and Olga's with ice cubes from a large silverplated bowl. Ice, he thought. That was one thing Russia had no shortage of. Everything else was in doubt.

''That's why I kept Vladimir's death quiet, even from my own men. I thought I might be able to follow a trail from him to his top boss.''

They were both silent for a long time. ''All prosecutors,'' Olga finally said, ''should be forced to get out and work in the streets with the police for a while. I have been just so out of touch and all of this is new to me.''

''Surely, you must have had some idea,'' he said, and again watched her face carefully.

''No,'' she said firmly. ''None.''

He hesitated only a second. ''Then I will give you even worse news,'' he said.

She looked at him with her large green eyes, made even larger by the reading glasses which were still perched on the end of her straight thin nose.

He took the glasses off and set them on the table. "It's like talking with a goldfish," he said. "Worse news is that somebody from the Mafia may have reached into the courts. Before I was interrupted tonight, I saw enough of Gubanov's records to think he was paying off somebody in the court system."

"I find that hard to believe," she said.

"Still . . . I saw initials and amounts next to them. And I saw evidence that just two weeks ago, money was paid to someone with the initials 'N.A.' When did Judge Nikita Alekhine become chief criminal magistrate?"

"Two weeks ago," she answered slowly. "I don't think it's possible," she said.

"Maybe not. I don't pretend to know," Rostov said.

She rose, excused herself, and went to the bathroom. When she returned, Rostov was rubbing the back of Trotsky, the cat, who was doing its bizarre little dance under the touch of his fingers.

"You really think she's in heat?" Olga said.

"Your little cat is very *mokraja* . . . horny."

She sat on the sofa again. "If somebody tried to kill you tonight, they might try again."

"That's possible," Rostov allowed.

"Would they know where you live?"

"Probably. I am sometimes too visible."

"Then you will sleep here tonight," Olga said.

He looked at her, then leaned forward and kissed her on the lips. With his face buried in her neck, he said, "Are you sure?"

"Yes," she whispered back. "All the little cats in this apartment are very *mokraja* tonight."

Chapter Eight

Lewisburg, Pennsylvania:

Even late at night, a prison was filled with noises. Generators ran, trucks rolled into and out of the yard, and all through the darkness, heavy iron gates were always clanging shut somewhere. If a person concentrated on them, he would never get any sleep at all.

The trick, Peter Kamen knew, was to register all the sounds and then to drop them off into your subconscious mind, so that they were no more than a background hum, always there, but never meaning anything.

It was a thing he had figured out when he was very young. His grandfather had told him that the earth was a large ball, streaking through the sky around the sun, and young Peter had rushed to an encyclopedia—Grampa's house was filled with books—and had learned to his amazement that the earth was not only rotating around the sun, but it was spinning on its own axis, tilting from side to side, and the whole solar system itself was moving through the galaxy.

So why isn't it noisy? Peter had asked himself. It had to be noisy with the wind and different parts groaning as it moved. Why didn't the racket keep everyone awake at night?

He thought about it for a long time before deciding that there really was a lot of noise but after centuries of centuries, no one heard it anymore. Mankind had just learned to file it away as some kind of background noise and then to ignore it. It was like listening to the Brooklyn Dodger baseball games from far-off St. Louis. At first, all he could hear was static, but then, after a while, he learned to concentrate on hearing the announcers' voices, and after a little longer, he stopped noticing the static. Its sound just vanished into background. So the earth . . . so a prison's noises.

Kamen lay in a cell in a wing of the Lewisburg federal prison that was sealed off from the main body of the prison by fences and walls and heavily guarded passageways. The local FBI man, Daniel Taylor, had lied to him. He had told Kamen that he would have an apartment and room to move around, while he was waiting for the witness-relocation program to make up its mind on where he was going next. Instead he was jammed into just another jail cell. It was true they had given him access to the library and he had a television set and there was a more-or-less-private flushing toilet behind a panel in a corner of the cell. But it was still just a cell.

Kamen pretended to mind more than he really did. He had been in jail cells before, he connected no social opprobrium with them, and he was content to wait here for the feds to make up their minds on what they were going to do—at least, he would wait for a while. After that, he had other things to do. He admitted, though, to himself that he would have felt a little better if he had known that Gesualdo Ciccolini, the Brooklyn mob boss, was in prison too, instead of out on the street, still able to threaten the few things in Kamen's life that Kamen really cared about.

He tried to shake that thought from his mind. He lay in the dark, concentrating on smoking one of the few cigarettes he allowed himself each day, forcing himself to listen to the background hum of prison noises that drifted through the night. So much noise to a man who really listened. So many ordinary sounds.

And one more sound . . . one that did not belong.

Kamen stubbed out the cigarette in the yellow plastic ashtray and tensed in bed, all his senses alert.

It was a shuffling sound and it did not belong. And then there was a whisper.

Instead of sitting up and causing his bedsprings to squeak, Kamen rolled his body over and let himself noiselessly drop out of bed onto the stone floor.

"Listen to him. Snoring like an old horse."

"He won't know what hit him."

"We don't want any noise. You cover his mouth. I'll get him."

"In the morning, they'll get a big surprise when they come looking for him."

"Screw him. I hate anybody who rats."

The two men in light blue prison garb moved softly along the stone corridor, past all the empty cells, toward the one from which they had heard Peter Kamen's snoring.

They paused near the cell and one man peered past the wall through the bars. Inside the cell, he could see the lumpen form of Kamen's body lying under the covers, curled up in the bed.

He squeezed the other man's shoulder, then went to

the door of the cell and quietly inserted the big steel key. The business end of the key had been coated with grease and so it turned smoothly, without noise.

He pulled open the heavy iron-barred door. Its hinges had also been oiled sometime during the day so it did not squeak. He put the key in his pocket and replaced it, in his hand, with a kitchen knife whose blade had been filed down, thin, to almost razor sharpness. He took a step into the cell.

When he had first heard the noise, Kamen had gotten up and quietly fluffed up the pillow and blanket on the bed to make it look as if he were still sleeping. Then he went into the small toilet cubicle and removed the porcelain lid from the back of the toilet tank. When he had moved into the cell, he had seen immediately that there was nothing inside that could be used as a weapon, so he had made his own preparations.

He had loosened the brass bar that connected the toilet handle to the styrofoam float, so that he could remove it immediately if he had to. The dumb FBI man had promised him he would be safe here in this cell, but Kamen knew better than to trust such a stupid promise. The word of his arrival at Lewisburg would have spread immediately and they read *TIME* magazine in prison too. Everyone would know that a half-million-dollar price had been placed on his head by Gesualdo Ciccolini and that the contract would pay off to anyone, to any convict who got lucky, even to a prison guard if one of them was willing to take the risk.

He gave the screw that held the brass toilet assembly together a half turn and it came off in his hand. He quietly removed the brass bar. It was about twelve inches long, a half-inch wide, and almost a quarter-inch thick. It was not as good as a knife, but in a surprise situation it would do. All the while he worked, he kept up a series of low rumbling artificial snores, the sounds a man fast asleep might make.

He knew, naturally, that there was no point in calling out for help. The guard was probably in on it and he would get only one chance at yelling before his throat was cut. Many might hear in other parts of the prison but no one would care.

He positioned himself in a corner of the cell, near the door, squatting low so that he would be less noticeable. Then he waited.

The first prisoner paused just inside the cell door for an instant. The knife glistened in his hand in the random splash of moonlight that entered the cell. Something did not ring true. Kamen had stopped snoring. Was he awake?

Too late.

Kamen rose from his crouch in the corner and jammed his right hand forward. The brass connecting rod hit into the prisoner's stomach, pierced it, and slid in like a knife. With his left hand, Kamen punched the convict's left wrist and the sharpened kitchen knife dropped and clattered onto the stone floor.

The stabbed prisoner screamed. The man behind him turned and fled and Kamen withdrew his homemade weapon and stabbed again, but this time the injured prisoner had recovered and he too turned and ran.

"You bastard," Kamen heard him call. "I'll be back."

"Bring doughnuts the next time," Kamen said.

He pushed the cell door shut, picked up the knife from the floor, then went back to the toilet to reassemble the brass float bar. It took only a few seconds. He flushed the toilet to get rid of any traces of blood that might be in the tank, then lay back down on his bed. He put the knife under his pillow but kept his hand on the grip. Nobody would come again tonight.

A few minutes later he was asleep.

"A big screwup," Daniel Taylor said. He was sitting in Kamen's cell, looking at the smaller man sitting on the uncomfortable bunk, cleaning his fingernails with an improbably-sharp-looking kitchen knife.

"Oh? How'd that happen?" Kamen said mildly.

"The guard had some kind of food poisoning. Somebody must have slipped him something and he had the trots. So he was off in the john and whoever it was sneaked in here. While his back was turned, so to speak. He's been transferred to another assignment."

Kamen searched the FBI man's face for a few long seconds before he said, "If you really believe that, Taylor, you're even dumber than I thought you were."

"What do you mean?"

"Grow up. The guard was reached. Somebody got to him and put some money in his hand and he looked the other way. Don't transfer him, fire him before he gets somebody killed."

"I'm sorry," Taylor said evenly, "but I don't go along with your paranoia. Everybody *wasn't* in on this."

Kamen grumbled something that Taylor could not understand.

"What did you say?"

"It was Russian," Kamen explained. "Something my grandfather used to say to me."

"What does it mean?"

"It means if I put your brain in a canary, the fucking bird would fly backwards. Forget it, Taylor. I'll take care of myself here. You guys decide yet what you're going to do with me?"

"We're looking for a spot. Someplace where you won't have too much of a chance to screw up."

"Fine. You've got a week."

"What do you mean, we've got a week?" Taylor snapped.

"Because after that I'm getting out of here," Kamen said.

"Why?"

"Because I've got things to do. So you've got a week. Seven days."

"We'll see about that."

"Yes, we will, won't we?" Kamen answered, then looked up at Taylor and grinned.

Kamen knew about the corruptibility of prison guards because he had already bought one of his own. And at four o'clock the next afternoon when the man came back on duty, he handed Kamen a plain white envelope without any address on it.

The envelope contained a letter that had been sent to a postal box in Rochester, New York. There it had been picked up by an old family friend who had opened the letter, thrown away the envelope, and resealed the letter in a plain white envelope. And then he had held it, awaiting instructions. The instructions came when the guard Kamen had bribed called, used the correct code word, and had the letter forwarded to his house by Federal Express.

Kamen thanked the guard and waited until he walked away before opening the envelope.

It began, "Dear Daddy."

The letter was a long chatty report from Kamen's married daughter, Molly, now living in California. It told about the exploits of his two young grandchildren—both obviously geniuses, at least in their mother's estimation—young Peter was ready to start kindergarten; Martha, named after Kamen's late wife, was the wow of the nursery school, already reading at three years of age. It reported how well Molly's husband was doing with his medical practice.

The letter came from a daughter that no one knew Kamen had, not the feds, not the mob, not anybody. Even when he was working with the mob, Kamen had been careful to keep his family out of that life. So none of his mob friends had ever met, or even known about, his wife. When she became pregnant, they did not know. And when she died soon after giving birth to Molly, no one heard of it. None knew of Molly's existence. She was raised by an old Russian aunt. She was twelve before she ever met her father.

Kamen had always been careful, and he knew that if the mob—or the feds, for that matter—knew about his daughter, his son-in-law, his two grandchildren, they could have put a squeeze on him to have him do a lot of things he didn't really want to do. If Ciccolini had learned of them, he would take them hostage until Kamen gave himself up for killing. And then he would probably kill them too anyway.

He knew he had taken a chance by bribing the prison guard, but he had to know how the family was. He had seen them twice in the past five years, just after the birth of each of the grandchildren. Even on those occasions, he had slipped into California quietly, heavily disguised, and had managed to meet his daughter and her children at a downtown hotel.

The letter was three pages long, written in a small, precise, yet delicate hand. His heart was filled with happiness as he read, until he came to the last paragraph.

"This is all probably silly, Daddy, but you've always told me to tell you anything that happens that strikes me as odd. Somehow, I'm getting the feeling that someone is watching us. Last week, I saw the same car, a big gray Lincoln, driving along after me and I didn't think anything of it, but then I think I saw the same car parked near Martha's nursery school when I went to pick her up. It's probably all my imagination and kind of foolish to bother you with, but I always remember what you said. We all love you and miss you. Molly.''

Kamen crumbled the letter in his hands and stared down at the floor. They were on to him and it was not the feds either. It was the bad guys. The big gray Lincoln proved that. Feds' would have used one of their normal nondescript cars, a Ford or Chevy, but the Lincoln was the car of choice of local wiseguys. Someone, somehow had found out . . . and now time was running out on him.

He went to the bars and called out loudly for the guard.

Chapter Nine

Moscow:

"He is here, General."

"Let him wait," said General Nikolai Budenko, fourth highest ranking officer in Russia's internal security agency, and former head of the old Soviet Union's militsia. He grabbed a sheaf of papers from his desk. "Have you read his report?"

Colonel Alexei Svoboda nodded.

"Well? What did you think?"

Svoboda had dreaded the question that he knew was coming. He had worked as Budenko's top aide for the past five years and he should have become used to the man's gruff, blunt manner, but the truth was that it still made him nervous. Budenko had a ferocious temper and he was quick to turn it onto others, especially if he asked for an honest answer and got evasion or somebody trying to say the politic thing.

Svoboda said unhappily, "There's nothing firm in it,

of course. Those initials don't, by themselves, prove anything. They might not even refer to Judge Alekhine. The numbers might not even refer to bribes. Still, with Alekhine's bizarre behavior in court yesterday, letting that drug dealer go, there might be some fire under all that smoke."

"Dammit, Alexei, if they ever give a prize for mashed-potato opinions, you will definitely be the winner. What we have here is a corrupt judge. The goddam criminals have bought their way right into our court system." He glared at Svoboda as if daring him to disagree.

The colonel, a precise neat man with a precise neat blonde mustache, simply nodded.

Budenko drummed his big fingers impatiently on the polished mahogany top of his desk. "Tell Rostov to wait," he growled. "I'll be with him shortly."

Crisply dressed in his military-style police uniform, Lieutenant Lev Rostov sat in the outer office, perched in military fashion on the front of his chair, his back ramrod straight. He was reading a magazine.

One true benefit of democracy, he thought, was that the quality of reading matter in Russia had improved immeasurably. Freed from the corroding touch of the political censor, magazines and newspapers could now make at least some kind of effort to tell the truth. The article he was reading now admitted, for the first time in almost a half century, that Russia indeed had been behind the massacre of six thousand Polish Army officers in the Katyn forest during World War II.

Tell us something we don't know, Rostov thought. The magazine blamed the atrocity on Stalin . . . lately it seemed that everything was being blamed on Stalin, but at least it was a step in the right direction. Rostov was not surprised by the revelation; he had no illusions about the morality of Soviet society. He wondered sometimes though what old people must think when they read something that upended all the lies they had been told for more than forty years. *Maybe that's what the Americans mean by culture shock,* he thought.

He saw Colonel Svoboda come out of the general's office. The deputy commissioner of the militia did not look happy and he was unnecessarily crisp as he snapped at Rostov, "He will be with you in a short time."

"Thank you, Comrade Colonel," Rostov said politely. *Yes, indeed, Colonel Svoboda is a very unhappy fish right now. And will I be next?*

He had met General Budenko only once before and that was in a mob scene at a ceremony in which fifty hand-picked militia had been graduated from a special training class in Western police methods.

He doubted very much that Budenko would remember him at all. And that was all for the good. He had been a policeman now for almost ten years, and one thing he had learned was that the less time you spent with generals and colonels, the less interference you had, the less explaining to do, and the more work you eventually got done. Also, generals and colonels had a way of vanishing with the shifting political winds, and if you got too close to them, you just might vanish too. There probably was nothing uniquely Russian about that, he thought. That just had to do with human nature.

Or inhuman nature, he thought, reflecting on what he had heard about the fabled temper of General Nikolai Budenko.

Inside his office, Budenko hung up his private telephone and looked again at the typewritten three-page report from Rostov.

He did not like people who rocked the boat, and Rostov was obviously someone who was going to have them all wash over the side if he was not stepped on.

The man had lied to his superiors when he had told them that the drug dealer, Vladimir Gubanov, had escaped. In fact, Rostov had killed him—on its face already a highly suspicious act—and then covered up the killing so he could go track the man's (maybe imaginary) Mafia bosses. That alone was enough to throw Rostov off the force.

And the man had given chapter and verse about operations that he had planned and that were somehow unsuccessful. Rostov complained that someone was leaking his unit's attack plans, but Budenko knew he could make at least as good a case that it was simply the Cowboy's own incompetence that had caused the failure of so many operations.

And what of Judge Alekhine? Nothing there but hearsay. No evidence at all, and no one dragged down a sitting judge just on the basis of some obscure initials and a string of computer numbers and a ridiculous judicial decision to set a drug dealer free. Sitting alone in his office, Budenko came as close to a smile as he ever did. *Hell, if stupid decisions were enough to purge judges, we would have nobody left on the bench.*

He pushed aside Rostov's report and opened the man's personnel file. Ten years on the force, Spetsnaz special-forces training, war service in Afghanistan, a good test taker obviously because his scores on written examinations were always at the top level. All the more reason to mistrust him, Budenko thought. He had never much cared for textbook policemen.

Still, there was more to Rostov than that. There were seven individual decorations for bravery in hand-to-hand operations in which Rostov could easily have been killed. And just yesterday, if his report could be believed, two men had tried to kill him with bullets and fire. Perhaps Rostov was more than a textbook policeman. He had studied American society extensively. *Maybe the man's a damned spy,* he thought.

What he knew was that Rostov had opened a large can of worms and now closing it might be worse than difficult; it might be impossible. And throwing Rostov off the force probably would be no solution at all. In the old days, you could fire someone and order him—under threat of death—to keep his mouth shut. But not today. Rostov could wind up in the newspapers and on television within thirty minutes of leaving Budenko's office. *The press would eat up this good-looking bastard*, he thought, looking at the photo of Rostov that smiled at him from inside the man's personnel folder. *They already have. He is in the press more than I am.*

Budenko decided it was his own fault. Without even knowing the man, he had given the okay to put Rostov in charge of a special drug-investigation unit that could be called in to work on any kind of case anywhere in Russia. He had thought it was a reward for good work; he had not realized that it was going to make the man a thorn in his side forever.

What do I do with him? he thought, as he pressed the buzzer on his desk to call the big policeman inside.

Rostov snapped off a crisp military salute and stood sharply at attention while Budenko looked him over. The two men were almost the same size. Rostov might be an inch taller, but Budenko, now in his mid-fifties, was thirty pounds heavier and they were not fat man's pounds. They were muscle and meanness. He had the shoulders and neck of a weightlifter.

He sat silently just long enough to remind Rostov who was the boss, and then stood up, leaned across the desk, and grabbed the other man's hand in a rough powerful handshake.

"Sit down, Cowboy," he said with a good-natured grin. "Sorry to keep you waiting."

No answer was called for; none was offered. Rostov

sat precisely on the edge of the soft leather chair facing Budenko's desk and the militsia's top man leaned back in his own chair and said, "Some say you see the Mafia everywhere."

"They would be wrong, sir," Rostov answered cooly. "But if by Mafia you mean a criminal organization . . . then, yes, organized crime exists and it gets worse every day."

"I get the feeling from your report here that you think this so-called Mafia might one day take over the country," Budenko said.

"That's a question for wiser people than me to answer, Comrade General," Rostov said. "But I think we might be facing what the United States faced sixty or seventy years ago, when the Mafia there became a force almost as powerful as the government itself."

"A lot of small little criminal organizations. How can they threaten us?" Budenko asked.

"Begging your pardon, sir, but they are not small anymore. The Gurov Report for the National Research Institute . . ." Rostov stopped. "I feel like a fool, General, telling you things you already know."

Budenko let slip a slight smile. "Pretend I know nothing, Lieutenant. I am sure that would confirm the suspicions of most members of the militsia anyway. Just go ahead. What does this Gurov Report say?"

"Everything it says, sir, is as you know confirmed by your men in the field. Official corruption in the 1970s led to more and more money being taken out of the state budget and being concentrated in the hands of some few private criminals who were fleecing the system. They were sharks, but upon those sharks, other sharks came to feed. There was an explosion in illegal activity. Strong-arm tactics were used to force these illegal businessmen to share their profits. For the first time in our history, kidnaping for ransom became a real crime. These were, remember, criminals preying upon other criminals and I suppose we did not give it the attention we should have. But then, as crime always does, it had to grow to survive. It began to move against legitimate businessmen. It began to pay graft to corrupt officials for protection. And all the while, this thing . . . this phenomenon of organized crime was growing and developing its own rules. It now has its own slang. Like the Japanese Yakuza, its members now favor tattooing their body and some special tattoos even show the criminal's specialty. I don't know how many pickpockets I arrested when I worked the streets before I found out that the tattoo they wear of a bug with a long nose is like an identity card. The point is, sir, that pickpockets now must pay protection money to the Mafia in their area to work. Whores are organized. They must pay too. Around this nation, Dr. Gurov suggests in his report, we may have as many as ten million professional criminals. And yet we know nothing about them. Obviously we have arrested some of the leaders. And just as obviously a new leader takes his place. We are losing, General. We are losing."

Budenko was silent for a few seconds, then said softly, "I too have read the Gurov Report, Lieutenant. And other reports as well. They all seem to agree that there may be as many as two hundred criminal groups . . ." He smiled. "I believe you crime experts call them 'families' . . . that there may be as many as two hundred crime families working throughout the unified nations. Is it possible that two hundred families can consolidate?"

"Of those two hundred families," Rostov said, "perhaps twenty were active in the Moscow area. Each ran its own whores, its own pickpockets, its own strong-arm men, its own narcotics operations. That was in the past. But now, I and my men sense that all the narcotics are coming together under one leader. If that happens, sir, yes, all the Moscow families must eventually be brought together. And if that happens in Moscow, it will happen everywhere. And the criminals will have free reign."

"Even your precious Gurov Report indicates that the families could not come together as one. Especially now after the breakup. The independent nations are too diverse for that to happen."

"Permission to speak frankly, sir?" Rostov asked.

"You had it the moment you came in that door," General Budenko replied.

"Then, sir, if you don't mind, bullshit. What all these experts have said was true perhaps five years ago. Maybe even three years ago. But no longer. Organized crime is driven by money. And there now is, we believe, an effort to consolidate the entire illegal narcotics business in Moscow and in this entire Russian republic. If that happens, the people at the top will have untold amounts of wealth. Vast riches. They will be able to buy anybody. If anyone opposes them, they will be able to hire the assassins to have him killed. Do you know that in Moscow, right this moment, one can hire a killer for fifteen thousand rubles? Five years ago, the price was five times that. We are facing a different world, sir, from the one the academics so glibly talk about. They were right *then*. But this is *now*."

"Obviously you think so." General Budenko picked up the blue-sheeted report that Rostov had filed. "You make serious charges in here, claiming that a sitting judge has somehow been corrupted by this perhaps-real, perhaps-imaginary organized crime syndicate of yours. I know Judge Alekhine. I have never doubted his integrity."

"I cannot argue, General. I do not know the judge. And I was making no charges. I was merely reporting the facts. If you asked me my suspicions, I would say, yes, I believe that Judge Alekhine is on some criminal's payroll, but, no, I cannot prove it now. However, I would have been disloyal both to you and to my profession if I did not state my true beliefs."

Passionate as well as smart, Budenko thought. *He really cares about this stuff.*

"I know I have told you to speak frankly, Lieutenant," Budenko said. "And I know how difficult that is for a subordinate officer. Do this, if you would. Pretend for a moment that I am not General Brass Balls Budenko . . ." Both men grinned. "Pretend instead that I am one of the men on your squad and sitting with you in a tavern after a dull evening. Tell me, Rostov, what do we do about this growing Mafia of yours?"

"We understand that the Mafia exists," Rostov answered immediately. "We understand that the mob is getting stronger. We understand that it is worth our while to stop them. And so we expend time and money and manpower. We infiltrate their organizations. We anticipate them and outsmart them, instead of always reacting too late with too little. Begging your pardon, sir, we declare war on these bastards and we put them out of business. We start with narcotics."

"And you don't think we've done enough?"

Careful, Cowboy, Rostov thought. *This is the loaded question, because he's just really asking you what you think of the way he runs the militsia. Careful.*

He told himself to be careful and then was not.

"No, sir, I don't think we've done enough. I think we have too few men with too few resources against a crime organization that will, before we know it, make contact and treaty with crime organizations in other countries. Out there, over the oceans, there are decades of experience in how to run a mob. We've had only months to try to figure out how to fight them."

"You think, then, this war is lost?" Budenko said, his face betraying no reaction at all.

"No, sir. We haven't even shown up on the battlefield yet."

The two men sat silently for almost thirty seconds, Budenko alternating staring at Rostov and looking at the file on the desk before him.

"And if you were me?" he finally said.

"Declare war."

"Just like that?"

"Just like that," Rostov said.

The general nodded. "All right. I'm happy that you have been so frank with me. When you leave here today, what do you plan to do?"

Rostov cleared his throat as if considering his answer, although he had made up his mind long before on his course of action. "Unless ordered not to, sir, I would institute surveillance on Judge Alekhine, his telephones, his family, his friends. I think he has been bought. I would try to prove it. Perhaps he might prove our passageway into this crime organization."

"I see." Budenko began to speak again but was interrupted by the buzzer on his desk.

"Yes, Svoboda, what is it?"

He listened for a long time. Rostov watched, but the general showed no emotion at all. He might have been listening to a weather forecast. Finally he replaced the receiver.

"You can forget about following Judge Alekhine," he said.

Rostov was not able to hide his disappointment. "Oh," he said simply.

"He has been found murdered. He and that man . . ." Budenko looked down at Rostov's report. ". . . that Pimen Spatsky. Both were shot to death twenty minutes ago in Sokolniki Park."

"Shot? By whom?" Rostov asked.

Budenko shook his head. "They were pushed out of a car. Then people inside the car shot them. The car got away. No description." He looked at Rostov and seemed almost pleased by the other policeman's confusion. "Well, at least, finally you seem to be speechless. What do you think about this?"

"Apparently someone wanted to make sure neither of them talked about anything. That is my opinion," Rostov said.

"And that is jumping to a conclusion," Budenko snapped. "For all we know, this . . . what was his name, Spatsky, maybe has been sleeping with Alekhine's wife. Maybe it was a lovers' quarrel."

Rostov nodded. *Why is he doing this to me?* he wondered. *He believes me or he doesn't. Why all this fooling around?* "Anything is possible," he said.

The telephone rang again. Budenko picked it up, spoke to Colonel Svoboda, and then his face seemed to lose color. He covered the mouthpiece of the phone and said to Rostov, "You may wait outside."

"Yes, sir," Cowboy said, and walked quickly from the office.

"This is General Budenko." The big officer waited on the telephone for over a minute before he was greeted by another voice.

"General?"

"Mr. President," Budenko said.

"What the hell is going on over there?"

"What do you mean, sir?"

"I mean that damned judge being shot down in the middle of a city park. I don't have enough problems but this whole country is turning into Cowboys and Indians?"

"My men are working on it, sir," Budenko said.

"That's not good enough. People don't just shoot down judges. Tell me what happened."

Budenko looked down at Rostov's three-page report in front of him. "Mr. President," he said smoothly, "we were developing information that Judge Alekhine was corrupt. That he was, in fact, on the payroll of some crime figures. They may have been afraid that he would talk to us."

"Well, that's something anyway," the other voice said after a few moments. "The Mafia, is it?"

"Yes, sir. We think so."

"Listen to me, General. Those bastards are sticking their noses into everything. This is a direct order. Go after them. Crush them and put them out of business. Do you understand?"

"Mr. President, I—"

"Do you understand?" The voice was almost shouting.

"Yes, sir. We are working on it right now. I need not remind you, however, that what happened today probably happened because we were getting closer to these criminals."

"Well, keep getting closer. I don't care if you have to get all the judges in Moscow shot. They're not worth a pail of spit anyway."

"Yes, sir."

"Continue to advise me on the Alekhine shooting. And within forty-eight hours, I want to know what you are doing about the Mafia."

"Yes, sir."

The phone clicked in his ear. *Fresh little bastard,* Budenko thought. *The first thing we do should be to get rid of all politicians. Especially those who are standing on the edge of the cliff already.*

He stood up, walked to the door, and yelled outside, "Rostov, get back in here. You too, Colonel."

When the two men were inside his office, Budenko said, "Rostov, you have a new assignment."

"Yes, sir?"

"Your group was formed to battle narcotics. Your mission has changed. Go after the Mafia."

Rostov hid his glee only with difficulty. "Yes, sir."

"This will be an undercover assignment. You can use the same team you have, if you wish. But there will be no publicity about it. You will retire that stupid cowboy hat that always gets you on television. In fact, I think the less your men know about what you are doing, the better. I want recommendations for an action program from you in thirty-six hours.''

Cowboy said solemnly, "Do I have to wait, sir?"

"What do you mean?"

Rostov reached into his pocket and brought out a sheaf of papers. "My recommendations are in here," he said.

"You think of everything, don't you?" Budenko said. "I won't ask you what is in your other jacket pocket."

"I think the general knows," Rostov said softly.

"Well, you can throw the resignation away. Or at least file it for now. You have other work to do." He held up his sturdy index finger. "One thing. You will report only—I repeat that, only—to Colonel Svoboda or me. No one else has any business knowing what you are doing."

"I appreciate this opportunity, General Budenko."

"Don't thank me yet. You said you wanted to declare war. Now it's been declared."

"Yes, sir."

"Just make sure our side wins."

Chapter Ten

Moscow:

The courts had closed early because of Judge Alekhine's death and Olga Lutska had left her office in the
early afternoon. She ran one errand, and when she returned to her apartment, Lev Rostov was sitting in his car
in front of her apartment building, waiting for her.

He had followed her upstairs; she had made them
drinks, but he was curiously reticent about the day. While
she had only known him for a day, she thought that she
knew him well already—*Has anyone ever really known
him before?*—and she decided he would talk when he
wanted to talk.

But what had happened? She knew that he had gone
to see General Budenko. Had he been sacked? Had he
been given a promotion? Finally, she could wait no longer
and she asked him and Rostov replied, "Give me a
chance to sort it out and I will tell you all about it. You've
heard, of course, about Judge Alekhine?"

"How could I avoid it?" she answered. She was in her office when the news came in shortly after noon and all the work of the Moscow court system had stopped. Sitting judges had recessed all their trials for the day; small clusters of people had traveled the court building from office to office, talking, sharing the sketchy information they had received, gossiping about Alekhine. "After what you told me last night about the judge, I spent much of the afternoon gathering gossip about him. No one had much liked him but no one ever thought he was corrupt. Not even a whisper of it and I am a prosecutor; I questioned subtly but hard. If he was controlled by crime, no one had any inkling of it."

Cowboy was buried in his own thoughts and merely grunted. She refilled his drink and he said, "Where is your sex-starved little kitten today?"

"That was my afternoon errand. She is at the veterinarian's. I took her to be neutered."

For the first time, Cowboy smiled. "There were other less radical treatments, you know," he said.

"None that appealed to me."

"I'm very sorry to hear that," Rostov said. She offered to cook dinner, but Cowboy insisted upon taking her to dinner at the Neptun Hotel Restaurant near Ismailovsky Park. He looked splendid, she thought, in his sports jacket and western hat, and she tried to look her best for him and thought she had succeeded, but at the restaurant, he only picked at his food and seemed distracted.

"You're not much in the way of company," she said.

"I'm sorry. I'm thinking of that old woman who died in the fire last night. When they attempted to kill me."

"Oh," she muttered, feeling very guilty for not understanding why he was out of sorts. "I'm sorry. I'd almost forgotten."

He nodded and shrugged.

110

"Were there no clues at the building on who started the fire?"

"Nothing," he said. "The building collapsed in on itself. I had men pick through it today but there was nothing to be found."

"I'm sorry."

"It has not been much of a day," Rostov said. "And then Alekhine. Just when we learn that he was probably corrupt, bang, that fast, before we even get a chance to put heat on him, somebody takes him out. A damned shame."

He watched her carefully; Olga merely nodded. They went back to eating; she found the meal curiously unsatisfying, even though it was the first dinner date she had been on in several months.

When they left, Cowboy drove them back to her apartment. He drove slowly along Semanyovska, then stopped across from the high-columned Motherland Movie Theater and silently watched a thin cluster of people who seemed to be loitering in front, with no intention of going inside the cinema. She noted that the movie *Rocky III* was playing.

"Are you interested in films?" she said.

He pulled the car back into traffic. "No," he said. "Drug dealers. Over there is Moscow's narcotics department store."

"If you know that, why don't you make arrests?"

"We did in the past. We would roar in and sweep up the petty little drug pushers by the dozens. We would send them to jail by the dozens. And by the dozens, they would be replaced by others. But now it has all changed. We come in to make arrests. We pick up people. And no one is ever carrying drugs," he said. "The sellers make a deal and then deliver the drugs later. And we don't know how and we don't know who. It is very frustrating."

* * *

111

They went back to her apartment and drank brandy while watching television. Rostov had still said nothing about his earlier meeting with his militsia boss, General Budenko. Finally, Olga went into her bathroom to change. Rostov heard the shower running for a long time and when she reemerged, she was wearing a silk dressing gown and, from the way her long legs flashed underneath it, it seemed, very little else.

She sat next to him on the sofa, leaning her head on his shoulder. Her right hand insinuated itself under his shirt and played with his nipples. She flicked her tongue into his ear. All the while he sat like a stuffed dummy and finally she said, "Your magnificent display of fore-play has raised me to new heights. Please take me inside and make love to me."

With an almost reluctant air, Rostov rose from the sofa and followed her into the bedroom. She arranged herself on the bed and untied her robe. Her lush long body looked shiny, oiled in the dim light from the single low-wattage lamp in the room.

Cowboy disrobed slowly, sitting on the edge of the bed, his back to her.

The telephone rang.

"Do you mind if I get that?" he said. "I've been expecting a call."

She turned on her side away from him. "Go ahead," she said crisply.

Wearing only his undershorts, Rostov walked out into the living room. He closed the bedroom door behind him.

He was gone a long time.

She heard the bedroom door open again, *But dammit, I will not even favor him with a glance. The rude self-centered bastard. When he leaves the next time, he can stay gone for all I care.*

She did not turn around even when she felt long soft

fingers trailing up her thigh. She felt his tongue on her belly, flicking in and out of her navel, and in the coolness of the room, she could feel his saliva, wet and cold, on her stomach, on her upper thighs, and yes, all over her body, and then his face was buried in her and slowly she turned over onto her back and felt his strong arms pulling her legs apart and he was kissing and licking her. She let it go. There would be time later to criticize him for his rude behavior . . . and then she felt her body begin to spasm.

His entire body was between her legs now and he entered her, so big, so hard, that she cried out with pleasure and raised her body toward him and wrapped her legs around the small of his back, and then felt his mouth on hers—*It is especially good when two tall people make love, isn't it?* she thought—and then she knew it was happening for both of them and she tried to pull him even deeper into her body and for a long moment they stopped, as if frozen in place, and then she felt him releasing into her and she let go too.

They rested in that position for long minutes as Rostov kissed her throat, then he raised himself up on his arms to look down at her face, and Olga smiled and said weakly, "Ride, Cowboy, ride."

Rostov laughed, and pulled himself from her body and rolled onto his side next to her, pulling up the thin sheet to cover their bodies.

She simply stared at the ceiling. She heard the click of his old-fashioned cigarette lighter and smelled the aroma of his vile Russian papirosy cigarettes and then he handed her one and placed an ashtray on the soft mound of her belly.

"So what do you have to say for yourself?" Olga asked.

"Olga Lutska," he said. "Thirty-two years old. An only child. Your father worked in the Moscow Street

Department right up until his death. You worked your way through Moscow Law School and now you are the sole support of your mother who is in the Happiness Nursing Home in Zagorsk. The extra charge for her care is sixty rubles a month. Your salary is three hundred rubles a month and after paying your rent and your mother's care, little is left. Your present bank balance is four hundred and twelve rubles. You have no hidden accounts. You own no car. You own no real estate. You have worked in the prosecutor's office for four years and in that time your bank balance has declined. You have no steady boyfriends and none of your relatives has ever been accused of a crime.''

"You bastard. You've been checking on me," she snapped. She was silent in the dimly lit room for a moment, staring at his sharp profile as he puffed idly on his cigarette.

"As the Americans say, you're poor but honest," he said.

"I could have told you that if you had asked," she said. "Is that what the telephone call was about?"

"Yes," he said honestly. "I had my men check on you."

"And I passed your test with bugles blaring?"

"Yes."

"Good. Now get the fuck out of here," she said.

"I don't respond well to subtlety," Rostov said. "What do you really mean?"

Despite herself, despite her annoyance, Olga chuckled.

"Why, Cowboy? Why?"

He stubbed out his cigarette, then hers, then put the ashtray back onto an end table and turned so that his face was only inches from hers.

"Because last night, I told you that I thought Alekhine was associated with the Mafia. And then today, he was killed."

"You thought I . . ."

"I had to be sure," Rostov said. "I told no one else about Alekhine. I had to see if you were, perhaps, on the wrong side."

"You insulting dimwit," she snapped. "How do you have the gall to suspect me?"

"Because Alekhine and the court system were not the only corrupt agencies mentioned on Gubanov's computer."

"No," she gasped.

"Yes."

"The prosecutor's office?"

"Yes," Rostov said. "I had to make sure it wasn't you. Don't be angry with me."

"No, of course not," she said sarcastically. "Why get upset about being called a stooge for the Mafia?"

"Why indeed, when you have been acquitted?" Rostov asked.

"So now are you going to tell me what happened today with General Budenko?" she said.

"Yes," he said. "But first this." And he moved his body over hers once again.

"That is a marvelous idea," she said later. "Do you think Budenko will agree?"

"I don't know," Rostov said. "I do know, though, that it's what we need. We don't have the experience here with organized crime. I may be the damned police expert on it and I don't know anything either. We need an expert on the Mafia and that means an American."

"What do they call those American police? The FBI? Is that what you mean?"

"Probably. Someone who can work with me and tell me what to look for, what to expect."

"When will you know if Budenko agrees?"

"He's a general and I'm a lieutenant. I guess he will get around to it in his own good time."

* * *

Colonel Alexei Svoboda disliked few things more than cocktail parties at foreign embassies, and the American embassy was the worst. Russian women seemed mesmerized by what they viewed as the power and glamour of Americans, so they came to these parties with their bodies half falling out of their dresses and they seemed to be offering themselves to every reasonably good looking, reasonably civilized American with whom they made eye contact. He had seen whores outside the Moskva Hotel act with more restraint.

It was not just that he did not like women, although that was the case also. He just did not like any Russian, man or woman, fawning over a foreigner. Thank goodness that the glory days of Patrice Lumumba University and all the visiting African students were finally over because he regarded those couplings as the most offensive at all. Although there had once been a young African student named Kwame whom Svoboda remembered with affection. Whatever happened to him?

The crowd was slowly thinning out as the evening wound down, and Svoboda found himself drawing closer to the American attaché for cultural affairs who was, everyone knew, the head of the CIA in Russia.

The American was a tall husky man, apparently of Italian descent, with large bad teeth, a pasty complexion, and a great deal of practical wits.

"Ahh, Colonel Svoboda," he said. "What a surprise to see you. Does this mean that all the criminals are off the Moscow streets tonight?"

Svoboda had no feeling this night for small talk. He said, "General Budenko has asked me to speak to you of something important."

"Can we talk here or should we go into one of the offices?"

"Here is better. All your offices are bugged," Svoboda said.

"Of course they are. You Russians put them there when you built the building. But here it is. What can I do for you?"

"We need a favor," Svoboda said.

"Anything short of nuclear weapons or money."

"We need a man," Svoboda said.

Chapter Eleven

Washington, D.C.:

"They want what?" In his office in the J. Edgar Hoover FBI Building, Archibald Semple listened to the phone intently again, then said, "Who the hell are we going to find who wants to go on temporary duty in Russia? Have you ever seen Russian women? There are three good-looking women in the whole country and they're all on *Playboy*'s payroll."

He listened some more, thought for a moment, then broke into uproarious laughter that brought tears to his eyes. When he recovered his composure, he said, "Just maybe I've got something that will work."

It was a grumbly kind of day, the kind of day when Daniel Taylor decided he did not like to fly at all anymore and if they kept calling him to come from Allentown to

Washington, D.C., he was going to start driving a bureau car.

People flew to save time, but between getting to the airport and getting where you were going and jerking around with cabs and luggage and airlines that were constantly late, you wound up saving no time at all. You were just as well off driving a car, eating at a McDonald's, and having all that spare time to think. Thinking was still a good thing, even for government work. And terrorists hadn't yet gotten around to bombing cars at random. Screw airplanes.

It was not just the usual flight from A-B-E Airport to Washington that had him annoyed. There was still the question of what to do with Peter Kamen. All Taylor wanted was to be rid of him, but Washington obviously had not yet found a spot for him, and so Kamen was still Taylor's FBI guest at the Lewisburg penitentiary. It was getting on Taylor's nerves, just as, obviously, it was getting on Kamen's.

The crazy bastard had called Taylor yesterday—where the hell did he get access to a telephone?—and told him that he had to be out of jail within twenty-four hours.

"Oh, you do?"

"Yes. A hard and fast time limit. I can't fool with you morons anymore."

"You'll get out when we say you get out," Taylor snapped.

"Listen. I've done good work for you people. I've handed up a lot of your enemies."

"No one disputes that."

"Well, I haven't told you everything I know. Not by a long shot. What I've given you is the tip of the iceberg. There's a lot more available."

"Like what?"

"Like a lot of things. Political fixes, special deals the

119

mob runs with the army. You ever wonder why toilet seats cost four hundred dollars? You ever wonder why there's so much shrinkage at your army ordnance depots? I've told you people what I had to tell you. But not all that I could tell you.''

"And now, out of the goodness of your heart, you're going to come clean?" Taylor said.

"Something like that," Kamen said.

"I'll talk to my superiors about it."

"Talk fast. I've got to get out of here. I've got things to do.''

"I'll talk to them as soon as I can."

"Either way, I'm leaving here."

"Don't try. It'd be a big mistake," Taylor said.

"I don't have any choice," Kamen had said.

That was the trouble with dealing with the crazy son of a bitch. Kamen never gave anybody any choice. He was born to complicate other people's lives, and all Taylor knew was that he wanted to be rid of him from his jurisdiction before the stoolie was found out and bumped off. If it happened on his shift, his next shift would be Anchorage, Alaska.

He wondered if he could drive to Anchorage, Alaska.

"I've solved all your problems for you," Semple said to Taylor.

"Oh? Tell you, Arch, I wasn't aware I had any problems.''

"Anybody who's got Peter Kamen in his bailiwick has more problems than mortal man should be subject to," Semple said.

"I'll buy that. He's talking now about a lot more information that he has for us," Taylor said.

"What kind of information?"

"Oh, government contracts, army fraud, you name it, he'll promise it.''

"What do you think about it?" Semple asked.

"Truth? I think he's bullshitting. I think he's just in a hurry to get out for some reason and this is the way he came up with."

"Good. Because if he had something, I wouldn't want to let him go. I'm going to take him off your hands."

"It can't be soon enough for me," Taylor said. "You've found a place for him?"

"Yeah."

"Where?"

"Russia."

Taylor started to laugh. Semple said, "What's so funny?"

"Russia?"

"Yes."

"Do you want to start the cold war all over again?"

Moscow:

General Budenko favored Alexei Svoboda with one of his rare smiles.

"You seem to have been very persuasive, Alexei," he said.

"Sir?"

"Yes. The Americans have agreed to send us an expert on Mafia operations."

"Who is he?"

"I don't know yet, but the ambassador has told me it is somebody who was on the inside of their organized crime for many years."

"He'll work with Cowboy . . . Lieutenant Rostov?"

"That's my plan. Yes," Budenko said.

"You think it'll make a difference, General?"

"We will see, won't we? If it does, perhaps we can get all these damned politicians off our backs." He sighed, and Svoboda thought it a curiously human gesture for someone as mechanically brusque as General Budenko always seemed to be. "Do you think life was so difficult under the czars, Alexei?" he asked.

Svoboda looked startled. It was obviously a question he had never thought of before and he had no idea on the politically correct way to answer it. Budenko recognized his discomfort and said, in disgust, "Get out of here and do some work."

Lewisburg, Pennsylvania:

The prison guard was sprawled in a chair, his feet propped up on a desk, leafing sideways through the latest issue of *Penthouse* magazine. When he looked up and saw the two men approaching, he tossed the book onto a small shelf behind him and rose to his feet.

"Evening, Warden," he said. He recognized the other man as that FBI agent who had been here before. Taylor, he thought his name was.

"We've come to see your guest," the warden said.

"He's inside, quiet as a mouse," the guard said. He took a key ring from his top desk drawer, then pressed a button on the wall. The heavy steel door that led to the cellblock opened with a noisy lurch.

"I'll take those," the warden said, and grabbed the key ring from the guard's hand. Then he led Taylor inside toward Peter Kamen's cell. The guard followed close behind them.

It was dark in the cellblock with only the light of the moon illuminating the ground floor and the otherwise empty cells.

When he got to Kamen's cell, the warden inserted the key in the lock, then looked up and said, "What the hell . . ."

Taylor pushed alongside him. Kamen's bed was empty. The panel that had hid the toilet from view had been lowered to the floor and there was a huge hole dug in the wall around the water-supply pipe.

"The bastard's escaped," Taylor snapped. He pulled open the door and ran into the cell. The warden and the guard followed him. In a moment, all were staring at the scarred, damaged wall and the guard finally had the brains to say, "Nobody got out through that. The damn hole's not big enough for my pet cat."

It was too late. They heard the cell door slam shut behind them, and as they wheeled around, Peter Kamen was locking the door with the heavy key.

"Good night, gentlemen," he said. "Nice of you to visit."

No! Don't let this happen to me. The son of a bitch was hiding under the bed, Taylor thought. *If he gets out or anybody gets wind of this, my ass has had it. They'll make me walk to Anchorage.*

The guard reached for his gun, but Taylor slapped the man's hand away from his holster.

"Kamen, wait!"

"What do you want?"

"I just came from Washington. They said you're free."

"Why is it that I don't believe you?" Kamen said.

"I'm telling you the truth. They've got a deal for you. That's why I came here."

"Ta-ta. Give my regards to J. Edgar."

"You bastard! Lock me in here and you're going to see him before I do."

Kamen laughed. He walked away and then Taylor saw the cell key skidding across the gray-painted concrete floor. It slid to a stop about four feet outside the bars.

It took them fifteen minutes to get out of the cell. The warden seemed to have the idea that even though the guard's arm was two feet too short to reach the key, if he stretched and tried harder, somehow he might be able to make it work.

Taylor, grumbling under his breath, watched their dog-and-pony act for five minutes, before he growled, "Let's stop the horseshit and get out of here. Give me your belts," He buckled their belts together to make a nine-foot leather lash, then tied the end into a loop.

He sat on the floor just inside the cell door and began trying to loop the belt around the key on the floor. Every time he did, he edged it forward, gaining three or four inches at a time before the belt slipped over the key.

Finally it was in reach and he leaned out, picked up the key and unlocked the cell door.

"I've got to sound an alarm," the warden said.

"What for?" Taylor asked.

"Escaped. The man escaped."

"I wasn't lying to him. I came to let him loose. Let's just let it be for a while, will you?"

"I just can't let people be wandering in and out of my prison," the warden said huffily.

"What we'll do is, from your office, we'll make some phone calls. In the meantime, we'll all calm down," Taylor said. He turned to the guard. "And you will keep your mouth shut, understand? One word and your ass is grass."

In truth, Taylor wanted some time to think. Washington thought it had solved the problem of Peter Kamen once and for all, but now the crazy bastard was on the loose and probably going into deep hiding. He had no family, no friends that anyone knew about. Where would he be? How the hell were they going to track him down? And he had let the man get away. *Next stop—Anchorage.*

From the warden's office, he had called his top office assistant and told him to get the full staff assembled at the FBI office. Sooner or later he would have to tell Washington what had happened. The warden had calmed down and decided that it wasn't his problem after all.

Whatever Taylor wanted to do was fine with him. The guard meanwhile had promised to keep his mouth shut, but after the fright wore off in a couple of hours, he would probably start yapping. And after that, it was every man for himself.

The guard escorted him through the door next to the steel door next to the prison's broad main gate and Taylor trudged through the intensifying rain toward his car, parked in someone else's private spot in the lot.

He unlocked the door, got inside, and put the key in the ignition. But before he turned the key on, in sheer frustration, he pounded both his fists onto the steering wheel again and again.

"Well, if this is the way you react to petty annoyances," a familiar voice drawled, "I'd hate to see what happens when it hits the fan."

He wheeled around. Peter Kamen sat in the middle of the back seat. He grinned at Taylor.

"What are you doing here?" the FBI man sputtered.

"Hey, if you want, I'll leave."

"No, no, no, no, no, no, no," Taylor mumbled.

"So you said you got a deal for me," Kamen said. "I want to hear about it."

"Why didn't you wait inside the joint? I would have told you."

"Because, in there, if I didn't like it, I was stuck. Out here, if I don't like it, I just walk," Kamen said. He paused and said, "So, I'm waiting."

"How'd you like to go home?"

"Show my face in Brooklyn again and I'm steak tartare by morning," Kamen said.

"Not that home. Your family home. Russia."

"You're kidding," Kamen said.

"Why should we be kidding?"

"Because the Russians don't trust us enough yet so you can start dumping your problems on them."

It sounded to Taylor as much the same thing he had

told Archibald Semple earlier in the day in Washington, D.C., but he felt no obligation to point that out.

"Look," he said, "the story is simple. Russia's got a growing problem with the Mafia."

"You mean from Sicily?" Kamen asked. "I know the Sicilians. They want to kill me too."

"No. Not Sicilians. Homegrown mobs. They call all mobs the Mafia," Taylor said. "Anyway, they want somebody to come over and help their cops fight against organized crime. They want somebody who can think like these hoods, can plan like them, can figure out what they're going to do next."

"And you figured to set a thief to catch a thief?" Kamen said.

"Something like that," Taylor agreed. "But think about it for a minute. Your family was Russian. You speak the language. Nobody knows more about how the mobs work than you. You could go to Russia, go onto their payroll, and that'd be the end of it. No more contracts on your head. In fact, in Russia, they'd probably make you a general or something, some kind of Hero of the Republic."

"They did that for Lenin and he's dead anyway," Kamen said.

"Nobody there wants to kill you," Taylor said. He turned around on the seat. "That's because nobody there knows you like I do, I guess. You want a smoke?"

"No. Never touch them," Kamen said.

Taylor lit one for himself. He had not smoked in three years, until he met Kamen. "Look at it this way. You always wanted to be a big shot. Well, this is a Lucky Luciano kind of deal. After the war, they let him go into Italy in exile because he helped in the war. The same thing here. You leave America. Exile if you want to call it that. But you can be a happy clam in Russia as long as you keep your nose clean. The way I figure it, you'll even be able to collect your lottery winnings there. An

American millionaire in Russia? They'll treat you like a king. I don't know, but it sounds like the home run of the world to me."

"Take me someplace and buy me coffee," Kamen said. "I've got to think about it for a while. And that prison coffee is the worst slop I've ever tasted."

After two cups of coffee, Kamen said he would think about it if he was able to convert his lottery winnings into rubles himself.

"Why's that?" Taylor said.

"Because if I let you guys do it or those other incompetents in Russia, they'll change it all at official rates and I'll wind up without enough rubles to buy a pound of pork chops. I convert it myself, I'll get some money for it."

"I don't think Washington would have any real problem with that," Taylor said cautiously. "I don't know about Moscow, though."

"Don't worry about Moscow. Get me there with my dollars in my pocket and I'll take care of my own currency conversion. What they don't know won't hurt them."

"Then you'll do it."

"I'm thinking about it," Kamen said.

After two more cups of coffee and after smoking a cigar which he made Taylor buy for him, Kamen looked up and smiled.

"I'll do it on one condition," he said.

"I don't know if Washington will agree to conditions," Taylor said.

"They'd better agree to this one. This is a real deal-buster," Kamen said.

Taylor sighed. "Then let's hear it," he said.

Chapter Twelve

Moscow:

Rostov was gone from the apartment before Olga arose at six forty-five A.M. She looked anxiously for a note in the kitchen or the living room but there was none. It didn't matter; she still felt wonderful.

How long has it been since I've been with a real man, not some statute-spouting legal mannikin? Too long. Much too long.

She puttered around the apartment, making coffee and thinking of the Cowboy, taking a shower and thinking of the Cowboy, trying to cook breakfast and thinking of the Cowboy, and she finally just sat down, sipped her coffee, and thought of the Cowboy. When she looked again at the clock, it was almost seven-thirty and she realized she had to hurry to get to the office on time. She dressed quickly and was gone at ten minutes till eight.

The telephone repair truck arrived fifteen minutes later. Two swarthy men with a peculiar Oriental cast to their features pulled two canvas bags of electrical supplies from the rear of the small van and went inside the apartment building to rouse the *dezhurnaya*.

"Telephone company, lady," one man said.

"I paid my bill," the woman said from behind the door that she stubbornly kept locked.

"It's not about your bill. Listen, mama, will you open this door so we can talk? We don't want to stand out here in the hall shouting."

With measured slowness, the woman opened the door, even though she kept the security chain in place.

"What do you want?"

"There's some kind of electrical problem on this street and we traced it to the phones in this building. One of them is shorting out. We've got to check them."

"Nobody's home. Everybody has gone to work."

"That's why we're here to see you. Give us the keys to the apartments."

"How do I know you won't steal everything?" the woman asked suspiciously.

"Because your telephone company doesn't steal things. We fix things. Come on, mama, we want to get done someday."

"You're pests. You're always pests," the woman said, but she shuffled away from the door and came back with a large jailer's ring holding a couple of dozen keys.

"They're all tagged with the apartment numbers," she said.

"Okay."

"I want them back," she said.

"Okay."

"And if anything is missing, I'll call the militsia on you."

"Nothing will be missing. We've come to fix your phones."

The woman handed the keys through the door. "Why don't you come to fix them when they're broken? Last year the phones didn't work and it took you two weeks to get here.''

''We're working every day to improve our service and to win your trust.''

''Don't steal anything,'' the woman said.

It took only three minutes to install the bug in Olga Lutska's apartment. One of the men simply unscrewed the metal base of the telephone and with a strong epoxy cement attached the coin-sized transmitter to the interior of the phone. Two small bare wires protruded from the listening device and the man fastened them around two contact screws inside the instrument. Now the entire telephone wire would act as an antenna for the microphone. While he worked, he tunelessly whistled the latest hit song. It was something he had heard on a jukebox two nights earlier by an American singer named Madonna. He did not understand the English lyrics, but somehow he did not think that it was a religious song, no matter what the singer's name was.

The second man, meanwhile, had gone down to the utility basement which opened directly into the small backyard of the building. Behind a clumsy wooden wall compartment built to house the fuses for the building's electrical circuits, he jammed a small tape recorder the size of a small loaf of bread. A pair of yard-long antenna wires protruded from the side of the recorder and he pulled them out to their full length and fastened them to the wall with tape.

He took a small earphone unit and plugged them into the jack of the recorder, raised them to his ears, and heard his partner's whistling. The man grinned, disconnected the earphones, and left the cellar.

They had been at work only four minutes.

They met back upstairs outside Olga Lutska's apartment. From there they walked upstairs to the top floor of the seven-story building and unlocked one of the apartment doors. A telephone sat on the kitchen table and they quickly disconnected it and replaced it with another instrument they took from one of their canvas bags. They were careful to lock the door behind them when they left.

"You're in luck, mama," the man called through the door.

"Why? Are you leaving?"

"Yes. We found it right away in . . . let's see, the Raskalovich apartment on the top floor. He had a short in his receiver. We replaced it. Want to see it?"

"What do I know about telephones?" the woman yelled back from inside the locked apartment. "Did you steal anything?"

"No."

The door opened a crack. "Then give me back my keys."

"Here they are."

The woman grabbed them from his hands, slammed the door again, and yelled, "And try not to bother me anymore."

As he was every Thursday, General Budenko was late arriving at his militsia office. Thursday was his day for conferring with the doctors at the Moscow Cancer Center where his wife, Ludmilla, was now a permanent patient.

The last of her fine blonde hair had fallen out. She was totally bald, and when her husband entered the room she shared with another patient, she turned her face away. He leaned over and kissed her cheek and she looked at him with tears in her eyes.

"I'm sorry I look so terrible," she said.

"You look just fine, Luddie," he said, and kissed her again and then he sat by the bed and held her hand as she dozed off. The truth was that she did not look fine. She had weighed only eighty-seven pounds last Thursday and seemed to have lost even more in the intervening seven days. There was little left now but skin and bones, hardly a trace of the tall, elegant proud woman with whom he had shared more than forty years of his life.

She had been in the hospital for over three years, suffering from a particularly virulent form of lymph-node cancer that now had free run through her entire body, slowly eating away at her internal organs. The doctors were very open in stating that there was no longer any hope; the only question left was exactly when she would die.

Still, Budenko met with them as he left the hospital room, to see if there had been any change for the better, if there were any promising new treatments available, if a change in scenery might effect some magical cure.

But always the answers were the same. *Sorry, Comrade General, but there is no hope. It is just a matter of time. There are no miracles.*

It had been a new pair of doctors this morning, young and oily and patronizing, and Budenko had disliked them right away, and when they finished their dismal report, he had stood up, towering over them, and said, "Suppose I told you I believed in miracles."

Frightened by his vehemence, the doctors had not the courage to stare him down and instead looked away toward the window. Silence hung heavy in the room for a few seconds and Budenko said sternly, "I will expect you to keep trying."

"Yes, General."

Walking from the hospital, Budenko thought that if those doctors had had the courage and the tenacity of Ludmilla Budenko herself, they would not have to be reminded to keep trying for a cure. It had been that courage that had put her in this hospital; it had been that courage that he knew, sadly, would cause her death.

He knew the exact day when Luddie had contracted her illness. It was April 26, 1986, and he was a division commander of the militsia, stationed far outside Moscow in a place called Chernobyl.

At 1:24 A.M., he was awakened in his bed by the roaring thump of a string of explosions. Ludmilla woke up at the same time and they ran to the window to see a ball of flame, rising on clouds of black smoke, high into the sky.

"The nuclear plant," he said, and instantly dressed to go to the office.

He was gone for thirty-six hours, working with the head policemen, the army, the KGB, the scientists, trying to dampen the damage from a deadly cloud, ten times more radioactive than the bomb dropped on Hiroshima.

Finally, on the direct orders of a higher-ranking officer, he peeled off his radiation-protection gear, showered, and went home to try to sleep. Ludmilla was not there. He went searching for her and found her two hours later, working as a volunteer in the hospital in nearby Pripyat, helping children who had been immediately taken ill after the blast.

He told her to come home with him. She said she would as soon as her work there was finished. She returned twenty-four hours later and as he looked at his wife, coming through the door, he could almost envision the deadly radiation that had by then found a home in her body.

He seemed to notice that her energy was flagging, and while he did not want to worry her unduly, he spoke to Russian doctors in the area. Nothing to worry about, they assured him and he thought, *Just as all of you assured everybody that there was nothing to worry about from the nuclear reactor*. The country ran on lies; deceit was its currency; treachery was its fuel.

Six months later, they were reassigned from Chernobyl to Moscow. Two years later, the slow-blossoming radiation poisoning finally took control of his wife's body and she was forced into the hospital. The day he took her, she said in a quiet, matter-of-fact voice, "I will never be home again, you know."

"Don't be silly," he said.

She went on as if she had not heard him. "When the end nears, do not let them keep me alive with their terrible machines. Let me die with grace."

And Budenko had wept for his brave and beautiful woman and she had put her arms around him in the back seat of their car and comforted him like a baby. "I love you," she said. "I will always love you."

Colonel Svoboda looked up as the general entered. The colonel was neatly shaved, his mustache impeccable, his eyes bright, and Budenko thought, *Poor Ludmilla who never hurt anyone in her life has to die while this pervert who spends his time spreading for other men is the picture of health. Where is the justice in this?*

"Good morning, Alexei. You look well."

"Thank you, General."

"Have Lieutenant Rostov come up here."

Budenko flexed a wooden pencil in his hands, delicately, to see how much he could bend it without the wood breaking. He looked over the top of it at the Cowboy.

"We are going ahead with your proposal," Budenko said. He saw Rostov's hands grip the arms of the chair in his excitement. "The Americans are sending us an expert on their Mafia. He will be assigned to you. You will be responsible for his happiness, his safety, his health, and his work. If anything goes wrong with him or with the program, it will be on your head. Do you understand?''

"Yes, sir," Rostov said quickly. "This man . . . who is he? From their FBI?"

"Even better than that, Rostov. They tell me that he was actually a member of the Mafia for more than twenty-five years until he decided to cooperate with the authorities.''

"A criminal? They are sending us a criminal?"

"A former criminal. Don't you believe in the redemption of the soul, Rostov? Lenin is dead. It is now an allowable doctrine. Yes, this man was once a criminal but now he is a changed man. He works now for truth and justice and the Russian way.''

Rostov seemed to bite back his words, and nodded through a long pause. Then he asked, "When is he coming?''

"Very soon. There are a few last-minute problems to be worked out. But very soon. I will leave it for you to work out the details with Colonel Svoboda.'' The pencil finally broke. "And remember, Rostov. Reports only to me or the colonel. No one is to know of this man's existence.''

"I will keep him as deep under the covers as my own bare feet,'' Rostov said.

Yes, Budenko thought. *Under the same covers you share with that delightful little public prosecutor of yours.* And the thought of it suddenly annoyed the general and he impatiently waved Rostov from his office.

Lewisburg, Pennsylvania:

Peter Kamen reached his hand through the bars of his cell and inserted the heavy key in the lock. He turned it until he heard it click softly, then quietly pushed open the heavy door and stepped out into the dark passageway. He did not like any of this but what other choice did he have? His daughter's life, that of his grandchildren, were all at stake.

The other door at the end of the corridor was open and Kamen ran quietly there, to the guard's small workstation. No one was in sight and Kamen said to himself, *Good work*. He took a heavy black raincoat from a hook on the wall behind the desk and put it on, along with a seaman's-style rainhat.

He found the ring of keys in the top desk drawer and started off down the west corridor. He needed no key to open the fire door at the end that led out into the small courtyard. The heavy rain pelted down, the big drops hitting the concrete yard with a string of plops that sounded like faraway gunfire.

Just where he expected it, he found a small gray panel truck. He crouched low behind the truck as the searchlights on the prison's walls swept the courtyard. When they had passed him, he clambered quietly into the truck. The keys were in the ignition.

Kamen checked his watch. Just a few minutes until midnight. He slumped down in the seat and waited.

At twenty seconds before twelve, he started the motor of the truck and, without lights, drove to the end of the courtyard where an open gate connected to another larger yard. He waited there, motor idling, without lights, until he saw a string of trucks, two large ones and four small gray panel jobs identical to his, pull through the large paved area. He flipped on his lights and pulled in behind the last of the panel vehicles.

The seven-truck caravan made its way to one of the large side gates of the prison compound where a guard casually checked some papers given him by the driver in the first truck, and then waved the vehicles on.

The caravan passed through the gate and out into the road that skirted the prison's big parking lot.

Kamen let the other vehicles pull away from him a little, then turned out his lights, and wheeled the truck into the parking lot. He sped to the far side of the lot and let the truck coast to a stop, then turned off the motor and pulled up the handbrake.

Leaving the keys in the ignition, he got out and saw a black Plymouth sedan about fifty feet away. Crouching low, he ran toward the car.

He had his hand on the doorknob when a voice suddenly echoed through the rain of the lot.

"Hold it right there, Kamen. FBI. You're under arrest."

Without hesitation, Kamen bolted away from the car and ran out of the parking lot into a grassy field that led toward a stand of trees several hundred yards away.

"Your last chance. Stop!"

Kamen turned and snarled, "You'll never take me alive, copper!" He reached toward the pocket of his raincoat. As he did, a single shot rang out and Kamen fell to the muddy ground.

Four men came out of the rain and Daniel Taylor, still holding his automatic in his hand, ran up to the fallen man and pressed his fingers roughly against Kamen's throat.

"That's the end of this pain in the ass," he said to the other three men near him.

Behind them, the prison lights came on. A siren sounded. Searchlights swept the parking lot, briefly illuminating them, passing on, and then swinging back to light on them again.

"You guys go over there and make peace with the prison guys. I'll stay here with the body," Taylor said. He looked down again at Kamen's body.

"Good riddance to bad rubbish."

Allentown, Pennsylvania:

Taylor sat in a hotel room, reading the morning newspaper's headlines aloud.

137

"UNDERWORLD INFORMANT SLAIN. Peter Kamen Killed by FBI in Escape Attempt at Lewisburg. New York Man Faced New Charges. Had Mob Contract on His Head."

He put the paper down, smiled, and looked across the small hotel-room table.

"Satisfied?" he asked.

Kamen took his last bite of a bagel with cream cheese and Nova Scotia smoked salmon and said, "So far, so good. Your guys don't suspect anything?"

"No. As far as they're concerned, your body's on its way to Washington. They'll bury you later. And you've been on the television all morning."

"And what about Washington? Everybody and his brother down there know what's going on?"

"Only the director's office and one man . . . my boss. Relax, Kamen, it's a done deal."

"If everybody keeps their mouth shut," Kamen said.

Taylor reached across the table to sip some of Kamen's coffee, then almost had to force himself not to spit it out because the coffee seemed laced with a half pound of sugar.

"I don't know why it's so important to you that the mob thinks you're dead. I don't know why just vanishing to Russia wasn't good enough."

"It's not for you to know," Kamen said. "But just because we're such close friends, I'll tell you. If they think I'm dead, they're not going to come looking for me in Russia." *And they'll leave my daughter and my grandkids alone,* he thought. *Peter Kamen's finished and so's the contract on his life.*

"You really think they could find you in Russia?"

"Yeah," Kamen said. "They could find me anywhere I hide. Just like I can find you if this goes sour and somebody opens their mouth and talks about Peter Kamen being alive and well in Russia."

"The thing I'll miss most about you is all the threats I'm always getting from you," Taylor said.

"You know what I'll miss about you?" Kamen asked.

Taylor raised his eyebrows and Kamen said, "Nothing." Then he grinned and said, "Well, on to Russia and my new comrades."

Chapter Thirteen

Paris:

Three weeks later, Daniel Taylor flew with Peter Kamen from Washington, D.C., to Orly Airport outside the French capital. They sat in the front of the first-class cabin, but Taylor seemed somewhat embarrassed by the entire thing and Kamen's attempts to start a conversation were met with grunts and nods and finally Kamen gave up and went to sleep.

Taylor waited with him in Paris until the departure of the giant Russian Aeroflot jet was announced, then walked with him to the gate.

"Well, Kamen. Good luck, I guess."

"Same to you. See you in the funny papers." Kamen joined the crowd and walked up the ramp toward the waiting jet. When he glanced back, he saw Taylor still waiting there, making sure that he got aboard.

He sat in the last row of the Aeroflot cabin. He had not known what to expect, but his ear had no trouble at all understanding the Russian speech that swirled around him. He had not spoken the language since his childhood, but it had all come back to him during the past three weeks as he had gone through a total-immersion course in the Russian language, customs, history. At the same time his dyed-blonde hair was dyed dark brown to match his natural hair color. Now, as his hair grew in, the new growth would match the dyed hair. It suited him just fine; one of the worst things with being a blonde was having to constantly have his roots touched up in a beauty parlor.

He amused himself by listening to the conversations near him. After spending six hours on a plane with Daniel Taylor, this was like traveling with a planeful of circus roustabouts. Even before the plane was airborne, before the stewardesses had a chance to take drink orders, bottles of Stolichnaya vodka were being passed around the cabin and Kamen guessed that at least a dozen of the two hundred people on board were drunk as skunks before the aircraft even took off.

And these are the Russian elite, he thought. *What must the simple folk do?*

He knew they were elite because the plane was not headed for Moscow Airport but for Vnukovo II, a special field outside the city, where politicians and officials regularly landed to avoid being herded around like the common folk. He declined a drink from the vodka bottle as it passed him, leaned against the window, and studied his passport.

He was no longer Peter Kamen. He was Pyotr Kamenski, Russian citizen of Odessa returning home after spending fifteen years in Israel and doing business all through the Western world. Pyotr Kamenski's smiling face stared at him from the passport and Kamen thought that it wasn't a bad face—at least not for a forty-six-year-old man who no longer had a country.

New adventures keep you young, he told himself. He replaced his passport in his jacket pocket and felt the

141

reassuring bulge of his thick money belt around his waist under his shirt. *And two hundred thousand dollars American can help make most new adventures bearable.*

I hope.
But we'll see.

Kamen fell in at the end of the line of passengers as they breezed along toward the customs counter. None of the bags was searched and the passports were given only a cursory check by an eager young male clerk who looked so starched and polished that it seemed he lived in fear of being reported for dress-code violations.

He glanced at Kamen's passport, and as he handed it back, he said in Russian, "Mr. Kamenski. Your party is waiting for you over there."

He pointed to a soft cushioned seat where a striking redheaded woman sat, smoking a cigarette. Their eyes met and Kamen nodded and the woman stood up and walked toward him as he came past the passport clerk.

She was very beautiful, he thought. *Who'd you think they were going to send? Madame Khrushchev?*

"Mr. Kamenski? I'm Olga Lutska," the woman said. "I will escort you to your party."

She looked at his face searchingly for a moment, as if to see if he understood the statement, but Kamen nodded and said, "Just who would my party be?"

"I am taking you to meet Lieutenant Rostov."

"*Lieutenant* Rostov?"

"Yes. Is there something wrong with that?"

"I sort of expected a marching band. At least a colonel," Kamen said, with a small grin.

Olga nodded and gave him a matter-of-fact, good-manners humorless smile. "I am sure the lieutenant will explain it all to you. Do you have any bags?"

"Nothing," Kamen said. When she looked at him

quizzically, he explained, "I lost all my belongings in a fire."

"Very well. Please come with me."

She led him away, a long-legged colt of a woman, and Kamen decided that Russia was breeding a better class of lady cops than he had expected.

It was a pleasant summer day with almost no humidity but the sky was discolored by the smog of factory smoke. He followed her to a small sedan that looked like the Russian equivalent of a Ford Escort. The nameplate on the trunk read "Lada." He had never heard of a Lada automobile.

He noticed that even though she had been parked right in front of the small air terminal, with a half-dozen blue-uniformed policemen wandering by, all the car doors were locked. *Were there car thieves in the "People's Paradise?" God, don't tell me that this is their 'crime wave.'*

But who would want to steal this car? It sounded like a lawnmower and seemed to sputter a lot as it traveled the dozen or so miles back into Moscow. The city was as gray as Kamen had expected it to be, but the air was smoggier, more polluted. It surprised him that the countryside seemed so flat. He had this idea of Russia as a land of mountains and valleys, but at least here, around Moscow, it seemed all to be one giant plain.

Olga Lutska was making an effort at small talk, asking him about his flight, how he liked the Russians he met aboard the plane, but all Kamen had on his mind was *Who is this woman? What does she know about me?*

He interrupted one of her chatty little comments to ask, "Are you a police officer?"

"No," she said in a voice that seemed surprised. "I am a public prosecutor."

"That's nice," Kamen mumbled in English, and turned away, fixing his stare outside the car window again. *A prosecutor,* he thought sourly. *The people with the biggest mouths in the world. What did you expect?* he asked himself. *Did you really think the Russians are going to be any less incompetent than the Americans? The damned FBI can't get the trucks out of the garage in the morning. What made you think the KGB, or whoever the hell you're going to be dealing with, could?*

This is going to be a long vacation, Peter Kamen . . . oops, Pyotr Kamenski. Or a short life.

Olga parked her car in an off-street space before the big gray apartment building and led Kamen through a side door, which she opened with a key, and up two flights of steps to the third floor.

Lev Rostov was waiting for them when she opened her apartment door with a key, and led Kamen inside.

What he saw first was a tall, long-legged man wearing blue jeans and cowboy boots, sprawling on the sofa. Unlike most of the Russians he had already seen, who looked as if they had skin diseases, this man's face was tanned and healthy looking with clear green eyes, a narrow straight nose, and a strong jaw. The man was reading *The Literary Gazette,* a thick tabloid newspaper, with a front-page photo of Yeltsin, holding his head in what looked like frustration.

The man hopped to his feet, tossed the paper onto the wooden coffee table, and with a big smile advanced across the room and grabbed Kamen's hand in his.

"Mr. Kamenski. Lev Rostov," he said in English.

"His Russian is quite good," Olga said. She was still standing behind them at the door.

"In that case, *zdrast'eh,*" Rostov said. "No bags?" he continued in Russian.

"No," Kamen said. He glanced back toward the door at Olga, who said quickly, "Excuse me but I must leave now for the office."

"Thank you for your help," Rostov said formally.

"A pleasure meeting you," Kamen said.

Olga favored him with her cold mechanical smile, then left and pulled the door shut behind her.

The two men looked at each other for a long moment.

"Can I get you a drink?" Rostov asked.

"I could use one," Kamen replied.

"Fine. Have a seat. Make yourself comfortable."

Kamen sat on the end of the sofa. He saw a big white cowboy hat tossed on a dresser near the door. He decided it must belong to this Rostov, because it was too big, even for the most fashion conscious of women, to try to wear. He glanced at the front page of *The Literary Gazette* and again saw the photo of the Russian leader, his head held in his hands, in apparent frustration.

Cheer up, Kamen thought. *You could be me*.

As she walked back down the side steps, to escape the snooping *dezhurnaya*, Olga saw a man in a telephone company uniform going through the basement door a flight below her. She thought for a moment about telling him that her telephone was faulty. Lately, there seemed to be a lot of clicking on the line. But she immediately put the thought from her mind. Some other time. With Rostov and the American in her apartment, she certainly did not want a repairman bumbling around.

In her car, driving to the courthouse, she thought that Pyotr Kamenski—was that his real name? she wondered—hardly looked like an expert on the Mafia. He looked more like a traveling salesman. But Cowboy had high hopes for him, so maybe something good would come out of this.

Rostov came out of the small kitchen with two glasses of vodka in his hands. One drink had been poured over ice cubes. He handed that one to Kamen. The other was straight, a full water tumbler. He put that one down on the table in front of where he sat. *They all drink like fish*, Kamen thought.

He sipped at his drink and Rostov said, "I suppose you are filled with questions."

"One for openers," Kamen said. "Who's the woman?"

"Olga is a lawyer in the prosecutor's office. She is a personal friend. You look like you have a problem with that."

"Yeah," Kamen said. "I thought my being here was top-secret."

"It is," Rostov said.

"Women can't keep secrets," Kamen said. "That's mistake one. Second mistake is prosecutors can't keep secrets either. That's mistake two. In a day, everybody in town is going to know about me."

Rostov smiled. "Relax," he said. "You're used to American women who spend their time chatting with fairies in beauty parlors. Olga is a Russian woman. She does not talk. And especially women who are Russian prosecutors do not talk because they are not allowed to. And I sent her today because I thought it would be better that you were not met by a police delegation. I checked the manifest of the plane and there was nobody aboard who would have any reason to be inquisitive, but I still thought it was better to be extra cautious."

"All right. I'll take your word for it."

"Please do," Rostov said. He drained half his vodka with one long sip from the glass, then turned halfway around on the couch so that he was facing Kamen. "Let's put cards on the table," he said. "I'll tell you what's going on around here."

"I wish somebody would," Kamen said.

* * *

Alexei Svoboda heard the bluff voice of General Budenko greeting the secretaries in the outer office and he whispered into the phone, "I'll talk to you later," and hung up. He buried his face down over the papers on his desk and pretended to be busy. While Budenko never questioned who Svoboda spoke to on the phone, it never hurt to be careful, especially since he had been talking to a new young man, Jan, whom he planned to take to dinner that night. What the general didn't know, didn't hurt him . . . or Svoboda, for that matter.

Budenko paused outside the door to the inner office for a moment. *That should give the little fairy enough time to get off the telephone*, he thought.

Then he pushed open the door and, when Svoboda looked up from his desk, nodded to him by way of greeting.

Svoboda scurried to his feet. "Nothing pressing this morning, General," he said. "But, of course, our American arrives today."

"Yes. Have you heard from Rostov?"

"Not yet, sir. He promised to report in after he got the man settled. Do you wish to speak to him when he calls?"

"Only if he is calling to report the total annihilation of the Mafia," Budenko said with an ill-humored smile. "Anything short of that you handle."

"Very good, sir,'" Svoboda said, and with his eyes escorted the general into the inner office. It was not like Budenko, he thought, to show so little interest in Rostov's operation. *Perhaps his wife had a bad morning in the hospital. Marriage is so very debilitating. Especially with a woman involved.*

"For the last two years," Rostov said, "I have been running a special drug squad within the MVD."

Three weeks earlier, Kamen would not have known what the MVD was. But the intensive briefing had filled those gaps in his knowledge. Nevertheless, he asked, "MVD. Is that like the KGB?"

"Former KGB. No. MVD is police, not espionage. It is the father organization for the militsia, the national police. I imagine it is sort of a combination between your FBI and all your local police departments."

Kamen nodded.

"We are not the regular narcotics squad. The militsia has those in every city; there are more than a hundred policemen in Moscow alone who work on that problem." He looked up to make sure that Kamen was following him. "My six men and I work primarily on trying to stop the flow of drugs into Moscow and the Russian republic."

"How have you been doing?"

"Rather well," Rostov said. "Until about six months ago when I began to recognize that there was a growing organization dealing drugs. Just from being on the street, it became apparent that there was less competition among dealers. People seemed to have certain territories staked out. There seemed to be a lot less narcotics coming into Moscow in the trunks of automobiles."

Rostov paused to sip at his vodka and Kamen said, "Mafia?"

"Yes. That is what I came to learn. More and more it became apparent that someone had stepped in to take over and to organize the narcotics traffic in Moscow. It could only be the Mafia."

"Why? Why not just some good manager?"

"Because the same thing is happening in the other major cities of the independent states," Rostov said. "It's maybe one of the sorry by-products of our new freedom, but the Mafia has gotten a strong foothold in our nation's life. Mind you, it's always been there. But it never amounted to anything until recently. Now, of course, with a publicly operated court system, with no more salt mines in Siberia, with a lot more regard for a citizen's rights, it has become worth the risk to be a member of the mob.

"At any rate," Rostov said, "it became apparent soon after that our organization was being compromised somehow. We no longer had to worry so much about small drug shipments. But when we found out about large ones, somehow the arrest would always fail when we got there. We were too late or too early. Or it wasn't drugs but something else."

"You've got a leak in your organization," Kamen said.

"Exactly. Six weeks ago, I took my men out on a training mission. At least, everyone thought it was a training mission. Actually, we went down near the Afghanistan border because I had word of a big drug deal being carried out there. No one knew where we were going. We stopped off in many towns along the way to run drug seminars for local militsia. No one knew we had a lead on this large drug shipment."

He stopped again to drink and Kamen said, "So what happened?"

"We broke up the drug deal," Rostov said. "Unfortunately, the ringleader got killed in the process. But when I got back to Moscow, I was able to find evidence of corruption in the courts, even in the police."

"Any suspects?" Kamen asked.

"Just one. A criminal court judge named Alekhine. He was murdered the next day along with a possible informant."

"Shot on the street? No witnesses?"

"Exactly," Rostov said.

"It doesn't sound like the Mafia. It sounds like the Wild West," Kamen said. He had still taken only the first sip from his drink; Rostov was up refilling his own glass.

"Perhaps," Rostov said. "I have this fear that someone is trying to unite all the criminals in the country under one big boss. I call that Mafia."

"It'll never work," Kamen said.

"Not in the United States perhaps," Rostov said. "But this stuff is all new. We don't know that it won't work here. Russians are different from Americans. And if it does work, then we face a crime problem that could . . . could destroy our plans for a free economy."

"Is that a bad thing?" Kamen asked.

He stopped and picked up a pack of cheap-looking cigarettes in a blue and white pack from the table. He twisted the end of one, lit it, and looked to Kamen. "Cigarette?"

"No thanks," Kamen said.

"At any rate, the Mafia must not be permitted to organize, to consolidate. As a policeman, I say it would be a tragedy. As a Russian, I say it would be a disaster. And so I asked for you. We have little experience here with Mafia organization. I thought you or someone like you would be able to help steer us in the right direction to fight these people. I am glad you came."

"Are you the only one who feels like this? What about your superiors?" Kamen asked. "Do they buy into this fight? Are they perhaps corrupt?"

"No. Without their support, I could not have gotten you here," Rostov explained. "I am only a lieutenant, after all."

"When do I get to meet your superiors?" Kamen asked.

"You don't."

"Why?"

"I think the fewer people who know about you, who have you on their mind, the better off you are. I haven't told any of my men you were arriving. In fact, that's why I sent Miss Lutska to pick you up today. My bosses have never seen you. As far as I know, only two of them know of your existence. All they're asking for, so far, is that I keep them advised of what's going on. I thought you and I might work better with no interference.''

"Is this Olga a girlfriend?" Kamen asked.

"Yes," Rostov said.

"Don't piss her off. First thing she'll do is blab.''

Rostov grinned. "I disagree but I bow to your superior wisdom.''

"I have other problems too. Not just the woman," Kamen said.

"Yes?''

"What happens when some crazy drug dealer puts a bullet in your head and your bosses know nothing about me? I'm a man without a friend," Kamen said.

Rostov reached down to a briefcase on the floor alongside the sofa. He pulled out a manila envelope and spread its contents on the table between the two men.

"Not really," he said. "You've got a Russian passport. Here is a Russian birth certificate. Here is a travel permit. Here is your residency card. It lists the address of your apartment. The rent has been paid for two months in advance. Here is a checking account that has been opened in your name at the Moscow State Bank. I've started it with one thousand rubles. That will be your monthly salary, by the way. Any additional expenses, let me know about and I will reimburse them. And then here's two maps of Moscow, in both English and Russian. And a map of the subway system. A historical guidebook of the city. You read it and you'll know more about Moscow and Russia than most people who've lived here all their lives. And here's five hundred rubles in cash for pocket money.'' He finished sliding the papers on the table and looked up. "As you can see, you are already a solvent, longtime resident of our fair city. When I get a bullet in my brain, you can just continue to live normally.''

Kamen smiled. "You seem to have thought of everything." He paused. "Well, almost everything. Do I get a gun?"

"No."

"Why not?"

"Because there is no reason for you to need one. I don't expect you to take an ax and start chopping down criminals' doors. I want you to be a new brain for us."

Kamen thought, and said, "That's all right for now."

"So? Do you have any opinions about what I've told you?" Rostov asked.

"Yes," Kamen said.

"And?"

"I've been studying Russian crime a lot during the past month or so. You've got more damned petty criminals in Russia than there are in America. The only way to tie them together is with muscle. The only way to get muscle is with money. The way to get money . . . real money . . . is by controlling the flow of drugs." He looked up. "I think you're exactly right, Rostov. I think the Mafia's come to town."

"Do you think that you will be able to help us?"

"I'm going to try, Cowboy. I'm going to try."

Chapter Fourteen

Rostov offered to drive Kamen to his new apartment, but since the day was warm and sunny, Kamen said he preferred to walk, "to start to get a look at this Russia of ours."

Once he was downstairs and away from Olga Lutska's building, Kamen hailed one of the yellow taxicabs that cruised up and down Lomonossovsky Avenue.

"And on this fine day, your pleasure?" the driver said. His Russian was fluid but oddly accented.

"Just drive around for a while," Kamen said. "I want to get a look at Moscow."

"You are a tourist then?"

"I haven't seen Moscow in many years," Kamen answered mildly.

The taxicab driver was a swarthy man with dark hair and mustache. It was impossible to tell while he was sitting but he looked short. His hands on the steering wheel were gnarled and lumpy. He turned around in his seat to look at Kamen.

He's looking at my suit to see if I'm Russian or not, Kamen thought.

The driver grunted softly and said, "I only accept payment in dollars."

Kamen smiled. "And I pay no other way," he said. He rolled down the cab's rear window and settled back in the seat to sightsee as the driver pulled away from the curb into the avenue, which, with eight lanes, was wider than most American superhighways.

The driver went over the Metro Bridge, spanning the Moscow River, as he headed north toward the city's center. Then he turned off the big highway, onto smaller roads, and as far as Kamen could tell, he was looping around the outskirts of the city.

Just as well, Kamen thought. *I've seen the Kremlin already in the movies.*

He quickly came to the conclusion that Moscow had to be the tail that wagged the Russian dog. In the United States, different cities were associated with different things. Detroit was where they made cars; Pittsburgh where they made steel; New York where they made money and muggers. But Moscow seemed to make everything. He saw automobile factories and steel works, almost cheek by jowl with large sprawling universities. There was a toy factory and across the street the headquarters of a ballet company.

And everywhere were statues—was there anybody in Russia who wasn't a hero? he wondered—and over it all, a pall of gray smoke that made the air bitter and turned a bright sun into a dullish orange globe in the sky.

"Where is the Sierra Club when you need them?" he mumbled in English.

"Beg pardon, boss?" the cabdriver said.

"Nothing," Kamen answered in Russian. "Just talking to myself."

"Sometimes it is the only way to get an intelligent answer," the driver said.

Armenian, Kamen thought. The accent was Armenian. He wondered why aliens always got jobs as cabdrivers in every city in the world. Maybe it was because it was one thing they could do without having to talk too much. *So why then do they talk all the time? Except this one.*

The driver had been silent throughout the entire trip and now, as the cab rolled past the high red brick walls that surrounded the Kremlin, Kamen realized that the cab had no meter and that the driver must be charging for his time because he kept looking at the watch he wore on the inside of his right wrist.

If Kamen asked a question, the driver answered it. The rest of the time, he remained silent and let his passenger watch the scenery. *They should send this guy to the U.S.,* Kamen thought. *He'd revolutionize the cab industry.*

"I'd like to change some dollars into rubles," Kamen said. "Perhaps we could stop by a bank?"

"A bank?" the driver said as if Kamen had just suggested they try walking on water. "We can do better than a bank," he said.

"What's better than a bank?"

The driver turned, while in the midst of heavy traffic and without paying any attention to the road, other cars, or pedestrians, and gave Kamen a big smile. "I am, boss," he said.

He turned back and swerved to avoid rear-ending a big black Zil limousine that had somehow drifted over into their lane.

"First of all, boss, you don't need rubles at all. Today, dollars do anything you need done. People see you with rubles, they don't want to talk to you. They see you with American dollars, they offer you their daughter in marriage."

"But if I want to look like a regular Russian, it would probably be a good idea to have *some* rubles," Kamen said. 'What's the exchange rate? How many rubles to a dollar?''

The cabdriver shrugged elaborately. "No one knows, boss . . . especially the geniuses who run the banks. One day they tell us four rubles, the next day they tell us a hundred rubles to a dollar. Forget the banks. I will make your exchange.''

"Two hundred dollars worth? Do you have that much?''

"If I had two hundred dollars in rubles, I would go back to Armenia. But I can get it.''

"Fine. Why don't you take me now to this address?'' Kamen read the address of his apartment building on Ogorodny Street from the resident's card in the manila envelope he had taken from Cowboy.

In response to Kamen's questioning, the driver said that he often worked twelve hours a day, from four P.M. until four A.M. The pay was poor, because Russians did not tip. "But what else is there for me to do?'' he asked rhetorically. "I have no other skills.''

"What is your name?''

"Omar.''

"How long have you been in Moscow?''

"Four years,'' the driver said.

"You know the city?''

"Four years of driving, I know every alley in this rathole. Anyplace you're going, anything you need, I am the man for you, boss.''

"Do you mean that?'' Kamen said.

"Exactly do I mean it. Anything. Anything.''

"Good. You're just the man I want,'' Kamen said and leaned over the seat to talk business to the man.

The cab pulled up into the driveway in front of another gray apartment building that looked identical to Olga Lutska's.

"How much?'' Kamen said.

"Five dollars. American."

Kamen gave the driver a ten-dollar bill from his pocket. "Keep the change," he said.

"Now I know you're not a real Russian," the driver said.

"But from now on, you're on salary. Eight A.M. until midnight. Seventy-five American dollars a day and I'll give you plenty of time off. Agreed?"

"Agreed, rich boss," Omar said.

"And you'll come back later with my rubles?" Kamen asked.

"As we agreed."

The *dezhurnaya* insisted upon seeing Kamen's residency card before she allowed him upstairs to his apartment.

"You are new here?" she said as she pushed the card back to him across her small table with a forefinger as if it had somehow gotten filthy dirty.

"Yes."

"Where are you from?" she asked crisply.

"None of your business," Kamen said with a cold smile.

She stared at him for a moment, as if deciding whether or not to challenge him, then grunted. "Walk. The elevator is broken," and turned back to her copy of *Pravda*.

The apartment was on the third floor of the five-story building and Kamen thought Rostov must have really gone out of his way to set things up.

The apartment was large by Moscow standards, with a separate bedroom but with the ubiquitous kitchenette in an alcove off the living room. Still the apartment had been outfitted with a large television set, a videocassette player, and a big selection of tapes. He looked at the tapes and smiled. Lieutenant Rostov's tastes seemed to match his nickname. Out of the two dozen tapes, twenty were of American western films. The other four were pornos.

"Debbie Does Dubrovnik," Kamen mumbled to himself.

There was an electric typewriter on a desk, but when Kamen looked at it, he saw that the keyboard was in the Russian Cyrillic alphabet and declared defeat immediately. He was a bad enough typist in English; in Russian, people would come from miles around to laugh at him. Paper and pencil would have to do.

The bathroom was stocked with soaps and razors and shampoos and towels, and another closet held sheets and blankets for the bed, and the kitchen cupboard was filled with canned and dried goods. Inside the refrigerator he found two quarts of milk in old-fashioned glass bottles, a collection of cheeses, heavy Russian bread sealed tightly in plastic wrap. None of the food looked very appetizing, but it reminded Kamen that he had not eaten since a brief lunch on the plane and he was hungry. But not hungry enough to eat his own cooking.

With the two keys Rostov had given him, he double-locked the door behind him, then walked downstairs. He passed the *dezhurnaya*, who did not even bother to glance up from her paper.

Outside, he looked both ways down the street but saw nothing that looked like a restaurant. Instead, it seemed like an unbroken string of ugly boxlike apartment buildings that stretched to the horizon. The soggy leaden air made him cough.

Even though it was late afternoon, the sun still struggled overhead to pierce the smog. He had forgotten how far north Russia was; the summer daylight would last a long time. But already there was a chill in the air and he told himself that tomorrow he must find a topcoat. *Just like that dumb FBI bastard to let me come here without the right clothes and freeze to death*, he thought.

He walked to the corner and turned down into a broad side avenue. Up ahead, he saw a uniformed policeman on the corner and approached him.

"I am a visitor. Can you tell me where I can find a restaurant?" he asked politely.

"Do I look like a tour guide?" the policeman snapped, and turned back to gazing out over the growing rush-hour swarm of traffic.

"No, you look like a jerkoff," Kamen muttered in English, and walked on.

Lev Rostov had never liked Colonel Alexei Sbvoboda. There was an unwholesome aura to the man, a sneakiness that always gave Cowboy the feeling that the man was staring at him when Rostov was not looking.

He knew very well of Svoboda's reputation as a homosexual, but always had some little doubt of it because of the military and the MVD training Svoboda had undergone. It was rigorous physically and tough psychologically, and while it had passed through more than its share of homicidal maniacs, Rostov could not recall any homosexual ever completing the training. Still, he had to admit that there was something feminine about Svoboda's manner, the way he listened, the way he constantly licked his lips as if to make them glossy with saliva, the way he spoke on the telephone with his hand over the mouthpiece as if sharing the latest gossip.

Still, he was the project boss for now, and Rostov waited in his outer office until he was nodded inside by one of Svoboda's secretaries. That was another thing. One of the fringe benefits of holding high position was having one's choice of the best-looking women available as secretaries. The three secretaries who worked for Budenko and Svoboda were middle-aged, frumpy, ferocious typists who filled the anteroom with a noisy clatter of typing.

Rostov tried a grin as he closed the door behind him and saw Svoboda looking at him from his desk.

"Well, Colonel, the eagle has landed," Rostov said.

"The eagle? Oh, the American gangster. Good. Did you have any trouble?"

"No," Rostov said. "I have him established now in his new apartment. He has all his identification papers. I thought after a couple of days for him to acclimate himself, I would put him to work."

"Sit down, Rostov," Svoboda said. He stroked his mustache as if trying to train the hairs to grow to the sides rather than down. "What exactly do you have in mind for him to do?"

"I thought I would take him through our records. Let him see our drug arrests and how lately they have declined and the distribution seems to be growing centralized. I planned to acquaint him, through the files, with the people we regard as major players in the drug Mafia. In other words, to get his feet wet. And then I plan to pick his brain to find out how we can jump the line and get to the top of this criminal organization."

"Are you going to let him look through all your records?" Svoboda asked.

For a moment, Rostov was confused. Slowly, he answered, "Yes, sir."

"I would urge you to use some discretion," Svoboda said. "Our records are our lifeblood. If they were to be compromised . . . there could be serious repercussions."

"Begging your pardon, sir, but I don't think we can get maximum use out of our man unless he understands the entire picture."

"The entire picture, yes. Each individual brushstroke is something else," Svoboda said. "You have to understand that what we are doing with this American is all very experimental. We don't want it to backfire with him announcing to the world everything we know or don't know. Discretion, Rostov. Discretion. That is what makes a good police officer.''

It makes a good bureaucrat is what you mean, Rostov thought. But he merely nodded. "I would of course consult with you before I do anything that might compromise us," he said.

"Please keep that in mind," Svoboda said. "The general has put me in charge of this operation day to day and I do not want it to reflect badly on any of us. I'm sure you understand." He favored Rostov with an oily smile, then reached across the desk and patted the back of Rostov's hand. "If there is any help you need from me, please let me know."

In New York City, the place would have been considered a hole-in-the-wall, Kamen thought, but the combination tavern and restaurant was packed with well-dressed people in their mid-thirties. Most of them stood around the bar, drinking raucously. Both men and women seemed generally to be wearing two-piece business-style suits, and Kamen decided there must be a big office building in the neighborhood somewhere, even though the only thing he had noticed outside was a mammoth steel television transmission tower only a block away that loomed over a small surrounding neighborhood park.

The restaurant was one big room with dining tables to the right and a bar at the left. He waited inside the door for a few minutes, but when no one came to seat him, he walked to one of the empty tables and sat down.

There were fifty customers in the establishment, but he saw no waiters or waitresses.

He waited at the table, alone, for five minutes, then went to the bar and ordered a scotch and soda. Heads turned toward him and people evaluated him as they heard him place the unusual—for Russia—drink order. When the bartender returned with the drink, Kamen paid with a twenty-ruble note from the stack Rostov had given him. When his change came, Kamen leaned over and tucked it all in the bartender's vest pocket. He smiled and nodded toward the man, who at first looked surprised, then pleased, albeit not pleased enough to say thanks. Kamen asked, "Could I get a waitress at that table over there? I'd like to eat."

The bartender, florid-faced, stared at the table where Kamen pointed for a moment, then nodded.

Kamen took his drink back to the table and sipped it while waiting for the waitress. He looked outdoors. Moscow women were prettier than he had expected. Maybe it was a city like all cities . . . attracting the best, the brightest, the most beautiful from the surrounding small towns.

Ten minutes later, the waitress came. She wore a dark blood-red one-piece uniform, wore an obvious brassy wig that looked as if it were on the cutting edge of polymer technology, and refused to make eye contact with Kamen as she tossed a menu in front of him and then walked away.

The menu was a single typewritten page and Kamen recognized a fish dish that his grandmother had liked when Kamen was growing up. He looked around to catch the waitress's eye but she had disappeared again.

It took another trip to the bar, another drink, another tip for the bartender, and another request for the waitress, to bring her out of the kitchen and back to his table ten minutes later.

"I'll have the boiled fish," he said.

Without any acknowledgment, she snatched the menu away from him as if he might soil it by looking at it too much and stomped away to the kitchen.

Meanwhile the place reverberated with the noise of people talking. Somebody fed coins into a jukebox in the corner and first the syrupy voice of Nat King Cole and then the demented staccato mumbling of some rap group seeped into the room.

It was another twenty minutes before the waitress returned.

She put a plate in front of him and said, "We didn't have fish left. So I got you this instead." She looked at him as if challenging a protest.

"That's fine. Could I have a knife and fork and a napkin, please?" he asked.

Another five minutes passed before she delivered them, just dropping them onto the table in front of his plate, and then stomping away.

By then, the food—some kind of ersatz meat loaf—was almost cold. Kamen ate it anyway, happy to be filling his stomach.

As he ate, he noticed another half-dozen people come into the restaurant. They too sat at tables where they were totally ignored. It did not seem to bother any of them, though, and they sat and talked and smoked . . . and waited.

The food, meanwhile, tasted as if it had been marinated in melted lard and Kamen was glad he had the scotch and soda to cut through the grease and clear his throat, especially since he had been given no water by the waitress.

He ate quickly, but despite his hunger, he could not finish the meal. He saw the waitress staring at him from across the room.

"Bill, please," he called out. She wrote something on a pad in her hand, then brought it over and dropped it in front of him. The meal cost exactly twenty rubles and Kamen left exactly twenty rubles on the table, along with the check.

As he passed by the waitress on the way out, he said in Russian, "Now you be sure to have a nice evening."

He stepped outside. A cab was waiting in front of the

restaurant. He got into the back and said, "Take me to McDonald's."

Rostov worked until after six P.M. in his office in the small annex building, only a few blocks from the main militsia headquarters. He was a man of habit. When he was annoyed by something—as he had been by Svoboda's stupid remarks—he usually went to his desk to cool off by shuffling meaningless papers around. He knew when he had had enough and it was time to quit, because his back began to hurt from too many hours sitting in a chair. It hurt now, so, confident that he could again face human company, he stood, rubbed his neck, and dialed Olga Lutska's number.

"If I bring the wine, will you cook the dinner?" he asked.

"It's already cooked," she said. "Hurry."

Olga set herself a test. She knew it took exactly eleven minutes to drive from Rostov's office to her apartment. Add five minutes in for buying wine. Sixteen minutes. Add two more for good measure.

Eighteen minutes. She set the table, and eighteen minutes after Rostov's call, she spooned the potatoes and carrots onto the plate, around the slice of beef brisket.

Now if he was late, not only the food would be cold but so would her ardor, because being late meant that it was not as important for him to see her as it was for her to see him.

A minute passed. She began to feel rejected. She rose from the table and went to the kitchen cupboard to get out two wineglasses.

As she walked back into the dining corner of the living room, she heard Rostov's key in the lock.

Close enough, she told herself. *Close enough*.

He came in carrying a bottle of red wine by the neck.

"Sorry," he said. "There was a line at the liquor store. Have you been waiting long?"

"I didn't even notice the time," she said. "So how was your day?"

"You can tell?" he asked.

"I can tell when you work hard at smiling to cover some kind of sour look. Something wrong with your American?"

Rostov shook his head. "No," he said. "It's that moron, Svoboda. Already he's trying to make my life more complicated than it has to be. He's worried that Kamenski might learn too much, snooping around our files."

"If he doesn't know what's going on, he's not going to be much good to you, is he?" she said.

The Cowboy grinned. "How come you can figure that out and our brave genius, Colonel Svoboda, can't?"

"Women are smarter than men basically," she said.

"Some women, some men," Rostov said.

"Forget Colonel whatever-his-name-is. What do you think of your American?"

"Very interesting," Rostov said. "From what I have been told, he spent most of his life working inside the American Mafia. But he certainly doesn't seem the sort, does he?"

"He looked like a stuffed-bear toy to me," she said. "Cute and gentle."

"Exactly," Rostov said. "*Mild* was the word that came to my mind." He drank sturdily from his wine goblet. "I hope the Americans haven't tried to sneak anything by us with him."

"Why would they do that? I think he is just what they said he was."

"Too mild-mannered," Rostov said, shaking his head. "Just too mild-mannered."

Peter Kamen put five hundred dollars in American money into his pants pocket. The rest he kept in the money belt around his waist. Tomorrow he would get a safety deposit box in a bank, but for the time being, his money was safer if he carried it, because he had no doubt that as soon as he left, that *dezhurnaya* would be snooping around his apartment under some kind of flimsy pretext. The less she found, the better.

He left the apartment at exactly 8:58 P.M.

The same woman was in the same place downstairs, reading the same page of the same newspaper.

"Going out?" she said.

"Yes."

"Have a nice evening." He glanced at her and saw that she was smiling. Had someone tipped her off that he was working with the police?

Omar's cab pulled in front of the door, exactly at nine P.M.

"Where would you like to go, boss?" he asked.

"Did you bring my rubles?"

"I have them right here."

"Good." Kamen handed two hundred dollars up to the driver and took back a packet of ten-ruble notes. He counted them carefully before sticking the roll into his pocket.

"All there, boss," Omar said.

"Always count the money," Kamen said. "Are you ready to be with me for the whole night?"

"Until four A.M.," Omar said. "After that, my wife starts to get nervous and think I am keeping a rich mistress someplace. At four-thirty she calls the police. At five A.M., she is ready to shoot me when I come in. But until four, I am yours. So where would you like to go?"

"I would like to buy a gun," Kamen said.

166

It was a rotten little piece of junk. A six-shot Italian Targa GT. But the semiautomatic weighed only about a half pound and was small enough to keep inside a holster hooked on the inside of his belt under his jacket.

The whole rig—gun, holster, and a box of fifty shells—had cost him two hundred dollars American, and while he knew he could have bought it in the States for only about half that, this was not the United States.

He had bought it from a grocer that Omar knew in the Armenian quarter of the southeast corner of the city. Omar had carefully parked his taxi a half block away and then had left Kamen in the vehicle while he went into the small neighborhood store to make the deal.

He came out a few minutes later with the gun wrapped in a cloth and showed it to Kamen.

"What do you think, boss?"

"I think it's *gavno*, crap. . . . But it'll do. Shells and holster too?"

Omar nodded. "Two hundred dollars American for everything."

"Okay." Kamen took the money from his pocket and handed it to Omar.

"Be right back, boss," the cabbie said. He returned a few minutes later with the gun, shells, and holster inside a brown paper bag, and while he drove off, Kamen loaded the clip and slid the holster into the back of his trousers.

"Now you seem dressed for the evening, boss. Where would you like to go?"

"Suppose somebody wanted to buy some powder to put into his nose?" Kamen said. "Where do you think he might find it?"

Omar cruised slowly as he turned in the seat to look at Kamen. *Christ, I wish he'd stop doing that*, Kamen thought.

"You're not some bad gangster, are you?" Omar said.

"Not me," Kamen said, shaking his head. "Just curious about Moscow life."

"You're not going to be one of those guys who pulls a gun on me at the end of the night and steals my money, are you?" Omar said, still looking into the back seat.

"Now what kind of fool would try to rob a man who has a knife in his sleeve?" Kamen said.

Omar laughed aloud and turned back to the road.

"You saw that, boss?"

"I saw it."

"You really want to know where to buy the devil's powder?"

"Yes," Kamen said.

"It is not my specialty. Money changing, women . . . I can find you very pretty women . . . games of chance . . . even, as you know, weapons. I can provide many things for you."

"Cocaine," Kamen said.

"Well, of course, I don't know about this myself since I am too poor to dabble in narcotics. But I have heard of a place."

"Take me there."

Chapter Fifteen

Kamen had expected Omar to take him to some dismal slum to purchase narcotics, but instead the cabdriver had sped to a large broad boulevard, just northeast of the Kremlin, and then parked across the street from a gigantic movie theater.

"Wait here, boss," Omar said. He hopped from the cab and Kamen watched him walk across the boulevard and then speak to one of the people hanging around in front of the showhouse. It was too far away for Kamen to see the man's face. He and Omar spoke for less than a minute and then the driver trotted back to the cab.

"Very strange, boss," he said.

"What is?"

"As I told you, with great passion, this white powder is not a specialty of mine. But this is the place where one could always buy it. This is a thing I know. However, I spoke to my friend and he says that no one sells this powder anymore on the street."

"In other words, you have accomplished nothing," Kamen said.

"I am cut to the quick, boss," Omar said, trying so hard to sound anguished that Kamen almost laughed. "They are not selling powder on the street. But they will sell it to you in another location."

"Then take me there. And forgive me for having underestimated you," Kamen said.

Omar turned and smiled. "I will add it to your bill, boss," he said.

"Again?" Kamen asked, and Omar laughed as he drove out into traffic.

Kutuzovsky Prospekt was the widest boulevard Kamen had ever seen. It stretched a dozen or more lanes across—it was hard to tell because there were no painted lane markers—and cars cruised along the street at high speed. In all, except the centermost lane.

Kamen asked about it and Omar replied, "That used to be the Chaika lane. You know, for big shots with limousines."

"Ahh, the people's paradise," Kamen said.

Not much more than a mile west of the Kremlin, the side streets off Kutuzovsky were filled with hotels and clubs, looking eerily to Kamen much like Manhattan near Sixth Avenue in the fifties.

Omar stopped in front of The Pink Elephant. The front of the nightclub was all flashing lights and fifteen-foot-high elephants twisted from pink neon tubing.

"This is the place?" he said.

"You go inside, boss. Have a drink and wait awhile. My friend will find you."

"This is a little strange, you know," Kamen said.

"Russia is strange."

The Pink Elephant featured a barn-sized dance hall and bar and restaurant in which almost all the interest seemed to be in the bar, which stretched forty feet long against the building's entire back wall.

Over the bar was a forty-foot-long mirror, and only the most regular of the patrons knew that the mirror was not an ordinary mirror at all, but a strip of one-way reflecting glass. On the other side was the second-floor office of Sergei Tal, the club's manager.

He was a tall husky man with a bullet neck that led up to a shaven-bald head. He was fair but pockmarked from an early childhood encounter with chicken pox and had the kind of skin that looked as if it would bruise easily. His eyes were a cold blue green, his lips thick and solid and rarely smiling. He wore expensive suits that were hand-tailored for him in Moscow and which disguised, but could not quite hide, the powerful ditchdigger shoulders, the tight waist, the barrel chest, the physical attributes that attested to an early life spent doing hard labor. He no longer did any such labor on his own, but he spent several hours a day in a private health club, lifting weights to keep himself trim.

He sat up there every night, watching the house, keeping an eye out for police who might decide to become officious or customers who might decide to become more boisterous than just ordinary drunkenness would call for. The former he would deal with himself. A few rubles spread around gently and the policemen on the beat found other establishments to "protect." In the case of rowdies, Tal picked up the telephone and called downstairs to his bouncers, two former Olympic wrestlers who sat in a booth in a dark corner of the room, drinking ginger ale, comparing muscles and tattooes, eyeing young male customers and waiting for Tal to call.

The front door opened, and for a moment the room was bathed in the harsh pink light from the neon elephants out front. As he always did, Tal looked down through the mirror to see who had come in.

It was not one of his regulars. The man was in his

171

forties, hatless, wearing only a suit and no topcoat. He had dark wavy hair and the first word that came into Tal's head was nondescript, except for the way the man walked. He seemed to strut with the cocky air of a sailor on leave with two months' pay in his pocket. But he seemed a little old to be prowling bars looking for women, and he was certainly too old to want to dance to the raucous rock and roll that a tape deck pumped into the room, and in his face there was none of the nervousness of an amateur trying to make a drug purchase.

His suit fit very well, and for a moment, Tal wondered where he had bought it. As Tal watched, the man looked up into the mirror and smiled broadly as if checking his teeth, then straightened his tie. Then he disappeared toward the bar beneath his window and Tal went back to looking through the paperwork on his desk.

There had been hell to pay when the militsia had confiscated the two truckloads of stolen weapons at the Afghan border and Vladimir Gubanov had turned up missing. Apparently, the load of cocaine had been burned in the raid. At least, that was the story that he had been told. But Tal had some doubts about that. Some of those thieving cops might have gotten their hands on it and were probably just waiting for the right moment to put it on the market themselves.

He would readily have believed that if it had not been for one thing: the raid had been carried out by the Cowboy's men. And no one had yet found a way to corrupt any of them. How the hell had they managed to stick their noses in anyway? They were supposed to be a hundred miles away, on some kind of dumb-ass training mission, and instead they had jumped right into the middle of the single biggest drug purchase in Russia's history.

Lieutenant Cowboy Rostov had better start looking over his shoulder. They could put up with him when he and his men were just an annoyance. But if they were going to be a threat to the whole operation, then they would have to go. This was a new world, he thought, and old-fashioned pests would have no place in it.

The two-way mirror over the bar was a nice touch, Kamen thought, as he came into The Pink Elephant and picked his way across the crowded dance floor. There had been a place on Twenty-Sixth Street in Manhattan that had the same kind of layout. It had been owned by a New York mob guy and he had used the room behind the mirror exclusively to make it with his girlfriend. She was a ditzy blonde refugee from an Atlantic City chorus line who got off on having sex in public. Ernie, the owner, had some problems with that but he was crazy about the woman and so he had the room built. The girlfriend—what was her name?—Lois—hadn't seemed to mind. She and Ernie would rut like farm animals in the hidden room and Lois would never take her eyes off the glass through which she could see all the people sitting at the bar.

Ernie had once confided to Kamen, "She's making me nuts, Pete. All she wants to do is screw. And always in that dismal goddam room on that lumpy goddam couch."

"Why don't you throw her out?" Kamen asked.

"You don't understand. This is love," Ernie had said.

Kamen shrugged. Some problems were beyond the capacity of even logic to solve.

At any rate, the problem solved itself a few months later, when Lois ran off with some dimwit with a video camera who was going to make a Porn-o-log of the United States. Ernie showed Kamen the note she had left. It explained that she and Hammer, her new boyfriend with the camera, were going to drive all over the country, screwing and filming it.

"You see, Ernie, we'll make it at Old Faithful, the gusher out somewhere near Chicago. And inside the Statue of Liberty. And by the Liberty Bell in Philadelphia. I think this can be an important thing that we are doing, Ernie, and I hope you will understand and wish us well.''

Ernie wished them so well that he offered ten thousand dollars for Lois and Hammer, dead, but before he was called on to pay off, they were arrested for public indecency when they were caught humping late one night on the steps of the New York Stock Exchange on the first leg of their transcontinental adventure.

By then, Ernie had calmed down. He wrote the whole thing off to experience and a week later sealed off the wall behind the one-way mirror and cut a door into the bar so the bartenders could use it for storing liquor. Very touching, Kamen had thought.

He wondered what was going on behind the mirror of The Pink Elephant. Somehow he doubted that it had anything to do with somebody trying out for the local Porn-o-log.

He found a couple of vacant stools in the corner of the bar, took the one closest to the wall, and asked the bartender for a scotch and soda.

The bartender here had greeted him with a smile and a hello and grinned, ''Sure,'' when Kamen had ordered his drink, and when it came, Kamen had tipped him the change and the bartender had said, ''Thank You.''

This must be a mob joint, Kamen thought to himself. *Everybody else in this goddam city is so rude they all ought to be shot. It's got to be a wiseguy hangout.*

It was strange, he thought, how people in the United States generally thought that places where Mafiosi hung out were bound to be filled with rude and surly types. But the opposite was generally true. The mob was primarily in the business of making money, and well-mannered staff was part of that. But in addition to having been told to be polite, staff people—waiters, waitresses, maître d's— were always on their best behavior because they never

174

knew who the next person coming through the door might be.

It might be one thing to be a supercilious maître d' and start abusing some old Italian whose suit didn't fit and who smelled of fried peppers and hair grease. And it was quite another thing to find out later that he was the head of one of the six families and you might as well write your will because your bad manners had just gotten you dead.

It was why the mob's hotels in Las Vegas had the most polite staffs of any hotel in the world, as far as Kamen was concerned. They never knew who they were waiting on and they weren't going to take any chances. Smiling beat dying any day.

Kamen leaned back in the corner and watched the dancers on the floor. The music from the stereo was just as incomprehensible as American rock-and-roll babbling, and the singers seemed mostly young, but they were not quite so weirdly dressed, not quite so ass-flashing wild as their American counterparts.

He figured out that the youngest people in the room sat at the tables surrounding the dance floor; the older folks hung around the bar. That took the age groups up to about thirty-five. There was not a section for anybody Kamen's age, and suddenly he felt very old.

From the corner of his eye, he saw a red flash, and the bartender picked up a telephone and listened for a few seconds, replaced the receiver, then glanced toward Kamen.

Kamen picked up his drink and walked away from the bar toward one of the small booths on the side of the room. It never made sense to make their work too easy.

"Tash?"
"Yes."
"Check out the single at table twelve."

"What's he supposed to have done?"

"I don't know. Boss's orders. Check him out."

Natasha Simunova nodded to the bartender. She ran her fingers through her thick blonde curly hair, then smoothed her tight skirt over her hips and walked back from the storeroom into the cocktail lounge.

She made her way through the tables, smiling at people, discouraging conversation, until she neared Kamen's booth. He was sipping from his drink, looking straight ahead at the other empty bench in the booth. *He looks harmless enough*, Natasha thought. *Pleasant even*.

She stopped by his table and waited for him to look up.

"Can I get one of the girls to freshen your drink, sir?"

"Ah, at last. The famous Russian quality-control department," Kamen said.

"I beg your pardon."

"Never mind. Just babbling to myself. No, my drink is fine."

"This is your first time here?" Natasha said.

"Yes."

"We have a small late-night menu. Snacks, chicken wings, potato chips, if you're interested."

"I am very interested," Kamen said. "I made the mistake today of trying to eat at McDonald's in Pushkin Square."

"And?"

"And I looked at the waiting line and decided that there was not enough time left in the universe for me to be served."

The woman laughed and Kamen looked at her broad, pretty face. It was strange, he thought, that the skin that he always felt looked so unhealthy on men looked so wonderful on women. On women it was close to peaches and cream; with men it looked like blood clots and scar tissue.

The woman had obviously been sent to find out who

176

he was. He could have drawn a lot worse. He looked up at the woman and smiled.

"I'm new in the city," he said. "And I've changed my mind. I *will* have another drink if you'll have one with me . . . ?"

"Natasha. They call me Tash."

"Then Tash it is," Kamen said. "And I am Pyotr Kamenski, once of Odessa, late of Tel Aviv and elsewhere, and soon to be the king of Moscow." *That should get a rise from her*, he thought.

Cowboy was wrong. Sergei Tal might be involved somehow with narcotics in Moscow, but it sure was not happening tonight at The Pink Elephant. Just as it had not happened anytime during the past three weeks that Georgi Golovin had been frequenting the place each night. It was a waste of time. So Vladimir Gubanov had worked at The Pink Elephant. That was hardly enough to connect the nightclub and its manager with the drugs that Gubanov had been trying to buy. This time, Cowboy was barking at a shadow.

Still, Georgi Golovin had no complaints. If somebody had to come here and watch this place, he was delighted that it was him. Not only was the militsia reimbursing him for his expenses, but also for what he spent on the women he brought each night to the club.

It also made him feel good personally. He was the youngest member of Rostov's narcotics squad and subjected to the usual insults and jokes that went with that status. But in his letters home to his family, back in Spas-on-Vodoga, which he knew were read aloud by his parents to the other thirty families in the tiny central Russian village, he was proud to report that he was now doing secret undercover work. Sophisticated Muscovites might look down on the militsia, but in Spas-on-Vodoga, no one before had ever risen to such a high station. And for a young man, only twenty-six years old, to already be doing secret work . . . well, obviously he was a success.

He just wished that he had more each morning to report to Rostov. But each night had been the same, dull and stultifying. Tal in the office upstairs. The two bouncers, Yuri and Viktor, sitting in the booth in the corner. The same hordes of young people, in and out during the evening, and yes, of course, every once in a while the men's room smelled of reefer or there was a telltale little trace of white powder on a countertop in the washroom, but none of it meant anything. It could have happened in any nightclub in the city. An occasional drug-user had visited the club; but none of it meant that Sergei Tal was doing anything illegal.

And why should he? He ran the most expensive and most packed nightclub in the city. He needed drugs like he needed . . . a head of hair? Golovin must have smiled, because the young woman with him, a flat-faced broad nosed brunette who worked in the militsia typing pool and was thrilled to be asked out by one of Cowboy's men, said, "Something funny?"

"No." The only thing unusual tonight was the man who had come in and eventually taken the corner booth. He was a little too old for a single customer—they tended to be in their twenties and thirties and cruising, trying to pick up women. And he seemed to find the music personally distasteful because he had a constant sour look on his face.

Golovin saw Natasha, the hostess, sit down at the table with the man. He had seen the hostess at work before, digging out information on strangers. *They don't know who he is either*, Golovin thought. *Now, what would make him interesting to anyone?*

How would Cowboy do this? he wondered. *Or Sergeant Federenko?* He looked carefully but saw basically just an ordinary man in his mid-forties, the kind one might find working in an office somewhere, or as a salesman in a shoestore. Not good enough he told himself. Cowboy or Sarge would notice something about his shoes. He looked but could not see his shoes. His suit, maybe? He looked and tried to see what he could notice about the suit. It was ordinary gray, maybe a little better weave than most because it did not seem to be wrinkled. But in the back of the neck of the garment, the jacket lay flat against the man's neck and back instead of bunching up the way—he glanced around the room to check his judgment—all the other suits in the room did. *What does that mean?* It meant that he was wearing a better suit than anybody else in here, or else that it has been tailormade for him. Which raises him out of the shoe-clerk category.

He sighed. *Or maybe he just has a lumpy neck. And maybe the hostess has not come to pump him for information but is really his long-lost sister. Who knows? Being a detective is hard work.*

He knew they had sent him here because he was the youngest and most able to fit in with the regular crowd, so he did not want to fail. He decided to keep an eye on the man.

Natasha Krasnova was a widow with an eight-year-old daughter. Her husband had been killed in the army in Afghanistan five years earlier, but there was no pension and the death benefit had quickly run out.

"So this is the best place to work," she said. "I can work nights when my little girl is in bed. During the daytime, when she's in school, I sleep. And then we have the weekends and evenings together like normal people."

"It sounds fine, *if* you can make a living," Kamen said.

"Mr. Tal is very generous," she said.

"Who's Mr. Tal?"

"The owner," she said.

"Then I'm happy for both of you. You, because you

179

found a good job that pays your way, and Tal, because he found somebody so charming and pretty to represent his establishment.''

"Keep up that kind of talk and you *will* be the king of Moscow," she said. "All the women will vote for you."

She touched his hand mockingly, but his fingers closed around the tips of hers before she could remove her hand. Her fingers were soft, almost liquid smooth, he felt, as he let them go. In the raucous sound of the room, her voice was not soft, not indistinct, not a child's voice, but a woman's—somehow sensuous, yet firm, at the same time. Kamen thought that she and Olga Lutska, Rostov's woman, were two totally different beauties. Lutska was tall, cold, reserved, a skittish nervous colt. But Natasha was different. She was not so tall, not so sharp-edged; she exuded warmth, and if Olga Lutska had fire, it was only a cool flame.

He looked at her eyes, even as he saw the man come into The Pink Elephant. He was wearing a pirate-style shirt with bloused sleeves and an open throat. The man was dark-haired, dark-eyed, and he openly looked about the room as he walked down the narrow walkway past the dance floor. His eyes lit on Kamen and lingered for just a split second longer than they had to.

But he walked past Kamen's booth, to the rear of the room, and sat down with the two bouncers. Kamen knew they were there because he had been watching them in the mirror, listening as they bellowed in loud voices about all the weights they had lifted that day in the gymnasium.

He met Tash's eyes again and then glanced past her to watch in the mirror the new man, talking to the two gorillas.

Was it something he had said? Kamen wondered why Tash was in such a hurry to leave, but before he could stand up to ask her, the swarthy man with the pirate shirt slid into her vacated seat.

"I'm Vilick," he said in heavily accented Russian. Kamen did not know enough to tell exactly what kind of accent it was, but he had to admit that he impressed himself by being able to tell native Russian from that spoken by ethnics from the provinces.

"A friend told me to look you up," the man said. "Your name is?"

"My name is unimportant," Kamen said.

"Then how will I know I speak to the right man?" the swarthy man asked.

"The friend who sent you . . . perhaps he likes Armenia better than Moscow?" Kamen said.

"Ahhhh, so we have a mutual friend."

"Yes. And you know what I am interested in."

"A visit to the land of snow, I believe," Vilick said.

"Spare me the poetry. Cocaine, how pure, how much?"

"Seventy-five percent pure. Two thousand rubles the gram. Five grams or more, the price drops to fifteen-hundred rubles."

Kamen nodded. Obviously Omar had not mentioned that Kamen was able to pay in American dollars. That could wait if it had to.

"So why," Kamen said, "did you speak to those two weightlifters back there if you came in to see me?"

"They know me," the man said. "I had to let them know I was here, or they might get nasty and try to throw me out."

"So you told them you're here, dealing drugs, and they said fine?" Kamen asked.

The man nodded. "More or less."

"How much less?"

"They will take a small commission for themselves," Vilick said, "from anything I earn."

"If you earn something. You have some merchandise?"

Vilick nodded. He reached his hand under the table and pressed a small glass vial into Kane's hand. Kamen dropped it into his pocket, then asked, "Where's the men's room?"

"I beg your pardon?"

"The bathroom. Where is it?" Kamen said, cursing himself for forgetting that Russians did not refer to men's and ladies' rooms, only bathrooms.

"Over there," Vilick said, pointing to a small hallway at the corner of the restaurant and dance area.

"Wait for me," Kamen said.

He rose and walked past the two weightlifters, who stared at him quite openly. The door to the bathroom said Men. No confusing cartoons on the door. *Sometimes being backward is being on the cutting edge of common sense*, Kamen thought.

Inside, he locked himself in the toilet booth, then opened the glass vial and touched his finger to the white powder inside, then licked his finger. Cocaine, he agreed to himself, although not very good. He pressed the vial to his fingertip, then upended it. A small sprinkle of powder stuck to his finger and he wiped it around his right nostril, then repeated the procedure for the left side of his nose.

He dumped the rest of the powder into a strip of toilet paper that was as rough and hard as an American supermarket shopping bag, crumpled it up, dropped it into the toilet, and flushed it away.

He washed out the vial at the sink, dried it with a cloth towel hanging from a hook and left the men's room. In case this was some sort of setup, they would be hard-pressed to find any cocaine on him.

He slid into the seat across from Vilick, then slid the empty vial across the table into the other man's lap.

"Good, is it not?"

Kamen leaned forward and spoke very softly, very slowly.

"Vilick, it is powdered-down crap . . . *gavno* . . . and I am not interested. I am deeply disappointed in you. I had hoped that you and I might be able to do business of some sort."

"But . . . really, this is the best material available in Moscow," the man said. He was almost sputtering.

"Well, then, I have a suggestion. You go back to your boss, to your supplier, and tell him you have met a man who can provide him with pure uncut cocaine at forty thousand dollars the kilo. And I have an unlimited number of kilos available. But I will talk only to your boss. I do not spend my time with those who cannot or will not make decisions. If your boss wants to deal, you can send me word through our mutual friend."

"Where do you get all this material?" Vilick asked.

"For many years I have lived all over the West. I now return home to participate in the spirit of democracy, openness, and to bring Western capital, Western equipment, Western machinery, Western business practices—and Western drugs. How I do it is my business. That I *can* do it may be the business of your boss. Him and him alone." Kamen reached into his pocket and took a fifty-ruble note, folded it, and placed it in Vilick's hand. "I want to thank you," Kamen said, "for your trouble. I hope we will meet again."

Vilick looked at him, then at the money, then stuffed it into his pocket, nodded, and left the table.

In the upstairs office behind the mirrored glass, Tash said, "I don't know, Sergei. He doesn't say much but he seems very pleasant."

"Is he a Russian?"

"Yes. From Odessa. But he said he's lived many years in the West. He's come back to live and to start a manufacturing business."

"And his name?"

"Pyotr Kamenski," the woman said. She stopped, looking at Tal, who was staring out the window, onto the brightly lighted dance floor. He turned back toward her and smiled slowly, then stopped. Only a few inches of space separated them.

"Thank you, Tash," he said.

"It's what I get paid for," she said.

"Among other things," Tal said. "You're looking very fetching tonight."

"Thank you, Sergei."

He put his hands on her hips, then reached behind her and cupped her buttocks in his palms.

"Tonight, I believe you will work late," he said. "After everybody else leaves."

His aftershave was overpowering her. What could she do? What could she say? That her babysitter had to leave early? She had said that the last time. That she wasn't feeling well? The time before that. If it was the price of a well-paying job in Moscow, then she would pay it. After all, did it really matter?

The telephone rang before she could say anything, and Tal released her and snatched it up.

He listened, then said, "All right. Let me know who is this mystery man."

When he hung up the phone, he sat in his chair and seemed to forget that Tasha was in the room. Quietly, she walked to the door and let herself out.

Kamen had watched in the mirror. He had seen Tasha go upstairs. He had seen Vilick, the drug dealer, start for the door, but make a brief stop first at the table of the two bouncers. They had not invited him to sit down so he stood and talked, but when he made a motion as if to leave, one of them grabbed his wrist and held on and then Vilick spoke some more.

Finally, the man freed his wrist and waved him away with a disgusted gesture.

It won't be long now, Kamen thought. He caught the eye of a waitress and signaled that he would like another drink.

The drink came. So did one of the two bouncers from the back booth. He slid into the seat across from Kamen, who was sipping his scotch and soda. The man had small eyes, pushed deep into a soft-looking beefy face, like peppercorns embedded in a piece of suet. He wore a blue turtleneck sweater, sleeves pushed up on his massive wrists and forearms. His knuckles appeared bruised and callused as if he had beaten a heavy punching bag into ribbons with his fists. His neck seemed as thick across as his skull and he reminded Kamen of pictures he always remembered seeing of football linebackers.

"Sorry, that seat's taken," Kamen said.

"I know. By me," the man responded in a voice gutteral even by Russian standards.

"Have a nice evening," Kamen said, and slid down the seat to leave the booth.

"Wait a moment," the man said, unable to mask his bewilderment. "I need to talk to you."

"About what?"

"About some merchandise you may have to sell," the man said.

"I told the other imbecile that I would speak to his boss if there was any business to be done. It is obvious that you are no one's boss. It is also obvious that I am wasting my time here. This is a low-class, small-time operation for low-class, small-time people. I will make other arrangements."

He pulled away from the booth, but the bouncer

grabbed his wrist in one powerful paw and squeezed. Kamen leaned back into the booth and poured his drink over the top of the man's head.

The big man sputtered and Kamen leaned close, whispering, "Let go now, or I break this glass and shove the pieces in your eyes. Now!"

The man released his grip and Kamen walked away. The other bouncer, younger, smaller, blond, came toward him and Kamen reached under his jacket to the back of his belt.

No one had noticed anything. The jukebox was still pounding out raucous rock and roll; the dancers were hopping around like St. Vitus victims; the only one who seemed to notice anything was the blonde young man sitting a few tables away with a slightly overweight woman who did not appear to be having a very good time.

The bouncer stopped when he saw Kamen's hand move and said weakly, "Wait."

"For what?" Kamen asked.

"Just wait a minute. Please."

"For a minute," Kamen said.

The blonde bouncer knocked lightly on the office door and walked in when he heard Sergei Tal respond.

"What is it?"

The guard closed the door tight behind him before answering.

"There is a man downstairs. He has told one of our street people that he has a lot of drugs to sell. Many kilos. But he will talk only to the boss."

"So, as bright as a brass button, Yuri, you came running up the stairs to tell me," Tal said.

"Yes," the bouncer said. "I knew you would want to know."

"It is possible that you are the only weightlifter in all

of Russia who is more stupid than his weights. The man is still downstairs?"

"Yes, sir."

"And now he knows that I am the one you talk to about buying drugs. By your pleasant little walk up the stairs, you have compromised me more than I have ever been compromised before. I hope you are proud of yourself," Tal said.

"I am sure that he is not a policeman," Yuri said in his own defense.

"I am sure of that also. And I am also sure that if he ever is picked up by the police and asked about drug-dealing, he will certainly remember this little evening. Get out of my sight, you brainless chicken."

The guard stumbled toward the door.

Tal waited a moment, then said, "Tell the man to wait. I will be right down. Tell him no—more—than—that. Do you understand?"

"Yes, sir."

The guard left, and when the door closed behind him, Tal reached into the back of his desk drawer, took out a small tape recorder, and dropped it into his inside jacket pocket. He clipped the microphone to his pale blue silk tie. Then he rose to go downstairs.

Tal coming downstairs? That's strange.

Georgi Golovin leaned forward in his uncomfortable wooden chair, and looked around as if searching for a waitress to take another drink order. He saw Tal go into the booth in a corner of the room and then saw the two bouncers leave the booth.

It was that stranger Tal was talking to. He knew he was not going to find out what they were talking about. But he certainly wished he could find out who the stranger was. Cowboy might like to know that. And it might mean something.

* * *

Tal did not offer a handshake.

"I am the manager here," he said.

"Your name?" Kamen asked.

"Is that important?" Tal asked.

"I always like to know who I'm doing business with."

"But you and I will do no business," Tal said. "Your name is Kamenski, is it not?"

Kamen nodded. So the woman had told Tal. So much for one pretty hostess. Another company spy.

"Now, Mr. Kamenski, I want to make things very clear, so if you will, please let me talk my piece."

"Please do."

"You have suggested that you might be interested in drugs to buy or drugs to sell. I am not sure which and I don't even care which. The fact is, Mr. Kamenski, that we will have nothing to do with drugs in this establishment. We don't buy them, sell them, or condone a market in them. My first inclination when my employee told me of your activities here was to telephone the police. However, since you are a stranger here and might have been misled, I thought I would explain it all to you in person and then give you the opportunity to leave peaceably. Do you have any questions?"

"Yes, actually I do. I was wondering what kind of body recorder you use for this close work. Oddly enough I always found the best one I ever owned was a Pierre Cardin, but I'm told the Panasonics are good too. What do you use? Are you satisfied with it?"

Kamen looked at Tal, smiled, and started to rise from the booth.

"Look, Mr. Tal. I don't mind you being cautious. I would be too. Fine. And now you have all your disclaimers on tape and everyone is happy. And now I'll give you one final word. I can provide a lot of drugs. Keep me in mind if you hear of someone who does business along those lines.''

"How do I know you are not a policeman?'' Tal said after a long pause.

"Because I'm not penniless,'' Kamen answered. ''I've got more money than your government. Keep me in mind. I'll be around upon occasion.''

He walked away, but in the mirror behind the bar, he saw the manager nod to one of the bodyguards. He had to go to the bathroom, but that would give the guard a chance to set up, so Kamen walked straight for the front door. He brushed by the same young blonde man who had been failing to meet his eyes all night. If he had to pick a policeman in the place, that would be the one. He just tried too hard to look uninquisitive.

The street was brightly lighted outside the club and reminded him of downtown Las Vegas, where you could read a newspaper at any hour of the night from the billboard and marquee lights all around. Only fifty yards away, the cars whizzed by along Kutuzovsky Prospekt.

Kamen saw Omar snoozing in the cab across the street, then heard the door behind him open again. He slid his hand to the back of his belt, under his jacket, as he heard a voice say, ''Hey, you.'' He looked into the angry face of the bodyguard on whose head he had dumped the drink.

"What do you want?'' Kamen said.

"You embarrassed me tonight,'' the man complained.

"It wasn't hard. And you should be used to it by now.''

"Is that another insult?''

"I certainly hope so,'' Kamen said.

The burly bodybuilder ran forward the two steps toward Kamen, raising his fists as he came. When he was within striking distance, Kamen brought his hand out from under his jacket. The .25 caliber pistol was in his hand and he put it on the bodyguard's nose.

"Now go away," Kamen said. "And don't come back at me ever again."

The bodyguard seemed to consider it all for a moment, but the gun barrel touching the tip of his nose was totally convincing and he turned back to the nightclub door. As he opened it, Tash Simunova came out. She saw the bodyguard, and before she could look at him, Kamen turned his side toward her and stuck the pistol into his jacket pocket.

So she's been sent out to see where I live, Kamen thought. *Well, maybe there's nothing wrong with that.*

He smiled at the blonde woman. In this garish string of night lights, she still looked good and fresh; her skin was not laden down with makeup, but still had honest healthy color to it.

"I have a cab," he said. "Could I give you a ride home?"

"No, that's all right," Tasha said. "I'm sure one will be along in a little while."

Very good, Kamen thought. *Disarm the pigeon. Never let him know that you're after him.*

"Well, if you don't have any objections, I'll wait with you," Kamen said. "These streets can get pretty dangerous at night for a pretty woman traveling alone."

"Thank you," she said. "I'd like that."

Omar still slept across the street. The in-service light atop his cab was off.

Kamen would not talk to the woman. He stepped out into the curb and looked left and right but saw no cab. He waited, watching.

After three minutes, Tash spoke. "I don't know where they all are tonight," she said. "They're always clustered around our entranceway."

"Maybe it's a portent, an omen."

"A portent of what?" Tasha said.

"That you should accept my offer. Let my cabbie drop you off."

"My father told me never to turn down a portent," Tasha said with a slight shy smile, and when she did, Kamen let out a wild New York City street whistle and Omar sat up sharply in the cab, looked over at him, and immediately brought the taxi by.

"We're going to drive the lady home," Kamen said.

"Very good. Your address, Madame."

Tasha recited an address only a few blocks away and Omar nodded and drove off.

Pyotr Kamenski was certainly different from the usual string of men she ran into, Tash thought. He was polite and charming and attentive. He made small talk easily, he kept his hands to himself, and when the cab stopped in front of her door, he helped her out and then leaned in to tell the driver, "Wait. But keep your motor running."

Then he took her to her doorway. She lived in a small apartment building, probably for only a dozen families. In some cities, it might have been regarded as a slum, but the building was painted in a bright pastel blue and Kamen thought it looked charming and homey.

She fumbled in her purse for her key and when she found it she said, "I'm sorry you told the driver to keep his motor running. I'd invite you in for coffee."

"Thank you," Kamen said. "But not tonight."

"My daughter is already asleep," the woman said.

"Maybe tomorrow night?" Kamen said.

"I'd like that. You can call me at The Pink Elephant," she said.

"Count on it," Kamen said and left.

Omar sat silently at the wheel even after Kamen got back into the cab.

"What are you waiting for?" Kamen asked.

"You caused me a great deal of trouble tonight, boss."

"How did I do that?"

"I sent someone to see you out of the goodness of my heart and what did I get for it, except to have my friend . . . my very dear friend of my entire life and childhood . . . abused and to have him curse me with names one would not call his sister's husband."

"Well," Kamen said, "that's why I'm overpaying you. And that's why I overpaid your friend. He *did* split with you, didn't he?"

"That son of a dog gave me nothing," Omar snapped.

"I gave him enough for both of you."

"Oh, the perfidy of it," Omar said.

"Well, let it be a lesson to you, Omar. Trust no one. Now take me home."

They pulled away from the curb, and a few moments later, Omar said, "There's a car following us, boss."

"I know," Kamen said.

"You want me to lose him?"

"No. But pretend to."

"I am sorry, boss, but confusion reigns."

"Make believe you're trying to lose him. But don't really lose him."

"In other words, let him follow us," Omar said.

"You have a way of getting to the heart of things," Kamen said.

Cowboy must have dozed. He woke with his lips on Olga Lutska's bare breast and her fingers trailing through the hair on his neck.

"Sleepy babe," she said.

"You must take something out of me," he said.

"Only what you keep putting into me," she said, and they both chuckled. He felt himself getting stiff and hard again, and because it felt good and he wanted to show

Olga what kind of power she had over him, he stood with his erection waving in front of him like a lance and said, "I will make a phone call."

"You need not call another woman. I can handle that," Olga said.

"In just a moment, we will see about that."

Conscious of his erection, wondering if she was impressed or if she thought he was just a foolish showoff, Rostov walked into the next room and dialed a number he found written on a card in his wallet.

Kamen answered the telephone on the first ring.

"Hello. This is Cowboy."

"Yeah. What do you want?"

"I was just wondering how your night was?"

"Peaceful, pleasant, and quiet until now. I was sleeping and you woke me up."

"I'm sorry. I wanted to make certain everything was all right. Are you enjoying Moscow?"

"I find it all very interesting."

"I thought tomorrow we might discuss business," Rostov said.

"Tomorrow would be fine," Kamen said. "Good night."

Cowboy hung up and went back into the bedroom.

"I'm sorry, Olga," he said. "But for some reason I was worried about our new American operative. I wanted to see if he was all right."

"And was he?"

"He was asleep. He is not the aggressive sort, I do not believe," Rostov said.

"Perhaps he was tired from all his traveling."

"I would be too. But I don't think I'd be able to fall right off to sleep without spending some time looking around."

"There are all kinds of different people in the world," she said.

"Yes, there are." He lay down beside her.

"For instance," she said, "there are men and there are women."

"I've noticed," Rostov said.

"Prove it," she said.

Chapter Sixteen

"So after a month of spending the government's money on wine, women, and song, you finally have something to show for it?"

Georgi Golovin grinnned back at Cowboy, and Rostov thought, *The little boy is growing up.* He remembered that if he had adopted such a mock-stern tone six months ago, young Georgi would have wet his pants. The boy from the marshy little country town was fast becoming a man.

"I have to tell you the truth, Cowboy," Golovin said. "Until last night I thought this was all a waste of time. The only thing I found out was that nobody who works at The Pink Elephant ever heard of Vladimir Gubanov, even though our records showed he was supposed to work there."

"Yes, yes," Rostov said impatiently. The young man leaned forward in his chair and rested his arms on Rostov's desk. "But I think something is brewing."

'What kind of something?''

'Last night, there was the usual activity. A few small drug sales made, none of them by the nightclub personnel. Just people who came in off the street, did a little business, then left. Streetcorner stuff. But then, a stranger came in, someone I'd never seen in the Elephant before. And later this petty pusher in this pirate shirt came in and joined the man at the table. Obviously they passed drugs.''

''You saw that happen?''

''No, sir, not actually. I could not see the actual transfer. But the newcomer went to the men's room, and when he came back, his nose was white. But then he was obviously unhappy with the drugs he had just bought, because I could tell that he was talking to the dealer, agitated, then he shoved some money in his hand and the dealer left.''

''Doesn't sound like anything out of the ordinary to me,'' Cowboy grumbled.

''But then, the two bodyguards who hang out there every night—I've told you about them, Yuri and Viktor—they came and talked to the stranger, presumably about the drug purchase, and there was almost a fight. I could tell the stranger was ready to break his glass. One of your old Wild West fight stunts, I think.''

'We can do without the editorial comment,'' Rostov said dryly.

''Finally the younger thug, Yuri, went upstairs and brought down Tal, who also talked to the stranger for five minutes. And then the stranger left.''

''If you pardon me, Georgi, I don't understand yet what you've found out.''

''The two bodyguards. I've made it a point of getting close to them in the last few weeks. They see me around every night and they think I'm harmless. I think Viktor, he's the ugly one, is in love with me.''

''Isn't everybody?'' Rostov asked with a smile.

''I heard them talking in the men's room later. It seems

as if this stranger wants to sell drugs. Large amounts of drugs. They stopped talking when I came in but I heard them through the bathroom door. And remember, this stranger talked to Tal. Maybe our little lead means something. Maybe Tal *is* some kind of drug boss.''

''Who is this stranger?'' Rostov asked.

''I couldn't find out his name and he eluded me, from the club. But he will be coming back. I heard the bodyguards talking about squaring accounts with him when he returns. Apparently he threatened them somehow.''

''That's excellent,'' Rostov said. ''Maybe something will come of this. Now what's today for you?''

Golovin knew what he meant. All Rostov's men understood that they were on duty day and night at Rostov's whim, and Georgi would never get credit for a full night's work just for sitting in a nightclub, keeping his eyes open.

''Viktor, the bouncer, told me he works out every day in a gym. He invited me. I thought it might be time to build my muscles.''

Rostov hesitated. If Tal was involved in drugs, if perhaps he was even the man behind trying to centralize all of Moscow's narcotics trade, Rostov wanted him and wanted him badly. But while the bouncers might be stupid, Tal wasn't. If Georgi started to pal around with them too much too quickly, it might get back to Tal and he might get suspicious. Better to wait, he thought.

''If this Viktor is really in love with you,'' Rostov said with a smile, ''you should play hard to get. Stay away from that gymnasium for a while. Go get some sleep.''

''All right.''

''And be back at The Pink Elephant tonight. And by the way, good work.''

Golovin smiled and left Rostov's cluttered office. It really was not such good work, Rostov thought. The young policeman should have found out what Tal and the newcomer were talking about. And he never should have let the man leave the club without calling in squad backup

197

to follow him. But nothing that could not be corrected, Rostov thought. It would work out. And maybe it was time to call in his new expert and see what Pyotr Kamenski thought of all this.

Of course Kamen had not been asleep when Rostov had called the night before. In fact, he had just gotten into the apartment from his night's tour of The Pink Elephant and taking Tash Simunova home. But he was not ready to tell Rostov anything about that.

This time, however, when the telephone rang, Kamen *was* asleep and it took him a few seconds to orient himself, to remember where he was, and then to reach over for the telephone next to the couch where he had decided to spend the night.

"Yes?" he answered, resisting the urge of years of habit just to bark out his name. First of all, Russians didn't answer the telephone that way. Secondly, his name was no longer Kamen and that might be the hardest habit to break.

The voice was male, harsh, guttural.

"Last night, Mr. Kamenski, you talked about a business deal. I would like to discuss it further with you."

"Who is this?"

"That isn't really necessary. It's enough that I am willing to do business with you."

"I never turn down a business opportunity. What might you be interested in?" Kamen asked.

"I think I need a new snow shovel for my business. Perhaps two snow shovels if the price is right."

Kilograms? Of cocaine? This is one ferocious buyer, whoever he is, Karmen thought.

"That sounds interesting," Kamen said. "What kind of price would we be talking about?"

"Some things are more expensive in this country and some in the West, but I would think thirty each."

Two kilos of cocaine for sixty thousand. Of course he's talking dollars. That's why the lunatic reference to the West.

"I think I could probably sell the same equipment for eighty elsewhere," Kamen said.

"Perhaps," the other voice said reasonably. "But it might take you months and the people you wind up dealing with might not have the money. Perhaps seventy would be fair all around."

"That is a reasonable number," Kamen said. "I can, you know, supply more of these shovels. Many more."

"Thank you and perhaps in the future. But for now, two shovels is all I need. When could you deliver?"

"A few days," Kamen said.

"I thought you had it available," the voice said, sounding a little annoyed.

"It's available. But I don't keep it in the toe of my shoe under my bed. I have to arrange to move it into the city."

"All right. I will call you tomorrow."

"Fine," Kamenski said. "You say we've met? I can't recognize the voice."

"That doesn't really matter," the man said, and hung up.

Kamen replaced the phone, then lay back on the couch, Of course, it was Tal. The nightclub owner had not actually made the telephone call himself, but he had been behind it. He was the only one who knew, probably from Tash, what Kamen's name was. And as Kamen had planned, his men had managed to follow him home the night before.

So he wants to buy drugs? Excellent. Perhaps we will have something good for the Cowboy before too long.

And Rostov, he thought, might be right about the amount of pressure his squad was putting on the city's drug dealers. If they were so willing to deal so quickly with a total stranger, their supplies were running out.

199

Kamen looked at the clock. It was almost eleven A.M. He reached again for the telephone to call Rostov.

The Cowboy had not intentionally thought about calling attention to himself, but it had just happened. With his American-style clothes and his cowboy hats, he had become a well-known figure.

He supposed it was stupid for a policeman—especially one working undercover against drugs —to be such a public figure, but he knew his ego was involved too and that's why he kept doing it. The fact was that he liked being recognized in restaurants and on the street; he liked getting good tables and good service. God knew there were few enough other fringe benefits to working in the militsia. His men made 250 rubles a month and he not much more than that. Just enough to starve on comfortably, he thought. No wonder some policemen were corrupt, at least in Russia. In New York City, he had read, policemen were paid some forty thousand dollars a year. That was at least ten times what a Moscow cop received and yet he had read that there was corruption on the New York force too. Maybe, for the greedy, no amount of money was ever enough money.

Ah yes, he thought, *Rostov the philosopher. And penniless. And, with God's help, going to stay that way.*

When he went into the small restaurant near the television tower, he knew he was recognized because he could hear the buzzing as he followed the waitress to a back table.

He was supposed to meet Kamenski outside the restaurant at one P.M. Outside, because Kamenski had said he did not know yet whether or not he would be hungry. "Play it by ear," he said, using an American expression that Rostov had never heard before. Well, by one P.M., the lunch crowd would have thinned, and if Kamenski was hungry, they could come back inside without attracting any attention. Probably Kamenski would not eat, he decided. Rostov had been surprised when the American said he knew the location of the restaurant. The only way that could have happened was if he had tried to eat here the day before. If he had, he would not want to return.

If he has eaten here, he's gotten an awful picture of Russian life, because the waitresses in this place are surely the most surly and incompetent in all of Moscow. The restaurant thrives just because it is the only place in the neighborhood.

He sat down and smiled at the waitress, who unfroze her stiff face long enough to try to don a pleasant expression, and asked for a bottle of cold beer, no glass. When it came, a pungent Finnish brand, he sipped from the bottle, drawing admiring glances from the people who crowded the other tables.

Olga Lutska arrived ten minutes later, right on time, and slid into the seat at his right.

It might raise eyebrows if he kissed her, but under the table he squeezed her thigh and she smiled at him. To anyone else in the room, the meeting would look like the meeting of a policeman and a prosecutor. Nothing unusual at all about that.

Rostov leaned over and said, "I'd like to make love to you on this table."

"Maybe if we wait long enough, everybody else will leave and then you can."

"I've never been that lucky," he said.

"Nor have I."

"So how has your day been?" he asked.

"I was warned today not to be corrupt," Olga said, the trace of a smile on her mouth.

Rostov leaned close and whispered, "Not in bed, I hope. I like you corrupt in bed."

"Silence, you imbecile," Olga said laughingly. 'We had a staff meeting with the prosecutor. He said that he has received a hint that some of our people might be too cozy with people we should know only from our attempts to put them in jail. Have you ever seen the prosecutor?''

Rostov nodded. ''But never spoke with him,'' he said.

''He is this giant blowfish with a pitted face and tiny little eyes behind bottle-bottom spectacles. He said 'I want you all to know that you are the primary bulwark of the law in this area. If one of us fails, we all fail. If any knows of anyone failing, it is your responsibility to tell me.' In other words, turn in people on rumors.

''I immediately thought of you,'' she told Rostov. ''What happens if they find out I am seeing you? What then? Will they take a look at that hat of yours and regard you as a dangerous corroding Western influence? Are you to be the end of my career?

''Anyway, my face must have had a smile on it because the prosecutor said, 'You find something amusing, Miss Lutska?' '' She lowered her voice in an imitation of her boss. ''So I said no. That if I had smiled, it was a smile not of amusement but of endorsement. I know that all my colleagues agree that we must be, as Caesar's wife, above suspicion. So that seemed to be that and he went back to business.''

''No mention of Judge Alekhine?'' Rostov asked.

''No. If they know anything about him, that is one secret they are keeping.''

''Good. He was, I am convinced, a corrupt bastard, but the less known about it, the better for my work,'' Rostov said. ''I like no one to know anything.''

Olga thought about it for a moment, then decided to tell Rostov the rest of what had happened. Right after she spoke and the staff meeting broke up, one of the other assistant prosecutors had sidled up to her and said, '' 'A smile of endorsement'? Indeed. Are you a fake or a brownnose?''

''Neither,'' she had answered mockingly. ''I am a righteous member of the judicial system of our land. I carry my responsibilities with full knowledge of their importance.''

"Stop it. You're making me sick. Lunch?"

"Sorry. I already have a date."

"Don't fall out of the saddle," the other lawyer said as he walked away.

She looked at Rostov. "It's pretty obvious that he knows about us."

"Just who is this attorney?" Rostov said.

"Anatoly Nabokov."

"I've never heard of him."

"You've heard of his father."

"Leonid Nabokov? The shark who got that prisoner released from Alekhine last month?"

"One and the same."

"Tell me about the son," Rostov asked.

"He is a person of very little brains. In this case, the talent in the family was all disbursed before he arrived. He is also a vile creature personally, constantly sniffing around me, making lewd remarks to the secretaries. You know the type." She paused. "No, you're not a woman, you probably don't know the type."

"But how did he find out about us?" Rostov wondered aloud.

"I don't know," she said.

"I have the answer," Cowboy said. When she looked at him in surprise, he said, "You constantly come to the office now with this dreaming look of satisfied passion on your face. Everyone knows only one man in Russia could produce such a response. And of course that is me."

She laughed aloud and Rostov felt good that he had lifted her spirits. But the question stayed in his mind: How had young Nabokov known about their very secret love affair?

* * *

203

Rostov was waiting in the car, parked in a no-parking zone, when Kamenski arrived in a taxicab and pulled up behind him outside the restaurant.

He leaned across the seat and pushed the passenger door open. Kamen looked inside cautiously until he saw and recognized Rostov, then got into the car and the policeman drove away.

"So how do you like Russia?" he asked.

"What a dump."

"No, no. It's not that bad."

"It's worse," Kamen said.

"You're jumping to conclusions."

"Right. I'll let you know when I change my mind."

"Did you ask for this meeting to complain, or have you decided to do some work?"

"What kind of work did you have in mind?" Kamen asked. They had driven north, past the television tower, and into a large park with vast fields of wild flowers in full bloom. It looked very un-Russian, Kamen thought.

He sat back in the car seat, his legs sprawled out in front of him. He used a small knife to clean his fingernails, but as Rostov glanced over at him occasionally, he saw that Kamen's eyes were always fixed outside, looking at locations, watching the streets, never once looking at his fingernails. *This one misses very little,* he said to himself.

"I thought it might be useful if you were to go over some of our files. It would give you an idea of what we're dealing with. Who some of the people involved are. From there, I thought you and I could produce some plan of action."

"I'll look at your files, but I'm not much on the value of files," Kamen said.

"What would be your approach?" Rostov asked. *Is it possible this man is lazy and doesn't ever want to go to work? That he just wants to sit around collecting a paycheck and doing nothing?*

"Well, maybe we could start here," Kamen said. "I need two kilos of cocaine."

"I beg your pardon," Rostov said.

"What's the matter? Is my Russian that bad? I need two kilos of cocaine."

"Well, of course," Cowboy said. "It's part of every Russian's weekly ration. Will it be all right if I have it delivered to your house tomorrow?"

"Don't be sarcastic and no, tomorrow is too late. I think I might need it before then."

Rostov swerved his car wildly into a parking spot, jammed on the brake, and the car rocked back and forth on its springs as he turned off the key.

"All right. What the hell are we talking about?"

"I am trying to infiltrate a drug mob," Kamen said. "I've convinced them that I have drugs to sell. I have to produce some goods."

"And then what happens?" Rostov said.

"And then your guys arrive in the nick of time to bust up the deal, but I escape with the drug people and I'm a hero and part of the mob."

"I've never heard of such a thing," Rostov said.

"Come on. This is like one of those American movies you're always watching. It's how you infiltrate the Mafia."

Rostov laughed aloud.

"Would you mind telling me what is so funny?" Kamen said.

"I was beginning to get the idea that you were unambitious and slow-moving," Rostov said. "And instead, here you are . . . well, I am impressed."

"Don't underestimate me," Kamen said. "Where I'm from, the people who did that are dead. Or in jail." He paused. "All except one."

"I will never underestimate you again. Tell me. Were you at The Pink Elephant nightclub last night?"

"Yeah. You had someone there?"

"Yes," Rostov said.

"The young blonde guy with the space in his teeth?"

Rostov stared at Kamen for a moment. "Was it that obvious?"

"No, he wasn't bad. It was just that he was watching everything a little too closely. And the girl he was with wasn't having any fun at all and he didn't seem to give a shit. I thought he had something else on his mind, and every time I looked up, he was staring at me and then he looked away real fast as if I had caught him doing something wrong . . ."

Rostov chuckled. "I'll have to warn Georgi about his technique." He pulled away from the curb, back into traffic.

"What did he say?" Kamen said.

"He said he thought there was some drug activity going on at The Pink Elephant. He said you went into the men's room and came back with powder on your nose."

Kamen nodded. "Yeah." He looked over at the big policeman, who sat with his hands drumming on the steering wheel. "Hey, don't get the wrong idea. I don't use that stuff. I hate drugs and drug dealers. In the bathroom I flushed it down the toilet, but first I rubbed some on my nose, just to make it look good. That was just to get a foot in the door."

"And now you have a foot in the door. So what has happened?"

Kamen told him about the morning's telephone call.

"It looks as if you are moving inside," Rostov said. "And here I was going to impress you today by telling you that we may have a lead into the Moscow drug network. And you turn out to be the one responsible for that lead." He whistled under his breath. "We've been watching Tal's place for a month. You come into town, and ten hours later, you accomplish more than we did in thirty days. How did you do that?"

"You people know police things. I know mob things. You're right, you know. There is someone trying to coordinate narcotics in the city—"

"The whole country," Rostov interrupted.

"If you say so. At any rate . . ." He stopped talking as they passed a cathedral. "How many churches are there in this city with gold domes?" he suddenly asked.

Rostov shrugged. "I don't know. I have never counted them."

"It's like living in ancient India," Kamen said. "Anyway, someone is consolidating drug operations. The sales on the street are being choked off. I just got lucky by contacting a dealer who sent me to The Pink Elephant. I was wondering why he did that. He could have sent me anywhere to meet me. I think he had business to discuss at The Pink Elephant, probably with those two musclemen who work for Tal. It was a big mistake. You can tell they're new at this; they're making a lot of mistakes."

Rostov swerved to avoid a car that darted out in front of them from a side street and then shuddered to a stop when the woman driver realized she had made a mistake.

"Ahh," Cowboy sighed. "I love equality, but women drivers should all be sent to work in the mines."

"There's hope for you yet," Kamen said. "So can you get me the cocaine?"

"I can try."

"Let's do better than that. When will you know?"

"I will make it my first priority when I return to the office."

"Fine," Kamen said. "I'll be back at the apartment later this afternoon. Call me then. Let me off here."

Rostov glanced over at him. "Do you know where you are?" he said, glancing around the old industrial area of the city, with its rickety warehouse buildings and deeply potholed streets.

"I'll be fine," Kamen said casually.

"Listen. This is not a good neighborhood. People get hurt down here all the time. Let me take you back to—"

"Thanks but just stop the car."

Rostov shrugged, and angled his car into the curbside.

"I'll talk to you later," Kamen said as he got out. He waited at the curb for Rostov to back out and drive away.

Then he stepped out into the street. A moment later, Omar's yellow cab turned a corner and pulled in to pick him up.

Three blocks ahead, Rostov saw the pickup in his rear-view mirror. *That's the damned cab that's been following us,* he thought, and wondered why Kamen would have a cab trailing them. *Does the bastard distrust me?*

He made a right turn into a side street, then quickly executed a U-turn and parked at the corner. He would wait there until the cab passed and then get its license number. Then he would be able to trace the driver. *Might as well find out who our American is getting close to.*

He waited.

Back down the main street, Kamen told the cabbie, "Make a U-turn here and go back the way you came."

The cop, he thought, *will be waiting for us so he can get this license number. Screw him.*

Omar's taxi roared around in the wide street and headed back to the center of the city.

Cowboy waited in his parked car for two minutes, then five, then cursed. "Devious bastard," he growled, then sped out into the street to go back to his office.

Chapter Seventeen

How could anyone have ever considered Russia one of the great powers? Rostov wondered as he slammed the telephone receiver back down onto the stand. The country was incapable of doing anything.

He knew for a fact that three blocks away, in the basement of the sprawling yellow complex that housed the Moscow militsia, the agency's property section held a vast assortment of drugs—cocaine, heroin, all contraband seized from smugglers and dealers.

Occasionally, it was burned in a public ceremony presided over by General Budenko, but the storage bin for narcotics was never completely emptied, since some was always needed for research work, analysis, and use by the police in ongoing operations.

That much was logical. What was not logical was the refusal of the captain who commanded the property division to release any of the drugs to Rostov.

"I need two kilos," Rostov said. "You have so much there that it can't cause you any problems."

"Don't you read the press, Rostov?" the captain said. "Or do you only read it when *your* photograph is in it?"

"What are you talking about, Captain?"

"Yesterday, General Budenko burned almost all our drug supplies. Part of the militsia's usual program of destroying contraband. His picture was in the press this morning, feeding it into the city incinerator. You should really keep your eyes open, Rostov."

"All right, all right," Rostov said. "But he didn't burn it all, I know. I know you have there what I need."

"But you can't have it," the captain said.

"Why not?"

"You have to have permission," the captain said.

"From whom?"

"From General Budenko."

"Fine. I will call you back."

Then Rostov had called Budenko's office. He spoke to Colonel Svoboda and told him that he needed two kilograms of cocaine for an undercover operation.

"Why are you telling me?" Svoboda said. "Tell the property room. That's where it is."

"I tried that. They said I need permission from the general." .

"The general left town last night. He will be gone for the next few days," Svoboda said.

God, Rostov thought, *I hate this perfumed little fop with his little waxed mustache and his spit-shined shoes.*

"Exactly, Colonel. Therefore, as the acting commander, it is necessary for you to call the property room."

"I couldn't do that without the general's approval," Svoboda said.

"I thought you were in charge in his absence," Rostov said. *Easy. Easy. Don't lose your temper. That will not make things easier.*

"I am," Svoboda said.

"So cannot you give this order yourself?"

"Not without speaking with General Budenko."

"I think it is important enought to speak to the general about," Rostov said. "Can you do that?"

"I should hear from the general," Svoboda said.

"If I may ask, when?"

"Probably tomorrow. He is doing much traveling now. He is probably out of reach."

"Tomorrow will be too late," Rostov said. "Can you try to reach the general now?"

'Well, if you're going to be insistent about it. . . ."

'Please, Colonel," Rostov said.

'I will call you back."

Rostov thanked Svoboda, hung up, put his feet up onto the desk and checked his watch. As he expected, the telephone rang ninety seconds later.

"This is Lieutenant Rostov speaking."

"Colonel Svoboda, Lieutenant. I have tried but cannot reach General Budenko. When I hear from him, I will relay your request."

The colonel hung up without waiting for a response. Rostov hung up the telephone precisely, looked at it for a moment, then stood in his small crammed office and screamed aloud.

The weakhearted faggot. Cock of the walk? This one is a capon.

He wondered how he would tell Pyotr Kamenski that it had all fallen through. In one day, the American had found a way to move into what might be the Mafia's growing centralized drug operation—the exact reason he had been brought to Russia—and now the police themselves were foiling his plans.

"No, dammit," he said aloud. "Not so easy as that."

He went to the door and bellowed, "Yevgeny, get in here."

Yevgeny Astafyev, darkly handsome and, after Sergeant Federenko, the most experienced member of Rostov's squad, walked warily into the office.

"Yes, sir," he said, almost hesitantly.

"Why are you so nervous?" Rostov demanded.

"I heard you scream a moment ago. When you scream, I run."

"I'm glad I intercepted you. I want you to call the Office for Hospital Supplies. We need two kilos of lactose."

"Lactose?"

"Yes. Are you deaf as well as stupid? Milk sugar. Lactose. We need it immediately. Get on it right away and send in Federenko."

A moment later, the grizzled sergeant stood in front of Rostov's desk. He seemed not to have shaved this morning and his eyes were red-rimmed and bloodshot.

"Yes, Cowboy."

"How much cocaine can you put your hands on immediately?" Rostov asked.

"Immediately. Like now?"

"Like ten minutes ago," Rostov said.

"I don't know. We've got some stashed outside. Some of the local police divisions should have some. Maybe a few hundred grams."

"Fine. Do it."

"Why don't we just call the property room?" Sergeant said. "They've got more than a hundred kilos over . . ." He stopped talking and his voice trailed off when he saw the expression on Rostov's face.

The sergeant paused at the door. "Is it okay to sign receipts for whatever I get?"

"Yes. If we're lucky, we will get it all back," Rostov said.

"Do you want to tell me what it's for?" Federenko asked.

"No," Rostov answered.

"I can live with that," the sergeant said, and left the office.

He had not been able to get through on a telephone line, even after telling the operator that it was official police business, so Yevgeny Astafyev had walked the four blocks to the Bureau of Hospital Procurement and Supplies.

"What do you mean, you don't have any lactose?" Astafyev asked.

"We don't have any. Our shipment has not arrived yet."

"When is your shipment due?"

"It was due six months ago. Last February."

"What have you been using in the meantime?"

"We have been using nothing," the supply man said.

"Where is the factory? Where is it coming from?"

"I don't know."

"You don't know where your supplies come from?"

'Sometimes it comes from here, sometimes it comes from there. I think maybe the lactose comes from Rumania. That's probably why it's late. They have been having much trouble in Rumania. Things are disorganized."

"And here they're not?"

"I really don't need abuse. I'm doing my best. I'm not the one who manufactures the lactose. If I ran the lactose factory, I would have lactose and I would give it to you. But I don't run the factory. I suffer just as you do."

"Not exactly," Yevgeny said.

'What do you mean?"

"You don't work for the Cowboy."

Yevgeny walked quickly down the street, back to his own office. When he saw a pretty young woman behind the counter of a pharmacy, he went inside.

213

He pretended to be buying a magazine, and when he felt the woman's eyes on him in the otherwise empty store, he looked up quickly, met her glance, and then smiled. She smiled back, almost embarrassedly.

Astafyev approached the counter, where the woman seemed to be waiting for him.

"Do you have any lactose?" he asked.

"No. We haven't had any since last month. We should get a shipment soon."

"From where?" Yuri asked.

"Czechoslovakia provides us with our lactose."

"Do you know anyplace that has any?"

"No. No one has any."

"Thank you."

She sounded almost disappointed when she said, "Will that be all?"

"My beautiful young woman," Astafyev said, "on any other day, it would not be all. On any other day, I would loiter here and charm you and invite you to dinner, all with a goal toward seducing you."

She just stared at him, uncomprehending.

"But since tonight I will have been castrated by the Cowboy, I think it best that you find someone else."

"Pardon me, rich man, but are we looking for anything special?"

"Just keep driving. I''ll let you know when I see it," Kamen said.

Omar grunted and hunched forward over the taxicab's steering wheel. *His feelings are hurt*, Kamen thought. *I'm paying him a month's pay every day and his feelings are hurt because I haven't made him my partner. What is it today, everybody's an artiste? Just drive. You don't want to be involved in my business.*

Omar was going through the side streets that were packed with small houses, painted in traditional cream

214

and white colors. Except for the cream and white colors, which Kamen saw all over the city and which he realized must represent some kind of traditional Russian color scheme for housing, the streets might have been found in the ethnic quarter of any city in America's northeast. Or on a Hollywood back lot.

If he stayed in Russia . . . if? Of course he was going to stay in Russia. He had no place else to go. What was he thinking of? He knew what. If he survived—that was what was on his mind—if he survived, he might someday try to get his hands on one of these pretty little houses. His apartment was . . . well, just an apartment and he wasn't much of an apartment guy.

Even as one of the guinea pigs in the U.S.'s witness-protection program, he had always insisted on living in a house somewhere. He liked backyards. He liked sitting in a lawn chair, *his* lawnchair on *his* grass, getting sunburned from *his* sun. He liked having tools, hammers and saws and screwdrivers, and getting a chance to use them. No, he didn't; he always wound up breaking the screwdriver by using it as a chisel, and mostly he wound up hammering his own fingers, and he had once owned an electric ripsaw and for ten years had been afraid to turn it on because the noise it made was loud and scary. He hated tools. But he liked the idea of owning tools. A man who owned tools wasn't a wanderer, a vagrant, a hobo. He bet Omar owned tools.

They were out of the housing area now and passing a large lot filled with boats of all sizes.

"What's that?" Kamenski asked.

"Boat station."

"I didn't think the river came up this far north," Kamenski said.

"No. That's Khiminskoye Lake. The city reservoir."

"All right. Keep driving."

A few miles farther out of the city, Kamenski saw a railroad terminal, stolid and gray, sitting like some kind of giant block in an old rundown area of housing and vacant lots. The air was, if possible, even worse here, the smoke from nearby factories black in the sky, dropping down in soot, coating parked cars, buildings, even the broken sidewalk.

"What's this?" Kamen asked.

"Rytsarya Train Station, boss," Omar answered.

"Park. I want to walk around."

"Keep your hand on your wallet, boss."

Kamenski nodded, left the cab, and walked away from the station toward a small maze of alleys that faced the old terminal building.

What had attracted his attention was that he had seen only two television monitor cameras outside the train station. Most public buildings he had noticed in the last several days seemed to have a dozen or more such surveillance cameras.

He walked down one of the alleys. Garages, rickety old frame structures, fronted the alley on each side; and from the alley, which was not more than ten feet wide, even narrower alleys trailed off at ninety-degree angles, leading to the rear of the garages and also to the back doors of the ramshackle tenements on the streets on either side of the rail station.

He turned into the first small alley. Ahead of him, perhaps fifty yards farther on, he could see into the next street. Here an old concrete-and-block wall bordered the alley next to one of the garages, and there were gaps in the wall where blocks of stone had fallen out or been chipped out by vandals. One opening in the thick wall was the size of a breadbox; it was mostly hidden by a corrugated steel fence and Kamen could reach the opening only by stretching his hand in behind the steel.

Good enough, he thought. *This should do fine.*

* * *

Federenko had been able to round up only a hundred or so grams of cocaine, about enough to fill a cup.

"That's it?" Rostov had said.

Federenko said, "It's all that's around, Cowboy. It's good stuff, though."

Rostov nodded. It might be enough, he thought, but that hope was shattered when Astafyev returned with the report that there was no lactose to be found anywhere in the city. "I've even called every nurse I've ever slept with, Cowboy. None in the hospitals even, none in the labs. Nowhere."

"Goddammit, the drug dealers never seem to have any trouble getting lactose to powder down their narcotics," Rostov growled. "Where do they get it from?"

"Let's face it, Lieutenant. The drug dealers are more efficient than the government." He hesitated. "That's an idea, though. Do you want me to go out and put some muscle to some of the drug dealers? That can get us milk sugar."

"No. Never mind. Let me think for a while. Get out of here."

Astafyev left and Rostov leaned back in his chair, putting his booted feet onto the desk. He had hoped, with a little cocaine and a lot of milk sugar, to fashion a couple of fake blocks of cocaine for Kamenski's needs. They might not stand close inspection, but if they were only going to be in the hands of the drug dealers for a few minutes, it might be adequate.

But now he could not even do that, because there was no lactose—the crystalline white powder with which narcotics dealers generally "cut" cocaine—to be found in the city.

He swore aloud. And only a few blocks away, in the property room, were all the drugs he would need for this operation and he could not get his hands on them. He swore again.

He felt, in a way, as if he were betraying Pyotr Kamenski. Whatever the man's background in crime might have been, the fact was that he had made a move into an organization that Rostov had been trying to infiltrate for a long time, and the American was willing—at high risk to himself—to set up a phony drug sale in order to penetrate deeper.

And the people who would benefit most, the government police, were providing him with no help.

And that was all very good and logical, he knew, but it was only a part of what he felt. The other and stronger emotion was anger because, dammit, he was Cowboy Rostov and he should be able to get something done, no matter what obstacles the bureaucrats threw in his way.

His grandfather, a career soldier as had been most of the males in the Rostov family, had long ago told him his own rule for life: "Swear three times, and if you're still angry, punch him in the nose."

Rostov swore for the third time and picked up the telephone.

When he got his number, he said, "Let me speak to Olga Lutska, please," and as she came on the line, he said, "Olga, I need a favor."

The other squad members were out on assignments and only Sergeant Federenko was in the office when Rostov returned.

He motioned for Federenko to follow him into the inner office, where Rostov opened a large briefcase, and took out two large blocks—each the size of two cartons of cigarettes—wrapped in heavy butcher's paper and tied with twine. He plunked them on his desk and grinned at Federenko.

"Courtesy of the property division," he said.

"How . . ."

"I stole them," Rostov said. "The prosecutor's office

218

made an unannounced inspection of the property room. The poor sergeant working there was so confused, he turned his back and I lifted the cocaine.''

"A wonderful plan," Federenko said dryly. "Maybe we can use it as a fringe benefit for recruiting. Each of us, two kilos a month for personal use."

"If they don't have a sense of humor, screw them," Rostov said.

Cowboy sat behind his desk, in high good humor, and with a penknife cut the strings around one of the brown paper packages, and folded back the paper. He touched his index finger to his tongue, then pressed it against the white powder, and touched it again to his mouth.

A bewildered look crossed his face.

"What the hell is this?" he said.

Chapter Eighteen

Omar's cab stopped when a woman with an armband halted vehicles in both directions as schoolchildren raced across the street.

Kamen recognized the neighborhood. He was just around the corner from Tash's apartment. He looked idly out the rear window at the children coming down the steps of the school. The building was physically connected to another of the giant gold-domed Catholic churches that dotted Moscow and he remembered reading, during the brief three-week indoctrination before leaving the United States, that the old Soviet government had seized tens of thousands of churches during its efforts to wipe out religion. The few churches that were left had been ordered to close their schools.

Seventy years of that kind of persecution, he thought, *and the government finally lets down its guard just a little and the church schools open right up again. Religion just dies hard.*

Kamen looked idly out the cab window at the children coming down the school steps, and then noticed the group of parents waiting at the bottom of the steps.

He said to Omar, "Pull over here and park."

"Yes, sir, rich boss," Omar said.

Kamen got out of the cab and stood behind it, watching Tash Krasnova across the street. She was wearing a simple white dress and a denim jacket. Her blonde hair glinted in the afternoon sun and, even in sneakers, her legs were curvy and trim.

He tried to guess which one of the kids coming out of the school building would be hers. He put his mental money on a pretty little blonde who could not have been more than seven years old. His eyes followed the girl down the stairs as she walked toward Tash. Tash smiled.

She looks like my own daughter when she was just a kid, Kamen thought. But then the blonde girl walked right past Tash and the woman stepped forward to embrace an equally small equally young brunette. The girl was as dark as her mother was fair and Kamen thought, *The old man must have had some powerful genes.*

It was too far away for him to hear, of course, but the little girl was jabbering excitedly at her mother, who had squatted down to hug her.

So now what? he asked himself. *So I just wanted to see her*, he answered himself. *Nice-looking kid. And at least Tash wasn't lying about having a kid.*

And hell, I killed myself for my kid, so who can blame Tash for handing me up a little bit for her kid?

The crowd in front of the school had thinned now and the guard waved the cars on in both directions. Omar leaned out of the cab and said, "Any plans, boss?"

"I'm going to walk awhile," Kamen said. "You go back and I'll see you at the apartment."

Omar looked across the street toward Tash and her daughter, obviously recognized the woman from the pre-

221

vious night, and nodded at Kamen with a grin. "You going to talk to her?" he asked.

"No. I just wanted to see her," Kamen said. "Go away."

Omar left, and on his own side of the street, Kamen followed Tash and the young girl as they walked back toward the corner. He stayed behind them, out of sight, until they vanished inside their apartment building.

He stood across the street, watching the building for a moment, then walked off quickly toward his own apartment, only about a mile away.

It was only on the fourth try over the period of an hour that Cowboy finally got an answer to the phone at Kamen's apartment.

"You had me worried," he complained.

"You worry too much and too easily," Kamen said. "Do you have our stuff?"

"Yes," Rostov said. "It's junk, but it could hold up under a brief inspection." He fingered the two wrapped packages on his desk.

"Why junk?" Kamen said.

"It's all I could get," Rostov said.

"All right. I don't intend to be dealing with it anyway. If everything goes the way it should, your men should confiscate it back when you arrive. You know, if you foul it up, I'm probably going to be shot."

"You can back out," Cowboy said.

"No. If I don't find something to keep me busy, I'll go crazy," Kamen said.

"Should I deliver the material to your apartment?"

"No," Kamen said. "I don't know if I'm being watched or not." He paused. "Let the lady deliver them."

"Olga?"

"Sure. I'll meet her for a drink at that gruel shop you call a restaurant. We'll make the switch there. Oh. And I need a small magnesium flare."

"What?"

"You know, something that throws out bright light and blinds everybody. Like a ship's flare gun. Have you got anything like that?"

Cowboy thought for a moment. "Yes. A small hand-held grenade. I can handle that. Why do you need it?"

"I don't know," Kamen said. "I just like to be prepared for anything."

Almost the instant he hung up the telephone, it rang again inside Rostov's office.

"Please hold on for Colonel Svoboda," a woman's voice said. Rostov recognized it as one of the old babushkas who worked at the director's office. *Now what does that homo want?* he wondered.

"Lieutenant Rostov, this is Colonel Svoboda," said the voice, almost seeming to drip oil.

"Yes, sir," Rostov said.

"If I hear from the general, how are things with our visiting expert, should he ask?"

Without hesitation, Rostov decided to lie. "Nothing yet to report, sir. He is still familiarizing himself with Moscow and I thought it best to let him get settled before putting him to work."

There was a moment's silence as Svoboda seemed to consider this. "Well, perhaps . . ." he said. "I hope he does not turn out to be just another useless and costly piece of unnecessary equipment."

"I think not, sir," Rostov said.

"Keep me informed."

"Yes, sir."

Svoboda hung up, and Rostov thought, *He never once*

mentioned my request for two kilos of drugs. Was that an
oversight or does he just not wish to deal with it?

Once, a long time ago, she had found children's bubble bath for sale in a store and she had bought three bottles. But they were long since gone and she had never found any more for sale, so Tash splashed a bar of soap back and forth through the warm bathwater, finally giving up after coating the top of the water with a sad-looking thin layer of bubbles.

She swept her naked young daughter, Rosa, up in her arms, hugged her and tickled her. The girl giggled as her mother carefully set her in the tub, then sat on the floor next to her and watched the young girl start to lather her body.

She hoped that she would hear from Pyotr Kamenski. He had seemed nice, he had promised to call, but it was probably just another misbegotten tavern romance.

She felt bad that she had told Sergei Tal the man's name. And then, right after she had gotten home, Tal had telephoned her and demanded everything she knew about Kamenski.

And she had told him. Everything she knew, which had not been much. It did not seem important to him, and after lying in bed, thinking for a while, she decided that Tal had already known. He had probably had their cab followed and called Tash just to see if she would tell him the truth. He was always testing people, as if he were afraid that somehow whatever it was he had could be brought down by untrustworthy people around him.

One did not refuse Sergei Tal. Especially in this city where decent jobs were hard to come by. And Tal, in truth, had not been the worst of employers.

When she had taken the job two years before, she

had known instinctively that part of her duties would be sleeping with the boss. She detested that part of it. And every time it happened, she came home as quickly as she could and soaked in the tub for an hour as if to wash the stain from her body and her spirit. But Tal paid her well, and he was understanding about her needing occasional time off from work, and at least he was not a brutal sodden drunk the way so many other Russian men were.

And maybe someday she would leave the job. *Certainly. The day pigs whistle.*

"What did you say, Mama?" her daughter asked.

"Nothing, honey. I was just mumbling to myself."

"You said pigs were whistling."

"Who ever heard of a pig who whistled?" Tash said, and reached under the tub water to tickle the little girl's belly.

Rosa giggled and Tasha thought, *No, dear. Pigs never get a chance to whistle.*

Cowboy looked around the room at the six civilian-clad officers who stood in front of his desk.

"Now, it's important," he said. "Anyone makes a mistake and he will be back to traffic duty. For the next forty-eight hours, I want all of you to be available to Sergeant Federenko at a moment's notice. If you're home, fine. If you go out, even to the corner store for a newpaper, leave word. He's got to be able to reach you immediately. Any questions?"

He scanned each of the six faces in turn. Georgi Golovin grinned. "I'll be at my usual post at The Pink Elephant," he said.

"And if you go anywhere else, let Sarge know."

"Big operation coming up?" one of the other men asked.

"Maybe yes, maybe no," Rostov said. "You'll all know about it when you know about it. Now get out of here. Sergeant, I want to talk to you."

As the men left the room, Rostov took the two re-wrapped packages of narcotics from a drawer and placed them on his desk. He and Federenko had carefully sprinkled the top of each package with the cocaine the sergeant had rounded up from other police squads, and in the top center of each block had carved out a little hollow and filled it with the cocaine. It would not stand close inspection, but it might fool anyone who just opened a package and dug a spoon into the top of one of the bricks.

Rostov closed the office door and said, "I'm sorry to confound any plans you may have had, but this might be important."

"Anything I should know about it?"

"It's not time to tell you yet," Rostov said.

The sergeant nodded and turned toward the door.

"One other thing," Rostov said.

"Yes, Cowboy."

"As you get time, start nosing around the property room. Find out who has access to the drugs that are stored down there."

"Officially?" the sergeant said.

Rostov shook his head. "As unofficially as possible."

"Just because of the bad drugs?"

Rostov shook his head. "Those two kilos I stole were marked as one hundred percent pure cocaine. And they were both one hundred percent pure milk sugar. Somebody stole the drugs."

Federenko grinned. "You mean, before you had a chance to steal them."

"Right. So see what you can find out."

The cafe near Kamen's apartment was again filled with late-afternoon drinkers. Apart from the language, it might have looked like any other five P.M bar anywhere in the world, except Kamen noticed that the men and women seemed to be wearing exactly the same clothing that they had the day earlier. He recognized a ghastly yellow polka-dot tie on a man with a blue pinstripe suit. And he recognized a pink-striped shirt, and two women's dresses were exactly the same. Maybe Russians had only enough American-imitation clothing to make up one outfit, he thought.

He was seated at a table in the far corner when Olga Lutska arrived, carrying a small leather bag that in New York might have held a model's makeup. She saw him and nodded as she walked back and sat at the table with him.

"Nice to see you again," he said. "A drink?"

"I think that sounds like a wonderful idea." She placed the bag on the floor between their seats.

Kamen waved to the waitress, who trudged over sullenly.

"The lady will have . . ." He looked to Olga, who said "Brandy."

He repeated that and pointed to his glass of wine. "And I'll have another of these."

The sour-faced waitress, the one he had first met there, snarled her understanding and walked away.

Kamen watched her leave and said to Olga, "Do you know that in the United States that woman would be fired her first night on the job?"

"Why?" Olga asked, with honest surprise.

"Because she is rude."

"She is a waitress," Olga explained.

"She chases people away from this establishment," Kamen said.

"Look around. It is almost full. She cannot be chasing away too many."

"In the United States, with polite waitresses, there would be a line around the block waiting to get in."

"I hate to wait in line," Olga said.

227

Kamen wondered if Olga had ever stood in line, like tens of thousands of Muscovites.

"How was your day?" he asked. Olga was wearing a light green business-cut suit, and Kamen thought that she was not really beautiful but there was an earthy cast to her face, full lips, heavily lidded eyes, prominent cheekbones, that made her look as sexy as hell.

"The same as all days," she said. "Trying to get degenerates off the streets."

'You know, you look very sexy."

Olga blushed and Kamen smiled. "I'm sorry," he said. "I'm used to being blunt."

"It's all right. It's . . ."

"I'm not making a pass at Cowboy's girl," Kamen said. "I just meant it as a compliment. Most prosecutors I've met in my life were men, homely, bald, and lisped."

Olga smiled at him. They stopped talking as their drinks returned, and as she sipped her drink, Kamen said, "You're a prosecutor. Is it allowed for you to hang out with a cop?"

'Everything is changed," Olga said. "In the old days, we were expected to consort with policemen because we did the same work. An arrest was political, the trial was political, and everything was cut and dried. But now, it is a different day and there is much more freedom. I don't think anyone cares anymore who I spend time with."

"Do you ever lose a case?" Kamen asked.

"Yes. Too damned many of them."

"Hooray for freedom," he said, smiling. "You ever lose any that Cowboy brought into court?"

"Just one," she said. "That was how I met him."

He touched his glass to hers in a toast. "Well, lucky for him," he said.

"And for me," she said. "He is quite a man."

"I'm glad you feel that way. I've never had many pleasant experiences with policemen."

228

"You were a criminal, were you not? That might make it difficult to have really deep relationships with policemen." She smiled at him slightly.

"I was involved in organized crime," he said. "But I was not really what you'd call a criminal. I was an accountant," he said.

"Oh, God," she said, and covered her mouth in mock horror. "The worst criminals of all. No wonder you had so much trouble with your American Gestapo."

"The FBI?"

"Yes. Aren't they all accountants too? They must have hated you as a traitor to your class."

"I never thought of that, but you might be right," Kamen said. "They used to be all lawyers and accountants. Now they are equal-opportunity morons. They didn't really care much for me."

"Lev is different," she said. "He likes you already. I can tell it."

"I know nothing about him. Does he have a family?"

"He was married once when he was much younger. But his wife died in a car crash. They had no children. He has been single since then."

"His parents must have found that difficult too. No grandchildren, I mean."

"His parents were already dead," she said. "His father was a colonel. A hero of Stalingrad."

Kamen resisted saying that he thought half of the adult population of Russia considered themselves heroes of Stalingrad. Instead, he just nodded.

They sipped their drinks and he said, "When did he decide to become a cowboy?"

"He must have seen too many Western movies," Olga said lightly.

"And his superiors don't complain about the jeans and the cowboy hats?"

"The important thing is results," she said. "He is

regarded as the best policeman in tbe country. Who would want to rein in that wild horse?''

The woman had a bad case of hero worship for Rostov, thought Kamen. But who knew? Some of it might even be true. If he had to go under, he would rather do it in the company of somebody who could at least try to get things done and who didn't worry too much about what the bureaucrats said. It was the thing that stifled efficiency everywhere—in police departments, he was sure, just as much as it used to in the mob. Everybody spent all their time watching out for their asses and no one had the nerve to make fast decisions.

Except him, he thought ruefully. He had always made fast decisions. And now here he was, officially dead, a man without a country, ready to get killed while trying to infiltrate some Russian drug mob. And what the hell for?

Because you had to get out of the United States to protect your family from Gesualdo Ciccolini. And because if you've got to be here anyway, you'd better do something or you'll die of boredom. Maybe that's how wars start. People just get tired of waiting around.

Olga finished her drink and Kamen gestured toward the glass.

She shook her head. "No, Pyotr. Thank you."

It still seemed odd to be called by his Russian name, even though he found now that he was thinking much more clearly in Russian than he had only twenty-four hours earlier.

She leaned forward. "The bag," she said.

"Take it with you," Kamen said. "When you step outside, a yellow cab will pick you up. The driver's name is Omar. Let him take you where you're going, and when you get out, leave the bag behind."

"With a cab driver? Are you serious?"

"This is a very special cab driver. Trust me," Kamen said.

She thought about it for a moment, then nodded, as if realizing it was indeed his show.

She stood and took the bag from the floor.

"Till next time," she said.

"Keep smiling," Kamen answered.

Chapter Nineteen

The rich boss certainly lived an interesting life, Omar thought as the trim red-haired woman slipped easily into the back seat of his cab.

He turned and smiled at her. The woman placed her traveling bag on the floor of the cab, then gave him an address down at the south end of the city.

A beauty. Again, a beauty, Omar thought. First the woman he had picked up at The Pink Elephant and whom he had gone today to see at school. And then this one.

He liked the looks of this one better. The one from the nightclub was Russian, soft, cuddly; but this one looked like an American, tall, elegant. The first was fire, but this one looked like ice, and Omar preferred ice because he liked to wonder how long it would take him to melt it.

If I had the money the rich boss has. If all these Russians are not careful, within weeks, within veritable weeks, he will have a hold on all their women.

He pulled quickly away from the restaurant and cut

recklessly across a line of traffic to make a left turn at the next corner. In his rearview mirror, he watched to see if his cab was being followed, but there was no car on the street behind him.

He made another quick turn into a side street.

"This isn't the way to my apartment," the redhead said.

"No, madam, I am sorry. I must have gotten confused. You will be home in a flash."

"Dammit, he got away," Viktor said. He pounded his hamlike hands on the dashboard of the car.

Yuri, the younger blonde man, was driving. "Better tell the boss," he said. As he leaned forward over the wheel in frustration, his shoulder muscles lumped up through the fabric of his pink silk shirt.

"Why should I tell him?" Viktor said.

"Because I talked to him the last time and he nearly bit my head off," Yuri said.

"You are a pansy. You will always be a pansy," Viktor said, and Yuri nodded, in total agreement.

From a curbside telephone, Viktor made a phone call.

"He met some woman and she left in a cab, but it got away from us," he said.

"Who was the woman?"

"We don't know. We're going back to watch the man again."

"You two are like a comedy team," the voice crackled back. "You'll lose Kamenski too." The phone went dead and Viktor looked at the instrument, resisting an impulse to crack it over his knee like a twig. With his luck, a policeman would pass by and he would be arrested for destroying public property. If Tal was angry now, that would put him over the brink.

He lumbered back to the car and Yuri drove back around the block and parked across the street from the restaurant. They arrived one minute too late to see Pyotr Kamenski come out of the restaurant, walk quickly to the corner, and pace away from the cafe.

Omar let the woman out of the cab, waving off her attempts to pay him, and saw her walk up the narrow steps to her apartment building. He glanced over the seat and saw the bag still on the floor.

He drove off, parked a few blocks away, and leaned back to lift the bag into the front seat next to him.

It was closed only with a zipper. *I should open it,* he thought. *After all, if the rich boss is doing something illegal, I should know about it. I can then protect myself. And raise my price.*

His hand reached for the bag.

Ahhh, but maybe the rich boss is in the armaments business. Perhaps this is a clever bomb designed to go off if someone opens the bag. Perhaps, Omar, you will not be so stupid as to do that.

Gingerly, he set the bag down on the floor in the front of the vehicle and drove back into traffic.

He picked up Kamen on a corner two blocks away from the restaurant.

Kamen hopped into the car and said, "Okay, let's go." As Omar sped off, the man asked, "See anybody following you?"

"I got into traffic quickly. I gave no one a chance to follow," Omar said.

"Good work. You got the bag?"

Omar picked it up and handed it back to Kamen.

"Drive out of this neighborhood," Kamen said. "Keep your eyes open. Then I'll tell you where to go."

He waited until Omar had driven off before he slowly opened the zipper atop the bag.

* * *

Colonel Alexei Svoboda was well aware of his reputation as a fussy nitpicking martinet, but he never let it bother him. He was, after all, General Budenko's top aide, which meant he was the second highest man in the militsia police. If he did not pay attention to details, who would? One could not run a national police department like a corner store, after all. Things had to be done right, things had to be accounted for, and if the job of assuring that fell to him, well, that was the way things were. No one was about to complain to General Budenko that his adjutant was a pest.

Svoboda told the secretaries that he was leaving early.

"Inspections, Colonel?" said one of the grim-faced ancient virgins who prowled the outer office.

"Exactly," he said, and was rewarded by one of the woman's rare smiles. *All those incompetents*, he thought, *are lucky that I conduct these inspections and not this vicious woman. She would have them in work camps for unshined shoes. They will never appreciate what I save them from*.

He walked from the office. The door closed behind him, and when it was securely closed, the old woman looked at the other two women in the office, then parodied spitting on the floor.

"Fairy," she snapped at no one in particular. The other two women smiled.

As Svoboda strolled from the building, he inspected his reflection in one of the glass entry doors. Satisfied that his gray gabardine dress uniform was immaculate and wrinkle-free, he walked into the pleasant warm afternoon, around the corner to the front entrance of the supply wing that housed the militsia's property room. It was called a property room, but it was, in truth, more like a vast warehouse of contraband and confiscated goods.

A lot of the goods were Western, seized by police from black-market merchants, and Svoboda remembered once running across a full case of men's silk bikini underwear,

235

the like of which he had never seen before. He had not been able to resist and a dozen of the garments had gone with him, inside his briefcase, back to his apartment. They had made several young men very happy and very appreciative. *It takes so little to make them happy sometimes.*

The night clerk on duty at the property room was lounging back in a chair, reading a magazine, when Svoboda entered. The young man, pimply-faced and thin, not Svoboda's type at all, snapped to attention as he saw the colonel approach.

With amusement, Svoboda noticed the man's frantic attempts to surreptitiously slid the magazine under a pile of paper on the desk.

"Colonel," the man said, standing stiffly at attention.

Svoboda nodded at him but did not tell him to stand at ease. He came to the young man's desk and pulled the magazine out from under the pile of papers. It was a pornographic publication in Swedish and Svoboda flipped through the pages. He found it all very revolting. It showed a group of young men and women involved in a long sequence of sexual gyrations. It was disgusting, he thought, even as he wondered how the producers of such pornography were always able to find young men who were endowed like stallions. Maybe there was one small family or tribe who shared those physical characteristics and maybe they starred in all the world's pornographic epics.

Cruelly, he let the young man stand at attention as he took his time leafing through the full-color pages of the publication. Then he tossed it back onto the desk and looked up. The young corporal was sweating and Svoboda finally relieved the tension by smiling and saying, "One of the fringe benefits of the job, Corporal. At ease."

When the young man relaxed, Svoboda said, "Keys, please," and the soldier scurried to the wall behind him and took a ring of keys from the wall and handed it to the colonel. It held twenty keys, each of them numbered to correspond with one of the large mesh-enclosed storage rooms that rimmed the walls of the room.

"Carry on," Svoboda said. He pointed to the magazine. "But please, no more of this trash during duty hours." He nodded, as if agreeing with himself, and walked away from the desk to the far corner of the room.

Lev Rostov was waiting for Olga when she let herself into her apartment. The television was on and he was sitting on the sofa, watching the early news.

He came forward and kissed her, then asked, "So, was your mission a success?"

She walked away, stripping off her jacket as she went. "I suppose so," she said. "I did what Kamenski said. I left the bag in a taxicab."

"You what?"

"I think he thought he was being followed. He had a cab waiting for me outside the restaurant. He told me to leave the bag there."

"Wonderful," Cowboy said sarcastically. "So now, we have some moronic cabdriver rolling around town with two kilos of cocaine."

As Olga poured herself a glass of fruit juice in the kitchen, she shook her head.

"No. Your Mr. Kamenski is very thorough, very organized. I am sure that bag is in his hands right at this moment."

"Let us hope," Rostov said.

"Dinner tonight?"

"I don't think so," Cowboy said. "I have to go back to my own apartment and wait for Kamenski's call. If it comes."

"Do you want company?" she asked.

He shook his head.

"I *want* company, but I don't think I should *have* company," he said. "I must be constantly alert, ready to fire out on a moment's notice."

"And I prevent you from doing that?" she said mockingly, peering at him over the rim of the glass.

"When I am with you, my underwear is always down around my ankles. I might lose precious seconds."

"I'll remember that the next time you *want* your underwear down around your ankles," she said.

"You are—what is that?"

"What?" she asked.

"I thought I heard a sound." He walked to the telephone and picked up the receiver. "A sound like a click."

"I heard nothing," she said.

Cowboy unscrewed the mouthpiece of the telephone and examined the innards. But it all seemed normal to him. He shrugged, reassembled the phone, and replaced the receiver. "Just more of Moscow's wonderful telephone service," he said.

"You were saying . . ."

"Hmmm? Oh, yes. I was saying you are a cruel and heartless woman to threaten me with your sex just because duty calls. On the other hand . . ."

"Yes?"

"I don't think I have to be at my home for at least another hour."

Olga laughed lightly, put down her juice glass, and beckoned him forward into the kitchen.

In the basement of Olga Lutska's apartment building, a man in a telephone company uniform carefully removed a large tape cassette from the sound recorder hidden behind the electrical panel board. It came out with a loud click as the electrical connection was temporarily broken. He replaced the tape with another, put the first cassette in his uniform pocket, and slid the recorder back out of sight.

Then, whistling, he left the building.

He got into a private car parked a block away, and placed the cassette into an envelope which he carefully sealed. Perhaps he would deliver the tape now, he thought.

No, he decided. He was not even scheduled to pick up the tape until tomorrow. It would wait, at least until after he had had a drink to celebrate the end of another glorious day of service to Mother Russia.

Omar waited in the cab near the Rytsarya railroad station and watched Kamen carry the leather bag off into a back alley that fringed a row of old tenement buildings.

He had stopped wondering what was in the bag. Whatever it was, Omar decided, it was not good for him. And if this crazy half-a-Russian with all the American money should be suddenly picked up by the police, Omar could honestly and very convincingly plead ignorance.

In his glove compartment he found a crushed half-empty pack of cigarettes that had been dropped in his cab by a passenger long forgotten. He lit one and waited.

Kamen found the broken spot in the stone wall, hidden behind the corrugated steel section of fence. He looked around to make sure no one was watching and that he was not in a direct sightline from any of the nearby tenements. When he was satisfied, he opened the leather bag and put the two butcher-paper-wrapped packages deep into the hole in the wall.

No one would find them there unless they were looking for them.

He closed up the bag and strolled quickly from the alley, walking briskly through the gathering twilight.

Omar saw him coming, and was surprised to see the bag still in his hand.

Kamen got in, dropped the bag onto the seat alongside him, and said, "Remember how to get to this place. Now back to my apartment."

"Am I to suspect that I am finished for the day?" Omar asked, as he started the motor.

"No," Kamen said. "This might be a long night."

Chapter Twenty

Cowboy was on the plastic-covered sofa in his small apartment, reading a copy of *Moscow Life*. The tabloid for a long time had carried the most insightful stories of all the press about the political turmoil inside his country, but lately it had seemed to be shifting its emphasis to flying saucers and Siamese twins connected by the soles of the feet, and Rostov, who used to like the publication because he thought it was important, now liked it just as much because he thought it was hilarious.

When the telephone rang, he tossed the periodical aside and snatched up the receiver.

"This is Kamenski. I'm going out."

"Is that wise?"

"I think so. I've hung around long enough for them to contact me. I think I should continue my regular life, let them see me around."

"Where are you going?"

"The Pink Elephant, naturally," Kamenski said.

"You're not bringing the stuff with you, are you?"

"Of course not," Kamen said.

"All right. I will wait to hear from you. Be careful."

"I always am," Kamen said.

Rostov hung up the telephone. It was ten-fifteen P.M. He wondered idly if having brought the American into this act was a good idea. Or would the man now known as Pyotr Kamenski eventually drag them all down into waters where none could swim?

Georgi Golovin saw the man in the American suit enter The Pink Elephant again and go, unaccompanied, to an empty booth in the back of the room.

Golovin was not surprised. The previous night, he had decided the man was up to something. Maybe tonight was the night it—whatever "it" was—would happen. And he would be ready.

Golovin saw Tash, the hostess, walk toward the table. *Maybe that's part of it*, he thought. *Maybe he has a thing for Tash*. He chuckled inwardly. *Good luck*, he thought to himself. *Many men have tried to get lucky with the Ice Maiden and I haven't seen one yet who succeeded*. He watched Tash and was surprised when she sat down in the booth, opposite the man. *Maybe this will be the lucky one*, he thought, then stopped paying attention when his date, a file clerk from the militsia's records bureau, started tickling the back of his wrist with her forefinger. When he looked up at her, she asked him to dance and, without waiting for an answer, rose and pulled him toward the small wooden floor. Golovin saw Tash still there, still talking.

"Nice to see you again," Tash said.

"Didn't you think I'd be back?" he asked.

Tash shrugged and smiled. "A lot of people wander through," she said.

"I'm not a wanderer," Kamen said.

They sat in awkward silence for a moment, and then Kamen said, "Did you go to school today to pick up your daughter?"

Tash looked surprised for a split second, then nodded. "Yes?"

"I thought so. I was driving by in a cab and I thought I saw you. Your daughter's tiny with dark hair?"

"Yes," Tash said.

"She's very beautiful."

"Thank you."

"It must run in the family," Kamen said, and Tash just averted her eyes, glancing down toward the tabletop, apparently unable to handle an honest compliment.

"Mr. Tal in tonight?" Kamen said suddenly, and Tash looked up sharply.

"Yes."

"I got a call from him last night," Kamen said.

"Oh, really?"

Kamen nodded and she said, "Well, I wouldn't know. I just work here. You know."

She looked at Kamen, but he had gotten what he wanted. When he mentioned Tal's call, a slightly guilty look had flashed momentarily across her face. She had spoken about him to Tal. And that was that. She was an enemy to be used, Kamenski realized.

"I should be working," she said. "Can I have someone bring you a drink?"

"Please," Kamen said. "A sweet wine on ice." She started to slide across the seat to leave the booth and he put his hand atop hers.

"Are you off any night this week?" he asked.

"Yes. Tomorrow night."

"I thought, perhaps we could have dinner?" He

gave the pretty blonde woman his warmest winning smile.

"I think I'd like that," she said carefully.

Golovin sat back at his table near the dance floor. He saw Tash leave Kamen's booth, but he could not tell, from the expression on their faces, what had happened, so he put it out of his mind.

His eyes kept sweeping around the room. Hanging out in a nightclub might sound like the best police duty in the world but the truth was that it was rather boring, doing the same thing night after night, always with different women whom he found basically unappealing, especially since they regularly drank too much and he had to make sure he never drank enough, just to prevent any eventual testimony from being impeached in court.

And he wanted very much to succeed in this job. Not just because it was his duty, but also because it would help the Cowboy. When the squad had first detected the changing patterns of drug sales—fewer pushers on the streets and even they were not carrying drugs but basically just taking orders for later delivery—Golovin had been excited. After all, didn't it show that the special squad was succeeding in its job of cutting down the flow of narcotics into Moscow? But Cowboy had not been pleased and Golovin had come to understand that Rostov thought it was just a signal of some single group moving in to take over the drug market and to impose new rules on it.

Maybe Cowboy worries about that, but I don't, Golovin thought. *If there's just one group, then it's us against them, and when we knock them out, the war is over . . . unless they win. But they can't win. We are the government.*

Still, he knew what his job was in The Pink Elephant. To try to catch any signs of major drug dealing, anything that might lead to some secret big boss who was running things. *I still am not sure any such boss exists but Cowboy says to be here and keep my eyes open, so I will be here, with my eyes open.*

He saw one man he had not seen in the club before walk to the men's room. A moment later, Yuri, the blonde bouncer, got up from his booth and walked toward the bathroom too. Golovin waited a few seconds, rose, excused himself from his date, and went into the bathroom himself.

The two men were not to be seen.

Then he heard noises coming from inside one of the two toilet stalls.

He walked slowly past it, as close to it as he could get without being obvious, and glanced through the crack alongside the door as he walked to a urinal.

Disgusting.

Two faggots, so far along in their own little world of perversion that they wouldn't have noticed him if he had started tapdancing. He had never trusted weightlifters or bodybuilders and it looked as if Sergei Tal's thugs were no exception to his rule. It was probably a good thing Rostov had told him not to go to that gymnasium today with the bouncers. He might have had to fight his way out.

He stood at the fixture for a moment, posing like a man urinating, then flushed it and walked back outside. Another false alarm.

That young blonde cop has either the worst bladder problem I've ever seen or he's very damned interested in what goes on in the men's room, Kamen thought as he watched Golovin go back to his table.

Tash worked her way carefully across the room, checking on the tables of regular customers, seating a few new arrivals, and eventually wound up at the stairs near the end of the bar.

Out of sight of Pyotr Kamenski, she walked quickly up the enclosed staircase, knocked lightly at Sergei Tal's door, and darted inside.

Tal rose and walked toward her. He was wearing a pinstriped suit that she thought looked gangsterish. His shaved-bald head glistened under the overhead lights while his jaw was faintly darkened with the shadow of stubble, despite shaving two times a day. Tal's body, she knew, was covered with hair, back, backs of his hands, backs of his legs . . . he was a mat of human hair and she had thought idly that he would have been a much better looking man if he had let the hair grow on his head and shaved it off the rest of his body.

"What's on your mind?"

He was standing before her now, and in a gesture that seemed only friendly, he put his big hands palm down on her shoulders. From her peripheral vision, she could see the dark hairs that sprung like wire from the backs of his fingers.

"That man who was here last night. Kamenski. He's back," she said.

"Alone?"

"Yes," she said. He was silent and she said, "I thought you'd want to know."

"Yes. Thank you."

"Do you mind if I ask—"

"Why I'm interested in him?" Tal finished her sentence. "No. I don't mind. I think he's a drug dealer and I think he might be thinking about using this place for his business. I just want to keep an eye on him."

"Oh," she said. Her tone must have said more than she had planned, because Tal smiled and asked, "Disappointed?"

"No," she said slowly. "It's just . . . well, he didn't seem the type."

"You never can tell," Tal said. "Look. Let's face it. You and I both know some people come in here to do little private drug deals and there just isn't anything much I can do to stop it. Not without ruining my business. But I'll be damned if I'm going to let the place turn into some kind of narcotics supermarket." He waited for a reaction and then said, "Keep an eye on him if you would. See if he meets anybody or anybody talks to him. And I'll have the boys see what they can find."

The boys. Tash knew that was Tal's name for his two gorillas, the two homosexual thugs who hung around the place just to run errands and throw out troublemakers. Kamenski had run into them last night, his first time in the place, and she thought she might tell him again— even if Tal might be upset—to watch himself around those two.

She nodded, and slipped out from under Tal's hands, which were still on her shoulders, and backed toward the door.

"I will keep an eye on him," she said.

Tal looked as if he wanted to say more, but then simply nodded and went back to his desk.

An hour and two drinks later, the two bodybuilders slid into the booth with Kamen. One got on his side, the other faced him.

"Well, well, Tweedledum and Tweedledee."

"Twiddledom, twiddledee?" Viktor, who was facing him, said.

"Forget it. What is on your mind?"

"We have business to do."

"The men's room is over there," Kamen said.

"It is business, not kaka." The man grinned, showing a mouth of snaggled teeth, separated by wide spaces. Yuri, to Kamen's right, laughed and pounded his own big fist on the table for emphasis.

"What kind of business?"

"You are selling. We are buying."

Kamen decided not to make it easy for them. "I don't know what you're talking about," he said.

"Listen. We know about you. You have material. We have cash. Now we go get it."

"My secretary makes all my appointments," Kamen said. He hunkered down over his drink and saw the blonde one bring his hand up onto the table. Hidden inside the big mitt was a small automatic, barely visible under his enormous hand.

"We'll forget your secretary this time," Yuri said. "We'll just go and get the material."

"Not until I see the money," Kamen said.

"That is reasonable," Yuri said, winking.

This is like a cartoon, Kamen thought. *These guys must think they're auditioning for "Godfather Part IV." The only thing they haven't done yet is make me an offer I can't refuse.*

Kamen paused as if pondering. Yuri put away his pistol and brought up a small attaché case he had on the floor next to his feet. He opened the case briefly and Kamenski was able to peer inside and see neat stacks of American hundred-dollar bills.

"Now the goods."

"You don't think I have them here, do you?"

"Where?"

"We will drive to them."

"All right. Our car is in front."

Kamen smiled and said, "So is mine. Two cars. You follow me."

The two men looked at each other for a moment, then Viktor nodded.

"That is acceptable," he said. "We leave now."

"We leave in five minutes after I go to the bathroom," Kamen said.

He pushed his way past the other man sitting next to him and strode quickly to the men's room.

As he entered, he saw Golovin get up from his table and start back toward that corner of the room.

Hurry up, Kamen thought. *Before these two morons wake up.* He waited just inside the door, and when the door opened again and the blonde walked inside, Kamen pushed the door shut behind him and leaned on it.

The young man looked startled.

Kamen said, "Listen, I don't have much time. You work for Cowboy?"

Startled, the man did not respond immediately.

"Dammit, you work for Cowboy?"

The man hesitated, then nodded.

"Call him now, immediately, at home. My name is Kamenski. Tell him you spoke to me. Tell him to have his men at the Rytsarya railroad station by midnight. You understand? Dammit, you understand?"

The blond man nodded.

"Quick, get over there."

He pushed the younger man toward a urinal, turned to the sink, splashed water on his hands, grabbed a paper towel, and dried his hands as he turned toward the door.

"Who . . . ?" Golovin started.

"Quiet," Kamen said.

The door pushed open and the two bouncers walked inside. Kamen tossed the paper towel into a garbage pail and raised a finger to his lips, ordering silence, as he nodded toward the blonde man standing at the urinal.

"Shall we go?" he said.

The two men nodded sullenly and followed Kamen out of the men's room.

The door closed. Golovin looked at his wristwatch. Eleven-twenty. His mind was spinning.

What the hell is going on? Who is this Kamenski that he knows about Cowboy?

He walked from the men's room in time to see the two burly men following Kamenski out the front door of the nightclub.

From his cab parked across the street, Omar saw the two men exit the club with Kamenski. It looked to him as if they were herding him along.

Trouble, he thought. For a moment, he considered driving away. *Leave the crazy rich boss alone with his problems.*

No. That would not do. Omar had honor. His entire family had honor. Until his father was hanged for stealing goats, he had had honor. Could Omar be anything less?

He started the cab's engine, then made a U-turn across the wide street and eased up in front of the club.

If I have to, I can still run for it, he thought.

When Tash came back to the bar from her service rounds, Kamenski's booth was empty and there was a fifty-ruble note on the table. She had not seen him leave, but she did not have time to think about it because the young man who had become such a regular in the last month was standing next to his table, reaching into his pocket for his wallet.

He was very finicky, always wanting a receipt, always counting his change, never leaving a tip.

She started toward him, but he simply pulled a note from his wallet, tossed it on the table, and walked quickly to the exit. The girl he had been with followed him slowly, as if reluctantly.

"Where to, boss?" Omar asked.

Kamen was twisted around in the back seat of the cab, as if watching Tal's two men wheel around in their

250

automobile to follow him. Actually, he was looking to see if the blonde cop had come out of the club. But he saw no sign of him.

He glanced at his watch. Eleven-twenty-five.

"We're going back to that railroad station," he said. "But I don't want to get there until five minutes after twelve."

"You know we're being followed."

"Yes."

"You want me to lose them?" Omar asked.

"No. They're going with us. Drive around, but don't make it look like we're going in circles. Five minutes after twelve at the station. That's the key."

"Cowboy, this is Golovin," the young policeman snapped into the pay phone near The Pink Elephant. His spurned date for the evening was across the street, huffily hailing a taxicab for herself.

"What is it?"

"I don't know. You know somebody named Kamenski?"

"Yes. What the hell is it?" Rostov snapped.

"He was in The Pink Elephant. He said to tell you to be near the Rytsarya railway station by midnight. What's going on?"

"Where are you?"

"On the corner by the nightclub."

"Wait there," Cowboy said. "We'll pick you up."

Cowboy pressed the receiver button, then called the sergeant's home phone number. It rang five, ten times, and the operator came back on the line and said, "No one answers there."

"Let the damned thing ring and get the hell off this line," Cowboy snapped.

Then the phone was answered.

"Sorry, Cowboy. I was in the bathroom."

"Get all the men you can. We meet in fifteen minutes by The Pink Elephant. Unmarked car."

"What do you think?" Yuri asked as he drove slowly behind Omar's taxi.

"I think they're driving around in circles."

"So do I. What should we do?"

"Keep following them. They have to stop someplace eventually."

"I don't like how any of this smells," Yuri said.

"Neither do I. But maybe he's just real careful."

"Who the hell is Kamenski?" the blonde policeman asked.

Cowboy tore away from the curb in his small Zil sedan. Behind him, Federenko and the four other squad members followed in another vehicle.

"Kamenski is someone who's working undercover for us," Cowboy said through gritted teeth. "What I want you to do now is to forget you ever heard that name."

Golovin was silent.

"You understand?" Rostov asked.

"Yes, Cowboy." He hesitated. "But I feel like a fool."

"Why?"

"Because I've been staking out The Pink Elephant for almost a month and then someone comes in over my head. Am I trusted or not? It doesn't sound like it."

His feelings were hurt, Cowboy realized, and he bit back his impulse to snap a hard answer at the officer.

"Think of it this way, Georgi. If you hadn't been on the job and if you hadn't been a good cop, prepared to make an instant difficult decision, that inside man would probably be dead by now."

He looked over at the younger man, then slapped him gruffly on the back. When the man looked up, Rostov grinned.

"Still think you're unimportant?"

He could almost sense the young officer swelling in confidence.

"Thanks, Cowboy," he said.

"Boss?"

"Yes?"

"Imagine that I told you I must stop to urinate. What would be your response to such a thing?"

"I would shoot you in the back of the head from point-blank range."

"Just asking," Omar said.

"I think we ought to call this all off," Yuri said.

"No. Let's just keep following him," Viktor responded.

"I think we're wasting our time."

"Probably. But let's wait and see."

At The Pink Elephant, Sergei Tal looked through the one-way glass at the nightclub floor below with a sense of satisfaction.

The place was filled, just as it was filled seven nights a week. All in all, not too bad for someone who had literally been raised in a gutter. Now, The Pink Elephant was a must-stop for almost all tourists in Moscow, and he had hosted ambassadors, diplomats, even a member of one of Europe's royal families, even though she had been a conceited little bitch who had tried to convince him to empty all the tables around her. As if she might touch a commoner and be contaminated.

He had politely declined. She had pouted and he had smiled and walked away. So she stayed and he gave orders to the bartender to put something special in her drinks. The bartender had, and after fifteen minutes, the little tramp was squirming around on the dance floor, skirt up around her neck, grinding like a two-ruble whore.

She had been with three fag pretty boys and when she was done acting like a tramp for the night, she had insisted upon coming upstairs to thank Sergei.

He had let her in the office and let the little fairies wait outside. It was obvious what she wanted, and for a moment, Sergei toyed with the idea of pulling down her panties and screwing her standing up, leaning over his desk, so that she could feel him inside her while she looked through the one-way window at the people still dancing downstairs.

Many women found that exciting. Why believe that a princess of royal blood would be different?

To hell with it, he had decided. That was one of the charms of running a nightclub. There was never a short-age of willing women, and so he had just perched on the edge of his desk, let the little tramp lean against him suggestively, and kiss his ear, and he put his hands behind her and pinched one of the cheeks of her ass. Hard. Hard enough for her to cry out.

"What'd you do that for?" she asked in English.

"Just to tell you that we don't like your kind here. Our regular customers are afraid of catching something from you so we'd be very happy if you took your trade else-where."

She looked at him, dumbfounded, then wheeled and left his office angrily, rubbing her butt.

He let her hear him laugh as she exited.

A princess. So what? He was Sergei Tal and he needed

no one. His place was always full and, even after taxes and payoffs and salaries, he was wealthy.

And that did not even take into account the sources of his real wealth.

He wondered where the two stupids were.

Chapter Twenty-one

There was no way to ignore midnight in Moscow. All over the city, bells in hundreds of the gold-domed churches sounded the hour, and to Kamen, listening through the open window of Omar's cab, the sound seemed to be coming from all directions at once. The ringing was all done by hand and so each of the bells had its own idea of precisely midnight and they sounded one after another, all over the city, carpet-bombing Moscow with sound.

When the very last peal died out, Kamen checked his watch. It was three minutes after twelve and he told Omar to pull up to the curb a block away from the Rytsarya train station and stop there.

The black car, driven by the two bodyguards, stopped directly behind them.

He felt his jacket pocket just to reassure himself that the small flare grenade was still there. He could feel his cheap automatic pistol pressing into the small of his back while he sat in the cab.

"Omar, you see those shacks up ahead to the right?"

"Yes."

"There's an alley that runs behind them. I want you to drive around the block and park on the other end of that alley. Keep your motor running and wait for me."

Omar turned in his seat and grinned. "If I hear shooting, should I still wait?"

"Would you?"

"Of course I would. You are the only maniac in the city who will pay me so much money for sleeping in my cab."

"Remind me to give you a raise," Kamen said. He got out of the taxi and Omar drove immediately away.

Viktor and Yuri approached him. Viktor was carrying the attaché case.

"Is this it?" he asked.

Kamen nodded.

"You drove us all around Moscow to get here."

"I drove all around Moscow to make sure we weren't being followed. Did anybody follow you?"

"What do you take us for? Amateurs?"

"Maybe you are. I don't know anything about you two."

"All you have to know is what's in this briefcase."

Kamen nodded. "Come with me," he said.

A few moments later, the three men walked past the massive main building of the train station.

Peering through a second-floor window, Lt. Lev Rostov saw them. Georgi Golovin, standing next to him, said, "That's him. That's Kamenski."

Rostov said, "I told you. Forget you ever heard that name."

He watched as the three men veered off across a broad plaza in the direction of a street of old tenements.

He depressed the button of the walkie-talkie in his hand

and said softly, "We've got them in sight. Georgi and I are coming down. Don't move until I get there."

"Got it, Cowboy," the sergeant's voice crackled back.

Youngblood looked at Cowboy and wondered why he was wearing sunglasses at midnight.

Kamen led the two men down the alleyway toward the ramshackle street behind. When he came to the passageway between the shacks, he glanced at the men and beyond them, but saw no one. *I hope the Cowboy knows what he's doing*, he thought.

"Okay, let's see the money," he said.

"You've seen it."

"I saw a couple of dollars on top. Let's open the case."

The two men looked at each other and the smaller one nodded. "All right," he said.

Viktor held the case on his arms, like a waiter balancing a tray, and the smaller man opened it.

Kamen came up and lit a cigarette lighter, as a signal in case Rostov had somehow missed him. He held the lighter over the open briefcase and thumbed through the stacks of hundreds.

He stretched it out as long as he could until Yuri growled, "All right, all right. It's all there."

"I guess so," Kamen said.

"Now where's the stuff?"

Viktor snapped the briefcase closed and held it again at his side.

"Right here," Kamen said. He moved into the alleyway between the shanties and pulled the two packages of drugs from the hollow inside the wall behind the corrugated steel panel.

Thank God this is Russia, he thought. *In New York, the drugs would be gone and probably the wall too.*

He turned and handed them to Yuri, who started to open one of the butcher-paper-wrapped packages.

He opened it just enough to touch a finger to it, sniffed it, then pressed the finger against his tongue.

"Looks good," he said to Viktor.

Behind them, in the direction of the train station, Kamen saw movement.

"Police. Hold it right there." Cowboy's voice barked loud in the chilly night air.

Next to him, one of his policemen slid his gun from inside his shoulder holster and Cowboy slapped his hand. "Put that away," he said.

"Police. We've been set up," Yuri snapped.

"Dammit," Kamen growled. He grabbed the two packages of cocaine up in his left arm. His right hand went into his pocket and fingered the magnesium flare.

"We surrender," he yelled. Softly, he said to the two men, "Move toward that alley. Run when I give the signal."

They stood still in their confusion and he pushed his way between them and the police.

"Here. You can have everything," he yelled back toward the policemen. He could tell by the shadows that there were at least six of them.

Slowly, so as not to draw a nervous policeman's fire, he pulled his right hand from his pocket, pressed the switch atop the magnesium flare and rolled it across the ground toward the policemen.

The area was instantly lit as if it were an athletic field during a night game. The flare sizzled; small tendrils of smoke leaked up. It was a small flare but it did its job. Anybody on the other side of it, trying to look at Kamen and the other two men, would have seen only the garish bright light of the flare's fire. Except, of course, for Rostov wearing dark glasses.

Kamen tossed the two packages of drugs toward the flare. They hit the ground and rolled forward toward the fire. He grabbed the two bouncers by the arm.

"They're blind. Follow me," he said.

Running down the alley, he could hear the pounding of the two men's footsteps behind him.

It was only fifty yards before they were on the next street.

Kamen saw Omar's cab at the curb, its motor idling.

He pulled open the back door for the two men, and himself jumped into the front.

The two Russians got in and closed the door behind them. The big one still held the briefcase with money.

"Get out of here," Kamen told Omar.

Then he reached behind him for his gun, turned in the front seat, and aimed the small automatic at the two men sitting behind him.

"I bet you two think you're real cute, don't you?" he said.

"They're gone, Cowboy. They must have gotten down this alley."

"Don't worry about it," Rostov said. "We've got the drugs." He pushed the sunglasses up on his head, then put the two packages of drugs in a plastic sack he took from his pocket. He noticed the sergeant staring at them and he caught the man's gaze and winked, as if sharing a silent secret. The sergeant nodded imperceptibly.

"Time to go home," Rostov said. "I want to thank all you men for your work tonight. You can return home. I'll handle the reports on this."

The men nodded.

Rostov said, "Sergeant Federenko, ride back with me and Georgi. I want to talk to you."

* * *

"What do you mean?" Viktor said, looking nervously at the small automatic in Kamen's hand.

"What I mean is, did you really think you were going to swindle me using some phony policemen?"

"Phony cops? What are you talking about?"

"Nobody knew where I had put that stash. And I didn't call any police, and somehow I don't think even you two are stupid enough to call the police about a drug deal. So how it breaks down is this: You have some friends follow your car and then, when we get to the spot, they come up and make believe they're cops and you try to rip me off. How stupid do you think I am?"

"We didn't . . ."

"Honestly. We swear it . . ."

Kamen stared at them a long time before slowly lowering the gun. "All right, relax. I don't know why but I believe you . . . at least for now. And I'm out two kilos of pure uncut cocaine." He saw Viktor tighten his arms around the attaché case of money and shook his head. "Stop worrying. The deal wasn't made. The money is still yours." He turned his head slightly but kept his eyes on the two men in the back seat. "Anybody following us, Omar?"

"No."

"Stop here. Let these two out."

"This is the heart of nowhere," Yuri protested.

"Just get out before I change my mind about the money," Kamen said.

"You two are the only two who will know," Cowboy said, turning in the passenger's seat to look at Golovin in the back. Federenko, who was driving, grunted and said, "The drugs are that stuff we phonied up today?"

Rostov nodded. "That's right. Georgi knows this because he bumped into him, but we're trying to place a man on the inside of the drug mob. His name's Kamenski."

"Local militsia?" the sergeant asked, and Rostov knew his feelings would be hurt if this Kamenski turned out to be just another cop, selected over one of Rostov's own men for the undercover work.

"No," Rostov said. "He's not even a Russian. We're using him to pose as a big-time drug dealer from out of the country. Anyway, that's all you have to know."

"If we gave him these drug packages to sell, why did we bust in on the sale?" Golovin asked.

"Because the drugs weren't any good. Just a fake . . . mostly milk powder and a little cocaine. If we had actually let him sell them, we'd have him dead as soon as somebody tested the shipment. So we tried it this way instead."

"Hope it works," the sergeant said.

"No more than I do," Rostov answered, and slumped down in the seat. "Anyway, no one is to know about this Kamenski. No one."

The other two policemen nodded.

"I am afraid, rich boss, that this will be where we sadly part company," Omar said.

"What are you talking about?" Kamen asked.

"Police, fleeing, a satchel filled with money, two kilograms of cocaine, this is all narcotics business and I will have nothing to do with it," Omar said.

"You hate narcotics so?"

"Yes," Omar said flatly. "With all my soul."

"But you made that appointment for me at The Pink Elephant with your drug-dealing friend," Kamen pointed out.

"Yes. And there we were talking about some small recreational drug use. I disapprove but I understand. Now we are talking about a major sale of major quantities of narcotics. The two are very different. I am sorry but that is the way it is."

"Will you listen to me and not ask any questions?" Kamen asked.

"I will hear you out," Omar replied solemnly.

"Two things. One. No matter what you think, no matter what tonight might have looked like, we are not doing anything illegal with narcotics. You have my word on that. Two. Tomorrow I will raise your salary."

Omar stared out the windshield of the car for a few long seconds, then turned back to Kamen with a broad smile on his face. "Where to, rich boss?"

Nightclub crowds in Moscow must break up earlier than in the United States, Kamen thought as he reentered The Pink Elephant. It was barely one A.M., but most of the crowd that had ringed the dance floor had left. Just three tables were still occupied and only a half-dozen people were seated at the bar.

He paused inside the doorway, looking around for Tash, but he did not see her. He walked toward the bar. The bartender was at the other end, talking to a young woman, and Kamen slipped past the bar and walked up the flight of steps to Sergei Tal's office.

He tapped on the door.

After a moment, a voice close to the door said, "Who is it?"

"My name is Kamenski."

He heard the lock being fumbled with and then the door partly opened. Sergei Tal stood inside, jacket off, shirt open almost to the waist. His sleeves were rolled up and a black-banded watch seemed overgrown by his furry forearm.

"Oh, yes," he said. "We met the other night. What can I do for you? I'm sorry I don't invite you in but I'm busy right now."

"You'll hear it from your men, but there was some trouble tonight. I just want you to know that I will no longer deal with those two morons you have working for you."

He turned to walk away and Tal said, "Wait. What are you talking about?"

He had opened the door more and now Kamen could see part of the office, including the mirror window in the front. In a faint reflection in the office light, he saw a woman sitting on the sofa in Tal's office. She seemed to have a sheet wrapped around her body and the blonde woman looked like Tash. He felt cold in the pit of his stomach.

"What are you talking about?" Tal repeated.

"Your men will tell you what I'm talking about, what happened tonight." He had only feigned anger when he first knocked on the door, but now he felt real anger from someplace deep inside him and he knew it was because of Tash in Tal's office.

What did you expect? That she was Mother Teresa? he asked himself.

He walked down the steps, back to the bar. It was only when he reached the bottom that he heard the door close behind him.

Now we'll see what we see.

Outside on the street, he got back into Omar's cab.

"Take me home," he said, but a few blocks later, he had the driver stop at an outdoor telephone.

He asked the operator to connect him with Rostov's apartment. There was no answer, a fact in which the operator seemed to take almost personal pride.

Kamenski gave her another number.

"Whose number is that?"

"It is the number of Olga Lutska, assistant prosecutor of the Moscow District, and if you have any sense, woman, you will connect this call and disconnect your mouth."

The call immediately went through. The phone rang almost a half-dozen times before Olga answered.

"Hello," she said. The sleep was obvious in her voice.

"This is Pyotr Kamenski. I have just tried to reach Cowboy but I was not able to. If you hear from him, tell him I am all right and I will contact him tomorrow."

"Is that the whole message?"

"Yes."

"Good night," Olga said.

Chapter Twenty-two

The story was on page one of *Pravda*, written in that curiously dry style that all Russian newspapers seemed to affect.

"Moscow militsia early this morning foiled a major sale of narcotics which was to have taken place at Rytsarya Railway Station.

"The three dealers were able to make their escape and police are searching for them. Officials said, however, that they were able to recover two kilograms of high-grade cocaine.

"Lt. Lev Rostov of the militsia said that police were alerted to the illegal activity by an anonymous telephone caller."

The news was delivered to many apartments in Moscow by the *dezhurnayas* of the building, the old concierges among whose jobs it was to distribute to VIPs copies of the early morning newspapers.

Colonel Alexei Svoboda read the story while drinking tea at the white wrought-iron table in the fabric-walled dining alcove of his apartment. He wore a white satin dressing gown and smoked a cigarette in a long ivory holder.

Two kilos. That is certainly a wonderful haul, he thought. He picked up the elaborate French-style telephone on the table and called Rostov's home phone number, but there was no answer.

He called Rostov's office, but Cowboy was not there either.

"No, sir. He left only a little while ago."

"Who is this?"

"Officer Golovin," a young voice said.

Svoboda remembered the boy, a nice-looking blonde lad, and he softened his rather imperious tone.

"Have Lieutenant Rostov call me in the office as soon as you hear from him, if you would, please," Svoboda said.

"Yes, sir."

General Budenko had gotten back early from his out-of-town inspection trip, and in his spacious apartment near the center of Moscow, he also read the news as he was served breakfast coffee by the young maid he had hired after it became apparent that his wife was never going to leave the hospital.

The young woman's name was Natalia and she had the broad Asian face of a Mongol, but she was well-formed and pretty in a savage way, and she regularly made it abundantly clear that she would have no moral problems about sharing General Budenko's bed if he asked.

267

He had never asked, and the young woman, who had grown up in a culture where women were meant to be taken, became at first disappointed and then almost surly in her manner. Budenko hardly noticed. He had many other things on his mind.

He read the story about the aborted drug arrest with interest. *Is this a product of Cowboy Rostov's American expert?* he wondered. *If it is, Rostov should have told me about it beforehand.*

He made a mental note to talk more often with Rostov so that he knew exactly what the wild men of his narcotics bureau were up to.

Leonid Nabokov read the story too. The newspaper had been delivered to the attorney's door at six-forty-five A.M., along with a package wrapped in dark brown paper. It had been left, the old woman reported, by a man at four A.M. who had quite noisily awakened her.

"He had been drinking, sir," she said, sniffing her eloquent nose as if she could still smell the man's breath.

Nabokov shooed the woman away, took his coffee and newspaper and package into the study. His young wife, Danielle, was still asleep, never having gotten over the late-rising habit she had developed when working as a model in Paris. Nabokov opened the package first and inside found an audio tape cassette. There was no note with it, but none was necessary. He knew where it had come from.

He put the tape onto a player, put earphones into his ears so that no one else could hear the tape, and read the paper as the tape played.

The two stimuli—the words on the newspaper page and the dialogue coming over the tape recording—battled for attention inside his head.

But the news story was brief. He read it, put the newspaper aside, and sipped his coffee as he listened to Lieutenant Rostov and the assistant prosecutor, Olga Lutska.

Most of the tape could not be heard clearly, but Nabokov could make out enough of the words to understand that the pair of them were in the woman's bedroom, making love. *Do these two do anything but rut?* he wondered.

He continued to listen, and finally, as clearly as if they were in the room with him, he heard the two of them speaking.

Rostov: "My American expert arrives tomorrow."

Lutska: "And what will follow?"

Rostov: "Perhaps finally we will make some inroads into this narcotics gang."

Nabokov bit his lip.

Why was I not told?

He tried to control his anger as he lifted his desk telephone and asked for a number.

Sergei Tal had not seen the newspaper. His attempt to bed Tash last night at work had been thwarted by the arrival of Pyotr Kamenski, and somehow after that, neither he nor the woman seemed able to recapture the mood. So now he was in bed with the young married woman who lived in the next apartment—her husband was an inspector of heavy equipment who traveled a lot, and when he was out of town, the sheets of her own bed got very little wear. They had both just awakened when the telephone rang.

"Yes," he said.

"This is your attorney. I have to see you."

"When?" Tal asked.

"As soon as possible. And do nothing until we talk," Nabokov ordered.

Tal felt the young woman's hand circle his penis.

269

"Well, hardly anything," he said, even as the lawyer hung up.

The new tenant certainly slept late, the *dezhurnaya* thought as she squatted outside Kamen's apartment, her ear to the door, pretending to refold the newspaper she had put there hours before. Almost everyone else in the building had already left for work and this one wasn't even stirring, at least not so far as she could hear.

And the copy of the morning paper that she had left in front of his door was still there, unopened, unread.

A criminal. Criminals keep these kinds of hours, she thought. *If he is not a criminal, why does he always have that taxicab waiting for him across the street?*

Olga Lutska had just opened the paper and scanned the headlines when there was a knock on her door.

Pulling her silken robe tighter around her body, she opened the door and saw Rostov in the hallway.

"Tea?" he said.

"Come in. God, you look terrible."

"Long busy night," he said. He kissed her once they were inside the apartment, and she wanted to press against him, but the kiss was as perfunctory as an everyday ritual and Rostov was already walking to the breakfast table.

When the man says tea, he means tea, I guess, she thought.

She was annoyed when Rostov took the paper from in front of her spot and was looking at it as she sat down. He smiled and grunted, mostly to himself, and then handed her the newspaper, pointing to the story on the drug raid.

"So this is what Kamenski was doing," she said, after scanning the story. "Did everything go all right?"

"I think so. I talked to Kamenski on the telephone before. At least he's alive."

"If he wants to remain alive, tell him not to call here in the middle of the night. He jolted me out of bed just to tell you he was all right."

"My apologies, madam," Rostov said. "Police work is sometimes not tidy. At any rate, he was able to escape with the other drug dealers. That is something."

"Surely you have enough information now to make an arrest?" Olga said.

Rostov shook his head. "Probably, we could arrest two underlings. That will not do. Nothing but infiltration in the mob. That is our goal."

"And then what?" Olga asked. Her robe slipped open, revealing the tops of her breasts, and while she knew it, she made no effort to pull the robe tight.

"And then we'll see," Cowboy said noncommittally. He eyed her breasts and rolled his eyes in a comic leer. Despite her pique with him, she laughed and closed up her robe.

"You're not telling me anything. 'And then we'll see.' See what?"

"If our suspicion is right and Tal and The Pink Elephant are involved in this drug operation, then perhaps Kamenski can get close. If he does, maybe we can close the Mafia down."

"Maybe," she said, and her voice sounded more mocking than she had wanted it to.

Rostov shrugged. "I'm open to suggestions," he said. "About work or anything else."

"Sorry, Cowboy. If you're going to be out all night, you can't come around here and expect me to be just waiting for you. I'm going to work. There are criminals to try."

* * *

271

Someone was outside his door. Unable to sleep since he had been awakened by Rostov's phone call, Kamen lay in the small bed, hearing a faint stirring, convinced he could even hear the breathing, a light asthmatic wheeze.

Wearing only his undershorts, he took his automatic from his holster and walked quietly, on bare feet, toward the door. He held the gun in his left hand. With his right hand, he held the deadbolt knob. Then he spun open the lock, grabbed the doorknob, and pulled the door open.

He jumped into the opening, leveling the gun into the hallway.

The old concierge was squatting on the floor outside the door. She looked up in shock, and then wailed, the sound of a professional sufferer attempting to scream. She rose to her feet and ran down the hall, and Kamen did not know whether it was the gun in his hands or the fact that he was wearing only underclothes that had frightened her so.

He saw the newspaper she had left behind and carried it inside.

Rostov sat stiffly in Colonel Svoboda's office, waiting for the man to enter. He came in, at last, through a side door. Even from across the room, Cowboy could smell his aftershave lotion. *Or maybe it's perfume*, he thought.

Svoboda was, as always, immaculate in pressed gray gabardines; his thinning hair was immaculately combed and slicked back, his pencil mustache without so much as an antic hair out of place.

He should have been an actor, Cowboy thought. *He could have made a living playing the assistant manager of a department store.*

Svoboda sat behind his desk and picked up a copy of *Pravda*. He jabbed angrily at the drug story with his hairless index finger.

"This one of your operations?" he asked.

"Yes, sir," Rostov said.

"I thought we had agreed that you would let me know everything that is going on," Svoboda said.

"I'm sorry, sir, but there just wasn't time. Kamenski . . . Kamen . . . only called at the last minute to tell me what was happening. And then it was very late."

"Lieutenant, in the future, I don't really care how late it is. I want to know what you are doing. What this American 'expert' of yours is doing. You must answer to me because I must answer to General Budenko. Understood?"

"Yes, sir. Understood."

"Now, this cocaine that you seized. Where is it?"

Please don't ask where it came from, Cowboy thought, certain now that if he had to he would lie about stealing it from the police property room and then finding out that somehow simple lactose had been substituted for the narcotics.

"Sergeant Federenko is taking it this morning to the police property room," Rostov said.

Svoboda nodded. "Very good," he said. "That's a serious amount of drugs."

"Yes, sir."

"Is it of high quality?" *Dammit, something's going on here that I don't understand*, Rostov thought. *Why is he so interested in the drugs we seized?*

"I'm not really sure, Colonel," Rostov said. "We haven't had time yet to have it analyzed. It didn't seem like a high-priority item, especially since we did not have a suspect to charge in the case."

"Yes, too bad about that," Svoboda said. "It would have been a good arrest. But you're right to put it in the property room."

What is this all about? Rostov thought.

"Now, what did Kamenski have to do with this episode?" Svoboda asked.

Careful, Cowboy, careful. "Somehow, he got in-

273

volved with these drug dealers and was along, I think, as an expert to testify on its purity.'' With a sinking feeling, Rostov realized that he had just turned a very large corner. He had flat-out lied to Svoboda, and if his lie was uncovered, Rostov could be out on his ear. Certainly, he would be tossed off the drug squad.

A voice inside him asked, *Why didn't you just tell him the truth?* and another voice answered the question: *Sometimes, you just have to trust your instincts, and my instincts say there is something wrong with the good Colonel Svoboda.*

Sergeant Federenko walked into the militsia storage compound with the two kilos of phony cocaine wrapped in a supermarket plastic bag.

He recognized Sergeant Navratsky. Navratsky was a veteran cop who had worked on the streets for fifteen years after getting out of training. And then a broken hip suffered in a fall while chasing a young hoodlum had immobilized him and wound up getting him the job in the property room.

Most cops would have loved the soft job, but Navratsky loved the streets. He hated desk work and Federenko had never heard him when he wasn't grumbling about it.

Navratsky was in a back room, putting on a civilian jacket, when Federenko arrived.

"Hey, you old cripple. Get over here. This is important police work."

Navratsky looked up quickly, then grinned when he saw Federenko. "How can it be important if you're involved in it?" he groused. "What do you want?"

"I have to squirrel away some drugs," Federenko said. "We real policemen seized them last night in a drug raid."

"Yes, I read the story in the paper. You let them all get away. Incompetent as ever," Navratsky said. He came out of the back room and started to look in his desk, coming out with a thick stack of multicolored forms in his hand.

"If you're going home," Federenko said, "I can come back later."

"No, I'd better do it now before I get a tractor running over my ass. The brass likes everything done to the letter." He looked around suspiciously. "And then that fag is always around over here. God help me should he find something out of place."

"Colonel Svoboda?"

Navratsky nodded. He started to fill in the lines on the form. There seemed to be room for fifty different entries on the page.

"Well, I'll make it up to you. Let's finish this up and I'll buy you a drink."

"You're not working?" Navratsky asked.

"Most of the night. Even sergeants get some time off to sleep."

"Or to drink," Navratsky said slyly.

"There's *always* time to drink," Federenko said, and the two men hunkered over the paper, filling out the seven copies of the necessary storage forms.

"I'm not really delighted about what you've done," Rostov said. He was in Kamen's apartment building, having entered through a rear door and walked up a back flight of stairs.

Kamen was sprawled out on the sofa, in a pair of slacks and a long-sleeved blue shirt open at the collar.

He shrugged. "What's the problem? We didn't lose any of the drugs. Your people wound up looking good and just maybe I might have an entry point into the mob. When they realized how I risked everything to save them and their money."

"And maybe they'll think it was very odd that you

were carrying a flare. And maybe they'll get the idea that you tipped us off yourself, as indeed you did. And maybe they won't touch you with Raskalnikov's dick.''

Kamen watched as Rostov lit another of those weird Russian cigarettes that was almost all tube with only an inch of tobacco at the end and the American finally said, ''Let's talk, Rostov. There's something on your mind and you'll feel better if you just tell me.''

This damned American can read minds, Rostov thought.

He took a long drag on the cigarette and blew out a plume of sour-smelling smoke. ''Very well,'' he said. ''I've told you how we have had a great deal of success in cutting off the flow of drugs into Moscow.''

Kamen nodded. ''And yet there is still an ample supply of drugs,'' Rostov said.

''It happens,'' Kamen said. ''Drugs are small; they're easy to smuggle.''

Rostov shook his head. ''No. I think not, not this time. I think that somebody has been stealing drugs from the militsia property division.''

''Are we talking a lot or a little?'' Kamen asked.

''I think we're talking a great deal,'' Rostov said.

The American smiled. ''And you think that someone in your department is providing the mob with drugs?''

''I shudder to think that,'' Rostov said, ''but it is a conclusion that I am slowly reaching.''

''Then somebody in your department is on the Mafia's payroll,'' Kamen said.

''It doesn't seem possible, but it might be,'' Rostov admitted.

''Don't feel bad. It may singe your Russian heart, but where there's a lot of money to be made, you'll always find crooks. And, yes, some of them wear uniforms. Do you have an idea who it might be?''

''Not yet, but my men are working on it,'' Rostov said. ''In the meantime, I have lied to my superiors about last night's operation. I said that you were involved only as an observer. I didn't mention that you and I had planned the whole thing."

"Was that wise?" Kamen asked.

"No. It was highly stupid."

"A man has to trust his instincts sometimes," Kamen said, and Rostov realized, *This man thinks just as I do*.

"There's another problem," Rostov said.

"I know," Kamen said. "If you have a high-level leak in your department, the bad guys are going to know I'm working with you."

"Exactly," Rostov said. "I do not like the responsibility of exposing you to unnecessary danger. If you choose to drop out of this mission, I will understand."

Kamen shrugged. "Nobody lives forever," he said.

The telephone rang and Kamen answered it. He winked at Rostov and said over the phone, "That will be fine," and then hung up.

"Sergei Tal," he explained to the policeman. "He wants to meet with me today."

Rostov sighed. "You asked me for a gun the other day. Maybe I should get you one."

"Don't bother. I already have one," Kamen said.

Tal replaced the receiver and looked across his desk at Leonid Nabokov.

"He will meet with me today," Tal said.

"Fine. And you know what to do."

Chapter Twenty-three

In the daytime, The Pink Elephant was closed, and Omar let Kamen off in a parking lot behind the building and the American walked up two exterior flights of steps. He looked back and saw Omar sitting in the cab, waiting for him, then tried the doorknob.

As promised, the door was unlocked and he stepped inside into a darkened hallway. As soon as the door closed, he sensed that he was not alone, but before he could react, the two musclemen who worked for Tal were standing in front of him. They had obviously been waiting in the hall to intercept him.

"What do you want?" Kamen snapped.

"Just checking for weapons," Viktor responded, grinning at Kamen with big yellow teeth. "Part of our routine, so don't worry."

Quickly, Yuri patted him down, and as Kamen expected, the blonde bodyguard missed the small gun that Kamen had stuck inside his undershorts.

Didn't you guys ever go to the movies? Kamen wondered. *Nobody around here knows how to do anything.*

"Okay, you're clean," the big one said. "Mr. Tal is waiting for you."

And if he counted on you two, I could put a bullet in his head, Kamen thought. *Just like he wants to put one in mine.*

"Another drink for my friend here," Sergeant Federenko said. He waved to the bartender in the seedy small tavern only a few blocks from the police property room.

"When did we become such good friends?" the other sergeant asked suspiciously.

"Aaaah, you just forget. We have always been comrades in misery," Federenko said.

"That's true enough," Navratsky replied. He watched carefully as the bartender poured precisely three ounces of vodka into a dirty-looking water glass. No ice, no chaser, no mixer . . . none of those things were requested much in a Russian workingman's saloon.

He clinked glasses with Federenko, who was nursing his drink. Navratsky was through work until after midnight, but Federenko had to be back in the office in a little while longer and he wanted to get there sober.

"So they're busting your chops too?" Federenko asked.

"When I got injured and took this job in the property room, I thought I would be able to hide out there. But you can never hide. Old Brass Balls himself comes down every couple of weeks to pick up drugs for the incinerator. And that little faggot assistant of his . . ."

Federenko just nodded at this reference to Colonel Svoboda.

". . . he is there all the time."

"What does he do to annoy you so?" Federenko asked.
The man shrugged. "Takes all my keys and then looks

into every room as if he expected me to be stealing evidence and taking it home.''

"You can't really blame him, I guess," Federenko said. "I mean, just the drugs alone would make a man rich if he had an inclination to steal."

"Steal? How the hell can you steal when that little ass-licker is always hanging around the drug room, counting bags and making sure that everything is the way it was. I couldn't steal enough to put in my nose."

"And he's not the only one, I guess," Federenko said.

"What do you mean?"

"You must have all kinds of officers . . ." He sneered as he pronounced the word. ". . . officers coming in to check up on you."

"I never thought of it, but no. Only the colonel, but he comes around all hours of the day and night and you can't even get any rest. I can barely nip a little drink now and then. You look at the sign-in sheet and he is always on it."

Federenko nodded. "And he always goes into the narcotics room?"

It was too much. Federenko knew it, even before he asked the question, but he had to try. The other policeman looked at him suspiciously and said, "You are asking many questions about our dear colonel."

Federenko tried to wash away the suspicion with a quip. "I'm bucking for his job," he said. "I want to know how he does it."

"How he does it is take off his pants, bend over, and grab his ankles. Are you ready for that?"

"Maybe that's it," Federenko said. "Maybe he's not interested in the contents of the drug room. Maybe he is in love with you. Did you ever think of that?"

"Disgusting. Even my wife sounds better than that."

"I wouldn't go that far."

* * *

Sergei Tal waved Kamen to a chair in front of his big steel desk. Kamen sat, and without asking, Tal served tea in two short glasses, filled from a steel pot on a small hotplate in a corner of the room.

"So, Kamenski, I guess we have a lot to talk about," he said. "First of all, I'm sorry for that search out in the hall, but, well, you know how it is . . . I really don't know anything about you."

"I would have done the same thing," Kamen said.

As he sipped at his tea, his eyes scanned the office. There was the leather couch on which he had seen Tash disrobed last night. The rest of the large room seemed filled with file cabinets. On a large table against the far wall were stacked what seemed to be a few weeks' copies of newspapers, but there were no paintings on the walls, not even a girlie calendar, and on Tal's desk were no photographs of wife or child or parent.

"My men admitted that without you, they would have been arrested last night," Tal said.

"I should have thrown them to the cops."

"Ah, yes, the militsia. One wonders how they happened to be there last night."

"That's easy," Kamen said. "Somebody tipped them off."

"But who? Was there anyone who knew of your plans?"

"No one. I never tell anyone."

"The cabdriver who was with you. Perhaps he has a large mouth."

"Perhaps he does. But he knew nothing about where I was going or what I was doing," Kamen said. "Not him."

Tal shrugged elaborately and Kamen thought, *This dumb son of a bitch thinks he's toying with me.*

"The press this morning said it was an anonymous telephone tip. Maybe it was. Or maybe the militsia was just in the area and stumbled upon you."

"Yeah. And maybe the Tooth Fairy whispered in their ear," Kamen said.

"I beg your pardon?"

"Forget it. What do you want with me?"

"Are you always this belligerent?" Tal asked.

"Usually, until I know what's going on."

"Fine. I will tell you. Until last night, I thought that you were perhaps some kind of undercover policeman."

"And now you don't?"

"Apprehending my two men would have been a worthwhile thing for a policeman to do. Instead you saved them. Yes, I think you are not a policeman."

"That much, at least, is correct. I am not a policeman," Kamen said, and thought, *I am just a liar while you are a major-league fool.*

"Then, I think we should have business to discuss. You can produce goods for sale?"

"Let's stop going in circles. 'Goods for sale.' I can provide high-quality heroin and cocaine. I have no supply problem. If the price is right, I can do it. Do you want drugs?"

"One always needs supply."

"You're doing it again," Kamen said. "Talk plain to me."

Tal seemed to consider Kamen's request as he sipped at his tea. "Yes," he said. "We need narcotics. At least for the short term until we make other long-term arrangements."

"You say 'we.' Who is we?"

"I'm sorry. I mean only myself. It's just a business habit. I have no partners."

"How long will it be before you make these other long-term arrangements?" Kamen asked.

"Several months, I suspect. In the meantime, well, I can handle whatever you can provide."

"At the agreed-upon price?"

"Yes," Tal said.

"I don't want to deal anymore with those two apes of yours."

"You won't have to. You deal only with me," Tal said.

"That's fine. Tell me, do you work only in Moscow?"

"Why do you ask?"

"It occurs to me that Russia is only one country. If you work only here, there are the rest of the independent nations for me to look to in the future."

"A grand idea. We have Moscow. You have the rest and with blessings."

"With or without them," Kamen said.

"But you may find that outside of Moscow, the rest is Siberia," Tal said.

"Even Siberians just want to have fun," Kamen said. "So what do we do now?"

"You make arrangements with your suppliers. Let's say for two to four kilograms. Let me know when you have it and we will consummate the contract."

"Fine," Kamen said, standing up. "I will be in touch."

Tal nodded and smiled. "This could be the start of something wonderful for us."

"I'm sure it will," Kamen said.

Sergeant Federenko came into Rostov's office and closed the door tightly behind him.

"It must be serious," Rostov said.

"Maybe serious, maybe not," Federenko said, "but certainly interesting."

Without waiting for an invitation, he pulled the small chair from the side of Cowboy's desk, turned it around, and straddled it, facing Rostov.

"Do you know who spends a lot of time in the property room? Your brave Colonel Svoboda."

"So? It's part of the job."

"Regularly inspecting the stores of narcotics? Is that part of his job too?"

Rostov leaned forward, his eyes narrowed. "He does that?"

Federenko nodded. "I found out from one of my comrades there. Every couple of days he comes in. He pretends to look around the entire place, but he always winds up in the narcotics locker. He does something, then leaves in a hurry."

Cowboy thought for a long moment, then shook his head. "No, it's not possible."

"Yes, it is."

"Svoboda couldn't be stealing narcotics from under the department's nose."

"I think he is," Federenko said. "Are you interested in proving it?"

"Of course."

"How?"

Cowboy thought a moment, then smiled. "I've got an idea," he said.

Were the judges like these in the United States? Or anywhere else in the world?

Olga Lutska wondered, as she sat in the first bench of the courtroom, waiting to go through the formalities of listening to a guilty plea from a small-time street thief who had grabbed a pocketbook and then been hunted down and beaten senseless by a group of neighbors.

He belongs in jail just for his stupidity if for nothing else, she thought. *Trying to grab a purse in broad daylight on a Saturday when all the factory workers are sitting around on their porches.*

So all she wanted to do was to accept the guilty plea on behalf of the state and get out of there, but this judge— the youngest on the Moscow criminal court—had decided to send a message to society in the form of an endless sermon to the young thief. *Maybe this will end street crime in Moscow*, she thought. *Make a record of this judge blabbering and play it to everyone who is thinking of committing a crime. That would make the devil himself go straight.*

She felt somebody slide into the seat alongside her but looked up only when the person nudged her shoulder. It was her coworker, Anatoly Nabokov, and he grinned conspiratorially and whispered, "Another eternal speech?"

She nodded.

"Well, at least it gives you time to think about your love life."

Which is exactly none of your business, she thought. He was just crude. Maybe there was something to the theory that outstanding men were doomed to have mostly moronic sons. Certainly, this one—apart from the diploma that said he was a lawyer—bore no resemblance to his dynamic, intelligent father who was the scourge of the court system. She said nothing.

"How is the Cowboy, anyway?" Nabokov asked.

"Ask him," she hissed.

"We travel in different circles. But I hear he's got himself a live one."

A live one what? She forced herself to turn and look at Nabokov, but still managed to hold her tongue.

"But I guess you know all about that," he said.

She had no choice. "What are you talking about?" she asked.

"Too complicated for here," he said. "You free for a drink? Or at least not too expensive?" He smirked at his own sad little attempt at a joke.

Again she was silent, and taking her silence for agreement, he said, "Four-thirty. At the usual place."

Before she could protest, he rose and left the courtroom, and as she watched him go, she thought, *Might as well find out what that imbecile is talking about.*

"And are you having a good day, rich boss?" Omar's voice had all the willing-to-please inflections of a man who knew he was going to get a raise.

"Excellent," Kamen said, and hunkered back in the rear seat of the cab. *Sure. I just meet somebody who says he's going to make me his partner in the drug business and he thinks I'm so dumb that I don't know he's going to try to kill me. At least in America, they kiss you on both cheeks and then you know you're dead. If Sergei Tal is the Mafia in Russia, then the Mafia's fallen on bad times. And Tash? Is she involved too? When the time comes, will she be ready to kill me, like just another of Tal's henchmen?*

Unbidden, the image of the pretty blonde, sitting on Tal's sofa, clothes disheveled, pushed into his memory. He spat an imaginary shred of tobacco from his mouth.

"Where shall we go?" Omar asked as he moved easily into a broad boulevard that circled around the high Kremlin walls.

Kamen looked at his wristwatch. "Let's drive by that school again," he said.

Rostov said into the telephone, "I just wanted to report that our men have turned the seized narcotics into the property room." He listened and said, "Thank you, Colonel Svoboda."

When he hung up, he looked across his desk at Sergeant Federenko.

"Can your man be counted on to keep his mouth shut?"

"Glue in his mouth. Count on it."

"Good. Then we just wait," Rostov said.

* * *

Tash was waiting in front of the school when Omar's cab pulled up across the street. Kamen sat in the back, looking at the woman through the window for a few long seconds, then opened the curbside door.

"Wait for me," he said. "But if I wave you away, then I'll meet you tonight outside my place. Eight P.M."

"I will be happy for the chance, however brief, to renew acquaintances with my wife," Omar said.

"How many children do you have?"

"Seven."

"You sound like you're very well acquainted already," Kamen said.

Tash's heart quickened when she saw Kamen cross the narrow street and approach her, and she wondered why he produced such a reaction in her. It was not that he was tall, dark, and handsome, because he was short, blonde, and ordinary. And moving into middle age.

Working in a job such as hers, there was never a shortage of eligible young men with more money than was good for them who tried to pick her up. If romance— even plain sex—had been a goal, the selection was very large and very good at The Pink Elephant. But sex was not much on her mind anymore. She slept with Tal when she was ordered to, but the passionate fire had gone out of her life with her husband's death. He had not been much of a husband and even less a father, but he had been a sexual acrobat and that had been, at least temporarily, a saving charm.

When he died, she was morose for several months, nagged by a woman's eternal fear that she was old, her life was over, no one would ever look at her "that way" again.

For two months, she worked to disprove that belief. She slept with almost everybody who asked her. Friends, neighbors, people who had known her husband. And then one night, just after a married man had sneaked from her bed, thinking that she was asleep, and skulked out the door to return to his wife, she understood that it was all unnecessary. She did not miss her husband at all. She had not ever really cared for him. And so she did not need any fervent sexual coupling to prove that she could still attract another man just like he was. Those kinds of men could be found in any tavern in Moscow. She changed the locks on her door and got a friend who worked for the state to get her telephone number changed.

Soon after, she found the job at The Pink Elephant, a good job that paid good money and that attracted enough tourists even to make some money in tips, since Russians themselves never tipped. And every kopek she made that she did not need for living expenses went into the education fund for Rosa. Because Rosa would be somebody.

She had thrown her life so much into her daughter's future that she thought she had gotten over men, needing them, wanting them, even liking them.

And then this one had come along. Pyotr Kamenski, and who was he? She had been in Sergei's office the previous night and Kamenski had come to the door. She hadn't heard the conversation but it was obvious they were having sharp words. And then Kamenski had left, and when she had tried to get Tal to talk about it, he had simply brushed aside her questions.

But something had upset him, because he never came back to the sofa with her. Instead, he looked at her and said, "We're not really in the mood for this, are we?"

She shook her head and he said, not in an unkindly fashion, "Get your clothes on and go home."

For that she was grateful to Kamenski, but gratitude did not explain the strong feeling she had toward him. She thought that maybe it was a premonition. Her old grandmother had told her always to believe her premonitions, and with this Kamenski, she had the feeling, the vision, that here was the man who would change her life.

* * *

Sergei Tal had been thinking of Kamenski too. He had been ordered to kill him, but you couldn't just shoot somebody during a meeting in a nightclub office. Suppose he had someone waiting for him; suppose that damned Cowboy knew where Kamenski had gone.

No. Pyotr Kamenski would die—and soon—but in such a way that no blame would attach itself to Tal. It was always easy for people giving orders to demand this and demand that, but they shared none of the risks. He would do it his own way. In the meantime, let the poor fool think that Tal really wanted to do business with him.

She had thought it would never end. The judge had pontificated and lectured and orated, but finally he had run out of fuel and had accepted the guilty plea and, running only two hours late, Olga had returned to the office that, because of her seniority, she shared with only one other assistant prosecutor.

She pulled out the stack of file folders on her desk, started to look through them, then snapped them closed and pushed them away.

To hell with it. Tomorrow comes soon enough.

For a moment she considered ignoring Anatoly Nabokov's invitation and just going home. Then she thought it would be rude. Then she thought that rudeness was just what Nabokov deserved. Finally she decided that all the conflicting viewpoints were correct. She decided to walk to the small restaurant by herself. It was the nicest time of year in Moscow. The air was cool and crisp and there was always some kind of breeze to wash away the smoke and pollution that turned the air over the city gray. And maybe, for the very first time in the two years she had known him, Nabokov might have something interesting to say.

He had never expected that there would be a neighborhood like this in Moscow. As Kamen walked with Tash along Arbat Street, almost within sight of the Kremlin walls, the first thought that came to his mind was "old Greenwich Village."

The warm weather had brought the street people out, and Arbat Street was filled now with jugglers and street magicians. Traffic was closed off and the entire street was a vast pedestrian mall with people wandering down the center of the block.

On one corner, a poet stood on a wooden box declaiming, in rhyme, the rapidly approaching end of the world. Rosa ran ahead of them and stood in rapt attention staring at a peddler who was selling King Kong masks and naturally was wearing one himself.

In front of a stationery store to their right, a long-haired young blonde woman was strumming a guitar, singing American folk songs. Her guitar case was open on the sidewalk to catch any spare coins that might come her way.

And for the first time, Kamen realized, he saw people in Moscow smiling. It was sunny, it was warm, the air for a change was clean and the crowds that packed the street—both old and young—seemed happy.

"This is wonderful," Kamen told Tash. "It's like . . . like Soho."

"So-Ho?" she repeated.

"A place I saw once in America," he said, and added quickly, "Don't say no. Rosa has to have that monkey mask."

"Oh, no. It is much too expensive," Tash said.

"Look at her," Kamen said. "How can you say no?"

Rosa had not moved from the spot, just staring at the peddler.

"Well . . ."

"Good," Kamen said, and walked forward to buy the mask. When the salesman asked for twenty rubles, Kamen nodded and reached into his pocket for a roll of bills. Suddenly, Tash was at his side.

"Thief," she snapped. "We will pay no more than ten."

The peddler looked surprised for a moment, then smiled. "Fifteen," he said. "And that's exactly what it cost me." He looked at Kamen. "Only because your daughter is so pretty," he told him.

Tash started to speak again and Kamen put his hand over her mouth. "For that compliment," he told the peddler, "take the twenty." Then he pulled Tash away before she had another chance to complain.

"You are a wild spendthrift," she said finally.

"Slow down and smell the roses," Kamen answered.

Rosa, holding her mask in her arms like a trophy, said "I don't smell roses; I smell candy."

"Well, we'd better find where that smell comes from before it is all gone," Kamen said.

"You will spoil her," Tash lectured him.

"And it will be my pleasure to do so for as long as you let me," Kamen said.

They glanced at each other. Their eyes locked for a long moment and Tash finally turned away and said, "Now that you've promised, we must find that candy stand."

Once inside the restaurant, Olga sat at a booth in a far corner and ordered herself a scotch and soda. Nabokov came into the place only five minutes later, went directly to the bar, got himself an ale and brought it back to the table.

This man just has no class, Olga thought. *He bought himself a drink at the bar so that he would not have to buy me one also. Maybe Daddy cut off his allowance.*

She looked carefully at Nabokov. Naturally, he would order ale, his idea of a very British drink. It was part of the new persona he had lately begun to create for himself. He had begun dressing like an Englishman, even to wearing a hat and carrying an umbrella, and his office garb now had grown very tweedy with patches on elbows and regimental ties and button-down shirts. She wanted to tell him that he still looked like a cretin. She thought it would be unkind. She thought it was well deserved. She decided to do nothing.

Do nothing. That's what I always do, she thought. *Nothing*.

"So what about Lieutenant Rostov?" Olga asked. Nabokov sipped at the frothy beer, then wiped the foam from his mouth with the back of his hand.

"Always business," he said. "Why can't you relax for a few minutes? You're like a woman constantly rushing to catch a train."

"Anatoly. It's been a long frustrating day. Why do you want to make it more frustrating?"

"I'm not. I want you to enjoy your drink. I want you to have another. I want you to calm down."

Biting her lip and resisting the impulse to crash the metal napkin holder onto his shiny, balding, silly-looking head, she said, "I am calm. Now what about Lieutenant Rostov?"

"All right," he said. "Nothing, really."

"Nothing? Really? And that's why I'm here?"

"It's just . . . well, I've heard that Rostov is in some trouble."

"What kind of trouble?" Olga asked.

Young Nabokov looked away as if to deflect her question, but when he again met her eyes, she was staring coldly at him.

"What kind of trouble?" she repeated.

"There are all kinds of trouble, you know," he said in an offhand manner.

Olga began to put her cigarettes and her wallet into her purse. When he looked at her quizically, she said, "You don't know a damned thing about Lieutenant Rostov, do you? This was just another one of your stupid attempts to get me to go out with you."

"And is that so bad?" he asked. "Or do you only like policemen?"

"I might like anyone who is not a frivolous gossiping fool," Olga said. She snapped her bag closed, but before she could stand, Nabokov put a hand on her wrist.

"He is in trouble, you know."

"And how would *you* know that?" she demanded coldly, knowing as she did that she had just challenged his honor. If this little fool knew anything, he would say it now.

"I heard someone speaking. . . ."

"Someone?"

"Yes. And he was talking about Rostov being removed from the drug squad for incompetence."

"Who? And who was he talking to?"

"I can't say. It was on the telephone." Nabokov now was almost cringing. He had lost control of the conversation and the meeting, and the only way to appear less wormlike to Olga Lutska would be to tell her the truth—and that he could not do.

"So you can't tell me who was talking or who he was talking to?"

"No."

"Good-bye, Anatoly."

"I think this is the best day of Rosa's life," Tash said.

"I hope so," Kamen said. The two adults were sitting at a curbside table, under an umbrella, sipping Russian coffee while Rosa sat on the pavement with two dozen other children, watching a Punch and Judy puppet show.

The Judy puppet grabbed a sword behind the tiny stage,

293

raised it over her head, and brought it down on Punch. Punch's head flew off his body and all the children in the street gasped in surprise.

First Judy strutted in victory and then compassion came over her. She picked up Punch's head and knelt down over his body. She tried to replace his head. She began to cry and beg Punch to come back to life, and then, to a cry of delight from the watching children, Punch leaped to his feet, his head back in place, kissed Judy, and, with their clinch, the curtain abruptly dropped.

The children applauded and Rosa ran back to her mother and Kamen.

"Did you like the show?" Tash asked.

"Oh yes, but I was afraid Punch had died." She looked at Kamen as if to see if he had been worried too.

He smiled at her. "Some puppets die harder than others," he said.

"And some children avoid homework much too long," Tash said in a stern voice. "Time to go home, child. Will you come for dinner, Pyotr?"

"Yes," he said.

"We do not have much in the house."

"Let's stop at a store."

"There is nothing in most of the stores," Tash said.

"I've heard that there are some stores that are always stocked."

"And they charge ten times what the others store charges. Their prices are sinful."

"Well, tonight, let us sin a bit," Kamen said. He took Rosa's hand—the other clenched the King Kong mask fiercely, as if someone were trying to steal it from her— and the three walked off Arbat Street the few blocks toward Tash's apartment.

Chapter Twenty-four

Sergeant Federenko waited behind the door in the closed hallway washroom.

It should be any minute now, he thought. He certainly hoped so. If he was discovered by one of the building's custodial workers, what was he going to tell them when they asked why he was hiding in the closet?

Oh, I was just peeing in the sink. Somehow that lacked the ring of authenticity and if they *did* believe it, then they would be sure that he was just too drunk to find a men's room. And on duty hours yet. And on to Siberia.

He heard the clicking of heels coming back down the concrete slab floor. Metal cleats on his heels. That would be Colonel Svoboda, the little fop.

He stayed in the closet until the footsteps had stopped sounding, then stepped out into the corridor. There was no one in either direction, so he turned and walked quickly down the hallway to the property room. He did not know who was working there now, but it would not be important.

From his accordioned jacket pocket, he took a flashlight with a purplish-looking lens. He leaned over the storeroom door, shielding the doorknob from the glare of the overhead light with his own shadow, and shone the flashlight onto the knob.

"Damn," he said aloud. *Nothing. There is nothing.*

He squatted down and shone the light again on the underside of the knob. *No. Nothing there.*

Sergeant Federenko stood up and looked around, but the long corridor was still empty. His face was masked with confusion. Then . . .

Of course, you imbecile. Inside. He didn't touch the outside knob when he was leaving.

He opened the door to the property room. The clerk across the big warehouse floor looked up at him from the magazine he was reading in his lap. Without acknowledging him, Federenko shone the purple-lensed flashlight on the doorknob. In eerie powdery texture, it glowed yellow, showing the imprint of someone's palm and fingers.

"Hey! What's going on?"

Federenko glanced up at the clerk briefly. "Routine maintenance," he called back. "Oiling the locks."

"Oh." The clerk, faced with the feeling that whatever it was, it was not likely to get him into trouble, nodded and went back to reading his magazine.

Federenko went back into the hallway and let the door swing shut behind him. He stepped off down the corridor almost at a run.

They were sitting in Tash's apartment. Rosa was watching a videotape of *The Little Mermaid*, the Disney film. But the tape—Tash explained she had gotten it as a gift from one of the visitors to The Pink Elephant— was in English, and while Rosa was fascinated by the beautiful graphics and animation of the film, she didn't understand a word of it.

So Kamen sat alongside the girl and began to deliver the dialogue in Russian, changing his voice for each character. Rosa giggled whenever he played the part of evil Ursula. And she started to roll on the floor laughing, when the film changed to one of its big musical numbers and Kamen got up from the sofa and began to dance around the apartment, translating the song and singing it in Russian.

He saw Tash watching him from the kitchen doorway, stopped, and grinned sheepishly.

"Don't stop," she said. "We hardly ever have entertainment for dinner. And dinner will be soon by the way."

Kamen sat back on the couch next to Rosa, and without taking her eyes from the TV screen, she put both her hands around his left hand.

"Pyotr, are you my friend?"

"Yes," he said, wondering why his voice almost caught in his throat, then remembering that he used to sit this way, watching television, with his own daughter when she was young.

"Then I love you," she said, and squeezed his hand.

"I love you too," he said. *But don't go complicating my life. Not you or your mother.*

"I have to talk to you." Olga Lutska's voice crackled over the telephone.

Cowboy said, "What is it?"

"I can't talk over the telephone. It's important."

"I'm sorry, Olga," Rostov said. "But it'll have to wait. Something important has come up here."

"Well, don't take yourself away from anything important for me," she snapped, and hung up the phone.

Now what the hell is on her mind? Cowboy wondered.

297

He had no time to think because the telephone rang again. This time it was Sergeant Federenko.

Omar did not like the looks of it. It was almost ten o'clock and he had been waiting across the street from Kamen's apartment for over two hours. He did not know which apartment was the rich boss's so he could not see if there were any lights on.

But he was being paid and paid well and he waited.

And now, those two muscle boys from last night were coming down the street toward the building.

It surprised him to see them. He did not think that Pyotr Kamenski would ever have them for guests. It certainly didn't seem as if he had any use for them.

Before reaching the building, though, the two men suddenly darted off the sidewalk into some shrubbery.

They were going around the back of the building. And there was only one reason for doing that. They did not want to be seen.

Generations of elders telling him to mind his own business now gave Omar pause. What should he do?

He thought about it for a long time by his standards, almost thirty seconds, and then got out of the cab and walked toward the front door of the apartment building. Through the glass of the door, he could see the old *dezhurnaya* seated at a table. She was either dozing or reading somethiing she had on her lap.

He almost turned and walked away, but could not. Instead he went inside. The elderly woman looked up when she heard the door open, and at the sight of him, her mouth pursed in displeasure. Omar wanted to ask her if she had an apartment to rent to him and his eight cousins and their families.

But he took off his cap and shuffled his feet in front of her table and said instead, "Mr. Kamenski asked me to pick him up. Is he home?"

"No. He has not come in."

"Are you sure?"

"I have been here since noon. I saw him leave. I did not see him return. He is not here."

"Thank you very much," Omar said.

"Are you going to keep waiting?" she called after him.

"I don't know," Omar said. He was satisfied and he had tried to do his job, to take the extra step, do the extra good deed. Kamenski was probably out. Good enough. Those weightlifting imbeciles would find an empty apartment if they were able to get inside. And later, Omar would tell Kamenski about their visit.

He walked across the street to his cab, but as he opened the passenger door to get inside, he felt his arms grabbed from behind in a pair of powerful hands. When he looked up, he saw the younger, blonde muscle man in front of him, grinning.

Trouble, Omar. Never volunteer to do anybody a favor. The words from childhood came back to him now.

Cowboy looked at the sergeant. "You're absolutely sure?" he asked.

Federenko nodded. They were in Rostov's office at headquarters. The room was lit only by an overhead fluorescent light that had been blinking defectively for the last six months. "He came out of the prop room and I tested the doorknob. It had the ultraviolet powder on it. The same stuff I painted on the two packages of cocaine."

Rostov sat behind the desk and sighed.

"So now what?" Federenko asked. His boss appeared distracted. Was there something else on Rostov's mind? he wondered. Maybe he was having trouble with his woman. There certainly wasn't anything unusual about that, though. He, Federenko, had had nothing but trouble with women his entire life.

"I don't know," Cowboy said honestly. "When you find out your boss is a thief, who do you tell?"

"*His* boss?" Federenko suggested.

"Maybe. Maybe I'll just send you, Fed. You go in and tell the general that his assistant is stealing narcotics. I'll come and visit you in the gulag."

"We can't just let him get away with it," Federenko protested. "We've been busting our asses trying to stop narcotics from flowing into this city, and this son of a bitch has been selling off police dope behind our backs."

"I know we just can't ignore it," Cowboy said. "But we've just got to be sure we do it right," Cowboy said.

"How about this? Let's just replace all the cocaine with rat poison, and the next time the fag bastard uses it, we'll be rid of him."

He half expected Rostov to jump all over him for insulting Svoboda that way. But instead Cowboy grinned. "Maybe you've got an idea there," he said.

Rosa had long before gone to bed and Kamen and Tash sat on the sofa, watching a very boring television documentary on the Kirov Ballet, and sipping coffee.

The dinner had gone beautifully, even though Kamen had to race into the kitchen at the last minute to rescue the two fine sirloin steaks he had bought at one of the private stores in the city. Each steak had cost him the equivalent of fifteen American dollars, but when he visited Tash's kitchen, she seemed to be preparing to cook them as if they had started out not quite dead.

"What are you doing?" he asked, looking at a thick brown goo that was bubbling in a cast-iron frying pan.

"Cooking them in gravy. Don't worry. Twenty minutes, they'll be done," she said.

"Madame," he said, "you've done enough. Please sit down and watch the master at work."

First he dumped the goo into the sink, washed out the

frying pan, and dumped in a quarter pound of butter. When it melted and was sizzling, he threw in the steaks and quickly clamped a cover on the pan.

"Reduces the smoke," he explained.

"Good thing, too," Tash said.

He made a big show of timing his performance by his writstwatch, and Rosa giggled as he sneaked up on the frying pan. When he lifted the cover after exactly one minute, smoke billowed into the room. Little droplets of butter spattered into the air and flashed into fire as they reached the gas flames under the pan.

With a fork, Kamen flipped over both pieces of meat. He replaced the frying-pan cover and turned off the flame.

"Done in exactly two minutes," he said.

"How long have you been a cannibal?" Tash asked.

"Mommy, what's a cannibal?"

"Someone who eats raw meat."

"For your information, Madam, I am not now and never have been a cannibal. I am a connoisseur of great steak."

Kamen was right. The steaks were cooked perfectly, rare, juicy, singed black on the outside.

"Admit it, woman. I am the steak chief par excellence."

"I bow before my master," Tash said, and their eyes met across the small kitchen table and Kamen thought, *Dammit, I like this too much*.

Now the steaks were just a memory and Tash had put her daughter to bed and they were alone. He had his right arm casually draped around Tash's shoulders. He raised his left hand in front of him and saw that his watch read almost ten P.M.

"Didn't you have to go to work tonight?" he asked.

"I called Sergei. He owed me a day off and I told him I had company. Somebody else is filling in."

"Good," he said, and they watched television some more.

301

Fifteen minutes later, he said, "I think I ought to be going."

Tash turned her face to him. "Do you have to?" she asked softly.

"I have to go sometime," he said.

"Why?" she answered, and now he turned to look at her, and when he did she moved her face close to his and kissed his lips. She put her arm around the back of his neck and kissed him hard, then dropped her other hand into his lap and touched his body through the fabric of his trousers.

"I want you to spend the night," she said softly in his ear. For a moment Kamen did not know how to react. It was not that he lacked any skill at seduction or that he lacked for experience. But somehow he knew that this was a serious event in his life, and he did not know how to approach it. He was painfully aware of her hand in his lap, still holding him. And then she took his hand in hers and put it on her breast, through the soft angora sweater she was wearing.

His voice, when he found it, was rough and gravelly.

"I'll stay," he said.

"You'll be glad you did," she said.

Omar did not know where Kamen was, except that he had let him off at the school, but he was not about to tell them that, not ever, not for a bribe and not for the beating that left him unconscious.

When the small Armenian had passed out, the two men threw him onto the floor in the back seat of their car and drove away from Kamen's apartment.

Omar came to. Carefully, he forced himself not to groan. He felt the car stopping. He heard the front doors open. *No, not another beating.* But then the doors closed and he heard the men walking away. He reached his hand up and rolled down the window so he could hear. The men's footsteps moved away from the car and Omar lifted himself, painfully, so he could see through the windshield. The men were at a pay telephone only a block from Kamen's apartment.

Omar quietly opened the door and let himself out of the car, then closed the door silently behind him.

They were on a broad well-lit empty street and Omar realized, with a sinking feeling, that there was no place for him to hide. No trees to vanish into, no shrubbery to hide behind, not even any buildings to hole up in. And, bruised and beaten, he could not outrun anybody. He did not know what to do.

Viktor got his number from the operator. When the phone was answered, he said, "It's Viktor. Kamenski's not there. We—"

"Forget that," Tal snapped. "He is at Tash's, spending a cozy evening."

"Should we?"

"Yes. But make it look like an accident."

"We've got Kamenski's cabdriver. What do we do with the greaseball?"

"Kill him too," Tal said.

As the two men walked back to the car, Viktor said, "He's at Tash's. We'll get him there."

"And the cabdriver?" Yuri asked.

"He goes too. And let's do it now."

But when they yanked open the rear door of their car, Omar was gone.

"Goddammit," Viktor shouted. He looked up and down the broad street but could not see the small Armenian. "The bastard ran off."

"Now what?"

"Aaaah, we don't worry about it. He doesn't know who we are, so the hell with him. We'll get Kamenski and then we'll find him and finish him."

303

"All right. Let's go."

The two men got into the car, pulled away from the curb, and sped off down the street. And at the curb, where he had been lying prone under the car, Omar rose slowly to his feet, saw the car speeding away, and ran toward the telephone.

Lev Rostov was still in his office. On a large white pad of paper in front of him, he was scribbling notes, but as much as he tried to make his mind focus on the problem of Colonel Svoboda, who might or might not be stealing and selling narcotics from the police warehouse, he kept coming back to Olga Lutska. What had made her so angry at him? He did not understand and all he knew was that he was unhappy about it.

He had sent Sergeant Federenko home and he had put on his cowboy hat to guard his eyes from the harsh blinking overhead lights. Funny how reputations are made. People thought he wore his hat in the office to prove he was a cowboy at heart, but it might be more truthful that he was just an aging tired man with eyes that suffered strain from bad lighting.

The telephone rang.

"Lieutenant Rostov."

"Listen, Lieutenant, and say nothing. You don't know me but we have a mutual friend."

"Yes?"

"His name is Kamenski."

The hair on the back of Rostov's neck tingled. His first instinct was to deny knowing any Kamenski. *What the hell is this, anyway?* Instead, he forced himself to remain silent.

"I think two men who work at The Pink Elephant are going to kill him. I heard them speaking about it. Mr. Kamenski is with a woman who also works at that club.

Her name is Tash and she lives at number sixty-four Burgas Street. The two men are on their way there right now. That is all I know. Good-bye.''

"Wait . . ." Rostov began, but the phone was dead in his hand.

Chapter Twenty-five

The front door of the apartment building was locked, but it was an old small building with no burglar alarm and no paid *dezhurnaya*, and Viktor wrapped the butt of his gun with his handkerchief and broke the thin plate glass of a window next to the door.

He reached inside, unlocked the door, and grinned at Yuri. "Let's go kill this bastard."

Yuri grunted. He was carrying a metal can of gasoline.

Three floors up, Peter Kamen lay in bed, lit a cigarette—a real American Marlboro he had found in the apartment—and smoked in the dark. Next to him Tash slept, sipping air softly and sibilantly through her lips.

Her last words before she had fallen asleep were, "I think I love you, Pyotr," and he had not been able to answer her. It had been so long since anyone had said that to him, and perhaps meant it, that he had trouble believing it and even more trouble understanding it.

She had made love like a woman who had not had a man in a very long time. She was yielding and pliable, frenzied and fierce, and she held her arms around him while they loved as if she would never loosen, never let him go. Like his wife.

His own wife . . . had it really been that many years ago? It had been almost ten years and in that time he had slept with a succession of women—they were always available to people connected with the mob—but they had been simple spurting acts of physical relief. There had been no long-term girlfriend, no special woman, no significant other. There had only been a succession of women who passed with him through the night and he, or they, were gone in the morning and neither ever bothered to look back.

His wife had been a sensualist too. She had loved sex, she had loved making love, she had been faithful and funny and smart and she had been cancerous too, and her body started rotting from inside at too early an age. He had never thought he would feel again the way he had felt making love to his wife, but there was much the same spirit of exploration, of tenderness, of surprise, with Tash. And the most important feeling of all to Kamen— possessiveness. It was as if he decided at that moment, for the first time in many years, *This is my woman. She belongs to me. And I belong to her.*

He smoked. On her pullout bed in the small living room outside the bedroom, Rosa cried out in her sleep. Tash stirred instinctively, and for a moment Kamen thought of getting up to see if the girl was all right. But then she was quiet again and Tash fell back into sleep.

It must have been a bad dream. We have a lot of those, kid, he thought. *Even grownups*.

He stubbed out the cigarette. He should go. No, he should stay. His illuminated watch showed that it was after midnight. Omar probably had gone home by now, and if not, what did it matter? Kamen paid him well for his hours. Omar had no complaints.

And leaving now would be wrong. If a man and woman woke up together in the morning, it might just mean something. But if one of them slipped away during the night, while the other was sleeping, it usually meant that they hadn't been making love. They had simply been fucking.

He would stay. He pulled the thin blanket up over his body and closed his eyes.

When he had been only a little boy, Omar had been told by his grandfather, "Keep your eyes open. Most of what you learn will be what you see. Believe only your eyes and very few of the words you hear."

His grandfather had been very old and so wise that he somehow had escaped the hanging that was the usual fate of the males in their family, so Omar had paid attention.

He kept his eyes open. One day he had taken Kamen to lunch and had seen him meet with the big cop in the cowboy hat. And then he had seen the same man two nights ago near the train station. And when he read the paper the next day, he had read about Lieutenant Rostov and his seizure of two kilos of cocaine and he had been able to put a name together with the face of that cowboy cop.

That was why he had called Rostov from the phone only a few blocks from militsia headquarters and then raced back to his cab. A few minutes later, when Rostov had come driving out in an unmarked car from the parking lot behind the building, Omar had recognized him and followed him discreetly.

It was important to learn what was going on and to see it with one's own eyes.

308

* * *

"How do we do this?" Yuri asked in a whisper.

"We get inside and bang them on the head. Serves the little tramp right for hanging out with that bastard. And then we torch the place."

"Doesn't Tash have a little girl?"

Viktor shrugged. "So what? Everybody's got a little girl."

"I don't like it."

"You don't have to like it. You only have to do it."

Yuri set down the twenty-liter can of gasoline outside the door of Tash's apartment as Viktor took a knife from his pocket.

He opened it, then crouched down, and began prying at the wooden frame of the door.

"Keep your eyes open," he said softly. "We'll be out of here in just a couple of minutes."

He heard a noise. Kamen opened his eyes and listened hard, with the intent skill of someone who had spent time in prison waiting to be killed, where every sound could be someone sneaking up on you.

It sounded like a scratching noise. But then it was gone. *Maybe they have terrible mice in Russia. They have terrible everything in Russia.* He glanced toward a clothes hook in the room where his trousers were hanging. His gun, he knew, was in the back pocket. He closed his eyes again.

"Got it," Viktor said, and he pulled the seven-foot-long piece of wooden door molding from the frame and set it quietly on the concrete floor.

"Now the lock's easy," he said. He squatted down

again. Yuri looked nervously up and down the corridor in both directions.

Viktor had the tip of the knife inside the lock housing.

"Now turn the knob," he said.

Yuri reached for the door just as a voice barked out through the hallway.

"Police. Stop right there. *Ruki nazad*." Hands behind your back.

The two men wheeled toward the sound. At the end of the hallway stood Lieutenant Rostov.

Viktor growled, "Fucking Cowboy," and pushed Yuri in front of him. Behind the cover of the other man's body, he pulled a pistol from inside his jacket pocket and, still in a crouch, fired down the corridor.

The bullet missed.

Rostov returned the fire, once, twice. Both men dropped. Viktor's gun clattered across the stone floor.

Rostov approached them cautiously. As he reached them, the door to Tash's apartment opened. Kamen stood there, wearing only trousers and no shirt, holding a gun in his hand.

He wheeled toward Rostov as the policeman approached, then let his gun hand drop.

"What's going on, Cowboy?"

"They were trying to break in."

Kamen touched both men with his toe. "Tal's men," he said. "Christ, you're a good shot. You got them both in the head."

Rostov bent over the men and pressed his fingers into their necks, looking for a pulse, but there was none. His hand touched the gasoline can.

"It looks like they were going to torch this place," he said. "I think maybe I've met these bastards before."

"And a little girl inside," Kamen said softly.

Rostov heard apartment doors opening behind him, and he turned and pulled his badge from inside his leather jacket.

"It's all right, folks. It's all over. Police. Go back to sleep. There's no danger."

"Uncle Pyotr, what's happening?"

Kamen turned and saw Rosa stumbling toward him, rubbing sleep from her eyes. Tash was running from the bedroom, clad only in a revealing thin gown.

Kamen stepped back into the room and pushed the door partly closed. He bent down and put his arms around Rosa. "It's okay, sweetheart. Just an accident in the hall. You can go back to sleep now." He nodded toward Tash, who lifted the little girl and carried her into the bedroom.

Kamen turned back to the door. The neighbors, used to obeying police orders, had gone back inside their apartments.

Rostov asked, "Can I use the phone in there?"

"Come on in."

The policeman came inside, leaving the apartment door open so he could keep an eye on the bodies. "Toss a blanket over them," he ordered Kamen.

As he did, Rostov called to militsia headquarters and ordered them to send over a police squad and a morgue wagon, then replaced the phone, just as Tash came back into the room. She now had a chenille robe on over her skimpy nightgown.

Kamen was staring at the doorway. He was mumbling to himself, over and over again, "With a kid inside. The bastards. The bastards."

"What's happening, Pyotr?"

"Somebody tried to break in," he said. "This officer stopped them. This is Lieutenant Rostov. This is Natasha Krasnova."

Cowboy nodded, as did the woman, and Kamen looked at the door again.

"The bastards," he said. He turned back to Rostov. "How did you know?"

"You must have a friend somewhere," Rostov said.

311

"I don't have any friends."

"Well, *somebody* called and said those two were on their way up here after you."

Kamen shrugged, then turned back to the door and said again, "The bastards."

When Rostov had parked haphazardly in front of the apartment building, Omar had stopped his cab a half block farther down the street. He kept the windows open and he heard the three shots fired. But he saw no one running from the building, as they would have if they had shot a policeman, so he decided to wait and see what happened.

About ten minutes after the shots sounded out, two police cars and an unmarked van arrived and parked in the broad street before the house. *From the morgue*, he thought. *Somebody is dead. Please let it not be my good-paying Mr. Kamenski.*

Five minutes later, while the uniformed militsia were inside the house, Omar saw a solitary figure come out the front door. He recognized him immediately, from his physique and his walk, as Pyotr Kamenski.

He started the motor and rolled down the street and softly swerved in alongside the walking man.

"Need a ride, rich boss?" he called out.

"Omar," Kamen said. "Just the man I wanted to see."

He got into the cab and said, "Did you happen to make a telephone call to the police tonight?"

Omar turned and grinned. "One makes so many telephone calls," he said, but Kamen slid forward on the seat and touched Omar's swollen face.

"Oh, Jesus, you look terrible. Did they do that to you?"

"It's fine, boss. Don't worry about it. My grandfather

312

used to beat me harder and he did it every day of his life.''

"They won't beat you again," Kamen said.

"Those shots I heard?"

Kamen nodded. "The cop you sent got there just in time. He got them."

"Our system in action," Omar said. "So where to?"

"I need to buy something. And maybe you can help."

Something had gone wrong. Sergei Tal knew it deep inside his bones, in that part of the human that was still more animal than man. His men should have called to say the job had been completed. Or they should have returned to The Pink Elephant. But they had not returned or reported in.

Maybe they had had trouble finding Kamenski. Maybe that was it. Maybe he had not been at Tash's apartment. Maybe he was somewhere else.

He had enough *maybes* to tie a ship to, but not a hope. He knew instinctively that something bad had happened.

He made a telephone call, woke somebody up, and said, "I'm going away for a couple of days. I'll call you when I can." He hung up before there was any argument. Then he took from his desk drawer the large stash of money he always kept there—five thousand dollars, just in case—stuffed it into his jacket pocket. He turned out his office lights as he stepped out into the darkened nightclub and walked down the stairs to the deserted dance hall.

His car was parked in front, as it always was, in violation of the city's parking ordinances. It would be a good night to leave the city for a while. Maybe a little fresh air would make him feel better. And if this was a false alarm and there was nothing wrong, the club could manage itself until he got back. And if there was something wrong, his friends would be able to take care of it. But first, he would let the dust settle.

He opened the front door from the inside and let himself out onto the sidewalk. The usual bright lights of the club were out now and the street was shrouded in darkness, broken only by two streetlights, each of them a half block away.

With a key from the ring he carried on his waist, he relocked the front door, and then with another key reset the burglar alarm.

Then he turned and started down the street toward his car, a black Zil limousine.

He looked up as he heard the sound of a car coming down the street. It was loud.

He saw a cab approaching. *Some people are always in too much of a hurry*, he thought.

He stepped off the curb in front of his car as the taxi approached and then he glanced up and saw Kamenski leaning out the back window of the vehicle. *Kamenski!* He reached inside his jacket for the pistol he carried. As it cleared its holster, a fusillade of bullets ripped from the cab.

They tore into Tal's stomach, his chest, and carved a tattoo across his body up toward his left shoulder. His gun clanked away. He grabbed onto the fender of his car, but his strength ebbed along with his consciousness, with his life, and he slid down into the street.

The cab wheeled around, raced back past him, then made another U-turn. As it approached him again, Kamenski again leaned out the window and riddled Tal's body and then Tal's car with two bursts from the automatic weapon he held to his shoulder. He grunted appreciatively as Tal's body jumped as the heavy slugs ripped into it.

Then Kamen sat back on the seat.

"Good job," he said to Omar. "Let's move now."

314

"Home?"

"No," he said. "Let's get back to the lady's apartment."

"The police are probably still there," Omar said in alarm.

Kamen said, "Exactly."

Omar said, "I think tomorrow perhaps we should talk about my salary."

"Where were you?" Rostov asked.

"I had to get out and walk around," Kamen said from the door of Tash's apartment. "Something about being a murder target makes me nervous, and when I get nervous I walk."

Rostov was making notes on a small table in Tash's living room. The bodies had been removed from the hallway and only two uniformed policemen were left there. The hole in the front door glass had been taped over on both sides, so no one would be cut on the glass shards.

Everything seemed to be proceeding nicely.

Kamen saw Tash in the kitchen, fussing with the tea pot, and walked up next to her. When he stood by her, she looked into his face. There was confusion spread on hers.

"How? Why?"

"Shhhhh," he said, and took her in his arms, holding her head against his shoulder. "Don't worry now. It's all over."

"But . . ."

"No 'buts,' " Kamen said, and whispered to her softly, "It's over forever. Trust me." He stood back and said, "Rosa?"

"She fell right back asleep. In the morning, she won't even remember that anything happened."

"We should all be so lucky," Kamen said. He turned

toward Rostov, who had looked up from the table and was watching them.

Kamen smiled. "I owe you one," he said. Rostov nodded and, seeming embarrassed, put his head back down toward his report.

Chapter Twenty-six

The young uniformed policeman came in from the hallway and spoke softly to Rostov, who bolted up from the table where he had been seated, rolled up the papers he had been working on, and stuffed them into his jacket pocket.

He turned toward Kamen, who was standing with Tash in the kitchen.

"Pyotr. Could I speak with you for a moment?"

He took Kamen out into the hall and said, "Sergei Tal has been shot dead." He hesitated. "Or maybe you already knew that?"

"What the hell are you talking about?" Kamen snapped.

"Somebody larded him with bullets as he was leaving his club."

"When?" Kamen asked.

"Maybe an hour ago. Maybe less," Rostov said.

"Then why are you asking me if I knew about it? I've been here with you, remember?"

"And you were out for a walk too, as I recall."

"You have a suspicious turn of mind," Kamen said. "While I was walking, I saw a lady with a dog. Question her. Maybe she did it."

"I'm going over there. Want to come?"

"Is it wise for us to be seen together?" Kamen said.

"No one has to know who you are," Rostov said. "Maybe you can help."

"All right. Can I tell Tash what happened?"

"Make it quick," Rostov said.

Back in the kitchen, Kamen said, "I hope this doesn't upset you, but Tal is dead."

Tash's eyes opened wide in shock. "Sergei. Dead? How?"

"He was shot outside The Pink Elephant. I'm going over there now."

Tash settled slowly into a kitchen chair. She looked up at Kamen with questions in her eyes. "Did he have anything to do with this?" She waved her hand about the apartment.

"Yes."

"And now he's dead?"

Kamen nodded.

"Is that what you meant when you said it was over for good?"

"I didn't know anything about it," Kamen said.

She reached forward and squeezed his hands. Her expression showed utter disbelief and total acceptance at the same time.

"Thank you, Pyotr," she said.

Quite a woman, Kamen thought as he walked away. *It isn't every woman who understands the virtue of revenge*.

* * *

Sergei Tal's body had been removed from the street where Kamen had last seen it, although blood was puddled in the street next to Tal's bullet-riddled car. A half-dozen uniformed policemen had set up portable searchlights on tripods, much like those used in photography studios, and they were looking in the street for shell casings.

It certainly isn't New York City, Kamen thought. There were no bystanders crowding around the scene. In New York, by now, it would have looked like a street festival.

Near the door to The Pink Elephant was another uniformed policeman, this one a lieutenant like Rostov, but Kamen could tell that Rostov outranked him somehow because the man nodded deferentially to Cowboy and seemed imperceptibly to come to attention as Rostov and Kamen came past the police barriers.

He was talking to a man in his sixties who was wearing a seedy-looking blue sports jacket with brown pants.

"This is the one who found the body," the lieutenant told Rostov.

"I was driving home from a party," the man stammered quickly. "I saw the body in the street and called the police and waited for them to come."

"Did you see anybody near the scene?" Rostov asked, but the other policeman was shaking his head before the man had a chance to answer.

"No. There was no one," the man said. His voice was firmer now, as if he was gaining confidence.

I wonder what he would think if he knew the killer was standing right in front of him, Kamen thought.

"Not a vehicle?" Rostov said. "No car . . . nothing?"

"No," the man said firmly.

"Thank you," Rostov said. "Lieutenant, my associate and I are going inside. We have business with the deceased's records."

"There's a crew up in his office, looking around," the other officer said.

"We will work with them," Cowboy promised.

"I am Rostov," Cowboy announced as he preceded Kamen into Tal's office. The two policemen inside came to attention and Rostov nodded them at ease.

"Have you found anything?" he asked.

"No, Lieutenant," one said. "We were looking through his desk for an appointment book. We thought that maybe he was supposed to meet someone which might give us a lead. But so far, we have found nothing."

"You have done excellent work," Rostov said, "and have proceeded in exactly the right direction." The two policemen visibly puffed up from the praise.

"We will take over now," Rostov said. "You two may go about your other duties."

"Yes, sir," they both snapped, and saluted as they left the office.

When he heard their footsteps vanish off the staircase outside, Rostov snapped to Kamen, "Imbeciles. Do they expect to find a schedule that says 'Midnight: go outside and be murdered'?"

"Well, you're the cop. Tell me what we're *supposed* to be doing here."

"Look. I don't care who murdered Tal. What I care about are narcotics. Before everybody comes traipsing through here, destroying everything, I want to look through his files and see if we can learn anything. We think Tal was a big man in the narcotics mob. Maybe, someplace, there is a record of his partners, his suppliers, something."

"All right," Kamen said. "I was an accountant. Paper I understand."

He rolled the desk chair over to the nearest file cabinet,

sat, opened the top drawer, and began to look through the file folders inside.

Rostov, meanwhile, was making a police search of the office, looking on the underside of desk drawers, behind cabinets, inside a clothes closet.

The two men worked silently for more than an hour before Rostov grunted in disgust. "You find anything?" he asked.

"Tal may have been a shit, but he was very well organized. Tax records, government forms . . . do you know he didn't own this place?"

"Naturally. Nobody owns anything in Russia. Well, not until a couple of years ago. This is a lease operation. The government is his landlord; he paid rent."

"And income taxes and a percentage of his profits and a fee on gross sales. Your government's as bad as those thieves in Washington, D.C."

"Then how was it you won the cold war?"

"I'll let you know in five more years. I've found his checkbook."

"Will there be anything in there? We're looking for illegal drug activity. It's hardly likely there would be any payments by check."

"That's true enough," Kamen said. "Anything illegal would be paid in cash money. But businessmen have a way of falling into the cracks. Maybe you're supposed to deliver some drug money to a hairdresser who's a crook. But to justify seeing him or her, you make an appointment for your hair and you pay that one by check and try to pretend it's a business expense. It happens all the time. I know Mafia bosses with a hundred thousand dollars in the trunk of their car who go to pay off somebody at dinner and the first thing they do is to steal a credit card so they don't have to pay for the meal themselves."

"That was America; this is Russia," Rostov said.

"Right. And crooks are crooks everywhere. I'm just looking for somebody that Tal might have done a lot of business with. If I can find that, maybe I have the name of his partner or his boss."

Rostov cleared his throat nervously, then said, "Keep your eyes open for anything that might involve someone named Alexei Svoboda." He looked around as if to check if someone might be listening in.

"Is that your boss?" Kamen asked.

"Yes."

"And you think he might be dirty?"

"I think he might be stealing drugs from the militsia property room and supplying dealers," Rostov said somberly. Kamen laughed aloud and Rostov looked pained.

"You've got some society here, Cowboy," Kamen said.

"Just keep looking, Kamenski."

It was almost dawn when Kamen said, "That's interesting."

"Did you find something?" Rostov asked.

"No. That's what's interesting."

"What are you talking about?"

"Tal's lawyer is someone named Leonid Nabokov," Kamen said.

"A very famous attorney," Rostov offered.

"With very high fees, I suppose," Kamen said.

"I suppose."

"He handled all the lease work on this place; he handles tax planning; he handled the financing for the remodeling; he writes all the letters to the bureaucrats to keep them out of the business . . ."

"Yes?"

"And Tal has not, in the past four years, paid him a kopek. I've been through the company checks and his personal checks. Nothing. No fees at all. Wouldn't you agree that's odd?"

Rostov sat down on the sofa and stared across the room at Kamen. "Try this for odd," Cowboy said. "When we arrested that drug driver in Afghanistan, Leonid Nabokov just happened to be in court, just happened to represent him, just happened to get the man released. A day later he was murdered."

"Bingo," Kamen said.

"What is this bingo?"

"A bull's-eye," Kamen tried.

"What is this bull's-eye?"

"Never mind."

Rosa woke early and chatted with Tash as the woman fixed her a breakfast of cold cereal with milk.

But she said nothing about the events of the night before, and finally Tash could stand it no longer and asked, "Do you remember waking up last night?"

"A little bit," Rosa said. "I must have had a bad dream. And then Pyotr was here and he made sure nothing bad happened."

Tash nodded and turned away. *That is the way it was,* she thought. *Pyotr was here and so nothing bad happened. And he promised that nothing bad will ever happen again.*

She thought about Sergei Tal, shot down in the street. *Was that Pyotr Kamenski too?*

What kind of man was he if he could kill so cold-bloodedly, she wondered, and then realized that she had spent no time at all grieving for Sergei Tal. He had been only her boss, her lover against her will. As a boss, he was worse than some, better than most. *But he is dead and good-bye. Now I have to wonder about whether or not I will have a job to go to tonight.*

* * *

"No mention of any Alexei Svoboda?" Rostov asked.

"No. No mention of anyone. These files are as clean as a whistle. Too clean, if you ask me."

"Then, I think that's about it," Rostov said. Through a small clerestory window high in the office wall, they could see that the sun had risen over Moscow.

"Good enough. I'm going to get some sleep," Kamen said.

"And I'm going to the office to catch hell," Rostov said.

"Have a nice day," Kamen said.

The telephone rang in General Budenko's office and he immediately recognized the sarcastic voice of the president.

"More Wild West shootouts? Now a nightclub operator dead in the street? What the hell is going on over there?"

"We are working on it, sir."

"What kind of country are we running if no one is safe in the street anymore? What do I say when the press harasses me about this incident?"

"You could tell them it is under active investigation," Budenko said dryly.

"Oh, yes. The famous 'active investigation' file. Where the shooting of Judge Alekhine a month ago now reposes, I presume?"

"The cases may be related. We are working on it," Budenko said formally.

"I want a full report on my desk by tomorrow noon," the politician shouted before slamming the telephone down.

Budenko looked at the receiver angrily, as if it had personally offended him, then hit the intercom switch.

"Yes, sir," said Svoboda.

"Get that goddam cowboy in here right away."

From his apartment, Kamen called Tash.

"How is Rosa?"

"She's fine. She didn't remember anything today except a bad dream."

"We should all be children," Kamen said.

"And Sergei?" she said. "It was as reported last night?"

"Yes. Shot in the street, no clues."

She sighed. "I wonder what will happen to the club. To those who work there."

Kamen thought for a moment before answering. "I'm sure something will be worked out."

"I am here to see Mr. Nabokov."

"Do you have an appointment, Mr. . . . ?"

"Trotsky. No, I have no appointment."

"Please have a seat for a moment."

The secretary, a crisp and pretty blonde who seemed barely out of her teens, left Kamen in the waiting room and went through an oak-paneled door. He had not known quite what to expect in a Moscow lawyer's office—maybe something nice in "Early Factory"—and, looking around, he got the idea that this one was not typical. It looked instead like the office of an advertising agency; the walls were covered with enormous color and black-and-white blowups of French-language magazine covers. All showed the same model, an improbably beautiful woman with long thick raven hair and jade-green eyes. One of the covers showed her full-length, wearing a corselet and carrying a top hat in an apparent parody of a dance hall girl's garb, and Kamen saw that the woman's figure was as breathtaking as her face.

"Mr. Nabokov can spare you a few minutes, Mr. Trotsky. I'm sorry to have kept you waiting."

Kamen smiled. "With such scenery to look at"—he nodded toward the photographs—"who notices time?"

The woman smiled. "Those are Mrs. Nabokov," she said.

"Then Mr. Nabokov is twice blessed."

"Twice?"

"Yes. By his wife and his secretary."

The young woman beamed and took his arm to lead him down the hallway.

A lawyer anywhere, Kamen thought as the woman led him into a paneled office where Nabokov was waiting. The Russian was smallish with thinning gray hair slicked back on his head. His suit was much too expensive for someone who made a living as an honest workman. His eyes were light blue and inquisitive and he wore a thin mustache that cut the same curve as the questioning arc of his upper lip. His fingernails, when he reached his hand forward to shake Kamen's, were manicured and polished and he wore large gold cufflinks in his shirt.

His office was an extension of the waiting room, filled with more magazine covers starring his wife, but also with huge enlargements of home snapshots of the woman. *When Mother Teresa dies, she'll be lucky to get a shrine like this one*, Kamen thought.

Nabokov waved him to a chair and said, "Well, Mr. Trotsky, what can I do for you?"

"I want to thank you for seeing me on such short notice," Kamen said. Nabokov waved off the courtesy as insignificant and Kamen added, "So I won't waste your time. My name isn't Trotsky. It's Kamenski."

The lawyer was a good actor, Kamen thought, and could have fooled most people with his apparent lack of reaction. But there was an almost-imperceptible cessation of breathing, the tiniest little stiffening of the shoulders, before they relaxed and Nabokov said, "That's certainly an interesting way of starting a conversation."

"I thought you might have heard my name and not

326

wanted to meet with me. I was involved in business with one of your clients, Sergei Tal.''

''Yes. Poor Sergei. You read about it, of course.''

''I know of his death,'' Kamen said. ''What I want to do is to take over his business.''

''The nightclub?''

''Yes. Did he have any other business?'' Kamen asked.

''Not that I know of,'' Nabokov said.

After a moment's hesitation, Kamen said, ''Sergei told me that you represented him. I understand he was leasing his club from the government. I want to take over that lease.''

''It is a terribly long, drawn-out process,'' Nabokov said.

''Sergei also told me that you were capable of cutting through the bureaucratic undergrowth,'' Kamen said. He turned his hands palms up and shrugged. ''Mr. Nabokov, no one . . . not the employees or the customers or even the government is well served if The Pink Elephant has to close its doors for any length of time. My proposal is this: You are familiar with the paperwork and the legalisms of the lease since I know you handled it for Sergei. Take my application and walk it through the government. Naturally I will pay your fees and whatever expenses might be involved—and I understand that they could be substantial.

''While this is under way, I think that the present assistant manager should be told by the government to continue operating the club. And, of course, if there are fees involved in that, I understand that also.''

Nabokov toyed with a pencil like a man studying a complicated problem. *He doesn't understand why the hell I'm here*, Kamen thought. *It's always the problem with lawyers; they can never take things at face value.*

''By assistant manager, you are referring to that woman . . . Natasha . . . Natasha . . .'' He snapped his fingers as if trying to summon her name from his memory.

"Mrs. Natasha Krasnova," Kamen said, nodding. "She is honest and intelligent and will be able to manage the place until the new lease arrangement is made."

"You have this woman's address; her telephone number?"

Kamen nodded and leaned forward and wrote them on a piece of paper he took from a sterling-silver note holder on Nabokov's desk.

He pushed the paper forward to the lawyer, then leaned back and said, "So, can you handle this for me?"

"I can try," Nabokov said.

"With the best attorney in Moscow on the case, I feel very secure," Kamen said.

"Thank you," Nabokov responded. "You say you were involved in business with Sergei. I don't believe I ever heard him mention your name."

"We did much business together until his tragic end," Kamen said. "Perhaps he felt they were things an attorney should not know about."

"He was a good client," Nabokov pressed. "I thought I knew of all his business."

"Apparently not," Kamen said with a small smile. "Now about your fee."

"I think one thousand dollars for a start," Nabokov said. "You understand, of course, that this is not totally my fee. As you said, there may be expenses."

"One thousand dollars will be fine to start," Kamen said, thinking, *So that's the going bribe for public officials in Moscow. Crooks come cheaper over here.* "I am newly returned to Moscow and I don't have a checking account yet. I will have the money delivered this afternoon."

"That will be fine," Nabokov said. "And I will get on the matter immediately. Will you please leave your name . . ." He smiled. "The real one, this time. And your address and telephone number with my secretary. So I can advise you of your progress."

"Of course," Kamen said. He stood and looked around the office. "Your wife is very beautiful."

"Thank you. Danielle was, as you can gather, a model before we married."

"And does she interest herself in your business?" Kamen asked.

Nabokov hesitated a moment, then shook his head. "No. She is like a butterfly. The law she finds boring."

"Count yourself lucky, Mr. Nabokov," Kamen said. "I think women should always stay out of business."

His eyes locked with Nabokov's for a moment, just long enough for him to be sure that the lawyer understood what he had just said. Then Kamen nodded, shook hands again, and walked to the door. "I'll be in touch," he said.

"Yes," Nabokov said softly.

Chapter Twenty-seven

"Pull over here," Kamen said.

They were in a grimy industrial section on the western outskirts of Moscow. Factory smokestacks chuffed grime into the air. Omar parked the taxicab and turned around in his seat, awaiting instructions.

"You did me a good service last night," Kamen said.

"I did not expect to be party to a murder, rich boss," Omar said. For just a moment, his eyes were wary, blinking too quickly, as if he had only just realized he was alone in a deserted section of town with a killer who might be interested in disposing of witnesses.

"Relax," Kamen said. "And don't think of it as a murder. Think of it as getting even . . . collecting on a debt."

"It is a very serious way that you do your bookkeeping," Omar said.

"It's the way I was raised," Kamen said. "Somebody tries to hurt you or your loved ones, you hurt him back.

Harder." He handed forward an envelope. "There's a thousand American dollars in there," he said. "It's for you."

"Is this to buy my silence?"

"Yes."

"Consider it bought," Omar said.

"This is only the beginning, Omar," said Kamen.

"Do you mean that every night we're going to drive around and shoot people? I don't know if my heart can stand it."

"No. Let's hope no more killing is necessary. But you've been a good soldier. Wherever I go, you go too."

"I hope you are not planning a trip to the grave soon," Omar said.

"We're not going down. We're going up," Kamen said.

"I will travel with you as high as one thousand dollars American takes me."

"Fair enough," Kamen said. "Now let's get out of here before we both choke to death on this damned smoke."

Rostov, immaculate in his blue militsia uniform, stood at rigid attention in front of General Budenko's desk. Colonel Svoboda leaned against the windowsill on the far side of the big room, as if trying to distance himself from what was going to come next.

Budenko was looking at some stapled-together blue sheets that Rostov recognized as his report from last night. Finally, Budenko looked up and seemed surprised that Rostov was still at attention.

"At ease, Rostov."

"Yes, sir." The cowboy snapped into a stiff position with his hands clasped behind his back.

"When I gave you permission to work on cracking the mob in this city, I did so against my better judgment."

"Yes, sir," Rostov said.

"But I thought to myself, this young man has enthusiasm and experience. Perhaps some fresh ideas might put a chip in the Mafia's armor."

"Yes, sir."

"But when I told you to clean up Moscow, I didn't expect you to turn it into Chicago."

"No, sir."

"Goddammit, stop yes-sirring and no-sirring me. Be quiet and listen and speak when it's appropriate." Rostov was about to say "Yes, sir" again, but Budenko pointed a finger at him in a cautionary gesture and Rostov was silent.

"Now I've read your report on last night's festivities in which three more have turned up their toes and now I ask you, what has this to do with our American operative? Perhaps you can explain this to me. To Colonel Svoboda and me."

He stared at Rostov, who saw that this time an answer was expected.

"The two men I shot fired at me first. I intercepted them while they were trying to set fire to an apartment where Pyotr Kamenski was staying. There was also a woman and a child inside."

"Yes. I read that in your report, although the press this morning called the two men unidentified burglars."

"I thought discretion was called for, sir, especially since Kamenski was to have been one of the victims. I did not want the press asking questions."

"At least that you did well. Now, who were these two men? Do you have any idea?"

"They were two thugs who worked for Sergei Tal. I believe they were drug peddlers."

"Ah, yes, that brings us to our next misadventure. The late Mr. Tal. Now, who killed him?"

"I haven't any idea, sir," Rostov said.

"Was it our Kamenski?" Budenko asked.

"No, sir. He was with me at the apartment scene the entire time." He added quickly, "Tal was, I believe, the head of the Moscow narcotics underworld. I think probably he was shot by another member of his own gang."

"Do you think these two men who tried to kill Kamenski knew who he was?"

"Apparently so, sir," Rostov said.

"Well, how did they find out?"

"It seems that there is a leak somewhere. If you'll remember, Kamenski had made some inroads into Tal's organization. But then Tal must have learned that he was working with the police and sent his men to kill him. It was just fortunate that I was there. I do not believe that Tal's killing was directly connected with the attempt on Kamenski's life."

"Do you know the pain and anguish all this is causing me?" Budenko said. Without waiting for an answer, he said, "The President is on the telephone every day. Now I have to have another report for him tomorrow. What would you recommend I tell him?"

"I would suggest, sir, that you tell him quick work by your militsia saved three innocent people from being burned to death by two thugs. I would suggest further that you mention to him that we are making sharp inroads into the narcotics network in this city. Police all over will tell you that there are no drugs to be had on the streets of Moscow. What we are seeing—in the death of thugs— is a mob in its death throes."

"And that goes too for Judge Alekhine and that other man . . . whatever his name was?"

"Pimen Spatsky," Rostov provided.

"Well, dammit, *he* might have been a thug, but Judge Alekhine was not a thug. He was a judge."

"And I am sure that eventually I will prove to everyone's satisfaction that he was on the payroll of the Mafia," Rostov said.

"The mob in its death throes, huh?" Budenko repeated. "Well, just maybe, I can get the President to bite on that one for a while. But I would like to remind you, Lieutenant, that our mission is not to kill criminals. It is to apprehend criminals."

"Yes, sir."

"To that end, I am now putting you on a short leash. Daily, from now on, you will report to Colonel Svoboda about what is happening with your mission. I want to know everything this Kamenski is doing. If he has an attack of diarrhea, I expect to hear of it. Do you understand?"

"Yes, General."

"Then get out of here."

The telephone rang just as Tash was ready to leave her apartment to pick Rosa up at school. She had spent a bad day alone in the apartment, and when she was sure that all her neighbors had gone to work, she went into the hall and scrubbed the concrete floor with harsh lye soap to remove the bloodstains from the two dead men last night.

She knew she was keeping busy so that she would not think too much. Would she still have a job at The Pink Elephant? The place would be leased quickly by someone else and maybe she would have a job for a while. But what then? Would a new owner want to replace her with someone . . . someone younger, someone prettier, maybe someone that *he* was sleeping with. What was next?

Even as she put on her light jacket, Tash picked up the telephone.

"Is this Natasha Krasnova?" asked a voice with the brittle brusque sound of the bureaucracy. Despite herself, despite knowing she had done nothing wrong and could not be in any trouble, Tash felt her stomach start to churn.

334

"Yes, this is she."

"This is the Ministry for Economic Development, Deputy Director Menchik speaking. We are aware of the death of Mr. Sergei Tal." He paused as if he had just announced something of great importance and was waiting for a response.

All Tash could think of to say was "Yes." *What is going on? Why is this person bothering me?*

"It is not in the best interests of the local economy that Mr. Tal's club, this Pink Elephant, be permitted to close because of his death."

Again the pause, again Tash's "Yes?"

"Therefore, we are appointing you as the acting manager until your application to assume the lease is approved."

The woman was dumbfounded by the statement. "My application."

"Yes. It should be acted upon within the next two weeks, although sometimes these things take longer. When a decision is made, your attorney will be notified. In the meantime, you will take over for Mr. Tal as if you already had purchased the controlling interest in this club. And it is my duty to remind you that we expect that all fees and taxes will be promptly and fully paid. Your attorney will explain the correct procedures to you."

"Yes. My attorney," Tash said. "Which of my attorneys filed my application to assume the lease?"

"Mr. Leonid Nabokov, of course," the bureaucrat said huffily.

"Oh, yes, of course. Then, thank you for calling."

She wanted to sit down with a cigarette and a cup of tea to think over this bewildering chain of events, but a glance at her watch showed that she had to hurry to be to school on time. Even if she hurried, she might be late, and that was not a pleasant prospect. The Moscow of today was not like the Moscow of ten, or even five, years before. Now, there were bad people out on the streets—

criminals, child molesters, drug pushers—and the damned religious imbeciles who ran the school did not even have the sense to assign one of the teachers to stand at the bottom of the steps to make sure none of the children were accosted leaving the building.

She would think about all of this later. Now she had to hurry.

After they had left General Budenko, Svoboda took Rostov aside in the outer office.

"You think there is a leak somewhere in the militsia?" he asked.

"Yes, sir. Why else would Kamenski be the target of drug dealers?"

"How many men in your squad know of Kamenski?"

"Only two, sir," Rostov said.

"And which two would they be?"

"Sergeant Federenko and Private Golovin."

"Ah, yes," Svoboda said. "Sergeant Federenko. And Golovin. If I were you, I would keep a watchful eye on them. It is easy for a low-ranking officer to be perverted by the easy money that comes from the theft and sale of drugs. Your men, dealing as they do with drugs, would be prime targets for those who corrupt."

This little fop stole drugs yesterday and now he has the gall to accuse my men. I wonder what he would say if I told him we had proof of this theft. I should strangle the evil bastard.

Instead of doing that, Rostov replied stiffly, "I doubt very much that any of my men has ever stolen any narcotics. For that, we must look elsewhere. Will that be all, sir?

"For the time being," Svoboda said.

* * *

336

The phone had done nothing but ring all day, and this time when Olga answered it, she was unable to keep the irritation from her voice.

"Calm down," a voice said. "This is Cowboy. I'm downstairs in the coffee shop. Can you meet me?"

"I'm very busy," she said coldly.

"Just coffee," he said.

"I had coffee on the stove last night for you. All night."

"I'm sorry," Cowboy said. "I was involved in a shooting."

"A shooting? Are you all right?"

"I'll tell you about it over coffee."

When she arrived, Cowboy was sitting at a table for two in the rear of the shop. Her coffee, black but laden with sugar, was already waiting for her.

"What shooting?" she said.

"Two people tried to kill Kamenski. I got them first. And then there was another killing, and before I knew it, it was morning."

"I'm sorry," Olga said. "I was acting peevish, like a fool."

"I'm sorry too. I should have called. You said yesterday you had something to tell me."

"It sounds insignificant now," she said.

"Try me."

"This lawyer here I mentioned to you. Young Nabokov. He accosted me yesterday and was full of hints that you are in trouble with your superiors. But when I tried to pin him down, he just slipped away. It was probably nothing."

"This is the second time he has brought up my name, isn't it?"

"Yes," Olga said. "Probably just to get a rise out of me. He is always hovering around."

Cowboy grinned. "Tonight I think you should re-

337

ward his persistence and let him buy you a drink after work.''

Tash saw Rosa's red coat as she turned the corner. Oh, no, the little girl was speaking to someone. A man. She broke into a run down the block, then slowed again to a walk when she saw who the man was.

Pyotr Kamenski was leaning over, chatting with Rosa, and then both laughed and sat down on the steps of the church school, obviously waiting for the child's mother to arrive.

Pyotr was talking with bold, waving gestures of his hands and arms and Rosa was giggling at something. Tash's fright evaporated and she smiled as she approached them. Rosa saw her first, jumped to her feet, and ran to her mother.

''Pyotr was telling me about Egypt and mummies,'' she said excitedly.

''A lot he knows about Egypt or mummies,'' Tash said in a mock-stern voice.

''Ah, yes, madam, a great expert I am about that,'' Kamen said, ''and many other things.''

''I can believe that,'' she said as Kamen rose, smiled at her, and stood awkwardly still for a moment. Then Tash leaned forward, offering him her cheek to kiss, and he did and his body seemed to unfreeze.

He took her hand and the three of them walked down the street, back toward Tash's apartment. As Rosa skipped ahead of them, the woman said, ''I need your advice. Something strange has happened.''

''I am also a great expert on strange things,'' Kamen said. She wondered if she should tell him everything, then remembered that last night he had been prepared to kill to save Rosa's life. *This is a man I can trust, now and forever*.

She let the story bubble out of her. The mysterious phone call. The request—no, make that a demand—that she take over as manager of The Pink Elephant.

"That might make some sense," she said. "But what of this business that I am leasing the club? What can that mean? I certainly cannot ask Leonid Nabokov. He is the most famous attorney in Russia. He will laugh at me. What can I do?"

She looked over at him and said again, "What should I do?"

"Silence, woman. I must think a moment." Kamen traced his fingers through the air, as if scanning invisible lines of script, then turned back and said, "Your course of action is clear."

"And it is?"

"Tonight, you go to The Pink Elephant. I will go with you to assist. You will become the manager. You will give yourself a salary increase. I will handle the bookkeeping. We will dazzle them with our brilliance."

"And what of this lawyer? What of Nabokov?"

"You will leave that with me. I will speak to Mr. Nabokov," Kamen said.

"You will?"

"Could I do less for . . ." He paused.

"For . . .?"

"For you," he said.

She stopped on the sidewalk and turned to him, staring into his eyes. Then she squeezed both his hands inside hers and leaned forward and kissed him on the mouth.

"Quick," she said. "Let's go back to my apartment."

"A fine idea," Kamen said.

"And maybe Rosa can go play with friends for a while," she said.

"An even better idea."

Kamen turned and waved to Omar, who was leaning

against his cab door, across the street from the school. He gestured that Omar should meet him again at six P.M.

Omar nodded and drove off in the cab. He found himself very happy that the rich boss had found a woman. *If he is in love, he is much less likely to get himself killed. And me with him.*

Chapter Twenty-eight

Kamen had been in his apartment only a few minutes when Rostov arrived. Without asking but after looking at the policeman's eyes, bloodshot and dark-ringed, Kamen brewed a pot of tea.

"I thought I would bring you up to date," Rostov said.

"Any luck in tracing the gun that killed Tal?" Kamen asked, although he knew very well that the gun was now resting on the bottom of the Moscow River.

Cowboy shook his head. "No. An army automatic rifle is the best we can do."

"A soldier? The killer was a soldier?"

Again Rostov shook his head. "It doesn't mean a thing. When everything fell apart in East Germany and Rumania, a lot of Soviet soldiers just sold their weapons. They're all over the place. Anybody can buy one. As you may already know."

"They sold their weapons? Doesn't anyone check on things like that?" The idea of military personnel selling their weapons sounded so . . . so . . . bush-league to him.

"A lot of things fall through the cracks," Rostov said.

"In this country, it seems everything falls through the cracks." Kamen went into the kitchen and poured two glasses of tea. "Sometimes I think you people would be better off if you'd leave the Mafia alone. At least the Mafia works. You can't get the trucks out of the garage in the morning."

"You'll get few arguments from me about that," Rostov said, remembering his own difficulties in trying to get cocaine for the sting operation from the militsia property center. "But whoever the killer was may have done us a favor."

He looked carefully at Kamen, who saw the suspicion in the policeman's eyes and responded by making his own face as open, honest, and nonconspiratorial as he could.

"What do you mean?" he said blandly.

"Drugs dried up totally on the Moscow streets last night. I have had reports from all over the city. So the killing of Tal had that effect. And who knows? Maybe he was the head of this entire thing. Maybe it is without a leader now."

It was Kamen's turn to shake his head.

"No," he said slowly. "Tal wasn't the head of anything. He wasn't smart enough to be a criminal boss."

"I never knew Mafia bosses had to take an intelligence test," Rostov said sourly.

"They take one every day and they pass it by staying alive. Not just in the United States, but here too. You don't get to be the boss because you're some fool and you're made out of cheese. Did you ever speak to Tal?"

"No."

"I did. He was filled with himself. He liked to show off his fancy suits, his fancy nightclub. He worked hard to prove what a big important man he was. The Mafia bosses I know—well, some of them anyway—carry sandwiches in a paper bag. They wear old suits. They go to church on Sunday. Their wives weigh 250 pounds, have only two dresses and both of them are black.''

"I thought that was old-fashioned. That it went out in the Twenties,'' Rostov said.

"Maybe a little. Maybe the suits are better now and sometimes the wives are a little leaner. But the bosses, at least the smart ones, stay out of sight, they're careful, and they're quiet. They don't talk to anybody, and if they do, they sure as hell don't brag about who they are.'' He shook his head again and carefully put his glass down on the table. "It wasn't Tal running anything. What do you know about those two thugs of his that you shot?''

"Very little. They had no criminal records. The driver's licenses they carried had false addresses. So far, I know nothing for sure except that they went under the names of Viktor and Yuri.''

"Check the gymnasiums,'' Kamen said. "They were bodybuilders. Someone's seen them around, lifting weights and sniffing each other's jockstraps.''

"Already, I am doing that. But whoever they were, they were small players. They worked for Tal and you insist Tal worked for somebody else. But who?''

"We just have to keep looking. Maybe more important is, why did Tal try to kill me? How did he know I was working with you?''

"I don't know,'' Rostov said. "Two of my men knew about you. I would trust them with my life.''

"It's not *your* life I'm worried about. But who else knew? Your girlfriend?''

"Olga knows who you are. My superiors know.''

"Well, if this operation is as tight as you say it is, then it's one of them. Who is this Alexei Svoboda, anyway?''

"The colonel in charge of this operation. I believe he has been stealing narcotics from the militsia property center. He is also a homosexual.''

343

He saw Kamen grinning and snapped, "What is so funny?"

"Your soldiers sell their guns on the black market. One of your top cops is a fag and maybe on the payroll of the mob. We've got a lot of work to do before we get Russia back on track."

"I'll be sure to give your ideas a lot of consideration when I am elected president. In the meantime, maybe we should stick to police work and forget the sociology."

"Sorry." Kamen looked at Rostov's face and said, "What's bothering you?"

"Do you have any vodka?"

"Sure. The man who got this apartment for me thought of everything," Kamen said, grinning. He poured Rostov a healthy glassful of the liquor, himself just a sip. "So?" he said.

"I brought you here to help us. I did not bring you here to be killed. I feel responsible. Even more so if the danger to you comes from within our own camp."

"You're worried about me?"

"Of course I am," Rostov said.

Kamen reached across the kitchen table and clapped the bigger man on the shoulder. "Cowboy, I am free, white, and twenty-one. I am here by choice. And you'll find that I do not die easily."

"Not up till now," Rostov said dourly.

Kamen went with Tash to The Pink Elephant. Omar stopped his cab in front of the building but Kamen said, "around the corner," and Omar let them out there. That way, Kamen was able to take the woman into the club without her having to walk past or over the bloodstains from Sergei Tal which were still on the street.

Tash had called all the workers of The Pink Elephant to meet her an hour before the club's normal eight P.M. opening time and most were there already when she arrived. Kamen went upstairs into Tal's office and sat at the big desk. Through the one-way glass, he could see Tash below, talking to about fifteen workers, being talked to in return. He could not hear the conversation, but the meeting seemed a little more heated than he had expected.

Idly he rummaged again through Tal's desk drawers but found nothing but paper clips and tape and ballpoint pens with the name of the club printed on them. Tal may not have been too smart, Kamen thought, but he was smart enough not to hang himself with too much paper.

Tash came into the office.

"Meeting over?" he said.

She shook her head. "A five-minute recess to let tempers cool."

Kamen was immediately annoyed. "What tempers? About what?"

"Why am I running the club now? Who am I to give orders? Why make any changes, in schedule or anything else? Why not just leave things as they were? Pyotr, they will not accept me as the manager."

Tears were welling in her eyes and Kamen rose and hugged her. "Sit down and rest for a minute," he said softly. "I'll be right back."

He put her into Tal's big leather seat, then walked downstairs where the dozen-and-a-half employees were clustered into groups of two and three, drinking liquor from water glasses, talking heatedly. No one noticed him at first, so Kamen took a heavy glass candle holder and slammed it down onto a table.

The sharp sound snapped all eyes toward him.

"Quiet and listen," he ordered. "The democratic portion of this meeting is over and now I will tell you how things are going to be."

He looked around, angrily challenging with his eyes anyone to speak, but no one did.

"I am Pyotr Kamenski and I will soon be the new owner of this club. I have appointed, with government approval, Mrs. Krasnova as manager. If you don't like that, you can leave now and no one will miss you, especially me since I think that you are a pack of overpaid, underworked slugs to start with. The door is that way.'' He pointed to the front door, but still no one moved or spoke.

"Fine. Now we are starting to understand each other. Mrs. Krasnova is the boss here. You will do exactly what she says or I will personally throw your ass out of this club. If you stay, you will make more money than you ever made before. You will also work harder. If you find that distasteful, go. In ten minutes I can have you replaced by people who will appreciate this job and appreciate the opportunity to work for such a fine woman. And now, since there are no questions and there are no resignations, I suggest you all get your asses to work. Now! Meeting adjourned.''

He turned and walked back up the stairs to the office. Tash was waiting outside the door and he smiled at her and she followed him inside. They stood side by side, looking below, watching the workers scurry around to clean up the club in preparation for opening.

"Did you mean it?'' she said softly.

"About your being a fine woman? Yes.''

"About your being the owner of this club?''

"No,'' Kamen said. "I lied. You are going to be the owner of the club.''

"But with your money, correct?''

"Does it matter?'' he asked her, turning to look into her eyes.

She paused, then smiled. "I couldn't think of a finer partner,'' she said.

After meeting Rostov for tea, Olga had gone back to her upstairs office. She detested it, but Cowboy had seemed to think it was important, so she walked into the outer office, past the desk where Anatoly Nabokov worked, and found an excuse to talk to a young woman, the office's newest attorney, who still seemed to find the work of the prosecutor's office absolutely and otherworldly confusing.

Olga chatted with her, leaned over her desk, stretching her skirt tight across her hips and butt, and listened to her rapidfire confusion for a full forty-five seconds before cutting her off with a friendly pat on the shoulder.

"Don't worry," she said. "Everything will become clear in a very short time."

She felt someone next to her and heard Nabokov's whiny voice. "And if you have any problems, Olga can always ride to your rescue."

Same old twerp, she thought. *An utterly predictable fool with his utterly predictable bad cowboy jokes.* What she really wanted to do was to hit him in the face; what she had to do was go out for a drink with him. Cowboy's orders.

"And if I don't know the answer," she said, turning back to the young woman lawyer, "you can be sure that Anatoly here does. And he'll be glad to help any way he can."

Fat chance, she thought. *The new lawyer was overweight and had bad skin. Anatoly is a bottom-feeder but he thinks he's a ladies' man. He will save his advice, worthless as it is, for the pretty ones.*

"I have to talk to you, Olga," Nabokov said, speaking softly, pretending to importance, as he always did.

"Sure. Speak."

"Not here. Prying ears."

Ears don't pry, you imbecile, she thought. "Where then?"

"Dinner?"

"Maybe. A drink first after work."

"Fine. I was just getting ready to go."

"Let me freshen up and I will be with you in a few minutes," she said.

He nodded and waddled off, overweight and silly, and Olga stifled a sigh. *The things I do for love*.

Systematically, Kamen began going through Tal's files again. There had to be something in writing somewhere that could tell him and the militsia what Tal had done in the narcotics trade, how he had done it, something that would give some scope on his operation. Something. Anything.

But there was little. He and Rostov had raced through them quickly the night before, but whatever was there to be found, they had found. The rest of it was a dreary mélange of letters to and from the tax bureau, personnel records, personal bills—but nothing that revealed anything except that Tal was a careful, meticulous businessman. The books, so far as Kamen could tell, were in order; bills were paid on time; taxes too; whatever Tal was, he was not an incompetent and not a fly-by-night.

He had just pushed closed the final drawer of the big filing cabinet when Tash entered the office, came up behind him, and kissed his neck.

"How is it?" he said. Relieved for a moment of his heavy concentration, he could hear the buzzing of people downstairs in the club.

"Busiest I've ever seen it," Tash said.

"I guess it's too early to credit it to new improved management, isn't it?" Kamen said.

"Sightseers. They read about the killing in the paper and they want to see where it happened. And then they come inside for a drink. Some of them stay."

"Those are the ones we want," Kamen said. "Those are the ones who might come back again."

"I know. And I have to tend to them. Bye."

"Just a minute," Kamen said.

The woman paused and looked back at him. "Yes?"

He was not sure exactly how to phrase it.

"Did Tal ever get any visitors up here? Or did people ever come into the club looking for him?" Kamen asked.

"Not often. Why?"

"But sometimes?"

She shrugged. "Sure. Liquor salesmen. People selling tablecloths. Usual business calls. Why?"

"Did he have an appointment book? Where he wrote down his meetings?"

"I never saw one. Why?"

This time he could not ignore her question. "I think Tal was involved in something more than the nightclub business," he said. "Maybe something illegal." He paused, but when she did not respond, he added, "Maybe something like narcotics."

"I never saw it," she said. "Maybe Yuri and Viktor . . ." She shuddered visibly as she thought of the two Tal bodyguards who had been shot in the hallway outside her apartment the previous night.

"What about them?" Kamen asked.

"A lot of people came in to see them. All night long. And then they went out every night to make bank deposits—there was always a lot of cash on hand, of course—but they were gone for several hours. But why, I don't know."

"Maybe some of the other people here. Maybe the bartender or the waitresses," Kamen said. "Maybe they know something more about Yuri and Viktor."

"I don't know. I'll see," she said.

"Please ask around," he said. "But be subtle. Do they know what happened to the two of them? That they're dead?"

"No. I said nothing."

"Good for you. Just nose around."

"Pyotr?"

"Yes?"

"Why are you interested?"

"I'm interested in everything," he said blandly.

"That answers nothing," she responded directly, almost with annoyance.

"I promise. I'll explain it all to you later," Kamen said.

"I'll hold you to it."

"I always keep my promises," he said.

She nodded and Kamen looked at her longingly as she walked from the room. Then his eyes fixed on the leather sofa across the office and for a moment there was a bitter taste in his throat, but he put it aside. *That was all then; this is all now. Let it go*, he told himself.

"So how is your cowboy?" Nabokov asked.

They had been seated at the cafe table for only a few minutes and already he had spilled part of his drink on his shirtfront and then spewed forth a blizzard of cracker crumbs which adhered to the wet spots on his shirt and made him look like a chicken piece being breaded for baking.

"I thought I would ask you that," Olga said. "You seem to be a fountain of information about him."

"One hears things," Nabokov said.

That's not the kind of answer I want, Olga thought. *That's the kind of answer one gives when he doesn't know anything and wants to pretend that he does. Am I wasting my time at this dismal cafe with this dismal excuse for a man?*

"It's no wonder one hears things," she said blandly. "Lieutenant Rostov is such a wild man, so irresponsible, so—"

Nabokov grinned as he interrupted. "It sounds as if the bloom is off the romance."

"You might say that," Olga said. *I wouldn't, but you*

350

can say anything you want, you fat toad. "We're just too greatly different. In personality, in the way we live, even in our sexual appetites." She leaned forward and talked softly as if revealing a confidence. "He is not really much of a police officer, or a man, for that matter. I guess one can never tell from the outside package." *Except with you, you cretin. You I know all about.*

"So he is no longer living with you?"

Now how did he know that Cowboy spends most nights with me? "No," Olga said. "We were never living together. How did you get that idea?"

"Oh, just gossip, I guess," Nabokov said. "You are well rid of him. Rostov is heading for a fall. As I said yesterday."

"No wonder," Olga said enthusiastically. "He is really a loose cannon, you know."

"I know. The ludicrous outfits are one thing, but do you know what he did that has really pushed him beyond the pale?"

"No," she answered flatly.

"He had this idea of bringing an American gangster to Russia to help him make war on the Mafia. Can you imagine that? As if we even had a Mafia."

"He sees too many American movies," Olga said. *How did this little bastard find out about Kamenski?*

"He did not tell you about that?" Nabokov asked.

"When it became apparent to me that he was not the kind of man I thought, we talked very little," she said. "Whoever heard of such a stupid idea anyway? Thinking of bringing a gangster here. Ridiculous."

"Not only thinking about it, he did it," Nabokov said gleefully. "And all that has happened has been chaos."

"Rostov will probably be disciplined. It will serve him right," she said in as firm and schoolteacherly a tone as she could muster.

"It might be worse than disciplining. He might very well be thrown from the force."

You bastard, you're making this all up, Olga thought. She said, "You seem to have a wonderful pipeline into militsia headquarters. The next time I try a case, I think I'll ask your advice on the police involved. I didn't know you counted so many of them among your friends." She tried firing in the dark. "Your father is so prominent an attorney and often so critical of the police, I'm surprised that policemen would even talk to you."

She sensed somehow that she had struck a nerve because Nabokov answered quickly, "Father's business is Father's business. Mine is my own." Too quickly.

She winked at him slightly. "Still, such an important man. I'll bet he can open many doors with officials. With the militsia. I'll bet you grew up surrounded by big shots. I suppose that's how you learned to deal with people so well."

The man was terribly stupid and seemed, almost visibly, to puff up with the praise. "Well, that could be true," he said. "My father does know everybody. I met the premier once, back when we had a premier. Generals, everybody. Everyone comes to Father's." He hesitated, as if checking himself. "But what I hear is what *I* hear. No one else."

"It just sounded like gossip from your father's breakfast table." He stared at her; his eyes blinked nervously. *I'm right*, she thought. *This does come from his father.*

Nabokov cleared his throat. "Around my father's table, they speak only of the latest in French fashions and where the best, most expensive vacations may be had."

"French fashions? Oh, yes. Your stepmother is French, is she not?"

"Not my stepmother. My father's wife."

"Isn't it the same?"

"No," young Nabokov said stuffily. "One label connects her to me, which I don't want. The other makes her exclusively the property and problem of my father. I am happy to leave it at that."

The mention of his father had seemed to turn Nabokov sullen, and it reminded Olga of a boy bragging about his new auto and then being embarrassed when it was revealed that the auto was actually his father's. Anatoly hunkered down at the table, shoulders up around his ears, staring at his bottle of beer, and Olga thought in surprise, *He wants me to apologize for something. Well, he can wait until hell freezes over. And without me.*

Without speaking, she rose to her feet and Nabokov looked up.

"I'm sorry, Anatoly. I have to be leaving now," she said.

"But . . ."

"Cowboy is waiting for me."

"I thought you said you were done with him," Nabokov said.

"I've changed my mind. I absolutely must have him tonight. Bye-bye."

"Nothing," Rostov reported glumly.

"How big nothing?" Kamen asked.

"Total nothing." Rostov's voice over the telephone sounded thick and groggy from lack of sleep. "My men and I have ransacked Tal's apartment. He paid his bills, he had a couple of girlfriends' phone numbers, a couple of snapshots taken when he was on vacation, and nothing else. At least nothing we're interested in."

"He had to have records somewhere," Kamen said.

"I know." Rostov sighed. "But I can't look for them anymore tonight. My men are trying to find where those two thugs lived, but I have to get some sleep."

"All right. We'll talk tomorrow."

"I forgot to ask," Rostov said. "Where are you calling from? I tried your apartment before."

"From The Pink Elephant."

"What are you doing there?" Rostov asked.

"Tash has been told by the government to manage the place. I just came down to help."

"Good. It goes without saying: keep your eyes open."

"Then don't say it," Kamen said. "Get some sleep."

The voice that answered on his next telephone call was a woman who spoke Russian in a curiously accented way. Her voice had the snap of silk, the warmth of velvet, when she told him that Counselor Nabokov was at dinner at the moment, but that if it was an emergency she would interrupt him, and Kamen remembered the photographs of the beautiful brunette that were all over the lawyer's office, and he said, "No, madame. That won't be necessary. Please have him call Pyotr Kamenski at this number."

She took a moment to write the number down, then repeated it, and said, "Will that be all?"

He wanted to say, "No, jump through this phone and I'll ravish you on the desk," but instead replied simply,"Yes, madam, thank you."

When he hung up the telephone, he still felt the electric chill of the woman's voice on the back of his neck. No wonder Nabokov was crazy about her. Who wouldn't be? He allowed himself to think for a moment of what she would be like in bed, then went back to Tal's files.

The lawyer called back fifteen minutes later.

"You certainly don't waste any time, Mr. Kamenski. I was surprised to see you calling from The Pink Elephant."

So he knew Sergei Tal's private number, Kamen thought. Good enough.

"Apparently, we both believe in moving swiftly," Kamen answered. "That's why I called. I wanted to thank you for getting the government to act so quickly on Miss Krasnova's application for a lease.''

''It has worked out?'' Nabokov asked.

''She is already running the place as manager, pending all the paperwork,'' Kamen responded. ''My thanks.''

''You're certainly welcome. Was there anything else?''

Kamen thought for a moment of asking if Sergei Tal had another office anywhere, a place where records might be kept. But he decided against it; the fewer people involved, the better. And he did not trust this lawyer, not one bit.

''No,'' he said simply. ''I'm sure I'll be in touch.''

''Fine,'' answered Nabokov. ''Call anytime.''

There had to be a paper trail. There had to be a record somewhere. There had to be receipts and payments and ledgers covering his narcotics dealings. But where the hell did Tal keep them?

The world lived on paper. Even the Mafia in the United States kept records. Somewhere there was an answer.

Kamen chewed the end of a pencil.

How did Tal's distribution system work?

The telephone rang again.

''Sergei?'' asked a man's voice.

Is there someone in Moscow who doesn't know that Tal is dead? Kamen thought.

''No, this is his partner. Can I help you?''

''What's your name?'' The voice was suddenly suspicious.

''Pyotr,'' Kamen said.

''I've never heard of you,'' the man said.

''I'll bet I've heard of you. What's your name?''

''Just tell Sergei that Blade called.''

''Is there a message? Should he call you back?'' Kamen asked.

355

"He knows what I want and he knows where I'll be," the man called Blade said. He hung up before Kamen could say anything else.

A mistake, Kamen thought. *Now there's somebody out there who's going to find out that Tal is dead, and when he does, he's going to remember this telephone call and Tal's "partner" who asked too many questions. Stupid, Kamen. Stupid.*

He went to the window and looked out over the club. Tash had been right. It was packed to standing-room. The noisy rock and roll of the jukebox seemed to rattle the floorboards under his feet, but precious little of the noise got into the office itself.

He tried to spot somebody in the crowd who looked like he was not what he should be, but had to give up. All Russians looked alike to him. In New York, in America, he could spot a wiseguy two blocks away on the other side of the street. Here, everybody was a foreigner.

With a sigh, he wheeled his office chair back to the file cabinet, sat down, opened the top drawer, and began to go through all the papers for the third time.

"I feel like a fool," Georgi Golovin said. "It was under my nose all the time." He had walked into Cowboy's office just as Rostov was preparing to leave for the night.

"What was?" Rostov said.

"Yuri and Viktor. I took the touched-up morgue photographs of them and showed them around. They were the drug delivery boys all right. A half dozen of our informants on the street confirmed it."

He pounded his fist on Rostov's desk. "I should have seen it. Every night they vanished for a while and I didn't think anything of it. I have to be the dumbest cop in Russia."

"Take it easy on yourself," Rostov said. "Your assignment wasn't to follow them. It was to keep an eye on The Pink Elephant. And you did that well.''

Golovin looked up hopefully. His self-esteem had taken a pretty solid bashing during the day, after learning that Rostov had shot the two big bouncers the night before.

"Let me ask you a question now that's very important,'' Rostov said.

"Yes?''

"When they left the club, did they carry anything? A briefcase, packages, anything that might be used to transport narcotics?''

Golovin looked at the ceiling while he searched his memory. "No,'' he said finally. "They carried nothing and they certainly didn't have anything hidden in their clothing. They were such fags; they always wore tight shirts and trousers to show off their physiques. There wasn't room to hide anything. They must have gone from The Pink Elephant someplace to pick up the drugs first, before distributing them.''

"And we don't have one idea of where they lived,'' Rostov said. He sighed. "Any suggestions?''

Golovin thought. "Maybe I should start to circulate around the gymnasiums where they might have gone. If they were members, they might have had an address.''

Rostov stepped around the desk and clapped a big hand on Golovin's shoulder. "Good idea,'' he said, even though he'd had the same idea hours before. "Why don't you get right on it?'' he said.

"Consider it done, Cowboy,'' Golovin said, and left the office almost on a run. Rostov smiled. It was important to keep your men's morale high. He turned out the light and left his office.

The health club.
It was at least the third time Kamen had seen the

receipt, but finally it registered on his mind. The bill from the Friendship Health Club admitting Sergei Tal as a member for a full year for two thousand rubles. The address was on Chernenko Street, and as he looked at the blue-carbon printed receipt, the address rang a small bell in Kamen's mind.

Where? What was Chernenko Street to him?

He closed his eyes and tried to remember, then lunged forward and pulled the personnel folder from Tal's file cabinet.

There were their names. Viktor and Yuri, and on both of their job application forms, listed under address, was simply "Chernenko Street."

He pushed himself, almost playfully, back on the rolling chair toward the desk and the telephone. It rang before he could touch the instrument.

"Hello. Pink Elephant," he said.

"Pyotr, this is Cowboy."

"Just the man I wanted to talk to."

"Why?" Rostov said.

"Tal's two bodyguards. I found a piece of paper with their names on it and the address, Chernenko Street. And Tal was a member of the Friendship Health Club on Chernenko Street. Maybe there's a connection."

"I'll be damned," Rostov said.

"I'm sure of that, but why specifically?"

"I was just calling to tell you that one of my men, the young one, just found out that Viktor and Yuri worked out at the Friendship Health Club. Did anyone ever tell you that you'd make a good policeman?"

"Not in this world," Kamen said with a laugh.

"If you're interested, I'll pick you up."

"No, too many people around here tonight," Kamens aid. "I'll meet you there."

"Twenty minutes."

* * *

"I'm closed. Go away." The man was talking from behind the locked glass door of the Friendship Health Club. In tight tee shirt and sweatpants, he was just a lump of muscle. He was also rude and scowling, which, Kamen decided, was the way everybody was who worked for a living in this damned city. Anybody who came to Russia talking about "the customer is always right" would be laughed out of town. How had McDonald's lasted? And where did they find their employees?

Rostov pressed his badge against the window. "You will open that door now," he said, "or I will bust it in and come inside and kick your pansy ass all over Moscow."

The health club attendant looked at the badge and then up at Cowboy's face, towering above him, seeming with his ten-gallon hat to tower above everybody in the city, and finally he nodded to himself and unlocked the door.

"What is it you want?" he said. All the bravado had gone out of his voice now when he saw closeup that Rostov was even bigger than he had appeared while standing outside.

Rostov brushed by him into the warm anteroom that almost felt moist with steam.

"We will lock this door and go into a room where we can talk," Rostov said imperiously. "Is there anyone else in the building?"

"No. We are closed. This is my night to lock up."

"Fine. Take us to the main office."

Russian bodybuilders must be a different breed from their counterparts in the United States, Kamen thought, as he and Rostov followed the bulky young man as he walked, rocking side to side the way people did whose thighs were too big, down the hallway toward the office.

They passed a number of equipment rooms, and in America, the walls would be covered with photos and posters of other men. In the few gyms Kamen had been in, Hulk Hogan, the wrestler, was a big favorite and so was Sylvester Stallone and Arnold Schwarzenegger. Here in Russia, the walls were covered with pictures of naked or near-naked women, a lot of them the ubiquitous *Playboy* centerfolds. Was it possible that Russian bodybuilders were straight? Then how did that account for Yuri and Viktor, who were two sick vicious fags if Kamen had ever seen any? Maybe they had been the token gays for the health club. And now they were the token corpses. *There's a spot in the world for everybody*, Kamen thought.

They followed the man into an office, which held a pair of paint-chipped gray metal desks and a half-dozen tall olive-green file cabinets along one wall.

The attendant turned toward them, querulously, as if not sure whether or not he should sit down. He leaned back against the desk. He was also unsure whether or not he should speak. He waited.

"What's your name?" Rostov asked.

"Alexander," he said. "Alexander Dropov."

"All right," Rostov said. "Alexander, I want to tell you that you're not in any trouble. At least, not yet. And you won't get in any if you answer our questions truthfully."

"Yes, sir," the young man said. He had been totally cowed by Rostov up till that moment, Kamen realized, but now he seemed to relax. Rostov was smarter than he looked. A man afraid would often hold back parts of the truth for fear it would get him in trouble. An assured man often had trouble *stopping* himself from talking.

Rostov fished into his pocket and brought out two small photographs. "Have you ever seen these men before? Their names are Yuri and Viktor?"

The attendant looked at the photos of the two corpses and his face paled. "They're dead. What happened to them?"

"I shot them," Rostov said.

"But . . ."

360

"Because they didn't answer my goddam questions. Have you ever seen these men?"

"I think I saw them a few times. I've only worked here for a few months."

"All right. Sergei Tal. You know him?"

"He died. I read about it in the paper. Did you kill him too?"

"No, he did," Rostov said, jerking his thumb toward Kamen. "Did you know him?"

"He was a member, but I didn't know him."

"You wouldn't recognize him if you saw him?"

"I don't think so," the young man stammered.

"Do you rent apartments here?"

"No."

"These two men—Rostov waved the photos again—"listed this as their permanent address. How is that then possible?"

"I don't know. Wait. We have two kinds of facilities here. There is the main gymnasium which is open to the public but we also have members' suites, with private equipment and baths and quarters."

"In essence, an apartment, you cretin," Rostov snapped.

The man seemed flustered. He looked toward Kamen for support and Kamen glanced away.

"Let me look." The man went to the desk and began looking through a membership index. He found Tal's name and looked up with a smile, wanting desperately to please the giant policeman. "Here it is. Sergei Tal. He has Suite A."

"Take us there."

"I don't have the keys to the private section," the young man sputtered.

"Take us there anyway."

They followed the man down a maze of hallways, past a sauna room and a steam room, past a large communal shower and a string of handball courts. Finally in a far

361

corridor, they reached a heavy metal door, inset with wired glass.

"There are several suites back there," the attendant said. "But I can't get inside. They have their own entrance to the street."

"You have no key?"

"No."

"Do you know where the key is kept?"

"No. I do not."

"What if there were a fire?" Rostov said. "What would you do?"

"Call the fire department."

"Go back to your office and wait for us," Rostov said angrily. "And make no telephone calls. This line is now being monitored by the militsia."

"Yes, sir," the man said. He hastened off down the hallway, almost at a trot.

"It's always nice watching Clint Eastwood at work," Kamen said.

Rostov grinned. "You think so, Pyotr? I thought I was a little too gentle with him."

"He will have diarrhea for a month."

"He cannot shit his brains out, however, since he has no brains to begin with," Rostov said. When he was sure the young man had indeed gotten back to his office, Rostov reared back and slammed the heel of his boot against the glass door, just above the lock. The door swung open and Rostov led the way through. In the corridor were three identical green doors, marked with letters of the Cyrillic alphabet. In the United States, it would have been A, B and C, Kamen thought.

Rostov tried the kicking trick again on Tal's suite, but the door did not jiggle in the frame. He leaned forward and looked at the sturdy cylinder lock.

"Call a locksmith?" Kamen suggested.

"Who needs a locksmith when we have Clint East-

362

wood?'' Rostov said with a grin. He pronounced the name as "Cleent Eastvud.''

He took his gun from his jacket holster and Kamen stifled a groan. Shooting out locks worked only in the movies. In the real world, the bullet just ricocheted off and you were lucky if it didn't wind up between your eyes.

Then again, this weapon of Rostov's might blow down the whole door. It was big enough to strike terror in Dirty Harry's heart.

Nevertheless, Kamen moved behind Rostov to be shielded from the bullet. But the big policeman turned the gun around, held it by its barrel, and slammed the butt down on the doorknob, which split off as if it had been sliced.

Rostov grunted over his shoulder. "Can't just shoot off the lock. You might get killed,'' he said. Then he inserted the barrel of his gun in the hole in the door, left by the knob, and fired. The sound reverberated like a cannon through the steel-walled hallway. Kamen heard the other half of the door handle rattling around inside the room.

Kamen tapped him on the shoulder. "Don't you need a search warrant or something to be doing this?''

"I am an officer of the law in the pursuit of my duty,'' Rostov said stiffly. "That is all the authorization I need.''

"Just asking,'' Kamen mumbled, but Rostov was not listening. Now he reared back and slammed his big boot-clad foot against the door just under the cylinder lock and the door popped open. The room was dark but it brightened as the door swung open and the light seeped in from the hallway. Rostov went inside and turned on a light switch which, moronically, Kamen thought, was located not just inside the door but about five feet down the wall away from the door.

They were in a small apartment. The large room held

a couch, a small table and chairs, exercise weights, and an electric treadmill. A gray-and-maroon warmup suit hung from a hook on the wall. Another door in the back led to another room where they solved the mystery of Yuri and Viktor. There were two small cots in there and a closet, which held men's clothing in two different sizes, with a remarkable preference toward pastels in general. Apparently, this had been the home of Viktor and Yuri. Off the bedroom was a small bathroom with a shower stall, sink, and toilet.

Except for the clothing, the closet was empty.

Out in the front room, Kamen saw a small file cabinet underneath the table, against the wall. He knelt down and pulled it out into the room. Rostov roughly shoved him aside and bent over to open the cabinet's single drawer. The cabinet was empty. The policeman snarled, "Damn it. I thought we had something."

"We did," Kamen said. "But somebody beat us to it."

"What do you mean?"

Kamen pointed to the front of the file where the paint had been rubbed off by someone's hand frequently opening it.

Rostov nodded. "And look at this," he said. He pointed to some slash marks, as if made by a knife or a razor on the top of the small table. He leaned close to the tabletop and pointed again to a few flecks of white powder caught around the rim of the metal edging of the table.

"What will you bet that that's cocaine?" he said, almost triumphantly.

He seemed surprised at the dejected look on Kamen's face.

"And what would you bet that someone's been here before us and took everything that was here—records, cocaine, and anything that would help us."

Rostov's angular face soured over.

"We are here now," he said stiffly. "So we will search the place from top to bottom."

"Jawohl, mein führer," Kamen said.

Together, they went through every garment in the closet, looking for something, anything, in a pocket. But Kamen found nothing but lint. Rostov stripped the cots and searched under the sheets, then turned all the furniture upside down and fished inside the hollow legs of the beds for paper, for notes, for anything.

After an hour they still had nothing.

Outside, Rostov gave the same upside-down treatment to the small table and the file cabinets, but the result was the same. He looked around and sighed.

"Wait," he said. "The sweatsuit." He yanked the two-tone garment down from the hook and searched through it, but its single pocket was empty. He was about to replace it on the hook when he said, "Somebody's left their wristwatch." He pointed to it hanging on the clothing hook where it had been hidden by the sweatsuit.

Kamen lifted off the watch, and as he examined it, Rostov hung the clothing back up and looked over his shoulder.

"Cheap American watch," the policeman said.

Kamen nodded. It was a black watch with a black plastic band. The brand name, printed on the face of the watch, said Casio Data Bank.

"It's Tal's," Kamen said. "I remember seeing him wear it."

"Keep it as a memento," Rostov said, but Kamen did not seem to be listening. He was pressing small silver buttons on the side of the watch and then he looked up at Rostov. The policeman thought the American's face looked absolutely gleeful.

"Guess what?" Kamen said.

Rostov cocked an eyebrow.

"Here's Tal's appointment book. Whoever was here before us stole all the records but they missed the watch."

"Let me see that," Rostov said. Kamen held the wristwatch out in front of him so Rostov could see its face.

"It's a small data bank," Kamen said. "I used to have one. You can store phone numbers and appointments in it."

"Well, what's in it?" Rostov asked impatiently.

"No phone numbers," Kamen said after clicking the buttons a few times.

Rostov growled.

"But one appointment. Tomorrow. At P.E. That must be The Pink Elephant."

"Who is the meeting with?" Rostov demanded.

Kamen handed him the wristwatch. Rostov read it and looked up, surprise on his features.

"Sicilians? It says 'Sicilians.' "

Kamen nodded.

"What does it mean?"

"It means the real Mafia is coming to town," Kamen said.

Chapter Twenty-nine

It was long after midnight when Rostov dragged himself, tired in mind and body, back to Olga's apartment. She had made him a doorkey so he could come and go as he pleased, but when he let himself inside, the woman lawyer was sitting on the sofa, reading.

Just a look at his drawn exhausted face told her all she needed to know and without asking, she went into the small kitchen and poured him a glass of vodka.

When she brought it back to the living room, he was slumped on the sofa. He smiled at her as he took the glass.

"Hello and thank you," he said.

"I won't ask you what kind of day it's been," she said.

"Don't. But I will tell you anyway. I think my American is crazy."

"Of course he's crazy. Do you think they would have sent you a sane one?"

"But this is even worse. Tonight we found out that Tal may have been planning to meet with the Sicilian Mafia."

"Are they important?"

"Pyotr knows a great deal about them. Apparently he dealt with them when he was in the United States. He says they were in charge of moving almost all drugs into America until Kamenski testified and closed them down. Apparently, Tal wanted to deal with them to supply drugs here as well."

"He's dead now. So what difference does it make?"

"Tal's meeting was scheduled for tomorrow night and Kamenski wants to go ahead with the meeting. To pretend he's Sergei Tal's partner and make a drug deal with them."

"What's the point of it?" she asked.

"The point? If he goes ahead, we can have a pipeline on all the drugs coming into Russia. They'll come in to Kamenski. Every drug dealer will have to come to him for supplies. At the right moment, we can move in and snap up every drug dealer in the country. And the Sicilian connections too."

"Then let him go ahead with it," she said.

"It's not that simple. If somebody up above has been protecting the drug operation, is involved in it, I'm afraid they may know about the Sicilian meeting. Kamenski could be walking into a trap where everybody knows he's working for the cops."

"Have you told him that yet?"

"Yes. But he doesn't believe it. He says he believes that Sergei Tal was free-lancing this meeting with the Sicilians without the knowledge of his partners."

"So?"

"So, that's just his belief," Rostov said. "He doesn't know that."

"What he doesn't know . . ." she started.

"Could kill him," Rostov said.

"No one can decide but you," she said.

"I know that." Cowboy lit a cigarette and watched the smoke drift toward the ceiling.

"There's just a chance that Pyotr is right. That the higher-ups don't know about the meeting. Maybe Tal was acting on his own," Rostov said. "Maybe he was going to pull it off and then show off by having the whole deal made. I don't know."

"A difficult decision," she said.

"You know what makes it really difficult?" Rostov said.

"What?"

He took a long time smoking before he answered, then jabbed the cigarette out in the black glass ashtray on her end table.

"A long time ago, before I joined the militsia and I was still a simple soldier, I was recruited for special KGB training. At least they called it that. But it was really a screening process to recruit members for Spetsnaz, the sabotage and terrorist unit of military intelligence."

"I didn't know you trained for Spetsnaz," she said.

"I managed to get out," Rostov said. He lit another cigarette. "Did you ever hear how they trained their members to fight?"

"No one ever hears anything about Spetsnaz."

"They used to bring prisoners into the training camp. These were serious criminals, tough people, thugs who had been condemned to death. We called them puppets."

"And trainees fought with them?"

"In a way," Cowboy said. "But not a regular fight. It was one man versus another man. Like a Roman arena. And it was barehanded. At one time we were allowed to kill them. In those days, there was no shortage of condemned prisoners. When I came in, we were not allowed to kill them anymore. But they were allowed to try to kill the trainees."

"Why?"

"Because it is necessary for men in Spetsnaz to know their missions deal with life and death. To learn that, they have to face death. These puppets would put you in that frame of mind. And remember, they would fight as hard as they could because it was their one way of staying alive. As long as they were able to fight, they were able to live. And we were not supposed to kill them in the fights. But we did anyway."

"Did you . . . ?"

"Yes," he said in a flat emotionless voice. "Just like anybody else would. I was fighting a multiple rapist in an arena, before spectators. He got me down and was choking the life out of me. I found a stone and I beat his head in with it. Yes, I killed mine. That was when I decided to leave the program."

"That's awful."

"I did not like the killing, but I did it. What I could not stand, though, was the thought of these poor condemned men willing to kill just to live a few days, a few months more, in captivity. All puppets died eventually. They were either killed by a trainee or else they were injured so badly they were sent back to prison and their regular death sentence was carried out. And nobody cared."

"And you don't want Kamenski to be your puppet, is that it?" Olga asked.

"Not mine and not the puppet of someone who might be above me in rank but is corrupt and wants Pyotr to die. I do not want that death on my hands."

She was silent a long time. Then she said, "Those puppets had no choice. Give Kamenski a choice. Let him decide. At least then it is not on your head."

"I gave him a choice," Rostov said. "I told him he might be wrong about Tal's free-lancing this meeting. I told him there was a very good chance that the Sicilians would know about him before the meeting."

"And what did he say?" she asked.

Despite his somber mood, Rostov chuckled. "He said 'Fuck it, nobody lives forever.' ''

"He has had a choice. He has decided and he is no longer a puppet and you must not feel guilt over it."

"I've told myself that. And I still do. I don't want that responsibility."

"It is not yours," she said.

"I wish I were as sure as you," he said numbly. And lit another cigarette.

Omar was under orders not to speak. Kamen had told him that he had to think, so when the cabdriver, on Kamen's orders, parked across the street from the luxury apartment building, Omar had sprawled out across the front seat and fallen almost instantly asleep.

Why have I come here? Am I going to learn anything by sitting in a cab across the street from an apartment building? I don't even know which apartment is his.

Kamen sat upright in the seat, his face close to the window, staring, thinking.

And I don't have anything but a hunch. Leonid Nabokov was Tal's lawyer but never collected a fee. He just happened to be in court that day to defend the drug driver from Afghanistan who just happened to get killed later. And when I met him in his office, he knew my name and he was afraid of me. He is in this. Somehow, he is in this.

He leaned away from the window as a gray chauffeured limousine pulled up to the apartment building's front entrance. Nabokov hopped out of the back seat with agility that surprised Kamen—*Why should I be surprised? Maybe he spends all his time exercising to better serve his young wife*—and stepped quickly around the other side of the car to open the rear door himself. *Odd. He should wait for the chauffeur to do that.*

He couldn't see who got out of the car's back seat.

Then the driver pulled away and Kamen saw Mrs. Nabokov, wearing a long white fur coat over a red sequined gown, standing next to her husband. Even at this distance, even under just the light from the apartment building's all glass entranceway, she was stunning. She was smiling now at Nabokov, who was talking to her, apparently earnestly.

She nodded and he took her arm firmly and guided her toward the apartment's front door. *Like newlyweds,* Kamen thought. *Or at least, he's like a newlywed.* As they turned their backs on him and walked away from Kamen's vantage point, he could imagine he could still see Mrs. Nabokov's face, her body, the sexual musk she seemed to exude.

The man is pussy-whipped, pure and simple, Kamen thought. A small smile crossed his face. He leaned over the front seat and tapped Omar on the shoulder.

"Let's go," he said. Omar awoke like an animal. He lay in the same spot, focussing mind and body, not flailing around as he climbed back to consciousness, then suddenly he sat upright, turned on the car key, and drove away from the curb.

"Home, rich boss?"

"Home, Omar," Kamen said. He had an idea.

Even when he had been living alone, on the run, on those nights when he hadn't been able to find a woman, Kamen had never spent any time looking at pornographic films. He knew that some people—mostly men—liked them and that for some, suffering through enforced loneliness, they were almost a form of therapy, at least some kind of psychological catharsis that could take the mind off the genitals, at least for a while. But they just never interested him. It was not even a question of morality, because when he had been working for the mob, Kamen had personally gotten involved in the financing for a string of porn parlors, X-rated film producers, massage shops, and it had all been just another way to make a buck for his bosses. If people wanted to screw in front of cameras, and they were over eighteen and doing it of their own free will, well, turn them loose. No skin off his nose. Just don't ask him to watch them. A matter of personal taste.

So what am I doing here watching this dismal dubbed Russian porn film? he asked himself when he was back in his apartment.

He had called The Pink Elephant, but there was no answer. The club obviously had closed for the night and Tash had gone home. He would call her in the morning. When he hung up the phone, he slid into his VCR one of the sex films that Rostov had left for him.

He sat on the sofa, drinking a large glass of wine and using the remote control to speed the film along. It was some kind of elaborate story that appeared to him to be a detective story, except that the detective never seemed to take any money for his work.

He was halfway through the film when there was a tapping on the door.

Kamen pressed the stop button on the VCR, and the picture vanished from the screen, replaced by a hissing staticky snow. He took his pistol from under the sofa seat before he went to the door, then held it at his side as he unlocked the door. Rostov. He expected the Cowboy but instead he saw Tash there.

She was smiling.

"Tash," he said, unable to hide his surprise.

"Happy to see me?" she said.

"Yes, but . . ."

"May I come in?"

"Oh. Sure." He realized he was still holding the gun in his right hand, and he leaned over and hid it on a table behind a small lamp before he unlocked the chain on the door and let the woman inside. She was wearing a long woolen coat that was nipped tightly at the waist and looked a far cry from the usual shapeless Russian garment he had seen so much of in the past few weeks.

He closed and locked the door behind her, then, as he turned to her, she stepped forward into his arms and kissed him hard on the mouth.

"I'm just surprised," he said.

"I know. I wanted to surprise you." She smiled her very warm smile. "I didn't know what this first night at the club would be like, so I made arrangements for Rosa to stay with friends. And I thought I would spend the night with you. Oh . . ." She looked around nervously. "Pyotr, you don't have a woman here, do you? I didn't barge in on . . ."

He laughed. "No. Just home alone."

Now that she was there, she didn't seem to know what to do. He took her coat and she looked around and said, "So this is where you live."

"Yes."

"It is a nice apartment," she said. "But small."

"Serviceable, though," he said.

"Rather like you," she said, and smiled again. She looked at the television's snow and said, "You were watching television."

"Just a tape. I'll turn it off."

She caught his hand. "No," she said. "I think I would like to watch television with you." She led him back to the sofa and pulled him down beside her. "And a glass of wine to share," she said. "What could be nicer?"

She kissed him again, her tongue searching out his this time, pressing her body against his. Their lips were together for long seconds and then she pulled back with a sigh and another smile.

"So. The film," she said. She reached for the remote-control device.

"You won't like this film," he said.

"Nonsense. I like all films."

She clicked the switch and the TV screen went dark and then the picture began again. The scene was shot from street level. Leaning out an upstairs window, showing a lot of cleavage in a low-cut blouse, a young blonde women spoke to a man in the street, obviously her husband. She wished him a good day and told him she would think of him every minute. He assured her the same.

As they spoke, the film's angle changed. The camera was behind the woman in the upstairs hallway. She was naked from the waist down, and even as she spoke with her husband, the film's private detective was standing behind her, plowing from behind. The film moved in for what Kamen knew X-film makers called "a monster shot," a huge closeup of the man's thick penis sliding in and out of the woman's body.

Kamen looked at Tasha. She was staring at the screen, in obvious surprise, her mouth partly open.

"Pyotr," she said. "I'm shocked."

"I told you you wouldn't like this film. Turn it off."

"No," she said. "I think I like it very much. Do you watch these often?"

"Never," he said.

"Why tonight?"

"I am looking for a woman," he said.

"In case you hadn't noticed, I am a woman," Tasha said. She kissed him again, then leaned back against the couch cushion to watch the movie. She put the remote control on her left side. With her right arm, she reached around Kamen's shoulders and pulled him back with her.

"I . . . I . . ."

"Shhhh. I think this is a good part here," she said. "And the dialogue is so wonderful. Listen. 'I can't wait until you get in tonight.' Isn't that clever?" She was smiling. She was teasing him.

"I really was working, looking for someone," he said.

"Then I will help you work. We will look together," Tasha said. "No one should have to do such hard work alone."

On the screen, the husband had finally left and the young blonde had turned, dropped to her knees, and was now performing oral sex on the detective.

"You must tell me all about the story so I am sure not to miss a nuance," Tasha said.

"I—"

"But later. During a dull moment. I do not want to miss anything. I might learn something," she said.

As uncomfortable as he had ever been in his life, Kamen sat next to her, held in place by her right arm around his neck, her hand idly touching his chest.

The onscreen couple had left the hallway now and were in a bedroom. A moment later, they were undressed and in bed where the woman showed that she was limber as well as lubricious.

Tasha put her lips to Kamen's ear. "I love this," she said huskily.

"I'm embarrassed," he said.

"Don't be," she said. "I am not teasing. I have never seen such a film before. I've heard of them, of course, but I have never seen one. I love it."

Kamen blinked hard in surprise and looked at her and realized that she was just an open honest woman telling him the absolute truth. A porn-by-mail operator had told him that once; that women bought almost half of the erotic videotapes but that they rarely watched them alone. Men watched alone; women watched with their lovers. Kamen had never really believed that until now, but looking at Tasha, he could. Her mouth was slightly open and she sipped air through her lips. Her left hand dropped the remote control and found its way to Kamen's lap where she unzipped his trousers, reached inside, and fondled him. To his delight, he was instantly erect and she licked his ear and said, "I will do everything to you that they do on this film."

"Careful," he said. "You haven't seen the part yet with the donkey."

She saw his grin and looked at him in mock horror. "Oh, and we haven't a donkey," she said. "I guess you'll just have to do." She squeezed his penis. "I think you'll do just fine," she said.

And then there wasn't any more point in watching the film because Tasha's face was in his lap, even as her hands reached up and began to unbutton his clothing. He was naked first and then he did the same for her and he said, "The bedroom's inside," and she answered, "No, here." He reached for the television control and she said, "No, leave it on. I want to watch," and then she knelt on the floor, her upper body across the coffee table, and Kamen moved behind her and her orgasm was instantaneous, just as he touched her body. He entered her gently and she gasped and squirmed her body back against him, never taking her eyes off the television screen, and they made love, in that position, that way, for more minutes than Kamen thought he could stand. She came again and then again, and the second time, he climaxed with her, wrapping his arms tight around her upper body, fondling her hard nipples, and she cried out in pleasure as the two of them just leaned forward against the table, exhausted, warm, fitting each other as if they had been joined since birth.

Finally, he pulled away from her and she looked up at him and said, "You are a very gentle man, Pyotr."

"And you are a very sexy woman."

"But only with you," she said. She saw something in his face and she said, "Yes, there have been other men, you know that. But it was never like this; it was never pleasure for me. From the time of my husband who beat me, sex was pain, sex was—"

He put his hand gently over her mouth. "That was the past," he said. "Forget the past."

Then he helped her to her feet and led her into the small bedroom and climbed with her into the big bed, under the heavy down comforter.

He cuddled up to her back, with his left arm reaching over her and holding her breast, and she said, "Forget the past? Can we? Is there a future?"

Kamen said, "You are a big nightclub operator now. Soon you will be rolling in money, able to support a donkey like me in fine fashion. Any man would be proud to make a future with you."

"Any man? Including you? Is there a future for us?"

"Especially me," he said. "And I don't want to see my future unless you are in it with me."

He heard her crying soft tears of happiness into her pillow and he held her in his arms until she slept.

And when she was deeply asleep, he went back outside, put on his underwear, and sat back on the couch and began watching the sex film all over again. But he could not stop thinking of what his future might hold.

Chapter Thirty

When Omar showed up at Kamen's apartment, the American had just reached Rostov on the phone. He asked the cabdriver to wait in the hall, closed the door, and went back to the phone.

"There's something you should find out," Kamen said.

"What is that?"

"When Tal was killed, was he carrying a key to his suite at the health club? And did those two goons of his also carry the same kind of key?"

Cowboy was quiet for a moment. "Of course," he said. "I will be back to you."

Kamen hung up and looked around the apartment to make sure that Tash had left no traces of her presence before she had left in the morning. The inspection was not really necessary; after all, Omar was his employee but Kamen considered himself just old-fashioned enough to care about appearances.

Satisfied, he finally opened the door and Omar came

inside. He looked around the small apartment and was obviously not impressed.

"Just temporary housing," Kamen said, "until I get settled. I need a photographer who can shoot videotape."

Omar nodded.

"And if he has some kind of studio equipment, that's even better," Kamen said.

Omar nodded again.

"Now don't tell me you have a brother-in-law who just happens to be in the photography business," Kamen said.

"No. Not a brother-in-law, but a friend of a friend," Omar said.

"The man must work rapidly, dropping all other jobs. It goes without saying that he will be well-paid," Kamen said.

"Brothers-in-law mean nothing. Everyone has a brother-in-law. But only to you, rich boss, would I entrust a friend."

"So it also goes without saying that he has to be discreet."

"How discreet?" Omar asked.

"This discreet: If he says one word of anything to anybody, I will put a bullet between his eyes."

"That kind of discretion does not come cheaply," Omar said. "Even from a friend."

"I know that, you Armenian bandit, and that is why I am going to have you negotiate for me. You will be my intermediary. I will never see this photographer and he will never see me."

"He will just hear the click of your gun if he ever speaks to anyone."

"Now you have it," Kamen said.

"I can have him in an hour. Perhaps you can tell me what it is he is going to take pretty pictures of?"

"There is a woman. Her name is . . ."

After Omar left, Kamen decided that he was ravenously hungry. His meals since he arrived in Russia had been, with the exception of the steak he cooked at Tash's, sporadic, unexceptional affairs.

In the kitchen he found eggs and bread but no bacon or ham. He would have to talk to Omar to get some fresh supplies for his refrigerator. Omar would know how, Kamen thought.

He scrambled eggs and toasted his bread on a fork over the gas burner when he could not find a toaster, and was just about to eat when there was a knock on the door.

This time it was Rostov who followed Kamen into the kitchen, saw his food, and said, "All that food makes me thirsty."

He went uninvited to the kitchen counter and poured himself a glass of vodka.

"You drink too much," Kamen said.

"All Russians drink too much. It is only too much when you cannot function any longer."

"Why is it that all Russians drink like this?" Kamen asked as he shoveled scrambled eggs into his face.

Rostov gave a large expressive shrug. He sat on the chair across from Kamen's. "Who knows?" the policeman said. "Maybe it is the long Russian winters."

"This is summer," Kamen said.

"Yes, but if you start drinking in the winter, it is hard to stop in the summer."

"I don't think the weather has anything to do with it."

"Neither do I," Cowboy said. "I think it has something to do with the fact that it is always winter in a Russian's soul. We are a dour, depressed people. There is little happiness in the life of most Russians. But there is always happiness to be found in a bottle."

"And cirrhosis of the liver. And God knows what

else," Kamen said. "You know, when I was growing up, I thought this was a people's paradise."

"Your grandfather's viewpoint?"

"No. I read the newspapers in America. They made this sound like heaven for the working man. Grampa always said that the Communists were as bad a bunch of thugs as the Czarists. The only difference, he said, was that the Communists were stupider."

"He was certainly right about that," Rostov said pleasantly. "Anyway, I talked with the morgue. Tal and his two men all had an identical pair of keys that were not for The Pink Elephant. Obviously, they were for the outside door and the apartment at the health club."

Kamen grunted.

"So naturally your idea was correct. Whoever broke into Tal's suite came in from the street and probably had his own keys. I found out who rented the other health club suites."

Kamen put down his fork to concentrate. "Imagine my embarrassment when one of them was in the name of my superior, Colonel Svoboda," Cowboy said.

"Maybe you were embarrassed, but you weren't surprised, were you?" Kamen said.

"I suppose not," Cowboy said. "One wonders how a mere colonel can afford such a thing."

"Maybe it's a fringe benefit of the job," Kamen said diffidently. "There were three. Who's the other one?"

"A well-known attorney in the city," Rostov said.

"Don't tell me, let me guess. Leonid Nabokov."

Rostov's eyes opened wider. "How did you know that?"

"He was Tal's lawyer but never seemed to get paid. He yanked a drug dealer out from under you in court." The American decided not to say that he had already met Nabokov.

"He is a well-known attorney. He represents many people," Rostov said. "Surely you don't think—"

"That Nabokov was Tal's partner in the drug business? Of course I do."

Rostov sipped his drink before replying. "Normally, with anyone else, I would say such a remark is beyond comprehension."

"Work on your comprehension," Kamen snapped, and started eating again.

"But Olga works with Nabokov's son in the prosecutor's office. He is always trying to talk to her about me; he knows about you, and Olga thinks such information could come only from his father."

"Case closed," Kamen said.

"But such a well-respected attorney . . ."

"Come on. Grow up to capitalism. You never heard of a lawyer who was a crook?"

Kamen, a disgusted look on his face, got up and went to the stove to pour himself some tea.

"Forgive me," Rostov said. "You are patently correct. It's just that . . . well, when I was a boy, I thought about being a lawyer. And Leonid Nabokov was my hero."

"A regular Perry Mason, I bet," Kamen said sarcastically.

"You joke, but it is true. Nabokov feared no one. He fought the state when no one else dared fight the state."

"A long time ago there was a cop on the payroll in New York City. He was a great crimefighter, a real gangbuster. He was always in the press rapping the mob, the criminals, the syndicate, the underworld. And he was on our damned payroll. We let him say anything he wanted because it helped give him credibility. No one would ever suspect him. So he had a pipeline into every prosecutor's office, every law-enforcement agency, everything. And when we needed to know something, he let us know."

"Are you saying Nabokov might be doing that same thing?"

"I don't know," Kamen said. "All I'm telling you is don't discount it."

Rostov nodded, rose, and poured more vodka. Some spilled on the wooden tabletop and he wiped it up with his handkerchief. Oddly, Kamen thought, it was a blue and white handkerchief, like the kind American railroad men used to carry. Or cowboys. Cowboys used to carry handkerchiefs like that. *Correct in all the small details is Lev Rostov.* Kamen liked that.

"It again brings up the question of tonight's meeting with the Sicilians. There is danger in it for you."

"I told you, I don't think Tal told anybody about the meeting. If there's danger, it's going to come from your end. From the leak in your department. Have you told this Colonel Svoboda about the meeting?"

"Not yet."

"Are you going to?" Kamen asked.

"It is my duty," Rostov said.

"Your dedication to duty can get me killed tonight," Kamen said.

"It is my duty, yes. But many other things are my duty also. I just may not get around to telling Colonel Svoboda about tonight's meeting. Perhaps not for days yet."

Kamen smiled.

"Suppose you have this meeting and suppose you survive. Then what do we do?"

"About what?"

"About Nabokov. If you are correct about him."

"With luck, the meeting will provide us with some ammunition. If not, well, there are other ways."

"What kind of ways?" Rostov asked.

"I'm working on them already," Kamen said.

"And you're not going to say anything."

"Not now, no."

"All right for now," Rostov said. "It has been a pleasure drinking with you." He rose and walked to the door, then saw atop the VCR two of the pornographic videos he had provided with the apartment.

"Glad to see you're enjoying the television," he said.

"More than you know," Kamen said without embarrassment.

No more than two minutes after Cowboy left Kamen's apartment, Omar knocked on the door.

Kamen suspected that Omar had come to the door, heard voices, and gone back across the street to wait for Rostov to leave. But he knew Omar would deny that fact, if asked, so he did not bother to ask.

"How did you do?"

"It was very difficult, boss," Omar said. "It was exceedingly difficult."

"Stop trying to raise the price. Let's just cut to the chase," Kamen said.

Omar looked puzzled. "There was no chase. We were never seen."

"Never mind. Just an expression. Tell me what happened."

"From sources known only to me, I found that the woman regularly leaves her apartment at eleven A.M., after her husband has gone to his office. We were ready for her in the taxi across the street. We photographed her leaving the building and getting into a limousine. We thought she might be on her way to an assignation, so I followed her in my taxicab. But, alas, boss, she went only to the department store. However, we shot much more film of her as she walked around. And at your request, many more shots of the parked limousine. Finally, she stopped in the department store to get her fingernails polished. Why is it that women do that, boss?"

"I don't know," Kamen said. "Maybe just to have something to do with their free time."

"I think you're right," Omar said. "At any rate, that looked like it might take a long time and I thought you might be in a hurry, and so I dropped the photographer off and I raced back here as fast as I could drive without attracting police attention."

"Omar, you are the charm of the world. Who has the videotape?"

Omar smiled. "I do, rich boss. Under threat of death, I would not let it out of my hands."

He reached into the inside pocket of his long shapeless denim jacket and handed Kamen a videocassette.

"Fine. And your cameraman is still available?"

"He waits only for our word to spring into action," Omar said.

"What was the woman wearing?" Kamen asked.

"A long red coat. Presumably a dress beneath it, although I did not see it and cannot swear to it. Black high-heeled shoes. A woman of very fine leg proportion, boss."

"Yes, I've noticed. You got a good look at her face?"

"To the dismay of my wife, yes. It is a face I will dream of for all nights to come."

"All right. Here is the next thing you must do. You must find a woman with the same color hair. You must find a long red coat and black high heels."

Omar was grinning.

"What is so funny?"

"I have no idea what we are doing, boss, but I am sure that already I like it very much."

"It gets better," Kamen said.

Two hours later, Omar returned.

"Mission accomplished, boss."

"You have the tape?"

"Yes."

"Let's take a look at it," Kamen said. He took the cassette from Omar and put it in the tape player under his television, turned on the set, waited for it to warm up, and then pressed the recorder's play button.

The picture was grainy and just a touch out of focus. It showed a young woman in a long red coat walking up the steps of an apartment house.

"It's in color," Kamen said.

"My friend says it will be no problem to transfer it to black-and-white," Omar said.

Kamen nodded and watched the tape again. The dark-haired young woman in the photos was obviously not Mrs. Nabokov but her hair was cut the same way and she was almost as stunningly beautiful as the lawyer's wife.

The film showed her walking up the steps of an apartment building, then turning at the top of the steps, then coming back down, only to walk up again. The photographer kept switching camera angles, shooting from various spots. Often he caught only the side of her face, or the back of her head with her ebony hair swinging. A little judicious editing, Kamen thought, and this could be perfect.

"Who's the girl?" he asked.

"I have this beautiful niece. She was only too glad to do Uncle Omar a favor."

"Family's always trouble," Kamen said. "She's going to tell everyone about the funny job Uncle Omar gave her."

"No, she will not," Omar stated firmly. "My loving niece and I already share many secrets. Since her sixteenth birthday, we have shared secrets. She knows that Uncle Omar will take care of her, as long as she keeps her mouth closed at inappropriate times."

Kamen had not taken his eyes off the screen. The girl was beautiful and sexily built, and without looking up, Kamen said, "You're a rascal, Omar."

"You have always known that, rich boss."

"How about a dirty old man?"

"I assure you that my niece regards me as a dirty young man."

On the television screen, the girl had vanished inside the apartment building. The next sequence showed her outside the door of an apartment; the camera seemed to have been hidden behind a banister or a potted plant, because only glimpses of the young woman's legs, her black high heels, the swirl of her coat, once in a while the flash of her hair, were ever visible.

"This is truly excellent work, Omar," Kamen said.

"Have I ever failed you?"

"No. Honestly, no."

"Then you will understand when I tell you I have incurred certain expenses on this assignment, that I am not trying to deceive you."

"Of course not. How much?"

"It was necessary to buy a red coat. There is not such a thing in my family, but the photographer assured me that even if we worked in black-and-white photos, a red coat could not be replaced by anything else."

"Right. A red coat it was. Anything else?"

"And high heels. Almitra—my niece—owned no such things. I bought them in her size and she will be happy—and silent—forever."

"How much?"

"Call it one hundred dollars American," Omar said.

"A bargain," Kamen said. The last frames of the tape showed side views, distant shots, of the young dark-haired woman coming down the steps of the apartment building, and Kamen nodded, stopped the tape, pressed rewind, and said, "Now the most important part. Your television cameraman is still on call?"

"Yes, boss. I have paid him enough money on your behalf to stay on call for five days."

"And he has editing equipment?"

"I do not understand what that is all about, but I asked him and he told me he did."

"Fine. Come over here with me and let me explain the instructions I have written down for him."

Chapter Thirty-one

"I've dealt with these bastards before. You don't have to tell me to be careful," Kamen said.

"You've dealt with these bastards before when they were in America. Now these Sicilians are Russian bastards and they may be different."

"Don't worry about a thing."

"When they come, just press this switch under your desk. That will activate the transmitter," Rostov said. "We will be in an apartment two buildings over monitoring everything. If anything looks as if it's going bad, we will move in."

"Fine," Kamen said. They were in the upstairs office at The Pink Elephant. Rostov had just finished installing a small transmitter under the desk. A wire, which served as its aerial, was taped along the back of the desk in a zigzag pattern. Kamen had insisted that the bug have an on-off switch. "How the hell could I get any work done here if I know you're listening in?'' Rostov had grumbled, but finally given in.

''Remember. We don't have any guarantee that they're coming tonight. Or any night, for that matter,'' Kamen said.

''I know. And if you don't want to do this, it's all right by me. I don't like the whole thing anyway,'' Cowboy said.

''In for a penny, in for a pound,'' Kamen said lightly. He glanced at his wristwatch. ''Go away,'' he said. ''For all we know, they've already got somebody watching the place.''

''Naturally. That's why I'm going out the front door, just like a regular customer,'' Rostov said.

''That explains why you're not wearing your cowboy hat,'' Kamen said.

Rostov nodded and walked from the big office that had been Sergei Tal's.

Through the one-way window, Kamen watched him stroll casually through the cocktail area and out the front door. Tash was busy with customers at a far corner table and did not see him. *Just as well,* Kamen thought. *One more question I don't have to answer.*

He was the same policeman who had shot the two men outside her apartment door. Tash recognized the big man, even though he was again wearing civilian clothes, as he walked quickly through The Pink Elephant and out the front door.

He had come down from the upstairs office where Pyotr was working. What was he doing there? What business did he have with Pyotr? And just who was Pyotr Kamenski? She made up her mind: She would ask him tonight.

* * *

When the knock came on the door, Kamen's hand strayed toward the speaker switch under his desk, lingered there for a moment, then moved away without touching the switch.

Sorry, Cowboy. Not this time, he thought.

He walked to the door. Three men stood in the hall. They were short and swarthy. They wore well-tailored suits and, thank God, he had never seen any of them before.

The man in the center stepped forward one pace. He was, perhaps, in his fifties with a pencil-line mustache and cold lizard-lidded eyes. Alone of the three, he wore a hat. The two men who flanked him were obviously his bodyguards; they were younger and their eyes flitted nervously about as the rock music from downstairs swept into the hallway. *That's right,* Kamen thought. *It's so noisy here that no one would hear a gunshot. But I won't shoot mine if you don't shoot yours.*

"Mr. Tal?" the leader said.

"Com'esta," Kamen answered in Italian. The faces of the three Sicilian drug merchants brightened.

"You speak our language?" the leader answered in Italian.

Kamen nodded. "Since my childhood," he said with a warm smile. "Some of my best friends are Italian. Please come inside."

Alexei Svoboda had been a bureaucrat in the militsia for so long he had forgotten how to be a policeman. So when he left his apartment for a pleasant evening on the town, he not only did not notice that he was being followed, he never even entertained the possibility and so never looked into his rearview mirror.

Anyone accustomed to seeing him in his military-style uniform, pinpoint-pressed and as dapper as a member of a drill team, might have had trouble recognizing him in his off-duty garb. He wore a white silk jacket with light gray threads in it, and a pair of matching gray linen slacks. His shoes were Italian leather loafers in gray patent leather, with long tassels hanging on the front gore of the shoes. His thought obviously was, no one knows me. Why even bother to look around?

So when he entered the small club in one of Moscow's sleaziest sections, he never noticed that three minutes later a young blonde man came in and sat alone at the bar.

By that time, Svoboda was already stalking his night's prey—a dark-skinned youth in a leather jacket, who wore eyeliner and earrings in both ears. The young man had come to join Svoboda in the booth he took at the back of the club.

George Golovin saw them talking. He saw them laughing and he saw Svoboda take a small glassine envelope from an inside pocket of his jacket, show it to the youth, and then replace it in his pocket.

Cocaine, Golovin thought. *He's got the nerve to come in here waving drugs around. Wait until Cowboy hears about this.*

"They're late," Cowboy said to Federenko. They were in an apartment two buildings away from The Pink Elephant. The apartment was regularly occupied by a cousin of the sergeant's, but she had been told to get lost for the night and was staying with friends.

The sergeant grunted. "My wife just read a book they're selling here now. *The Godfather*. You ever hear of it?"

Cowboy nodded, and stared glumly at the small radio receiver that sat silently atop a dismal metal kitchen table.

"It's all about Italian gangsters. From what my wife tells me, they're never late. They're always on time."

"I don't think so," Cowboy said.

"Argue with the book. That's what it said. Italian gangsters are always punctual. Neat and businesslike too. She said to me that she wished we had only Italian gangsters to deal with because they were all so nice and professional."

"Books have been known to lie," Cowboy said.

"Only the ones written by Marx and Engels," the sergeant said.

Cowboy grinned. "Heresy," he said. "Off to the gulag with you."

They called Rostov a cowboy, but the Sicilians were the real cowboys, Kamen thought. They rode through life like it was a Wild West show, shooting left and right, not caring who they hit, not once looking around.

They came from a country in which criminal behavior was a normal part of normal life. So they don't worry about who's watching or what they're doing or how they're doing it, and when they get outside of Sicily, they're in trouble.

The three men followed Kamen into the office and sat, next to each other, on the sofa to which he waved them. Again the two younger men flanked the third. Kamen offered them a glass of red wine which he had brought up from the bar before the club opened, and when they agreed, he poured them glasses. It was an American table wine, wildly overpriced in Moscow, but they smiled and fussed over it as if it were the prize of their local crop.

"Yes, a fine wine, Mr. Tal," the man said, which prompted a pair of nods from the others.

"I'm not Sergei Tal," Kamen said. "I'm his partner."

The three men looked shocked for a moment. "We were supposed to meet with Mr. Tal."

"Sergei is dead," Kamen said.

"Oh." A pause. "I'm sorry to hear that."

"I'm not," Kamen said. "I killed him." He sipped at

his wine and glanced over the glass at them. Their faces showed very little reaction. This now was something they understood . . . killing a friend or a partner. *What animals these people are. But then you've always known that, haven't you?*

"But I was his partner and I am now in charge of the business, so we can proceed with our discussions as if nothing had happened," Kamen had said. "What point had you reached with Tal?"

"I think we would like to speak among ourselves for just a few moments," the older man said.

Kamen nodded. "Caution is the food of long life," he said, and thought, *How easily all this babble comes back to me, all this mock pseudo-polite bullshit. And in pidgin Italian, no less.*

"I will go downstairs for a moment to check the cash register," he said with a smile. "And then I will return. If you are here, we will discuss business. If you have left, well, then I hope you have a pleasant flight home."

Kamen went out into the hall. This was the critical moment, whether their greed could triumph over their caution. He had very little doubt about the outcome of such a contest, since caution did not come easily to them and greed was their sole reason for living. Still, he went downstairs. He spoke to Tash briefly and told her he was in a meeting.

"I won't disturb you," she said. "I don't have time to be a nuisance. Look at this crowd. When does the novelty wear off?"

"Maybe never," he said. "Then you can be wealthy and I can live off your labor." He smiled at her and touched the side of her face. *If I stay alive to live off anyone,* he thought.

She smiled back and walked again out into the lounge to check on her waitresses, and Kamen went back upstairs, knocked on the door once, and let himself inside.

The three men, like stuffed toys, were sitting in the

same position on the sofa. The oldest man rose and nodded. "It would be a shame to have come so far and to do no business," he said. "What is your name?"

"Kamenski."

"We can talk to you. That is our decision."

Kamen nodded. *Time now to give them some bad news.*

Alexei Svoboda spoke to the waiter, a young man clad in leather shorts and cowboy boots and a leather vest without a shirt, then dropped a bill upon his tray. He led the young sloe-eyed man toward the door.

From his seat at the bar, Golovin heard him call the youth "Elvis."

He does look like Elvis Presley, the young police officer thought. *And now these two are going to rock and roll.* He picked up his change, left no tip because he doubted he would ever return to such a place, and waited no more than thirty seconds before following the two men out the door of the club.

"Where the hell are they?" Rostov said.

"Only a traffic accident could make an Italian gangster late for a meeting," Sergeant Federenko said.

"They're an hour late."

"Calm down, Cowboy. You have somewhere else to go tonight?"

Once having decided to cast their lot with Kamen, the Sicilians wasted no time in telling him everything he wanted to know.

They had never dealt directly with Tal. A month earlier, a lawyer in Palermo had visited The Pink Elephant while on vacation in Russia. He and Tal had met and Tal had asked him to arrange a meeting with somebody from the Sicilian drug operation.

The lawyer had been reluctant to do so but was persuaded by Tal's promise of a ten-thousand-American-dollar fee.

The Sicilian family was contacted and by telegram had set the meeting for this night.

"And it was your belief that Sergei wanted to talk to you about supplying all the narcotics used in Russia?" Kamen said.

"That is so," the older man said solemnly.

"That is correct," Kamen said. "We have had a problem maintaining a regular supply of goods. Russia is in such turmoil now. We thought that your family could provide all the 'goods' we need . . . first for Moscow. Then for this Russian republic. And finally for all fifteen republics of the former Soviet Union. We know of your reputation and we know that you could meet all our needs. And of course on this end we would provide the operation with police protection, with transport, with people. You would supply at a regular market price. You would supply. We would run. Was that your understanding, my friends?"

"Yes."

Kamen smiled sadly. "It would have been a very fine arrangement," he said.

"Would have been?" the older man said.

"Yes. I am afraid complications have arisen." Kamen sat down heavily on a soft chair, as if overcome by the travail that filled his life.

"Perhaps you should tell us of these complications. Complications often have a way of working themselves out."

The smiled an oily smile, and Kamen allowed himself to look cheered as he raised his head.

"It is the Americans," he said.

"What have the Americans to do with this?"

"Don Gesualdo Ciccolini. He is from New York. . . ."

"We know where he is from," the older man said with a hint of snap in his voice.

"He has contacted me. He has said that he will send over many men, much equipment, much supplies. He has offered . . . no, that is not the correct word. He has *told* me that he and he alone will run the drug business in Russia and in the rest of the nations. We here will have nothing. Our salesmen will be out of work. Our suppliers will be thrown to the wind. All who come to rely on us will be in the hands of strangers."

"And what did Ciccolini offer you in return?" the older man said.

Kamen noticed that the older man had dropped all the "Don" and formalistic crap now. Don Gesualdo Ciccolini was in their way and all of a sudden he was just "Ciccolini."

"He said that we would be paid ten percent of the gross receipts of his organization."

"Do you believe that you will ever see a penny of that money?" the older man said.

"Of course I do not. But I am just one man and ours is still a small organization. I do not have the . . ." He paused as if trying to find the correct word. ". . . the muscle to oppose one such as Don Gesualdo Ciccolini. I would much rather deal with you, but what choice do I have?"

"You will not have to oppose Ciccolini. This is all some sort of mistake," the man said.

Kamen wrinkled his brow as if to ask a question.

The Sicilian nodded. "Our family has done business with Ciccolini. We have an agreement that we supply him in the United States. For that, he stays out of all other countries. It is our agreement."

"Then he has decided to toss your agreement into the garbage, because he has ordered me to deal with him and

398

not with you. And I cannot disobey the commands of one so powerful.''

"Those commands are invalid,'' the older Sicilian snapped.

Kamen shook his head. ''As long as there is a Don Gesualdo Ciccolini, I must obey. I am responsible for the well-being of all those in my family.''

"He is not permitted to issue such orders,'' the man said angrily.

"Yet he has.''

The older man sipped his wine again. ''How much are we talking about in the way of product? In American money.''

"We would start off by buying fifty million dollars of supply from you. That is just at the beginning. As we expand outside Moscow, as we consolidate the other cities, all the republics, we might one day be looking at five hundred million dollars of supply. Every year. In American cash. Who knows?'' Kamen smiled. ''If we are as successful here as you have been in other parts of the world, perhaps that is only a fraction of the final numbers. Maybe, gentlemen, we are talking about billions of dollars. Remember, Russia is an awakening giant. So are all our other satellite nations in Eastern Europe. There will soon be money of all sorts. More than we can imagine now. I would have liked for you all and your family to have been in at the beginning with me.''

The old man stood stiffly. ''Mr. Kamenski,'' he said, ''You may count on it. We will be in with you.''

"But Don Gesualdo Ciccolini? His representatives have warned me to speak to no one else. To tell no one about this. And especially . . .'' He paused. ''Do I dare?'' he said.

"You are among friends. You may speak.''

"Especially, I was told, to mention nothing to the Sicilian donkeys who pretend to be businessmen but are instead nothing but baby-rapers.''

The anger on the old man's face was undisguisable. He snapped his fingers and the two younger men preceded him to the door. The old man stayed behind for a moment.

"You will hear from me here tomorrow," he said. "I think I can promise you a solution to your problem."

"I will wait to hear from you, wise counselor," Kamen said. And then, as if overcome by the passion of the moment, he threw his arms around the older man and squeezed him in a gesture of undying friendship.

The man stood stiffly, taking the demonstration as if it were his due. When Kamen released him, the man nodded curtly. "Tomorrow night," he said, then turned and led his men out the door.

Kamen watched them go, then went to the hot plate and poured himself some tea. He sat at the desk, sipping from his cup, watching the crowd milling around the dance floor below. He waited a full ten minutes.

Then he pressed the switch under the desk.

"Cowboy," he said. "It's Kamenski. It looks like our Sicilian friends aren't coming tonight. Sorry."

He flicked off the switch, then went over to quickly wash out the four wineglasses and put away the bottle, in case Rostov decided to visit again.

Chapter Thirty-two

It had not been one of Cowboy Rostov's best nights. First, the Sicilians had failed to show up. He had intentionally failed to notify his superiors about the meeting and now he had nothing to show for it. It was the kind of mistake that got people thrown out of the service. Fortunately, the only other person who knew—besides Pyotr Kamenski—was Sergeant Federenko, so his secret was safe for now. But only for now. Sooner or. later, something would leak. It always did, and when it did, his career might be over.

And then his surveillance of Alexei Svoboda had produced exactly nothing.

What had he expected? That Svoboda would go down to the theater and sell drugs on the street? Drugs that he had stolen from the militsia evidence room? Or maybe even that he himself would wind up in the meeting with the Sicilian drug merchants?

But none of that had happened. All Svoboda had done was to pick up a nancy boy in a homosexual bar.

"And they went straight to Svoboda's apartment?"

"Yes, Lieutenant," said Golovin. "He and the young man." He paused and looked around as if someone might be listening even though they were inside Rostov's closed office. "They went to the apartment house and they stayed there for two hours. At two A.M., the young man left and I thought it made more sense to follow him than to stay outside the apartment building. I trailed the man to a dingy apartment next door to another fag bar. He stopped first at a restaurant for tea and I was able to get his name from the waitress. I hope that was correct."

"Correct in every detail," Rostov said, politely but not enthusiastically. "You are not to blame if not much happened." He looked at the young policeman and said, "You've been going a long while without sleep. Get some rest."

"I'm sorry, Cowboy. I wish I had more to report."

"Sometimes, the lack of action is as informative as action itself." He nodded sagely, even though some voice inside his head said *What the hell are you talking about, Rostov? Is this a children's show on educational television? Or do you think, perhaps, that you are Sherlock Holmes?* He wanted to scream in frustration, but instead he looked down at the small piece of notepaper that gave the young homosexual's name and address, and nodded again with great surety.

"They call the young man 'Elvis,' like Elvis Presley," Golovin said. Rostov grunted and the young officer said, "I'll be back in a few hours."

"Take your time," Rostov said. *We've got plenty of time because nothing is happening.*

Kamen had gone home with Tash, after The Pink Elephant closed for the night. The ubiquitous Omar had been waiting in his cab across the street and he pulled up in front as the two of them came out.

"Where to, boss?"

"Where to?" Kamen asked Tash.

"My place," she said.

Before Kamen could say anything, Omar pulled away from the curb.

Tash leaned close to him and Kamen squeezed her hand affectionately. She let her hand remain in place just long enough to make her response ambiguous, then took her hand away and settled it in her lap.

Something was bothering her, Kamen realized, and he knew what it was. She was waking to the fact that she knew almost nothing about him. *And what will I do if she asks me point blank, Who is Pyotr Kamenski?*

After Omar arrived at her apartment and Kamen had helped Tash from the cab, the driver asked him, "Should I wait, boss?"

Go home, Kamen. Go home. He looked up and saw Tash marching stolidly toward the apartment's front door and made up his mind.

"No, Omar. You go home. I'll see you tomorrow at my place. Bring the videotape."

"As you speak, boss, so shall it be."

Kamen followed the blonde woman into the building.

Olga had waited the entire evening for Rostov to call, but she had finally tired and gone to bed. But sleep had not come easily and her mind kept drifting back to the Cowboy.

Despite his cocky mannerisms, she knew Rostov was at heart a very traditional man, and the possibility that his colonel, Alexei Svoboda, might be in the employ of the criminal enemy weighed heavily on him. In the last week, she had seen the strain start to tell. He was smoking constantly now and drinking too much, and policemen

403

who did that were prone to mistakes, in a profession where mistakes were often fatal.

Perhaps it was time to spirit him away for a vacation. A week or two at a Black Sea resort might be just the thing to revive his flagging spirits. Deep inside, she knew that it would probably be easier to get milk from a bull than to get Rostov to take time off, but the thought was still cheering and she fell asleep smiling.

Kamen waited until Tash had paid the babysitter and dismissed the teenage girl, then said, "All right, what's the problem?"

"I think we've got a lot of problems," Tasha said. "Such as just who are you?"

"It's what I hate about women," Kamen said mildly. "All you have to do is fall in love with them and the first thing you know, they want to know who you are."

Love? It took her by surprise, Kamen could see, but she was tough. Only just for a split second, and then she shook her head and said, "Where there is love, there are no secrets."

No, darling, that's wrong, Kamen thought. *There are always secrets, and secrets kept in love are the most secret of all.* He thought then of his daughter and her family, out in California, who were alive only because he had kept his family secret from the mob he had worked in. Their lives, his own life, all now depended upon an FBI man keeping secret the fact that Peter Kamen was not really dead.

He had come to Russia to start over, to put all the burdens behind him once and for all, and now he was buying in again. He did not want to, but he looked at Tash and realized that he could not help it.

"Sit down," he said. "I'll make us some tea and then I'll tell you everything."

Rosa was asleep in the small bedroom. Apparently she

slept with her mother most nights, and on those occasions when Kamen—or somebody else—God, have there been a lot of someone elses?—slept over, Tash moved her daughter to the pullout couch in the living room.

Kamen heated water on the gas stove and made two cups of coffee using the last of the powder that was in the small brown grocery bag. Tash sat inside on the couch, unmoving, silent, obviously not willing to soften the mood at all, lest she let him off the hook.

Finally, Kamen came back inside with both cups of the thick goo that Russians pretended was coffee.

He put a cup in front of Tash and then said to himself, *Formal you want it? Formal it is,* and instead of sitting next to her on the couch, sat on the easy chair at the end of the coffee table, at right angles to her.

She sipped her coffee and looked at him, her dark perfectly lined eyebrows raised quizzically.

"What would you like to know?" Kamen asked.

"Everything."

Kamen took a deep breath and said, "I'm a career criminal. There is a worldwide murder contract out on my head. I'm now working undercover for the police. Sergei Tal, your boss, was the head of the Moscow drug ring. He tried to kill me—and you and Rosa—and I killed him instead. I pulled the trigger myself and I would do the same thing again without hesitation. Tonight I set in motion another killing. At any rate, I certainly hope so. I'm buying you The Pink Elephant because I'm rich and I'm in love with you and I'm going to spend the rest of my life in Russia and I want to spend it with you. The only problem is that the rest of my life isn't likely to be very much since my life expectancy is, I guess, about two days. Now where would you like me to start? Or would you rather I just left?"

She did not answer and Kamen put down his cup and began to rise from his seat, but Tash put her hand on his wrist as if to hold him in place.

"Start with your childhood and don't leave anything out," she said.

"I hope you have more coffee," he said.

Rostov walked softly up the dingy steps. On the first floor of the old stone building was a metal stamping shop, and the owner obviously had decided to make some money out of the housing shortage by illegally converting his second and third floors to furnished rooms. Golovin had told him that the young homosexual lived alone on the third floor, but that did not seem logical, since certainly more than one room could have been built on that entire floor.

When he reached the landing, Rostov saw that the rest of the third floor was used for storage of supplies for the metal shop and that there was only one small door that could lead to living quarters.

He walked over and tapped on the door. When there was no answer, he tapped again.

Finally, he heard a voice. "Who is it?"

"Elvis, it's me. Open up."

He heard the lock being turned, and when the door opened a little, he put his shoulder against it and pushed it open, tearing a security chain from its housing as he did.

"Elvis" was a slight young man with dark hair and alabaster skin. In the dim light from a small reading lamp, Rostov could see the man was wearing eye makeup. He was dressed in jeans but was barefoot and shirtless.

"Who are you?" the young man demanded in a voice high-pitched and lisping.

Rostov closed the door behind him.

"I am the police. You are a pervert. Such activities are against the law. If you wish not to be hauled off to jail, you will answer my questions. Do you understand?"

"I want to see your badge," the youth said, and now

his voice trembled. He could not have been more than twenty years old and was probably younger.

"This will have to do," Rostov said as he drew his big Magnum-style revolver from his holster. He pointed toward the small cot where the young man obviously had been reading. "Sit down over there and speak only when you're spoken to."

Without hesitation, the youth obeyed and Rostov snapped again, "And if you lie to me about anything, God will have your soul before breakfast."

Visibly shaken, the young man nodded. He seemed unable to wrest his gaze away from the pistol in Rostov's hand.

"You were in a degenerate club this evening. You left with a man. Who was he?"

"His name is Alex," the youth said. "He comes into the club often. He says I look like Elvis Presley."

"You look nothing like Elvis Presley, imbecile. Where did you go when you left the club?"

"To his apartment."

"What did you do there?"

"We made love."

"Don't call it love," Rostov snapped. "You mean you had sex with this Alex?"

"Yes. He gave me fifty rubles."

"And then what happened?"

"He wanted me to stay the night, but I refused."

"Why?"

"Because he promised me that he had a lot of good cocaine. He had almost a half kilo, but it was all milk powder."

"Did you try this cocaine?"

"Yes."

"Did Alex?"

"Yes."

"Did he agree that it was milk powder?"

"Yes."

"What did he say about that?"

"He said that someone obviously had stolen his drugs and replaced them with garbage."

"He called them 'his drugs'?"

"Yes."

"What happened then?"

"I asked him if he had other drugs, but he said he did not and so I left."

"Did he promise to get more cocaine?"

"Yes. He said that he has a large supply of it on his job."

"What is his job?"

"He did not say. He just said he would have good drugs tomorrow night. He invited me back."

"What did you say?"

"I told him if he got real drugs I would return. For another fifty rubles."

"Are you supposed to telephone him first?"

"No. I should just go to his apartment at eleven P.M. I don't have his telephone number."

"Does he have yours?"

"I don't have a telephone," the young man said.

"What is Alex's last name?"

"I don't know."

"But you say he comes into this club often."

"At least once a week for the last year, I would say."

"Does he always leave with someone?"

"Yes. Why else would he come to the club?"

Rostov nodded, and holstered his revolver.

"You have answered truthfully, my little faggot friend," he said. "I will not arrest you."

He turned away and stepped toward the door.

"But . . ."

"But what?"

"What I should do? About Alex?"

"Tomorrow night you mean?"

408

"Yes."

"You should keep your date with him, of course. We wouldn't want to disappoint him, would we?"

Tash and Kamen, still fully dressed, lay side by side atop the covers on the pullout sofa bed. It had taken him more than an hour, but Kamen had told her his entire story, leaving nothing out.

When he was finished, she had said a most peculiar thing. "Your life has been very sad," she said.

He thought about that quietly for a moment. It had never occurred to him to regard his life as sad. Complicated, yes, and dangerous, certainly. But sad? He felt compelled to protest.

"Don't make me some kind of a victim in your mind," he said. "Whatever I did, I did willingly, with my eyes open."

"Yes, but sad nevertheless. I make no moral judgments, Pyotr. But this mob you once belonged to. You could have been its leader. Certainly you are intelligent enough. But they held against you that your ancestors were Russian. And then when the police moved, these 'friends' of yours tried to make you the scapegoat. And then their threats to your daughter and your beautiful grandchildren whom you never see. No man should have to die so that others might live. I call this a very sad life."

He turned his head and kissed her lightly on the lips. "It has had some good moments," he said. "This is one of them."

"It will have many more," she said. "But first you must end this assignment with the police."

"I don't know that I can," Kamen said. "I was allowed in this country to assist the police. If I tried to stop, I think they'd just throw me out." He realized he was tired, and rubbed his eyes. "Besides, I have never liked drug dealers and I signed on to help get rid of them. I plan to do that."

"Then guard yourself, Pyotr. And when you are done . . . well, I think you will make a very good nightclub proprietor."

"We'll see," Kamen said as he closed his eyes. "We'll see." But he was a long time falling asleep. *How to tell her the truth. How to tell her that I can take over this Russian Mafia. First in Moscow and then everywhere. I was smarter than all of them in the United States and I'm smarter than all of them here. I'm a mobster and this could be my mob. And I can probably do a lot more that way to make this country work than any thousand lying politicians you can elect.*

But there was no way to say it and finally he slept.

"There is simply no alternative," Olga said. "You must report Svoboda to General Budenko."

"But will he believe me? Or will he sweep it all under the rug and me with it?" Rostov asked.

She put her cup down on the kitchen table with such force that some of the liquid splashed out.

"The man has been stealing narcotics from the militsia property center. He uses them to entice minors into illicit relationships. It is altogether possible that while you and your men have been closing down the flow of narcotics into Moscow, he has been undermining your work by providing the criminal drug market with narcotics. Police narcotics! That is not only criminal; it is an obscenity. You must speak to General Budenko."

"What will you do when your boyfriend gets thrown off the militsia and is unemployed?" Cowboy asked her.

She reached across the table and touched his hand. "Then I will work twice as hard to support us both."

Chapter Thirty-three

When he walked down the hospital corridor, General Budenko saw two of those insufferable doctors spot him and walk quickly in the other direction, so he knew things were bad and he tried to steel himself.

But he was still shocked when he pushed open the door and walked into his wife's room.

Almost overnight, Ludmilla had seemed to shrink away. Only a few weeks before, she had weighed eighty-seven pounds, but now he would not believe that she weighed seventy. Her silken yellow hair had long ago vanished but now her bald head seemed evil, a scabrous-looking thing blotched red and yellow. Her breath came only in gasps and the odor of her exhalations smelled like gas from a sewer.

He sat alongside her and took her hand in his. Her eyelids fluttered, but her eyes remained closed as if she no longer had the strength to open them.

"Oh, Luddie, Luddie," Budenko said, unable to disguise his torment. "Why did they do this to you?"

Of course she did not answer; this morning there was not even an answering squeeze from her fingers, which he held in his hands.

But because he knew nothing else to do, he began reciting the week's events.

"It's a fine and lovely day today, Luddie. Sunny and warm . . . the kind of day when we would sit on our balcony and drink tea and watch the people passing in the street."

He looked at the oscilloscope mounted next to her bed, monitoring her heartbeat. A small, weak sine curve slithered across the green screen and he tried to convince himself that while it was weak, at least it was regular.

He paused and searched his wife's face, but there was no expression, no indication that she had heard even a word and he thought guiltily that if she could hear at all, his anger and frustration did nothing to comfort her, so he began to speak again of the boats sailing on the Moscow River and the sounds of children playing in the parks and he talked for almost an hour and her eyes never once opened.

But still the monitor traced its silent curve across the screen. She still lived, and as long as there was life . . .

Was there hope? No, he understood sadly, there was no longer any hope. He had always been careful not to weep in her presence, but now she could not see, so he surrendered himself to tears and they flowed down the harsh planes of his face.

Finally, he could take it no more. He stood and folded his wife's hands across her chest, over her sunken breasts. He wiped his eyes with his handkerchief, leaned forward and kissed her one last time on the mouth, and then walked to the door. He knew he would never see her alive again.

Rostov did not trust himself to see Colonel Svoboda in person. What he would like to do would be to grab the little faggot by the throat and squeeze the truth of his transgressions out of him, but he knew he would not do that. What he might do, however, would be to reveal by expression or gesture more than he wanted to, so he telephoned instead.

"Good morning, Colonel," he said, attempting a cheeriness he did not feel. "Is the general in?"

"What does it concern, Lieutenant?"

"I'm sorry, Colonel, but it is a personal matter about which I can speak only to General Budenko."

"I am his assistant, you know," Svoboda sniffed. Rostov could picture him twisting the ends of his mustache. Only God knew what they might be coated with.

"I know that, sir, but this is a personal matter."

Svoboda sighed. "Well, the general is not in the office."

"Will he be in later, Colonel? This is quite important."

"No. The general's wife has taken a turn for the worse. I believe he has gone to his dacha, perhaps to await bad news. I do not expect that we will see him here until Monday at the earliest." He paused. "So perhaps it would be best if you discussed this 'personal business' with me."

"No, sir, I prefer to wait for the general's return," Rostov said.

"Have it your own way," Svoboda snapped. "And just because the general is out of town, do not think that you may avoid turning in the regular report on your alleged antimob program."

Why, you smug little turd, Rostov thought. He said, "I will be certain to do so," then held his office phone away from his ear while Svoboda hung up by slamming the phone down onto its base.

Now what? Cowboy thought. *With the general off at his country house, what do I do about that drug-dealing bastard who is his assistant?*

Kamen walked back to his apartment from Tash's and, when he got there, he saw Omar's cab parked across the street. The wiry Armenian was already clambering out of the taxi; his shrewd eyes had seen Kamen before the American saw him.

They met at the front door and Omar followed Kamen in silently, past the glare of the *dezhurnaya*, who did not like people coming into the building in the morning when respectable people should be leaving the building to go to work, and who especially did not like ethnics of any sort.

Once inside Kamen's apartment, Omar wordlessly handed Kamen a videocassette that he took from inside his jacket.

"Good," Kamen said. "Have you looked at it?"

Omar smiled slyly. "Indeed, rich boss. I could not control the curiosity. It is too bad that my niece will never know that she was a fraction of a movie star."

"It may have to be enough satisfaction for her to realize that her uncle Omar was a man of wealth able to buy her many red coats."

"From your lips to God's ears," Omar said. "Should I wait for you downstairs?"

Kamen nodded and Omar quietly left the room.

When he was gone, Kamen poured himself a soft drink from a bottle of Russian imitation cola he found in the refrigerator. One sip convinced him it tasted like rancid root beer, and he poured it down the sink drain. Then he sat down to watch the new videotape.

It was better than he had hoped for, and he made a mental note to give Omar some extra money as a bonus for the cameraman who had made the tape. Whether or not the money would ever pass from Omar to the cameraman was questionable, but Omar knew his people and Kamen could live by his rules.

The tape was a mix of three other videos. The first was of Danielle Nabokov, the second of Omar's niece, and the third was bits and pieces of one of the porn tapes that Kamen had found in the apartment.

In the lab, the cameraman had spliced them all together, first in black-and white, and then had softened the focus slightly, so the pictures were a little fuzzy and looked like nothing so much as film shot from a hidden camera.

The film, as finally assembled, showed Mrs. Nabokov coming from her apartment building and driving off in the family limousine. Then, after several shots of the limousine parked, a woman—whose face was not really visible but clearly appeared to be Mrs. Nabokov—walked up the steps of a small neighborhood apartment building. Then again, more tape showed an identical dark-haired woman having sex in a king-sized bed with a man whose face could not be seen.

Danielle Nabokov had the misfortune, Kamen thought, of being too good a model. Her face was always expressive and the cameraman had clearly shot a lot of footage of her, wandering harmlessly around a department store, then stopping to get her nails done. He had blown some of that tape up into large closeups of the woman's face, and then spliced them into the scenes that featured Omar's niece and the actress from the smut film.

It was absolutely a topnotch job, Kamen thought. Only a real expert would have been able to detect that the film was a fraud and did not really show Mrs. Nabokov leaving her home by limo, entering a small apartment building, and then having afternoon sex with some unidentified boyfriend. At the end of the tape, the cameraman also had cleverly cut in more shots of the lawyer's wife getting again into the limousine and had managed to make them look as if they were taken as she left her afternoon assignation.

Now he had it, and all Kamen had to do was to figure out what to do with it. *And while I'm at it, I might as well figure out what I'm going to do with me.*

Rostov sat alone in his office, feet up on the desk, his cowboy hat pulled down over his face to protect his eyes from the glaring overhead lights.

It all comes down to this, he thought. *Svoboda has been stealing narcotics from the militsia. He has been using them to seduce his little boyfriends. Worse, he has been providing them to the drug mob that we have been risking our lives to close down.*

And I don't know if I can prove any of it.

Rostov tried to sort all the facts out in his mind. Svoboda made all-too-frequent inspections of the property room and always managed to wind up in the narcotics stall there. Rostov's men had sprinkled an invisible powder over two packages of narcotics that were in the property room, and after Svoboda "inspected" that day, he had left traces of the powder on the doorknob when he left the room. What else had he done but steal some of the narcotics? Further proof: the narcotics had been almost all lactose with just a sprinkling of cocaine, and Svoboda's latest fairy boy confirmed that the colonel had tried to give him just such worthless drugs.

And even though Rostov's squad had intercepted massive drug shipments into Moscow, Sergei Tal and his organization had still seemed to have narcotics for the illegal trade. And when Rostov had gone to Tal's private suite at the health club, there was evidence that it was used as a drug distribution center, but all the records had been stolen—apparently by someone who had a key to the private suites. And who was Tal's health club neighbor? None other than Colonel Svoboda.

Dammit, Cowboy thought, *perhaps it would not be enough in a court of law but it is enough for me. Svoboda is guilty and General Budenko must be told of it.*

And the general will either believe me and I will be proven right or I will be thrown off the force in humiliation and disgrace. But do I have any choice?

Still, he did not move. He heard his men moving around in the outside office in what seemed a sudden frenzy of activity. They must have guessed his mood, because none had come into his office for the past two hours.

He rose, opening the office door, and looked outside. Sergeant Federenko was strapping his large duty-revolver to his belt. The other members of the squad stood at the door, as if waiting for him.

"What's happening?" Rostov asked.

Federenko glanced toward him. "We just heard that two city patrol officers have been shot. Apparently they interrupted some sort of drug deal. We're going there now. Are you coming?"

Rostov shook his head. "Go on," he said. "And be careful."

His men left and Rostov went back inside the office. Two policemen shot . . . another drug deal. And these would not be the last. The violence would go on and on, just so long as narcotics were peddled, just so long as people like Colonel Svoboda let that happen.

No, Rostov, he told himself, *sometimes a man just doesn't have a choice.*

He picked up the telephone and asked to be connected to the Moscow Cancer Center. He finally reached the office and asked for the condition of Mrs. Ludmilla Budenko. "She is the wife of our commander," he explained.

A crisp nursey voice answered: "Mrs. Budenko remains on the danger list. I'm sorry, Lieutenant, but I don't think it will be much longer."

417

"Thank you," Rostov said, and replaced the telephone. *She is not dead and the general is not yet in mourning. He will have to see me.*

Kamen was in the upstairs office at The Pink Elephant, trying to make some sense of the haphazard pile of receipts from the previous night's business, when there was a soft tapping on the office door.

Omar, he thought. He had told the driver to wait for him downstairs in the private off-street parking lot. Still, as he walked to the door, he lifted the small Targa automatic from the back of his belt and held it inside his right pocket.

He opened the door cautiously. One of the two young Sicilians from the previous night's meeting stood there. He was about to speak, when he noticed something and his head twisted suddenly to the left. There, Kamen saw Omar standing, his right arm dropped at his side, and Kamen knew he had his knife in his hand. He must have seen the young man enter and quietly followed him up the back steps.

"Easy," Kamen said to Omar. "It's all right." He looked at the young Sicilian, who took his eyes off Omar only reluctantly. "He is my assistant," Kamen explained in Italian.

"Very good," the man said stiffly, but his eyes still betrayed his nervousness. His fingers reached gingerly for his jacket pocket and he said, "I was told to give you this."

He brought out a piece of paper and pushed it forward to Kamen. It looked like paper from a large roll, the kind he had once seen on a teletype machine in a newspaper office, and one end was rough as if it had been crudely torn from such a machine.

It was a news bulletin from Tass, the state's information service. It read:

NEWS BULLETIN

"Gesualdo Ciccolini, a well-known American Mafia figure, was shot to death early today as he left his home in Brooklyn, a suburb of New York City. He was 53 years old." (FURTHER DETAILS TO FOLLOW.)

Kamen read the brief notice, then looked up at the man. "Thank you for sharing this information with me. And tell your master I await his pleasure," he said in Italian.

"We will be in touch," the man said, and turned away, but he kept his eyes carefully on Omar until he was almost halfway down the stairs. Then he moved more quickly and pushed his way outside into the bright afternoon sun.

"Omar, are you a drinking man?" Kamen asked.

"On my pitiful income, boss, I have little opportunity. But, yes, I have been known to drink."

"Then come inside and share a glass of wine with me."

"It will be my pleasure. Are we celebrating something good in your life?"

"Yes," Kamen said. "Something very good."

Chapter Thirty-four

Rostov walked to the nearby courthouse and called Olga's office from the house telephone in the lobby.

When she came down, she said, "I know, don't tell me. Our dinner date tonight is off."

Cowboy smiled. "Perhaps," he said. "And just perhaps I may get back early."

"Where are you going?"

"To General Budenko's dacha. He was not in the office today."

She looked around to make sure no one was in earshot. "And you will tell him of Colonel Svoboda?"

Rostov nodded.

"Good. I will wait for you to return," she said. She smiled, but there was no answering smile from the big policeman.

"Does this worry you?" she asked.

"Yes. But I have no choice."

"No. You haven't." She squeezed his hand affectionately, then watched him all the way out the front door. *It must be hard for him,* she thought. *He has dedicated his life to enforcing the law, and then to find that others, in higher positions than he, make a mockery of dedication . . . The ones who care the most are always the ones who are hurt the most.*

She turned toward the elevator to return to her office.

Because she had to leave early for a dentist's appointment she had waited six weeks to get, Leonid Nabokov's secretary had juggled his appointments to keep the rest of the afternoon open. So when the young blonde left, Nabokov locked the front door behind her and retreated into his oak-paneled private office to research a complicated estate case he was working on.

He thought for a moment about taking the afternoon off himself and going home and surprising Danielle, but he knew she would not be home. She seemed to have set for herself the task of buying a dress in every store, large and small, in Moscow and so she would be out shopping. The truth was, he did not mind at all. Danielle's eye for clothing was perfect, befitting the magnificent mannikin she once had been, and he loved her to model for him, when he went home, all the day's acquisitions. He hoped she had bought undergarments. He especially liked for her to pose for him in lingerie. He looked at the photos of his wife that adorned the office wall, lingering for a long time on one that showed her on a French beach in a mesh-topped bathing suit, and then he sighed and opened the thick legal book on the desk before him.

He was so engrossed in his work that he did not hear the front office door slip open and he was unaware that he was not alone until he looked up, in total concentration, and saw the man he knew as Pyotr Kamenski standing in the open doorway of his office.

Behind him was another man, roughly dressed and swarthy.

It took a split second for Nabokov to smile, then he rose and said, "You startled me. I thought the outside door was locked."

"It was," Kamen said. He turned to Omar and said, "Make sure we are not disturbed." The cabdriver nodded and strode off, and Kamen entered Nabokov's private study and closed the door behind him.

"I really don't have anything new to report," Nabokov said. "Mrs. Krasnova's application to lease The Pink Elephant has been filed and . . ." His voice slowly trailed off as he stared at Kamen's face, hard and unyielding. *This man is a Mafia killer and I am here alone with him.*

"I didn't come to talk about nightclub applications," Kamen said. He still stood just inside the office, his back to the closed door.

Nabokov sank into the chair behind his desk. He felt a trickle of perspiration in his armpits.

"I have come to do you a favor," Kamen said.

"I've never been known to turn one down," Nabokov said, but Kamen continued as if he had not even heard the pleasantry. "I am closely connected with a certain police official," he said, "and I have come to tell you that your life is in danger."

Nabokov stared at him for a second, then said, "I don't know what you're talking about."

Kamen came forward and sat on the chair across Nabokov's desk. "Let's make it simple," he said, "and save ourselves a lot of time, before I get bored and change my mind. You are involved up to your neck in the drug trade. Don't insult either the clock or my intelligence by protesting. I really don't have all the time in the world and I have taken a risk by coming here."

How much does he know? Nabokov wondered. He looked at Kamen's eyes, trying to measure the man, and the man's cold piercing gaze answered his question. *He knows everything.*

"I know who you are," Kamen said. "But I don't think you know who I am."

There is no point in dancing around, Nabokov thought. *He knows. He knows.*

"I know that you are an American gangster who was brought here to infiltrate the Mafia," Nabokov said.

Kamen surrpised him by laughing. "Did you really believe that?" he said.

No reaction seemed more appropriate, and the lawyer could only shrug.

"I was not brought here," Kamen said, "to *infiltrate* the Mafia. I was brought here to *organize* it. You were naturally not told because it was thought that you might be part of the problem. And of course you were. You and Sergei Tal had tried to organize all the drug dealing, but it was beyond you. I told this to Tal. He was a fool. His response was to try to kill me and now he is dead. And you are left."

Kamen leaned forward and opened a wooden humidor on Nabokov's desk. He took out a cigar, rolled it between his fingers, and sniffed it deeply.

"I've always had a weakness for Cuban cigars," he said, and slowly, carefully lit it. Then he blew a long plume of smoke toward the ceiling and sighed with satisfaction. "One of life's many pleasures," he said.

Nabokov watched him, wondering if his life was in any danger. Should he try to run for it? *But what was the point? The other one is waiting outside.* His body now was bathed in perspiration. He almost recoiled when Kamen leaned forward and put his elbow on the desk.

"So Tal was in the way and now he is dead. But he was a thug and you are something different. You have done me no disservice and shown me no ill will. In fact, you have been helpful to me in the matter of The Pink

Elephant. And so, at some risk to myself, I have come to give you a chance to save yourself.''

''I don't think we should be discussing this. Not alone,'' Nabokov said. ''There are others involved.''

''Only one of whom counts,'' Kamen said. ''And if you involve him, then not just you, but I also, will die. Here is what I want. I want all the records that were stolen from Tal's suite at the health club. I want all the drugs that you have stockpiled, since—with the death of Tal and the two imbeciles who worked for him—you no longer have any mechanism for distributing them and the addicts are getting restive. And when I have those two things—the records and the drugs—I want you and your wife to retire to France.''

''You must be joking.''

''Perhaps we are different,'' Kamen said coldly, ''but I do not regard your life and that of your wife as a joke.''

''But . . .''

Kamen thumped a fist on the desk. ''Do you think I am acting on my own?'' he said. ''Are you really that foolish? I am not telling you what *I* have planned. I am telling you what others have planned for you. Mr. Nabokov, you are going to take the fall, as we call it in America. The thought right now is simply to kill you. I have argued against that. Killings have a way of multiplying. I may have won that argument but I may not have. I don't know. All I can tell you is that whether by death or by humiliation, your life here is ended.''

''Humiliation? How could I be humiliated?'' Nabokov asked.

Kamen rose and said, ''The process is well under way.'' He reached into his inside pocket and removed a videocassette, which he stepped across the room and inserted into the player built into the lawyer's television set. ''This is the product of a secret police camera. I will wait outside for a few minutes while you watch it,'' he

424

said. "You will understand why I leave the door open. A phone call by you would not only guarantee your death but mine also. I regard that as too high a price to pay, just to do you a favor."

He turned on the television, pressed the play button, and stepped out into the hallway. He stood on the side of the open doorway. He nodded and winked at Omar, who was lounging in the front office, reading a magazine, and then leaned back against the wall and savored his cigar. *I almost feel sorry for him,* he thought. *But not much. Has he ever felt sorry for anyone whose life he ruined with drugs? Screw him.*

The entire tape was about ten minutes long, with the sex starting about four minutes in. He checked his wristwatch, waited five minutes to make sure Nabokov got the full flavor of the tape, and then walked back into the office.

The lawyer's head was down on the desk, buried in his arms, and Kamen walked across the room, turned off the television, and ejected the cassette from the video recorder. Nabokov was weeping and Kamen hardened himself with the thought, *Weep for all those you've helped kill,* then returned to his seat and puffed on the cigar.

He heard Nabokov muttering.

"Nikolai. Goddam Nikolai." The attorney looked up at Kamen. "Why is Budenko doing this to me?"

Budenko! Good Jesus, Kamen thought, and said, "Because all people who deal in drugs are slime and Budenko is even more slimy than you."

"And what does that make you?" Nabokov asked, still weeping, not even bothering to wipe his eyes.

"I am the worst of all," Kamen said. "And now I need an answer from you."

"Do I have a choice?" Nabokov said.

"No. None at all."

General Budenko's dacha was located in a forest on a lake, less than an hour's drive west of the Kremlin in a small town named Nikolina Gora. The area was clearly "dacha country," the summer homes of the rich and powerful, Rostov realized, because the narrow roadways were well paved and the fields bordering the roads were trimmed and mowed. As he moved into the forest, he could see glimpses of estates, giant stone-and-glass homes, built back into the woods. High on a bluff overlooking the lake's sandy beach was a startlingly modern home which he had seen in magazines and where he knew a famous writer of children's books lived. Here and there, he could still see a simple log hut or a frame cottage. The scent of pine trees was redolent in the air, and through an occasional break in the trees, he could see fishermen sitting on the edges of wooden docks, lines in the water, hoping to catch a late-swimming fish for the evening dinner.

But in the midst of all the ostentatious splendor, Budenko's dacha was a surprise. Despite his rank, which entitled him to better quarters, his home out of the city was rustic, not much more than a sprawling log cabin, with a large plank porch around the entire structure. The roof was made of striated shingles that looked as if they had been hand-hewn from the cedar trees that fringed the water only fifty yards behind the house, and if Rostov had been a betting man, he would have wagered that Budenko had built all or most of the home with his own hands.

Cowboy saw no guards, no signs of increased security in the area. That did not mean there weren't any, but, in truth, Rostov realized, there was probably very little call for security measures here. Despite its faults—or perhaps because of them—Russia had escaped most kinds of terrorist attacks and it had probably never occurred to anyone living out here to worry about his security.

He parked his small auto in the long driveway behind a nondescript black sedan. *Budenko even drives like a poor man,* Rostov thought. Probably, he decided, the general's chauffeur would be by to pick him up and bring him to the office on Monday.

He walked up the crunchy gravel driveway toward the house, slowly, as if inviting someone to distract him from his mission with something important, like an invitation to go for a walk. But no one interfered with him and, once on the porch, he took a deep breath, then rapped on the door with the brass knocker in the shape of a lion's head.

There was no answer, and after waiting as long as one should at a general's house, Rostov rapped again, harder and longer this time.

A few seconds later, the door—which obviously had been unlocked—was pulled open. Budenko stood there wearing a sleeveless nylon undershirt and sweatpants. A thick tan leather weightlifter's belt was buckled tightly around his waist. Sweat rained down his face and a towel around the back of his neck looked as if it were soaking wet.

He was obviously surprised to see Rostov.

"Well, the Cowboy. What is it, Rostov, that brings you to my home?"

Behind the big bulk of the general, Rostov could see the living room, rustic furniture with floral-print slipcovers, a ceiling-high stone fireplace, and in the center of the floor a complicated weightlifting machine that was a conglomeration of cables and bars, and next to it rested a half-dozen barbells of assorted weights. If Rostov needed any proof that Budenko's wife had been confined to the hospital for a long time, this house, so clearly the quarters of a man who lived alone, provided it.

"I have to speak to you on a matter of great urgency, General. May I come in?"

"Of course. I apologize for the place. It has lacked a woman's hand for a while."

"I have heard. I am sorry about Mrs. Budenko."

The general nodded and walked away, leaving Rostov to close the door and to follow him.

The living room was lowered two steps from the entrance. Budenko waved him to a chair and asked, "Would you like a drink?"

Rostov hesitated, and Budenko smiled and said, "You're with me, Lieutenant. It's all right."

Rostov returned the smile. "Vodka then, please."

"Of course." The general poured them each a drink, straight, into a pair of large water tumblers, then sat on the sofa facing the lieutenant, waved his glass in a salute, then drank almost half of it. Rostov did the same.

"So? What is it?" Budenko said.

"I want you to understand, sir, that this is very difficult for me," Rostov began.

"And it will only grow more difficult if you beat around the bush. Get to it, man."

"Very well. In recent months, I have had the suspicion that someone inside the militsia has been undermining the work of my narcotics squad. I have not brought this to your attention because it was only a vague feeling, but I felt it was necessary to pursue it myself," Rostov said. He thought, *Why am I talking like this with all this rodomontade? Why can't I just come out and say that Svoboda is working for the mob?*

But he could not. When the general nodded to go ahead, Rostov said, "In the past few weeks, other information has come to light that I could no longer ignore and I have to bring it to you."

"And I'm sure you will. Any day now," Budenko said dryly.

All right, Rostov thought. *You want blunt, you get*

blunt. "Colonel Svoboda has, I believe, been stealing narcotics from the militsia property section. He has been using them for the purposes of seducing young men. Or at least one young man that I can prove. It is also highly likely that he has been providing narcotics to the mob, which accounts for the fact that even though we constantly interdict drug supplies, there is always an ample store upon the streets. I believe it comes, through the agency of Colonel Svoboda, from our own police contraband." He spoke as rapidly as he could, and when he was done, he took a deep breath and exhaled slowly.

All the general said was, "Svoboda? Colonel Svoboda?" He seemed to be having difficulty restraining a smile.

"Yes, sir."

"These are very serious charges, Rostov."

"I know, sir, and I have been reluctant to make them until now."

"Suppose you tell me what facts these charges are based upon," the general said. Rostov heard the gentle emphasis on the word "facts," and he thought, *Here goes my career down the sink.*

Rostov nodded. He told the general how he had searched Tal's suite at the health club, and that he had found evidence of drug paraphernalia but that the records had all been missing along with any supply of drugs that might have been there. The theft, he explained, had probably been committed by someone with a key to the set of suites at the club and the suite next to Tal was rented by Colonel Svoboda.

He told him about the trap he had set by sprinkling ultraviolet powder on seized narcotics in the property room and how Svoboda had left the same powder on the doorknob when he left, after completing one of his very frequent inspections of the drug bin there.

He told him about his run-in with "Elvis," the young homosexual who called Svoboda "Alex," and said that the colonel frequented the gay club and was a ready source of supply for narcotics. And even as he was recounting all that he knew and guessed, Rostov felt with a sinking sensation that it was all nonsense; it was not evidence, it was all guesswork and hearsay and conjecture and hardly the kind of thing on which to destroy a militsia colonel's career.

He finally finished and met the general's eyes, where he hoped to find some hint of approval, or at least understanding, but Budenko's gaze was flat and blank, like a shark's.

Finally, the general said, "If what you said was true, Colonel Svoboda has grievously compromised our department. What is your opinion on what should be done to someone who violates his personal oath in this matter?"

"I think such a man should be tried and made to stand witness to his crimes," Rostov said firmly.

"You have thought that through carefully?" Budenko said.

"Yes, sir, I have. People die every day—many policemen—from the scourge of drugs. Anyone involved in such activity is a criminal and should be treated as a criminal."

"You are a very hard man, Lieutenant Rostov. Very hard," Budenko said.

"Olga, this is Pyotr Kamenski. Where is Cowboy? I've called everywhere for him."

Olga could tell from the crackle in Kamenski's voice that this was not just a social telephone call. "He had to go out of town," she said.

"Where? I have to talk to him on a matter of life and death."

"He went out into the countryside. To the dacha of General Budenko."

There was a long silence and finally Kamen said, "Oh, Jesus. Olga, where is that dacha?"

"I don't know. I think it's near Nikolina Gora. That's west of the city. But I'm not sure."

"Find out. I will call you back in a few minutes."

After spilling his entire story to Budenko, Cowboy had drained his vodka glass in one long nervous gulp, and without being asked, Budenko did the same, picked up both glasses, and refilled them. When he set Rostov's in front of him on the coffee table, the general went back across the room and behind the crudely made wooden counter that he obviously used as a bar.

He sipped and looked at Rostov over the rim of his glass.

"You understand, Lieutenant, that everything you've just said to me is circumstantial. It could all have a reasonable explanation."

"I . . ." Rostov began but the general silenced him by raising his hand.

"For instance, the drugs that you doctored with ultraviolet powder, the same powder which later showed up on Colonel Svoboda's hands. It is quite possible that Alexei was merely inspecting those drugs to make sure that your men had not adulterated them, thus keeping some of the drugs themselves to later sell illegally. He may be doing his own undercover work."

Rostov seemed ready to interrupt, and again Budenko silenced him with a gesture.

"Please let me speak," he said, and Rostov thought that, oddly, there seemed to be a faint smile on the general's broad face. Budenko seemed finally to have stopped perspiring, and he wiped his forehead with the towel around his neck.

"And Colonel Svoboda's frequent inspections of the

property room? Well, one might choose to cast those in a bad light, but one could just as easily say that they were the work of a man deeply involved in his duties. As for his providing drugs to homosexuals . . . well, sadly we are all aware of Alexei's sexual proclivities. However, we have nothing factual there and we might be maligning him on the sole, unsubstantiated word of some male prostitute who would say anything for a fee.''

What is he doing? Rostov asked himself. *I didn't say I had a case that I was ready to present in court, but there is certainly enough here that he should not be mocking it.* And he thought, with sudden ferocity, *I will not have this.*

"So you see," Budenko said, "there is probably a very logical explanation for everything and perhaps you have overstepped yourself in your zeal for your job. And perhaps we should just let this matter die here in this room between us." Budenko was smiling again and Rostov rose to his feet angrily.

"No, dammit, I have not overstepped myself and I have not overstated my case. Two city policemen have been shot today in some drug-related incident and I have no intention of letting the men of my own squad be shot, with bullets fired at them from within. You may regard this as nonsense, General, and that is your right. But I have rights too. I have the right to resign and to let the public know, through the press, exactly what I think and I am prepared to do just that. If the colonel is helping the mob, he should be treated as the mobster he is. There is no way to 'let this matter die between us.' " He tried unsuccessfully to keep the sarcasm out of his voice when he repeated the general's phrase. Now he glared at his superior across the room.

"Sit down, Rostov," Budenko snapped. His voice was cold now and there was no longer any smile.

Cowboy sank back onto the chair and Budenko said, "Only a difficult man does not compromise sometimes—

and you are a most difficult man." Rostov did not answer and Budenko finished his glass of vodka. "Let us continue," he said. "You think that Colonel Svoboda emptied out Tal's suite at the health club because you found Svoboda's name listed as the tenant of another suite. I can tell you that Alexei Svoboda has never been in a health club in his life. Certainly not the Friendship Health Club, which is aimed solely at weightlifters. And you should have kept in mind, Lieutenant, that Colonel Svoboda signs many things in my name. For instance, that suite at the health club has always been one of the small benefits that the head of the militsia has. But, lest anyone someday accuse me of using my position for personal gain, I had Alexei sign the contract."

For a few seconds, Rostov had been wondering what Budenko was driving at, but now, suddenly, it became all too clear. Cowboy jumped to his feet.

"You! You are the traitor," he said.

"Traitor?" Budenko said. "That is all really a matter of viewpoint, isn't it?" And then his hand, which had been below the bar, was resting on the counter and a large pistol was aimed at Rostov's chest. "Sit down, Lieutenant. Sit down."

"Where the fuck is it?" Kamen snapped.

"Easy, we are here." Omar turned onto an unlighted road covered over with trimmed strips of asphalt roofing material.

"All right. And there's his car. Turn out your lights."

Omar turned off his lights and his motor and coasted to a slow stop behind a gravel driveway where two old cars were parked.

Kamen opened the door, and as he did, Omar slapped his hand over the ceiling light to cover its glare. Then Kamen closed the door softly.

"I will wait, rich boss," the driver said.

"Thank you, my friend," Kamen said. He put his hand over Omar's and squeezed, then walked away, his hand already reaching behind his back, under his jacket, where the gun was.

"You are too young, Rostov. You have never been betrayed the way this state has betrayed me."

Rostov looked across the room at General Budenko. He had always respected the man, always been in awe of his reputation as "Brass Balls Budenko," but at this moment, he felt nothing but contempt for him. "Many feel betrayed by the state; few become traitors," was all he could bring himself to say.

"A traitor? You throw that word around a great deal, Cowboy. I will tell you what treason is. Treason is making someone believe that he is part of something noble and grand, some great experiment, and then throwing it out in the morning like yesterday's soup scraps. Treason is telling a man that he and his family are safe and then turning the horrors of Chernobyl loose upon him." Budenko's voice rose with his anger. "Treason? This entire goverment is treasonous to everyone who has lived in it. Yes, Rostov. I stole drugs. I pretended to burn them every month at a big public ceremony and instead I stole them and I burned talcum powder. I put narcotics out on the street and I controlled their sale. With others, I have tried to create a race of addicts, because the sooner we do, the sooner this whole country will vanish into the mists of history. You talk treason. I talk hatred. Yes. With my longtime friend, the lawyer Nabokov, and with that fool Tal, we controlled the narcotics market in this city. And now Tal is dead, and although you will not admit it, I know your American has killed him. And it does not matter. Because you will be gone and so will your American fool and I will continue to sell drugs, I will continue to create a mob that will somehow try to run this country, I will continue to try my best to destroy this evil power that somehow has taken rule of us. The former Soviet Union now is dead. And anything I can do to help bury it, I will do. And maybe . . . perhaps . . . someday, Russia—the real Russia—will live again, and maybe I will have helped create it." He looked across the room at Rostov; his eyes squinted. "What do you think of that?" he demanded.

Despite his position, despite the fact that his life hung by a thread, Rostov could not control his anger. "I think you are giving me a lot of sociological bullshit excuses about why you were a corrupt *apparatchik* whose life was built on stealing. I see no hospitals that you and your drug-peddling friends have built with your ill-gotten gains. Spare me, General, the bullshit of your deep and fine motives. You are a thief like all corrupt policemen."

Rostov said all that, and wondered how he could possibly get his hand to his revolver, which was under his tan corduroy jacket.

"Your trouble, Rostov, has always been your nickname. Like the cowboys we read about, you think that things are always black and white, that the hero wears white and the villain wears black. That there is good and evil and nothing else. But you are a fool, Cowboy. The world is made up of grays and nothing but grays. We strive, if we strive for good, to pick a lighter gray over a darker gray. But none of us pretend ever to find a white. Only you zealots."

"So what do you do now, General?" Rostov said, and realized how idiotic it was to still apply rank to this man who was a drug dealer obviously bent on his death. "What do you do now?" he repeated.

"I kill you, Cowboy, and bury your body. No one will know and no one will care. And next week, when she dies, I bury my wife. And then I return to Moscow, I return to my office, I return to my mission of destroying this country. And then I die a happy man."

435

A voice barked through the room.

"You drop that gun now, or you die unhappy and off-schedule."

Budenko's head snapped toward the rear of the building. Inside the door that led down to the lake stood Peter Kamen. An automatic in his hand was aimed directly at Budenko. The general looked at him for a moment, then seemed to weigh the fact that he had a much larger, much more powerful gun in his own hand.

"Don't even think of it unless you have an urge to become wallpaper," Kamen said, in a voice that could score glass. All the while he spoke, he walked into the room. As he did, Rostov rose from the sofa and took his own gun out from under his jacket and leveled it at Budenko.

"It's all over, General," Rostov said, unable to break the habits of a decade. "Put the gun down."

Budenko looked at him, then across at Kamen, and then slowly laid the gun on the bar and crossed his hands in front of him, as if to show they were empty without suffering the indignity of raising them above his head.

"And you, I guess, are Pyotr Kamenski, the Mafia thug," he said. "At last we meet."

"And you, I guess, are General Budenko, the real Mafia thug," Kamen snapped. "And never meeting would have been soon enough." Budenko shrugged.

"Get that gun," Kamen snapped, nodding toward Rostov, who walked forward and picked up the general's pistol from the bar.

"It's all over, General," Kamen said. "Nabokov talked. He talked about everything. About how you both planned this. How Tal's men cut the drugs in the health club and how they distributed them. How you tried to take over the drug trade so you could take over everything else. How you stole the drugs. Even how you put out the order for Tal's men to kill that thieving judge. It's all done, General, it's all done."

Budenko turned his massive head slowly toward Kamen. He said, "All good things end in time, don't they?" After a pause, he asked, "And Nabokov?"

"He is gone, General. His last words were to curse your spirit," Kamen said.

Budenko sighed. "I knew it was a bad idea to bring you over from the United States. I guess I just didn't realize exactly how bad an idea."

"People do often wind up thinking that about me," Kamen said. "It must be my fatal charm."

Cowboy's head was swimming. *What do I do now? Do I bring in General Budenko like a common criminal and try to put him in jail? What jailer will turn the key on him? How do I convince anyone that I am lawful and he is not? This cannot be done.*

Before he could speak, Budenko said, "I am ready to go with you. I would like a moment to get ready."

And before Rostov could answer, Kamen said, "That will be fine. We will wait on the front porch for you. Of course, we have other men out there. I did not come alone."

He walked to the bar and picked up Budenko's service revolver. Then, holding it in his hand, he waved toward Rostov and the two men walked toward the front door. Rostov glanced nervously over his shoulder, but Budenko stood stolidly at the bar. He smiled at Rostov, then picked up the bottle of vodka and raised it to his lips, draining a long gulp.

Kamen ushered Rostov outside. The two men stood on the planked decking. Rostov saw the taxicab parked in the driveway behind his car and he looked at Kamen and said, "Now what do we do?"

"We wait just for a moment," Kamen said. "Calm down. Light yourself a cigarette."

Rostov fished in his pocket for his pack of papirosy. He twisted the end of one and lit it. As he did, he looked through the glass of the front door and saw Budenko still at the bar, still draining the bottle of vodka. When he flicked on his lighter, for a few seconds he was able to see nothing. He inhaled deeply and put the lighter back in his jacket. Just as the vision was returning to his eyes, he heard the terrible explosive sound of a gun firing.

He tried to duck, to cock his own pistol, to look through the door window—all at once. But Kamen put a hand on his wrist and said, "Easy, Cowboy."

Then Kamen walked to the door, opened it, and looked inside. He walked up behind the bar, bent down, and picked up a small revolver that looked just like the one Kamen had been carrying when he entered the house. He put it back in his pocket, then stepped over Budenko's body.

Rostov entered the room, but Kamen was already walking toward him. "He must have taken my gun when I wasn't looking," Kamen said.

"But. . . ."

"Let's go back to Moscow, Cowboy."

Chapter Thirty-five

He had asked just everybody he knew, just absolutely *everybody*, and every one of them had said that if the cop had been so big and so good looking, why hadn't he just . . . well, you know, and he had said, But the big sonofabitch had a big gun pointed at me and they had said, Oh, aren't you the lucky one, and the simple fact was that when you needed advice, sensible advice, a fag was the last person to ask.

So "Elvis" had had to decide for himself, and what he decided to do after talking to just absolutely *everybody* and then taking off only a few minutes to go buy that new purple sweater, was that he was leaving town, faster than anyone had ever left town before.

Except that he wasn't fast enough. Just as he came out the door of his disgusting apartment building—and if he never saw that place again, it would be years too soon—a young blonde man walked up alongside him and Elvis smiled, but it was not a smiling situation, because the

439

blonde took out a badge, grabbed Elvis by the wrist, and said, "Don't you have an eleven o'clock date?"

And that was how it was that Elvis wound up knocking at eleven P.M. on the apartment door of Colonel Alexei Svoboda. And the truth was that he was so nervous and so absolutely flabbergasted by the events of the last twenty-four hours that he did not have time to tell Alex about anything that had happened before the doorbell rang.

Alex had pushed him into a bedroom, but he opened the door a crack and listened anyway.

Outside the door, in the hallway, stood Lieutenant Lev Rostov.

Colonel Svoboda, resplendent in a corn-yellow dressing gown, said stiffly, "What is it, Lieutenant? What do you want?"

"I have to come in and speak to you, Colonel," Rostov said.

"I'm afraid it will just have to wait until morning at the office," Svoboda said.

Rostov pushed the door open and, elbowing Svoboda aside, stepped into the apartment. He turned and grinned at Svoboda. "Don't worry, Colonel. Elvis won't mind that I'm here. He and I are old friends. But what you and I have to talk about, I think, would be better said if he is not here. So send your little boyfriend home, why don't you? One of my men is outside and will escort him."

Tash saw Rostov, when he came through the front door of The Pink Elephant. She waved to him and he nodded, then walked past the bar and up the steps to the second-floor office.

The door was open and he stepped inside. Kamen looked up from the desk where he was writing numbers in a ledger book, and Rostov nodded and said, "It is done."

"Good. And now you'd better sit down, because I have some things to tell you."

Tash came up the steps to talk to Pyotr, but from outside the door, she could hear the sound of raised voices. She listened for a moment, but could understand nothing except that the men inside were yelling something about Sicilians. She knew nothing of any Sicilians and she thought that she would let them argue and come back later. She had time now. She had nothing but time.

"What do you mean, you met with the Sicilians and you did not let me know?"

"Well, try it this way. I met with the Sicilians and I did not let you know," Kamen said.

"Why?"

"Because you yourself said that there was a leak in your organization. I didn't know whether you were that leak or one of your superiors or your prosecutor girlfriend or one of the cops who works for you. I could not take the chance that somebody would come jumping in here and blow us all to Minsk. So I held the meeting in private. Sorry, Cowboy, but that's the way it was. And I just talked to them again while you were out harassing your colonel."

"Perhaps, then, you will tell me what was discussed. I might even find it interesting," Rostov said.

"More than just interesting," Kamen said with a smile. "Maybe just wonderful. The Sicilians are going to send in a squad. They are going to bring in a year's worth of narcotics for the city of Moscow all at once. I am going to pay for the drugs and arrange for all the major independent drug dealers of Moscow to meet with them and buy junk."

"You have been a busy little man, Pyotr," Rostov said.

"And my work is never done. When this meeting is all set up and ready to take place, I am going to give it all to you and you will simply come in and seize a year's worth of drugs, a half-dozen Sicilian bandits, and every drug dealer worth a ruble in Moscow. And then don't say I never did you a favor."

"After tonight, after General Budenko's house, I would never say that," Rostov said earnestly.

"Good. Because I need a favor in return," Kamen said.

Rostov said, "Anything except asking me to give you control of the Russian Mafia."

Kamen was deadly serious as he answered. "I wouldn't need your permission for that, Cowboy. I could take this thing over in three days and I could run it better and tighter and cleaner than you could ever imagine. And don't think that would be such a bad thing, either. The fact is that your country—the institutions, the people—there's no way they can convert from what they got to what they need. The only way for Russia to go to capitalism is to get some capitalists in power, and the only ones you've got—the only people in this whole country who are willing to work hard—is the mob. I'm giving you the Mafia on a silver platter, Cowboy. But someday, you might not think that I did you any service."

"We'll just have to wait and see about that," Rostov said. "You said you needed a favor. What is it?"

"First, do I get it?"

Rostov smiled. "You know, once I worried that you were a puppet and people were pulling your strings and dragging you right to the edge of the precipice. But you are no one's puppet, are you, Pyotr Kamenski?"

"Everyone is a puppet," Kamen said. "Me. You. They were pulling your strings too. Some of us are just strong enough to yank away from our strings and wrap them around the puppetmaster's neck. Do I get the favor?''

"You saved my life tonight. Somehow, and I'll never know how, you have delivered to me all of Sergei Tal's records of drug dealers in this city. You have produced for me nine kilos of drugs that were stolen from the militsia. Everything I have tried to do for years, you have done in a matter of just days. Yes. You get the favor. Whatever it is. You have earned it.''

Kamen smiled again. "You'll never regret it," he said.

"Somehow I doubt that.''

"No. You will never regret it. Trust me.''

Epilogue

A month later, after the tragic death of General Nikolai Budenko in a hunting accident at his lakeside cottage was reported in the press, Colonel Alexei Svoboda quietly retired from the militsia on pension.

The city's elite had been shocked by the general's death, nearly as shocked as they had been by the departure earlier of noted Counselor Leonid Nabokov and his beautiful French-born wife, Danielle, back to her native Paris to live.

The press never mentioned the quiet wedding of newly promoted Captain Lev Rostov of the Moscow militsia to Olga Lutska of the city prosecutor's office, or the elaborate reception thrown for the couple at the Pink Elephant nightclub by its new owner, Omar Ararat, an Armenian émigré whose rise from cabdriver to businessman was hailed by the government as an example of "the new, free enterprise economy."

But even if the Rostov-Lutska wedding had been covered, hardly anyone would have noticed, because only two days after the marriage, Captain Rostov was involved in one of the largest police operations in the history of Moscow.

In the FBI office in the Lehigh Valley in Pennsylvania, Special Agent Daniel Taylor was idly reading the *New York Times* when he saw an interesting story datelined Moscow.

The story detailed the police seizure of hundreds of kilos of raw drugs in the largest drug bust in the history of Moscow. More than a hundred policemen under the aegis of a special drug squad swooped down upon a city health club and arrested seven drug couriers from Sicily who had tried to smuggle the illegal narcotics into the city.

Then police, in a classic "sting" operation, had taken the place of the couriers and calmly gone ahead with all the illegal narcotics deals with most of Moscow's major drug pushers and had then arrested the dealers. In all, more than one hundred arrests were made and police said they had broken the back of the illegal narcotics trade in Russia. And in addition, valuable information was garnered about Sicilian drug traffickers and forwarded to authorities in Italy, where more arrests were expected momentarily.

The arrests had not been made without cost, however. Police reported that an undercover informant, whose name was given only as "Kamenski," was shot and killed in the operation.

Agent Taylor read the story and pushed the paper across the desk, away from himself.

So you finally bought the farm. Kamen, you poor shit, I just knew it would end like this. Taylor sighed, and thought, *Well, better in Russia than here.*

It was too bad, he thought. Gesualdo Ciccolini, the

445

Mafia boss who had put the hit order out on Peter Kamen, had been killed in a gangland rubout only a month earlier. With him out of the way, it might even have been possible for Kamen to return to the United States one day. *Kamen, you were always an unlucky bastard*, he thought.

High above the Atlantic, on a Russian Aeroflot flight to Kennedy Airport, where they had a connecting flight to Los Angeles, were Mr. and Mrs. Peter Krasnova. Their shiny new U.S. passports showed that they had just concluded a two-month vacation in Russia. Traveling with them was their eight-year-old daughter, Rosa.

The family had been escorted to the airport by a policeman in a tall white hat who had formally shaken hands with Mr. Krasnova at the boarding gate and said, ''Farewell, good luck, I hope I never see you again.''

And Mr. Krasnova had said simply, ''Don't count on it, Cowboy. Don't count on it.''

WARBOTS by G. Harry Stine

#5 OPERATION HIGH DRAGON   (17-159, $3.95)

Civilization is under attack! A "virus program" has been injected into America's polar-orbit military satellites by an unknown enemy. The only motive can be the preparation for attack against the free world. The source of "infection" is traced to a barren, storm-swept rock-pile in the southern Indian Ocean. Now, it is up to the forces of freedom to search out and destroy the enemy. With the aid of their robot infantry—the Warbots—the Washington Greys mount Operation High Dragon in a climactic battle for the future of the free world.

#6 THE LOST BATTALION   (17-205, $3.95)

Major Curt Carson has his orders to lead his Warbot-equipped Washington Greys in a search-and-destroy mission in the mountain jungles of Borneo. The enemy: a strongly entrenched army of Shiite Muslim guerrillas who have captured the Second Tactical Battalion, threatening them with slaughter. As allies, the Washington Greys have enlisted the Grey Lotus Battalion, a mixed-breed horde of Japanese jungle fighters. Together with their newfound allies, the small band must face swarming hordes of fanatical Shiite guerrillas in a battle that will decide the fate of Southeast Asia and the security of the free world.

#7 OPERATION IRON FIST   (17-253, $3.95)

Russia's centuries-old ambition to conquer lands along its southern border erupts in a savage show of force that pits a horde of Soviet-backed Turkish guerrillas against the freedom-loving Kurds in their homeland high in the Caucasus Mountains. At stake: the rich oil fields of the Middle East. Facing certain annihilation, the valiant Kurds turn to the robot infantry of Major Curt Carson's "Ghost Forces" for help. But the brutal Turks far outnumber Carson's desperately embattled Washington Greys, and on the blood-stained slopes of historic Mount Ararat, the high-tech warriors of tomorrow must face their most awesome challenge yet!